A CERTAIN FUTURE: BOOK TWO

A CERTAIN MERCY

LINDA DINDZANS

Scrivenings
PRESS
Quench your thirst for story.
www.ScriveningsPress.com

A Certain Mercy reminds us why we read stories about the past—to understand ourselves. The characters in Dindzans' novel feel astonishingly real, their struggles achingly human. You don't just read this story, you live it. No doubt this is part of the author's painstaking research—Dindzans knows her stuff. You'll enjoy reading every page of *A Certain Mercy*, and it might just change your life. This is Historical/Biblical fiction at its finest, and the easiest 5 out of 5 stars I've ever given.

— Vincent B. Davis II, author of
The Sertorius Scrolls

From the very first page of *A Certain Mercy*, Linda Dindzans launches an epic, evocative, and thrilling historical novel—one that feels born of a lifetime of faith, study, and reflection. You walk beside Yeshua, hearing his words in a Biblical cadence that draws you into a powerful journey through evil, revenge, joy, and courage. *A Certain Mercy*—Book Two in *A Certain Future* series—is a triumph for both reader and writer, a testament to Dindzans' growing mastery as an author of substance and remarkable insight. I dare you to put it down.

— Peter Van Sant, 5-time Emmy Award-
winning Correspondent, CBS News,
podcaster

A Certain Mercy transports readers to the first century where the characters are tangible and real and the plot-line compels you to read the next paragraph. It's creative writing tethered to biblical conscientiousness.

— Brian Dainsberg, Lead Pastor, Alliance Bible Church, Mequon, Wisconsin, *The Brian Dainsberg Podcast*

One of the most wonderful things about our Savior's time on earth is that He taught profound biblical truths through the power of story. Stories have a unique way of reaching the heart and communicating truth and life principles far more deeply than mere instruction ever could. In *A Certain Mercy*, Linda has done exactly that. Through this beautiful narrative, she weaves lessons about love, struggle, relationships, and forgiveness, inviting readers not only to enjoy a compelling story but also to encounter timeless biblical principles that transform the heart.

— Richard Marks, Ph.D. Founder, RelateWell Institute

Dindzans is a masterful storyteller. In *A Certain Mercy*, she paints a vivid tale of forbidden love with richly drawn characters, relatable struggles, and the promise of mercy. The story carries the reader into first-century Jerusalem and into the heart of a hurting woman forever changed by Jesus. Exquisitely written and deeply redemptive, this novel reminds us that God's mercy reaches into the darkest corners and brings light and restoration. I highly recommend this page-turner.

— Charlsie Estess, Author of
When the Ocean Roars

In *A Certain Mercy*, Linda Dindzans has once more made the time when Jesus walked the earth come alive for her readers. She has created an intricately woven story filled with realistic characters that deal with the age-old problems of forgiveness and trust. They capture our hearts, but the consequences of their actions create suspense that keeps us on the edge of our seats from beginning to end.

— Deborah Sprinkle, Award-winning author
of *Death Under the Ice*,
Golden Scrolls Novel of the Year 2025

Blessed are the merciful, for they will be shown mercy. ~ *Sermon on the Mount*

This novel is dedicated to those who will forge our family's future—Andra, Maisie, Karen, Lauren, Karlis, Viktors, Greg, Mikey, Henry.

May they be blessed and bless others as they journey along the path of a certain mercy.

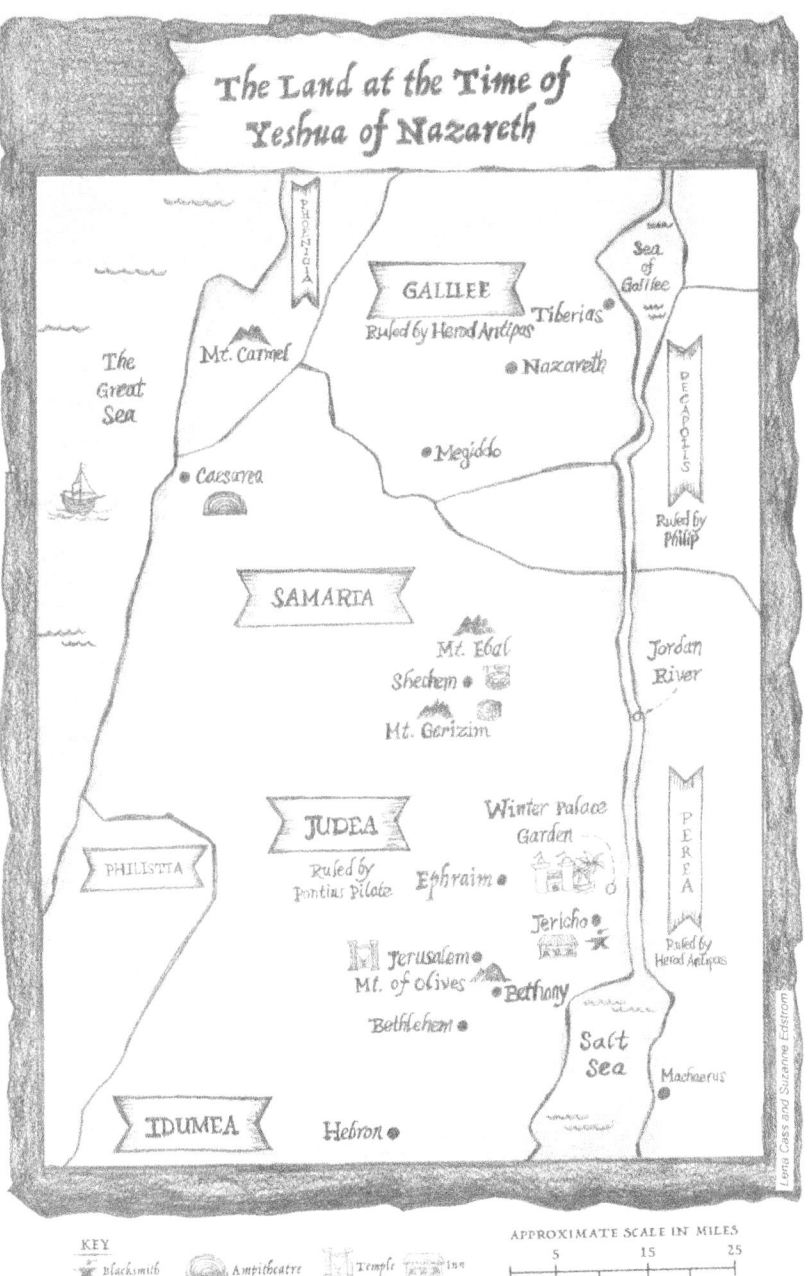

The Land at the Time of Yeshua of Nazareth

PHOENICIA

GALILEE
Ruled by Herod Antipas

Sea of Galilee

Tiberias

Nazareth

Mt. Carmel

The Great Sea

DECAPOLIS
Ruled by Philip

Caesarea

Megiddo

SAMARIA

Mt. Ebal

Shechem

Mt. Gerizim

Jordan River

Winter Palace Garden

JUDEA
Ruled by Pontius Pilate

Ephraim

PEREA
Ruled by Herod Antipas

PHILISTIA

Jericho

Jerusalem
Mt. of Olives

Bethany

Bethlehem

Salt Sea

Machaerus

IDUMEA

Hebron

Lena Gass and Suzanne Edstrom

KEY
Blacksmith
Jacob's Well
Amphitheatre
Village
Temple
Altar
Vine

APPROXIMATE SCALE IN MILES
5   15   25
0   10   20

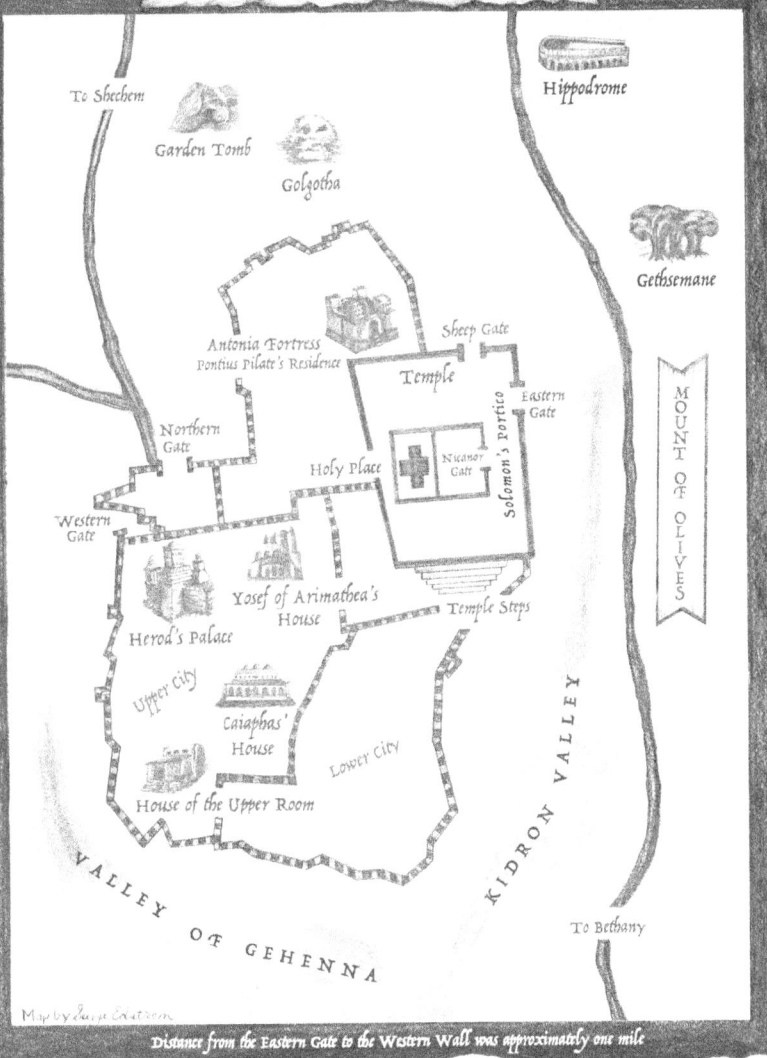

Jerusalem at the Time of Yeshua of Nazareth

To Shechem

Garden Tomb

Golgotha

Hippodrome

Gethsemane

Antonia Fortress
Pontius Pilate's Residence

Sheep Gate

Temple

Eastern Gate

Northern Gate

Holy Place

Nicanor Gate

Solomon's Portico

MOUNT OF OLIVES

Western Gate

Yosef of Arimathea's House

Temple Steps

Herod's Palace

Upper City

Caiaphas' House

Lower City

House of the Upper Room

KIDRON VALLEY

VALLEY OF GEHENNA

To Bethany

Map by _____

Distance from the Eastern Gate to the Western Wall was approximately one mile

A Certain Mercy: List of Characters

Legend:

* Historical figure
+ Biblical figure
# Fictional character
^ Also appears in *A Certain Man* (Book 1)

Abram #—Infant son of Shamara (Mara) and Samuel
Auriga Maximus (Auri) #—Famed slave charioteer
Barabbas +—Criminal released by Pontius Pilate at Passover
Barid #^—Innkeeper at the Jericho Inn
Caiaphas +*^—High Priest of Jerusalem during Yeshua's time
Chuza +—Herod's chief steward; husband of Joanna
Dex #^—Blacksmith in Jericho; husband of Sophia
Emet #—Young slave in the House of Lazarus
Gaius #—Young son of Sophia and Dex

Herod Antipas +*^—Tetrarch of Galilee and Perea during Yeshua's ministry

Herodias +*^—Wife of Herod Antipas; formerly married to his brother

Ira #—Steward over Zara's inheritance

Joanna +—Wife of Chuza; Zara's kinswoman

Johakim *^—Retired High Priest of Samaria; obscure historical figure

Jonathan *—High Priest of Samaria at the time of the crucifixion; obscure historical figure

Joram #—Zara's husband

Lazarus (Amon) *+—Friend of Yeshua; brother of Martha and Mary

Lyra #^—Daughter of Samuel and Zosi, his deceased comfort woman

Magdalena (Lenah) +—Mary Magdalene, delivered of seven demons by Yeshua

Mark (John Mark) +*—Young man at Gethsemane; later author of the Gospel of Mark

Martha +—Sister of Lazarus and Mary of Bethany

Mary of Bethany +—Sister of Lazarus and Martha

Miriam +^—Mother of Yeshua

Ozri #^—Woodworker at Samuel's woodshop

Reah #—Handmaid to Zara

Samuel +^—The Good Samaritan; husband of Shamara; not named in the Bible

Shamara (Mara) +^—Wife of Samuel; the Woman at the Well; not named in the Bible

Simon the Leper +—Host of banquet in Bethany

Sophia #^—Wife of Dex; mother of Gaius

Theo (Etan) +^—Disfigured servant at Jericho Inn; victim in the Good Samaritan parable; not named in the Bible

Yeshua of Nazareth *+^—Jesus, the Christ; the Promised One

Yonah (Salome) *+^—Daughter of Herodias; not named in the Bible

Yosef of Arimathea *+^—Wealthy Sanhedrin member; provided the tomb of Yeshua

Zara (Zera) #—Wife of Joram; secretly in love with Auriga Maximus

Chapter One

Jerusalem
Under Roman Rule of Tiberius Caesar
After Sukkot or Feast of Tabernacles, Tishri 22 (October)

Zara

She could think of no one else. Zara's neglected lips tingled at the thought of Auriga Maximus. Golden-haired. Famed charioteer. And her husband Joram's slave.

Zara sat in front of her dressing table. Every time she was in Auriga's presence, her yearning for him lingered longer and grew more vivid with each stolen glance.

"When is the charioteer expected to arrive?" Reah lifted a polished bronze mirror.

"He will sup with us at sunset." Zara's breaths quickened, captives to her longing. She drew in calming air. "My husband has sent word he wants me to look my most alluring."

"Mistress, look in the mirror. For the banquet, I will hide

your right eye with this draping tendril." Then Reah brushed Zara's curls upward and secured them with her amber-studded comb. "The comb will set off your cinnamon brown hair. And my lady, your hair draped in this fashion will add mystery to your appearance." Reah stepped back and studied Zara. "Of late, your husband has been in high spirits. The golden tunic clinging to your slender form is so tempting." Reah touched Zara's shoulder. "Perhaps he will come to your chambers tonight."

"Do not torment me. You well know that during the first three years of my wedded life, my husband doted upon me. Now, for nigh on three more years, I am an unbedded wife. I have kept a thousand lonely vigils. Why should this night be any different than the others?" Zara could not keep the bitter tone from her voice or the sour twist from her stomach. "From the day Joram won our charioteer while casting dice with King Herod Antipas, my husband has come to me only to beg for lucre to back his wagers at the hippodrome." Zara removed the comb. "Pin back the draping tendril."

"Mistress, why flaunt your flaw? Since birth, it has been the source of such superstition and shunning."

"Auriga will not flinch at my gaze. He chose this comb to match my eyes." Zara turned back to the mirror and studied her blemish. In the place of a small dark circle, the slit of a cat eye gleamed.

Soon, Auri would stand before her. Soon, he would feast upon her carefully crafted appearance. Soon, they would share the evening meal. And her husband would never know of her secret hunger.

Something soft brushed against Zara's toes.

Mmrrr ... Mmrr.

Two black kittens had escaped the willow basket tucked under the dressing table.

She scooped up one in each hand and cradled them against her cheeks. "These little ones are hungry." She turned to Reah. "Did you bring the fresh goat milk?"

"Yes, Mistress." Reah poured milk from a pitcher into a silver bowl meant to mix kohl to paint around the eyes. She set the bowl on the floor and looked up at Zara, who still cradled the kittens against her cheeks. Reah giggled. "Your eyes mirror the color of the kittens' eyes."

Zara released the kittens onto the floor. They scrambled over each other, racing toward the dish. She smiled at their antics, having learned to cling to any scrap of joy. "The kittens miss their mother."

"As you and I both miss my beloved mother." Reah's voice faltered.

"I remember her fondly." Reah's mother had been Zara's nurse. "We both coddled you from the day you were born. You were my first doll. Now you are my only friend."

Reah sighed and seemed to gather herself. "Mistress, may the gods bless you for saving the kittens. I did not want to watch that fish merchant drown them."

"Auri reveres Bastet, the black Egyptian cat goddess."

"You dare call him a fond name ... Auri?"

"Auriga means charioteer, but my husband was amused when I suggested we call him Auri, which means golden. His victories in the hippodromes have amassed us a fortune. A fortune my husband is quick to stake on his next wager." Zara strove to suppress the caress in her voice when she spoke of Auri and the loathing in her tone when she spoke of Joram.

Reah's eyes flickered with something Zara could not read. "Is this Auri pleasing to look upon?"

Zara's cheeks heated from a passion that was growing harder and harder to deny—and harder to hide. She flashed a soft, shy smile toward Reah. Zara considered Auri's son-of-a-gladiator build, his strong charioteer arms, and his soothing voice. A voice that sent pleasant shivers down her spine. One that made her stomach flutter and her face flame.

"Reah, you may judge for yourself. My husband has arranged a sumptuous banquet for the three of us to celebrate Auriga's victory today. You will help serve."

The kittens licked the bowl clean, and Zara lifted them, moving to her raised sleeping pallet. She motioned for Reah to join her in the nest of embroidered pillows where they lazed in comfortable quiet.

Zara rested her palms on the sleeping kittens and listened to them purr. The rise and fall of their tiny chests tickled her hands and called to mind how much she craved any loving touch from her husband. She missed a husband who sought to know her thoughts and desired to sleep within the circle of her arms. She mourned the loss of a husband who loved her without restraint. Her husband had been stolen from her by a new obsession, a new mistress—gambling on the chariot races.

Zara sighed. The sigh of an honorable woman whose soul is pulled in two directions. "Auri bought the comb in my hair with his portion of the last victory purse. I want to give him a special gift in kind. Since he honors Bastet, I will give him one of the kittens. Which should I offer him? The male or the female?"

"Tread lightly, my lady. Your husband may become jealous."

"Joram will not be moved to jealousy. Or even the anger of insult. For months, Auri has looked on me with undisguised admiration. He praises me in Joram's presence. Once, Joram mocked my cat eye, and Auri saw my humiliation and stepped between us. He presented me with the precious comb, telling me that my eyes were enchanting. The eyes of a goddess. The eyes of Bastet."

"Any other husband would have sentenced Auriga to the arena. What did Joram do?"

"His face remained unmoved. No trace of jealousy. My husband's heart is no longer mine." The shame roiling in her stomach sent a burning wave of humiliation up her throat. "Then, most mortifying of all, Joram nodded to Auri, sneered and waved toward me as if he would reward his prize-winning charioteer with the favors of his wife."

"Take care. Joram may divorce you."

"He will not. I have asked him three times to set me free from the shackles of this insufferable marriage. But Joram refuses—he will not return my dowry as prescribed by my wedding contract."

Reah rose and stretched. "Your father never meant to leave you languishing in a loveless, lifeless marriage."

"That is why my father charged his faithful steward with the oversight of my inheritance." Zara stood and smoothed her robe. "Enough of my troubles. Which cat should be my gift to Auri?"

Reah lifted the female. "The champion charioteer praised Bastet. Give him the one that brings to mind his most favored goddess. But the kitten is young and will need care."

"I will keep her until she is able to survive and thrive in the stables and give Auri reason to visit me often."

Auri's past looks of admiration were locked in Zara's mind. But the new flickers of desire in his eyes had unraveled her resolve. And temptation threatened to push her to the brink of seduction.

A chill coiled in Zara's chest like a snake ready to strike.

Suddenly, the heavy cedar door swung open and thudded against the wall. Joram strode in and waved Reah away.

She swept up the kittens and left.

Zara turned to face Joram. She had seen this look before.

Lips curled tightly in a feigned smile— eyes darting refusing to meet hers. At first, she had thought this look was guilt for his neglect of her, but now she knew it was greed.

Joram's face was flushed from wine and impatience. He clenched a fist and slapped his palm. "Do not dawdle. And do not protest. Give me your ruby armband." He grabbed Zara's arm and shoved her toward the jewel box.

"Do you not recall? You took that weeks ago when you bet on Auri's team."

"And see how it has enriched us." He pawed through her jewel box and lifted a clump of necklaces. "A sure win has been whispered in my ear. We must not miss this chance for great gain. It is so sure I can feel the gold in my hand. But I must have the wager recorded within the hour."

Each strand of jewelry Joram pulled seemed to tighten the tangle. He tossed the knotted jewels down. His face darkened and he reached for the precious comb in Zara's hair.

She leapt back. "Remember, there are no chariot races to bet upon today." She desperately wanted to keep the comb.

A storm of obsession raged across Joram's face. His eyes were the eyes of a man gone mad. He again reached for the comb.

Zara turned away, leaving Joram's fingers pinching air. "Peace, husband. Come, sit on the sleeping pallet. I will look through my other jewel box and find something much more precious than this comb. Something worthy of this grand chance."

He sat, wiped his brow with his sleeve, then slid his palms along the lap of his robe.

Zara stooped at the dressing table and lifted a carved box tucked behind the wicker basket. She carried it to the sleeping pallet, opened it, and studied her jewels. Many were missing, already confiscated by her husband to secure wagers. Only two pieces would rival the worth of the comb. Both were the only remaining jewels left to her by her *ima*. She picked up her mother's emerald brooch hidden at the bottom of the jewel box and brought it to her lips in farewell. Joram grabbed it from her hand and rushed from the room. Praise HaShem. She would hide her *ima*'s sapphire ring.

Reah returned at a run, her face forlorn. "Joram took your *ima*'s emerald broach."

"I gave it to him." Zara's chest tightened around a breath-robbing realization. Just as her husband was obsessed with risking his whole fortune on a foolish wager, she was obsessed with a never-ending desire for Auri.

Chapter Two

Jerusalem, House of Joram
Same day, early evening

Zara

Zara held a bronze mirror and watched Reah edge her eyes with kohl. "Joram has misused me. I am dead to him. It is as if he has murdered me and left me abandoned in the road."

"I hear your desperate loneliness." Reah colored Zara's lids with malachite dust. "This soft green dust sets off the amber of your eyes. And I purchased this new cream made from berries and rose petals to stain your lips the red of dawn."

"You are truly a gifted *cosmetae*. Many of the Roman women in Jerusalem vie to buy you from me for your makeup skills alone."

Reah drew in a quick breath and dropped the lip brush.

Zara turned to face her handmaid's watery eyes and trembling hands.

"Would my lady like to add sparkle with the powder made from silver fish scales?"

Zara took Reah's hand. "Surely, you know I would never sell you, no matter the price. Now let us try the sparkle powder on my cheeks and neck."

Bonggg ... Bonggg ...

"The call of the gong. The private banquet awaits." Reah applied the glint and blew gently across Zara's face, clearing any loose powder. "I must finish." Rhea took the cherished bejewelled comb from its secret drawer and drew Zara's hair back. "My lady is ravishing. Now you must go."

"Let the men wait for me. Did not your *ima* teach me the enchanting power of a lady's entrance?"

"You remember my mother's lessons well." Reah smiled at the hint of their shared secrets. "I will go to the kitchen and present myself for service at supper." She scurried from the room.

The sound of Reah's mouselike pitter-patter made Zara smile. But she would not scurry. She moved along the portico like a lioness on the prowl. Her stride lengthened, becoming more graceful, more fluid, more feline. She neared the wide archway that led into the triclinium where the banquet was laid. Both Joram and Auri's voices drifted to her, but she could not discern the content of their conversation. She slipped between the two massive pillars that bolstered the dining room arch and posed—the statue of a patrician woman.

Both men gradually sensed her presence and looked at her. A silence hovered over them. An expectant silence.

Zara captured their gaze and glided forward to the three-sided banquet table and reclining couches. The center section was laden with food, ready for the slaves to fulfill the requests of the guests.

Joram occupied the left table, positioned so he could see

both couches across from him. He motioned her to one of the couches.

Zara stole a glance toward the couch next to her, but her view of Auri was blocked by Reah filling his wine cup. Other servants travelled the central aisle, filling silver platters and golden plates.

Reah hurried to help Zara drape her robes elegantly across the couch and gracefully recline.

Zara met Auri's eyes and suppressed a gasp. She had never expected to be looking directly upon his face. From a distance, she had always thought his eyes were deep blue, but in the golden hour sunlight, they flashed blue flecked with green.

For a moment, Zara could not make sense of the arrangement of the reclining couches. She studied Auri's couch. Joram had positioned his slave to recline on his right side, forcing him to use his left hand to eat. Zara and Auri were reclined face-to-face, eyes-to-eyes. Their couches were so close, so intimate, she wondered if Auri could hear her heart flail like a songbird trapped in a cage.

"Wife, you seem perplexed."

Another ambush from her cunning and cruel husband. He must suspect her feelings for Auri. He was tormenting her. Testing her.

"Husband, it is my mistake. Auri is reclining on his right side." She dismissed the servants with a wave and watched them leave. "Forgive me, I did not oversee the new servant who placed Auri's couch."

"There was no mistake. I ordered the reclining couch set so that Auri faced left."

Zara's anger sparked. She must choose her words, but she would not leave Auri's honor undefended. "Surely you did not mean to suggest that your faithful and prize-worthy slave is sinister—left-handed—untrustworthy."

Joram stood. "No, by Zeus." He sneered toward Auri. "If he ever betrayed me, he would find himself in the arena fighting fierce gladiators, not in the hippodrome racing a four-horse quadriga."

Auri smiled the steady, subdued smile of a man who never concerns himself with foolishness. "And if I were ever to fight in the arena, my gentle lady would learn that there has been no insult. I fight with the gladius, the short sword, in my left hand. Sinister-handed gladiators have the advantage and are no more deceitful than any other men."

"But you are a charioteer, not a gladiator."

"Wife, surely you have not forgotten our golden slave was the son of a gladiator."

Auri lifted his left hand, palm up. "Some may not recall that my father was left-handed. Much feared. Much revered." Starting with the smallest finger, Auri slowly curled each inward. A gesture of homage. "My father was a slave who won his freedom in the arena. Respected for his loyalty to the hundreds of gladiators he trained."

"Wife. No insult to our prized slave, Auri, was ever intended."

Anger and anxiety seared Zara's cheeks. She fisted her hands as if she could fend off her husband's mocking tone.

Would Auri think she was a shallow woman? A woman whose mind was consumed with childish things.

Joram's cutting words left her feeling unsure. She turned back to Auri. "How then did the son of a gladiator who gained his freedom come to be a slave charioteer?"

"It is a long tale." Auri looked toward Joram, seeming to ask permission to continue.

Reah rushed into the room. "My lord, a runner is at the gate. His message is urgent."

Joram gestured to a male servant. "Bring him in. But first,

make sure he is unarmed." Joram faced Auri. "I am sure your tale would captivate Zara, but it will have to wait."

A gaunt, young runner scuttled to Joram's side and whispered in his ear. A wide-eyed look of frantic panic flitted across Joram's face, but he quickly buried it beneath a stony mask. The runner withdrew to the entry arch.

Joram rose and looked from Auri to Zara. "I am called away. Wife, I trust you will amuse our guest with all the admiration and affection he so richly deserves."

Zara's anger awakened the lioness within. She wanted to leap for Joram's throat, knock him to the ground, and scratch his taunting eyes.

He reached into his robe and handed Auri a white stone. "We have drawn the Whites as our opponents in the next race."

Auri tossed the stone from one hand to the other. "Winning will be a challenge for our Goldens." He threw the stone back to Joram. "You have seen them race. I have not. We must devise a plan."

Joram grabbed a wedge of cheese and a round of bread. "Our banquet was meant to last many hours, so I had chambers prepared for you here. As the Fates have decreed, I am called to deal with matters that will take all night. We will meet in the late morning."

Zara's brazen husband dared to tempt both her and Auri to indulge their passion for each other.

Joram seemed to gaze through her—his expression devoid of any remnant of his early love.

"Husband, I know your mind wrestles with an urgent matter, but even your impeccable reputation would be sullied if you choose to leave Auri and me here alone. The gossip geese will gather in the streets, spreading slander. They may even charge us with adultery."

A look of calculated cruelty crossed his face. "We are

Herodian Jews. We eat in the Roman style. Our homes feature Roman design. In Rome, patrician women visit gladiators privately. I daresay some visit charioteers. Even here in Judea."

"I am not just any woman. I am your wife." Zara wanted to run from her humiliation. She wanted to run from her husband. But most of all, she wanted to run from the temptation of Auri's adoration.

Joram strode forward, grabbed her cheeks, and pinched hard. "Do you think yourself beautiful enough to attract the notice of the gossips? Why would anyone ever believe that even a slave would want you?" He dropped his hands. "You disgust me."

Disgrace cinched Zara's chest, binding her breath. Her heart drummed a sad, slow rhythm of lost hope. Tears blurred her vision. She could not see Joram, the man she desperately wanted to escape, or Auri, the man she desperately wanted to embrace.

Zara wiped her tears and risked a glance toward Auri. Was that tenderness or pity she read in his eyes? She did not want his pity. And she would not wallow in the sinking sands of sadness.

Fire simmered in Zara's spirit. "Six years ago, you thought I was beautiful—beautiful enough that you wanted to win me. Six years ago, you courted me, swore to love me, swore to protect me. And married me."

"Six years ago, your father demanded a hefty bride price." Joram grabbed her shoulders and shook her. "But your dowry was colossal. Marriage to you was an opportunity for wealth beyond my wildest imaginings."

Auri tensed and sat up.

Zara sent him a restraining look. He must not make any move to protect her. If he were to manhandle his master, he would suffer a slow, torturous end. She would not be the cause of Auri's death.

The messenger returned to Joram's side. "Please, sir, my master cannot wait."

Joram shoved Zara back onto the reclining couch and rushed after the runner.

She sat, straightened her tunic, and gazed at Auri. It was not a slave's place to speak first. "Joram's heart has been poisoned. Poisoned with the love of money. And that love of money has supplanted his love for me."

"I am sorry, my lady. The love of money has seduced Joram to risk wagers that teeter on the brink of madness." Auri's tone seemed to brim with understanding and afforded her comfort.

She studied his face. As with any great warrior, Auri's face was most often a mask. His thoughts and feelings hidden. But now he looked at her with an open gentleness she had never seen. He seemed to read her heart.

Zara met his eyes with questions of her own. Did he care for her? Did he want her?

Auri leapt up and sat on the reclining couch at her feet. "My lady, you are deserving of a gentle man. I have witnessed Joram bruise you with words, but never before have I seen him grip you with his hands. Only a coward would harm a woman. My father's tribe held women in high regard."

"You must never challenge Joram. He would have you crucified."

"Joram would gain no gold by my crucifixion. Instead, he would sponsor a preposterous match in the arena. One that would pique the bloodlust of a crowd. Spectators would come from afar to place wagers and watch Auriga Maximus—champion charioteer and son of their famed gladiator—fight to the death."

"How would your death serve Joram?"

"In secret, he would wager vast sums against me."

Zara moved closer to Auri. "You were so quick to state your fate."

"Joram threatens me with the arena if I raise the slightest protest. Until now, his promises of shared victor's purses have secured my submission to his schemes." Auri covered her hand with his.

At Auri's touch, pinprick shivers ran up Zara's arms.

He gazed at her with a look that drew her deep into the sea of his blue eyes. Zara turned her hand over and let Auri's hand softly settle into her palm.

Could it be that Auri had read her wayward longings? She gazed through the entry arch. Like the sun setting behind the Temple roof, tonight any ember of love for her husband had been snuffed out. Her feelings for Joram were as cold as mountain snow.

Could it be she had captured Auri's heart as he had won hers? "Call me Zara."

"I dare not."

"Come, we are alone, and I would hear my name on your lips." She lifted Auri's strong, callused hand between her slender, smooth palms. "Look at me. Read my eyes."

Auri leaned close and studied her face. He did not flinch at the sight of her cat eye. He stroked her cheek, touched her lips. "Forgive my trespass ... Zara."

She ran her fingers through his hair. "Auri, you must know. I would forgive you anything."

Chapter Three

House of Joram

Same day, after sunset

Zara

Zara stared at the emerging stars from the portico of her sleeping chamber. "I left the banquet and Auri more than an hour past, yet my thoughts are still consumed with him."

Reah placed a basin on the table and dropped rose petals into the water. "If your *abba* knew about your desire for Auriga, he would leap from his grave to keep you from this appalling sin."

Zara's mind and heart were divided, but she could not help but wonder what ripples her choices this night would create. She walked inside and sat on the stone window ledge near Reah. "If my father, my *abba,* knew of my plight, he would demand a divorce and redeem his daughter from her abject loneliness."

"He never intended for you to suffer at Joram's hand."

"My *abba* could not have known Joram's love would turn cold." She took the comb from her hair and returned it to the secret drawer. "Where is Auri now?"

"He has gone to our Roman bath, where Joram's slave attends him. Auri will sleep in the chamber your husband ordered for him. A chamber next to this one."

Zara placed her palms against her burning cheeks to cool the scarlet flush she knew had spread across her face.

Reah looked toward the far panelled wall. "Does Auri know of the secret door that connects his chamber with yours?"

"No. But it taunts me." If Auri knew of the door, would he come to her? Would his passion conquer his caution?

Reah dipped a cloth in the rosewater and took Zara's hand.

Zara pulled it away. "I do not want to lose the lingering touch of Auri's hand covering mine."

"Where the mind goes, the heart begs to follow."

"Where did you hear such wisdom?"

"When we journeyed to Galilee, a handmaid and I secretly slipped away to a hillside. There, Yeshua of Nazareth taught those gathered that anyone who looks on a woman with lust commits adultery in his heart."

"Why should we heed the words of a mere teacher?"

"This rabbi is a worker of wonders. Many believe He is a prophet. Some say He is The Baptizer returned to life. Others hope He is the long-awaited Messiah."

Zara shook her head. "The wonders He works are beyond belief. Many call Him a conjurer, a magician, even a sorcerer."

"But I have seen Him heal with my own eyes. Seen the blind gain sight, seen the crippled rise and walk." Reah knelt in front of Zara, her hands lifted, her face aglow. "Yeshua's power must come from HaShem."

"Is it not more likely He is a charlatan? A master of deceit?"

"He healed the sight of a man known by all to be blind since birth. He is no charlatan. There was no deceit."

Zara waved Reah away and stood. "Enough talk of this Yeshua."

"Yes, my lady, I will be still, but another question tugs at me. You know women throw themselves at the feet of Auriga Maximus. Do you believe this man truly loves you?"

Zara's heart flipped like a racing chariot cut off by a rival team. "I do not know. When Joram wooed me, he told me that with every couple, one is the Lover who seeks to please and the other is the Beloved who is content to be indulged. He claimed I was his Beloved." Zara hugged herself and rocked from one foot to the other. "Tell me. What is love?"

"Yeshua teaches that the greatest love is the willingness to lay your life down for a friend." Reah opened an ampule of perfume. "Would Auri die for you?"

"Again, I do not know. But I would be content to be the Lover, never the Beloved."

"My lady, how could that kind of love ever satisfy?" Reah dabbed perfume on Zara's wrists.

She breathed in the sweet scents. Myrrh ... rose ... and some other subtle fragrance. "I am parched for love, like a wilting flower whose roots reach for any drop of water. Only my waning sense of honor restrains me from sin. I crave the slightest kind word, gentle glance, loving touch."

Reah lifted a silver pitcher and poured. "Perhaps a cup of warm spiced wine will ease your mind and summon sleep." She motioned Zara to the sleeping pallet piled high with inviting pillows.

Zara settled herself and accepted the wine. The cup brushed against her lips. Lips. Three years since Joram's lips had spoken sweetly of her. Three years since her husband's lips warmed hers. For three long and lonely years, she had been left untouched, unbedded—shunned—without hope of bearing a child.

Tonight, Joram had all but offered her to Auri—whether to torment him or humble her, she did not know.

She stared at the panelled wall, longing for it to open. But sleep called to her. Her eyelids drooped and her hand faltered.

Reah took the cup from Zara and brushed her hair back from her brow. "My lady ..." Reah's voice was soft as the whisper of a butterfly wing. "I pray you do not walk down a path that offers no way of return."

Three days later

Zara walked across the sunlit triclinium and dropped onto her couch facing Auri at the banquet table. "Joram has not returned for three days and two nights." Auri's prolonged presence tempted her sorely. Only by the sheer strength of her iron will and Reah's vigilance had she not succumbed to sin.

"Joram must be enjoying strong drink and the harlots of the hippodrome." Auri met her eyes. "Forgive my wounding words."

Sunset crowned Auri with fiery golden light. He resembled Belenus. The image of the Gauls' sun god was fashioned in gold on Auri's chariot—a face encircled by long hair and a long beard fanned out like rays of the sun.

Reah poured wine into Auri's goblet. "This is sweet and well-watered."

"Many thanks. I never partake of strong drink. It is fool-hardy for a charioteer who intends to survive the sudden swerves of a racing chariot."

Reah filled Zara's goblet. "My lady, at midday, Joram's

servant returned here and took a treasure chest away with him."

"My husband must be casting charmed dice. Each day, treasures have been delivered."

"The dice may be turning against Joram." Auri raised his cup toward Zara. "We have spent countless hours together." He glanced toward Reah. "Always under the watchful eyes of your handmaid."

Did Zara detect a growing impatience in Auri's voice? Would he tire of his pursuit of her and turn to another? She had ordered Reah never to leave them alone. And since the night Auri occupied the chamber that shared a wall with hers, Rhea slept at the foot of Zara's pallet.

Zara rested her hand on Auri's forearm. "This morning you began to tell me of your father, the gladiator."

"It is a long tale of suffering and sorrow. A tale I am loath to share."

"Would you not share it with me? One who will listen with the ears of her heart?"

Auri glanced toward Reah bringing fresh fruit to the serving table. He leaned close to Zara. "My father's story rankles my bones and rakes my mind. But I will trust it to the one woman I know would soothe my wounded soul."

Hearing Auri confess his trust in her sent Zara's heart skittering. She took several deep breaths but failed to coax her heart back to a steady, sedate pace. She brushed her fingers along his arm, touched the hollow of his neck, then let her hand drop into her lap. "You must not tempt me to trespass the binding covenant of marriage." Her words honored her wedding contract, but her inviting glance, her sultry voice, her sensuous touch betrayed her dishonorable desire.

Auri picked up a dripping sweet-cake and fed her a bite. Honey ran down her chin, and he swiped it away with his finger and brought it to his moist lips. "Have you not tempted me beyond bearing?"

"Perchance it is you who have tempted me to the brink of the Law."

"My father taught his gladiators—in the arena or in the battle for love—all tactics are deemed fair. No feint, no ruse, no deception is forbidden."

Reah flashed a warning look that should have made Zara send Auri away. But she wanted nothing more than to hear his secrets and set his hardened heart free.

Zara looked back at Auri. "Reah. Leave us."

Reah dipped a towel in water, crossed to Zara, and patted her sticky chin. "With respect, is my lady certain?"

Zara's double-minded silence seemed to grow, take on weight that yoked her to Auri.

His eyes searched hers.

Zara read the attraction in his eyes. But there was something else. Something he guarded. Something he kept hidden.

"Reah, leave us." Zara had devised a plan to fend off her wanton desire and temptation. Reah knew thrice she must be ordered to leave Zara and Auri utterly alone before her faithful handmaid would obey. "Go. I would hear Auriga's tale."

Reah's worried look flickered with foreboding.

"Reah, fear not, all will be well."

Even though her handmaid's face was filled with dread, she nodded and slipped through the archway.

When Reah was well out of sight, Zara gestured for Auri to share her couch.

He joined her and reclined on his back, his head resting on his clasped hands.

Zara turned on her side, her head on her arm. "Tell me of your father."

"Armor your heart, for this story takes courage to hear."

Auri's voice trailed into a sigh. "My father, chieftain of a tribe from Gaul, was captured, paraded in chains, and sold on the Roman auction block to Herod the Great. The king spared no expense to have my father trained by champion gladiators in Rome. When Herod the Great returned to Judea, he brought my father to the arena in Caesarea. There, he achieved fame and a loyal following."

"Your father won a fortune for Herod as you have for Joram."

"I also race to win for you."

The sensual rasp in Auri's voice flustered Zara.

"One day, after a thrilling gladiator match, the adoring, riotous crowd demanded my father be set free. In exchange for his freedom, my father oversaw a gladiator school and split all the winnings with Herod."

"Auri, come rest your head on my shoulder."

Auri lay his head down, put an arm around her waist, and drew her close.

"Your father was a free man, but you are a slave."

"Because my mother was a slave. When Herod the Great died, I became part of the inheritance passed down to his son, Herod Antipas. My father vowed to my mother, when she died at my birth, that he would keep me from the fate of a gladiator." Auri's tone dulled, and his voice hitched as if overcome with unspoken sadness. "Ask me nothing more. If I am to finish, I must tell this tale without pause."

Zara traced the contours of his strong arm, then let her hand come to rest.

"Once my father amassed a fortune, he went to Herod Antipas to buy my freedom. The Old Fox had me brought before him. Though my life had only spanned twelve wheat harvests, I was already a giant of a man. Antipas refused to redeem me for even double the gold. He was sure crowds would flock to see the son of their champion gladiator win crowns in the arena. I will never forget the look of loathing on my father's face."

Zara wanted to stop her ears, but Auri needed her to hear his tortured past.

Auri sat up and turned to her. "I faced a future where the spectre of Death hovered over my head."

Auri hated Herod Antipas with good reason. Zara must never share that her father had once been a steward for Herod Antipas in Jericho.

Zara rose and took his arm. "Come into the garden with me. The flowers, the birds, and the sunlight will give you peace." She led him under the arch and out onto the garden path.

"My father argued that it would be years before I could fight and my victories in the arena were not sure. Antipas stroked his beard, then asked if my father had a proposal."

Walking the path seemed to offer no peace. Auri continued his story with the same single-minded fervor.

"My father told Herod to promote a series of contests. He would come out of retirement and fight the three best gladiators in Judea. Herod would keep the winnings as payment for my freedom."

After the span of several breaths, Auri stopped and turned to her, his face filled with revulsion. "In order to attract the largest crowds and the highest wagers, Herod said the matches must be fought to the death."

Zara shivered at the thought of what horror she might next hear. She led Auri down a path that would lead them farther away from the house to make sure he was not overheard.

"My father's face darkened like the visage of an angry god. He told Herod he refused to kill gladiators he had trained. Herod finally relented, proclaiming that the first two matches would not be to the death. But the third would be fought against a champion gladiator brought in from Rome, one my father did not know. And that pairing would be a fight to the death."

Zara pressed her lips together so she would not cry out. Herod's cruel scheme echoed the threats Joram had made to her Auri. She should not have been astounded. Joram was Herod's kinsman, both by bloodline and shared depravity.

"My father clutched the Belenus amulet around his neck. He pleaded to his sun god for protection in the arena. Then Herod laughed, the howling bark of a jackal. I will never forget that predatory laugh, the one that sealed my father's fate. And mine. He said that my father had not heard all his terms."

Auri stopped walking and met Zara's eyes. "And I will never forget, nor forgive, what Herod said next. That I would never be freed, but he would take payment to keep me from ever fighting in an arena."

Auri reached up and withdrew an amulet from the neck of his tunic, handling it with great reverence. "I feared that my father would strangle Herod. But thankfully, my father tamed his temper and knelt in total submission."

Auri turned to Zara, his face an ever-shifting storm of emotion. His eyes dimmed as if he no longer saw her but stood with his father before Herod in an all-too-vivid past. "In that moment, I came to understand. A man—even an honorable man—must, at times, suffer humiliation to survive."

"Humiliation is an ever-present stone under my foot, one that stabs me with every step." Zara linked her arm in his and walked with him back into the triclinium. He sat at the foot of her couch. Zara sat beside him and moved so close that her knees grazed Auri's thigh.

"Herod plotted to use me to increase his fortune, so he sent me to the hippodrome to train as a charioteer. I was trained by champions from the Circus Maximus in Rome."

Auri met her eyes. "I was so young, so ignorant. My heart swelled with pride at the chance to become a famous charioteer. I gave no thought to the dangers of the hippodrome."

He retreated into an anguished silence. A silence teeming with sorrow.

Zara reclined, calling for him with open arms. He settled next to her and pulled her into his chest. She could feel him try to smother his sobs.

After what seemed a night and a day, Auri shifted and faced her. "My father won the first two matches. The third lasted for hours, sapping his strength. He died, that I might live."

Auri's rough whisper sounded like a voice from the grave.

"The willing sacrifice of a loving father." Zara stroked Auri's brow. "The greatest love one can offer is to lay down your life for another."

"My life was redeemed at a great price. I will never let my father's sacrifice be in vain. Each time I am slotted to race, I remember him. My preparation for a race exceeds that of any other charioteer. Whether racing in the hippodrome or walking the road of my life, at every turn, I will always choose the path of survival. No matter the humiliation, no matter the cost to my honor."

An unexpected chill wrapped its fingers around Zara's heart. A chill as cold as lost love. A chill as cold as death.

Chapter Four

The ring of a high-pitched bell startled Zara and Auri from their embrace.

Reah shouted, "Mistress, mistress. We have an unexpected guest."

Zara stood, smoothing her robe and dishevelled hair.

Auri hurried to his reclining couch.

"*Shalom*, Ira." She smiled at the short, wizened man whose quick tapping steps matched the speed of his brilliant mind. His hair and beard had silvered over the last months, but he seemed as spry as ever. "What brings my faithful steward here at this hour?"

He bowed. "My lady, we must protect you."

Auri rose, his hand touched the hilt of his dagger. He scanned the room, ready to confront an ambush.

Ira raised a palm toward Auri. "You mistook my meaning. We must secure the lady's goods, not her person."

Auri's stance relaxed, but he remained standing.

Ira tugged on the hand-stitched cloak that covered his long robe. "My report is for my lady's ears only."

"You may speak freely. I trust Reah and Auriga Maximus with my life." Zara offered her hand.

Ira brushed her fingertips and dipped his head.

Auri came to stand beside Zara.

"Joram has been casting dice." Ira's mouth drew in as if he had tasted wine gone to vinegar.

"When is Joram not hunting down the next wager?" Zara's sour tone sounded as if she drank from the same cup as Ira. "He has not been home for three days. Yesterday, he sent large chests full of his winnings. But today, two of the larger chests were collected by creditors."

"There will be many, many more creditors before last light tomorrow."

Zara's arms prickled with dread.

Ira swept both hands wide open. "Make haste. I must take your entire inheritance for safekeeping, far away from the thieving hands of Joram."

Zara dragged in a deep, slow breath. "Reah, go and direct the servants what things they should pack."

After Reah left, Auri took Zara's hand.

"Ira, does the whole city know of my husband's mountain of losses?"

Ira stared at their joined hands. A flash of reproach glinted in his eyes. "Not yet. My kinsman Chuza is Herod's chief steward. He sent word an hour past that unless Joram's fortunes turn, he may be taken to debtor's prison this very night." Ira headed for the archway. "Under no circumstance are you to send valuables that allow him to continue to wager."

Auri picked up his cloak from the reclining couch and swung it across his shoulders. "If I find the game of dice, perchance I can persuade Joram to stop."

Zara ran to him and clung to his cloak. "I forbid you to go.

A Certain Mercy

Think. If Joram catches sight of you while the wager-fever is upon him, Herod Antipas might goad Joram to risk you as the surety for his next wager. Herod has often pleaded with my husband to give him a chance to win you back."

Fear flickered across Auri's face, then gave way to a look of disdain. "Joram will never risk losing me. My next victory purse is his only hope of recovering his riches quickly."

Ira stopped under the archway, turned, and stared. "Auriga. There are no chariot races for weeks."

"Without my winnings, what can be done?"

"We must plan for the worst. Much is already in hand. Because Zara's father had no male heirs, when he knew he was dying, he arranged for his only daughter to inherit. He named me steward and ensured that Joram's foolhardy wagers would not drag her to debtor's prison with him."

Auri joined Ira under the arch. "Tell me what I must do for Zara."

"Lend your strength. Come with me to Zara's chambers. We must clear every bit of treasure. Every trinket, arm cuff, pearl strand, and ring must be recorded and taken where it will be guarded."

Zara and Auri ran down the portico and into her chambers. She grabbed Reah's arm. "Our time runs out. Empty every shelf, every hidden nook in the panel wall, and every cranny under the loose floor tiles beneath the sleeping pallet."

Reah rushed to do Zara's bidding and piled the treasures on the sleeping pallet.

Ira removed a small tablet and stylus from his robe, sat at the table, and listed all that was to be entrusted to his care.

Zara walked to the wall shared with Auri's chamber. It was covered with decorative cedar wall panels, each a false front covering a hidden nook filled with coins. As each nook was opened, she scooped them into the front of her robe and spilled them into a large basket at Ira's side.

"Auri, could you please empty the highest panels?"

He joined her and reached up. "Is every front false?"

"Yes."

He emptied the remaining nooks, but the last would not yield. He pounded his fist.

The panel opened just enough for him to see there was a hidden passage between her chambers and his. Auri turned to her, his eyes full of the knowledge that he could come to her chamber unbeknownst to anyone.

Zara pulled the panel shut and put her fingers to her lips.

Ira put down his tablet and stylus. "My son will soon be here with an oxcart."

"My lady ..." Reah's face turned as pale as spent ashes, and her eyes sparked with terror. "If the master cannot lay his hands on riches to steal, he will sell me at the daily slave auction to feed his need to wager."

Zara rushed to Reah. "That will never come to pass."

Ira stood and gave them a reassuring nod. "Fortunately, unlike Auriga Maximus, you are Zara's slave. Joram cannot sell you."

"Never?" Reah put her hands together. "Give me your word."

"Never. From my mouth ..." Ira touched his lips. "... to the Lord's ears." He pointed toward the heavens. "You will never be sold while my lady Zara draws breath."

Thanks to Ira, Zara was still wealthy and safe. But Joram's odds of escaping debtor's prison worsened with each wager he placed. She had once foolishly trusted Joram with her heart. Now, if Joram went to prison, mayhap she could be with Auri. Did she dare risk handing her heart to him?

Zara sat on her empty sleeping pallet. "I had not foreseen that the packing would require so many hours for so many hands."

Reah handed Zara a plate of crusty bread and crushed spiced olives. "Auri will soon return from escorting Ira and his son home with the treasure-laden oxcart."

"I am too spent and too distracted to eat. Help me into my nightshift."

Reah went to the wooden chest at the foot of Zara's sleeping pallet and took out several nightshifts. "Which one most pleases my lady?"

"Which one most suits me?" Zara's low, lilting voice betrayed her forbidden desire.

Reah helped Zara change into her most alluring, silky, golden nightshift.

Zara's thoughts clamped around a rising fount of rebellion against her mock marriage. She had rightly earned her husband's trust and heart. And he had abandoned her. She walked to her dressing table and stared at the panelled wall where the secret passage loomed.

Reah tapped lightly on her shoulder. "Sit here, my lady."

Reah brushed Zara's long hair and arranged it across her bare shoulders.

"Perfume my wrists and hair with the scent of roses and cinnamon."

Reah dabbed the open ampule of perfume to Zara's wrists with trembling hands. "My lady, consider the Law."

"Joram has broken the Law. He has denied me my marital rights. Not only has he withheld the pleasures of the marriage bed, but he has denied me any chance of an heir. An heir to love and cherish. An heir that would provide for me in my widowhood."

Reah waved the ampule around Zara's hair, the fragrance filling the air. "My lady will go to Auri this night?"

"Never. Auri must come to me."

"Beware. Your choices may reap a dire harvest." Reah glanced toward the secret panel.

"Faithful handmaid, cherished friend, go. Leave me to my fate."

"As my lady commands." Reah's words shared her obedience, but her face belied her objection.

Hours passed. Many times, Zara traded fitful sleep for flustered pacing. Did Auri truly care for her? Perhaps his attentions had been born of pity and not affection. Perhaps he did not want her as much as she wanted him. She returned to the sleeping pallet where she dozed. Some small sound awakened her. She stared through the window at the shining stars.

The watchman on the wall blew the cockcrow trumpet, signalling the end of the third watch.

Auri had not come. He would not come. She had misread his eyes, his face, his touches. His desire did not equal hers.

Zara rolled away from the panelled wall and pulled a blanket over her shivering body and quivering heart. Auri had warned her that he would never risk his life.

She would forever be alone.

"Zara." The whisper was so soft. Was it merely the wish birthed from her desperate loneliness? Could it be a phantom come to torture her shattered soul?

"Zara."

"Auri." She turned and saw him standing at the open passage.

Something stirred in the pit of Zara's being and made her hesitate. But she brushed aside her caution, threw back the blanket, and ran to him.

Auri lifted her and cradled her in his arms.

Zara settled into the warmth of his embrace, but shards of cold shivers pierced her heart. She was walking a dangerous path toward an enticing cliff. Once she leapt, there would be no time or room for repentance. She could only pray for a soft landing.

Auri's lips met hers.

Her veins flooded with a passion for the forbidden. A searing passion she had never known.

A still, small voice spoke to her soul.

From this moment forward, and for all time, you will be known as an adulteress.

Let it be so.

Zara studied Auri as he slept. The room brightened under the glow of the morning star. The kittens stalked and pounced on a lone grasshopper. Later, the crescent moon further lightened the dark. At long last, golden sun rays streamed through the window and haloed Auri's face.

She touched his arm. "The morning shineth. You must return to your chamber."

"Do not banish me so soon." His mumble was heavy with sleep.

Joram had never once returned from a night of debauchery this early. Zara eased her back into Auri's chest. He threw an arm across her waist and drew her closer. Auri's small snore seduced her back into a light sleep filled with dreams of a future with her lover.

A loud crash startled them awake. The cedar door broke free from its hinges and smashed onto the floor. Joram's men surrounded Auri.

Zara's heart stopped, then started racing like a stallion in the hippodrome. She wrapped the linen sheet around herself just before Joram pulled her from the sleeping pallet. "Sinner. Harlot. Adulteress." Joram's furious face filled her sight. "The wage of sin is death."

"Joram, grant me a divorce. I beg you."

He shoved her toward his slaves outside the door, and they pushed her along the portico.

No outcry from Auri.

Had his throat been slashed? Or would he suffer a slow tortuous death? Her knees turned to water. *Lord, do not credit my sin to Auri. Lord, let him live.*

Joram caught up, grabbed her by the hair, and dragged her through the courtyard to the gate. He tossed her into the street at the feet of three oncoming Pharisees on the way to morning prayer. "My wife was caught in the very act of adultery." Joram spit on her. "Take her to the Temple for judgment."

The Pharisees did not deign to speak with an unobservant Jew.

Joram motioned for his slaves to surround her. "Go with the Pharisees to the Temple. Make sure this vile woman does not escape judgment."

Zara could not move, could not speak, could barely grasp what was happening. Had Joram gone mad? He had taunted her that the marital bed meant nothing to him. He had even seemed to offer her to Auri. But now he threatened her with death.

When the eldest Pharisee prodded her forward with his walking staff, she saw the servant of the youngest Pharisee slip a small packet into Joram's palm.

What dealings could a strict Pharisee possibly have with Joram, an unclean Jew? One who blatantly transgressed the Law.

But Joram's schemes no longer mattered to her. Her life was in the balance. They were taking her to the Temple for judgment. She was without excuse, without defense. Her life was forfeit for her sins of the flesh. Unless she could escape, she would be stoned to death before nightfall.

She pulled the sheet up under her arms and tied it tight. She would break free. Or die in the attempt. Watching for an opening, she bolted through a gap between the slaves.

They chased her through the narrow streets. She raced up stairs to a rooftop room, lowered herself to a short wall, then into a garden. When she slowed to tighten her slipping sheet, a pursuer caught her trailing leg and hauled her to the ground. He brought her back to the road.

Now she was prodded forward by three walking staffs.

She stumbled and a sharp stone gashed one knee. She reached out, breaking her fall, her hands scraped by the gravel on the road. She would not whimper. She would not cry out. This was only a small glimpse of the fate that awaited her.

Joram would come to her trial as the Accuser. She must find a way to speak with him alone. To speak reason into his poisoned mind. To beg mercy from his hardened heart.

She stood, blood trickled down her leg, her sheet loosened, and she pulled it closer.

Someone put a cloak around her. Shame kept Zara from looking up.

"Take some water." A woman offered her a cup. Zara reached for the water and drank deeply. She knew that voice. She looked up into the face of her kinswoman Joanna, wife of Chuza. "I am deserving of death, but I am so afraid."

"I will not leave you or forsake you." Joanna squeezed her hand.

"My name has been blotted from the Lord's Book of Life."

"Have faith. Though the Lord's justice is sure, you may rely upon the Lord's unfailing mercy."

"Thank the Lord. When I die for my sin, I will not be alone." Zara struggled to her feet. "Perhaps I can gather enough courage to die well."

Chapter Five

Jerusalem

Temple Mount

Early Morning

Theo

Theo swung his crutch and struggled through the crowd heading for the Temple Mount. He moved with the masses across the foundation for the Temple designed by Herod the Great. He hesitated. *Dare I ask for my miracle?*

Theo pictured himself able to walk without effort, without weariness, without pain. Run, like the children chasing through the crowd. He could almost feel his leg straight and strong. Healed and whole. His hope moved him forward.

Several paces ahead, his friend Barid stared up at the golden roof of the Temple glinting in the early morning sun. The imposing Temple made Barid, a giant of a man, seem small.

Theo hobbled forward, lifted his crutch, and jabbed Barid's leg. "I fear the crowd will trample me underfoot. Please help me move closer to Yeshua."

Barid crouched down. "Hand me your crutch and climb onto my back." They made their way through the gate, past rows of twisted columns, onto the expansive Portico of Solomon. Barid plowed a path through the crowd swarming around Yeshua of Nazareth.

Theo slid down from Barid's back. Brimming hope loosed Theo's tongue. "What think you, dare I ask for my miracle?" His mumbled whisper quaked with fervor and fear.

"I will never forget the day Samuel the Samaritan carried you, a badly beaten Jew, to my inn on the road to Jericho. Ten years have passed since you were maimed and left for dead. Be bold. Your time for healing is come." Barid prodded him forward, making Theo stumble into a man and woman by the courtyard wall. Theo barely righted himself with his crutch.

The couple stared at his lame, misshapen leg—the man with pity, the woman with revulsion.

Theo's cheeks heated at his clumsiness and deformity.

The woman looked at Barid's blue eyes, short Roman tunic, and hobnailed sandals. She cupped her hand and spoke to the man, who shot a curious look at Barid. The Portico of Solomon was the only place a pagan was tolerated at the Temple in Jerusalem.

Barid glared a warning and gestured for the man and woman to look ahead. "The miracle worker is still teaching."

Yeshua of Nazareth sat on a low wall. His disciples had spread their cloaks and sat near him. "Have I not taught you? Ask and it shall be given you. Seek, and you shall find."

Theo's chest lightened. Perhaps he *could* gain his miracle.

Even while seated, Yeshua was tall. And despite His humble homespun robe, He seemed kingly. Every listener leaned in as if each word were a note of heavenly music. Though not comely, Yeshua was a man of riveting presence and persuasion.

Theo found himself trembling. "I have heard Yeshua teach and heard reports of His miracles, but I have never seen His healing power. And I tell you, I am afraid."

"Come, man. Why so afraid? You met Him. You have even partaken of a Sabbath supper with Him."

"Yeshua teaches that the Lord grants forgiveness to those who forgive. But what if He sees more of my past than I can recall? What if He requires that I forgive those who maimed me in exchange for healing?" Pain pounded through Theo's twisted leg. A pain that hardened his heart.

"Travelers at my inn say He heals all who come to Him."

Bitterness coiled in Theo's chest, tightening with each heartbeat. "I will never relinquish my right to vengeance."

Yeshua stood, a sign he had finished teaching. And the crowd moved back to make way for the press of incurables craving a cure.

"The sickly are flocking close. Yet you hang back." Barid's voice rang with the urgency Theo felt. "Are you content to remain a cripple?" Barid's face was as laden with compassion as his tone was laced with challenge.

A man stepped close to Yeshua and stood silently, patiently. Yet there was no outward sign of any affliction.

Barid leaned close and whispered into Theo's ear. "Perhaps he is given to fits."

Yeshua studied the face of the man before Him, then cupped His hands over the man's ears.

A curious quiet settled across the gathering. Hope seemed to shimmer in the silence.

"Be opened." Yeshua lifted His hands from the man's ears.

A gust of wind slipped through a crack in the courtyard wall.

The man touched his ears. A look of wonder dawned on his face. "Wind! I hear the wind again." He raised his hands to heaven. "The wind sounds like the satisfied sigh of a well-fed man. Since I was a child stricken with a summer fever, I was sentenced to a life of silence." He laughed, took the hand of a man nearby, and began to lead a dance that circled the courtyard. Other men joined the dance, rejoicing and praising the Lord. Some of the children in the crowd skipped behind them.

Nothing had been required of the deaf man. Perhaps Theo could be healed without surrendering his pursuit of vengeance. A heart-stilling, breath-stealing rush of hope raced through his veins.

A woman stretched a shrivelled hand toward Yeshua. He offered her His open palm, and she placed her hand in His. Her gnarled fingers opened like a wilted flower given fresh water. Living water. Tears streamed down her cheeks. An awe-filled silence descended upon the gathering. Before their very eyes, her hand was entirely restored.

Murmurs came from the crowd.

"This man is a prophet."

"Our prophets have been silent for four hundred years."

"John the Baptizer spoke of the Coming One."

Like a burst of lightning strikes during a summer storm, each revelation sent jolts of excitement through the throng.

"Yeshua heals with the spirit of Elijah."

"Could He be the Messiah?"

Then, as sure as thunder follows lightning, shouts of amazement, astonishment, and awe rumbled nearby.

"Theo. Now is your chance. Yeshua's healings were granted without condition." Barid shouldered an opening between two onlookers. "Move."

With short, stuttered steps, Theo drew in courage and edged himself near the young woman who was now closest to Yeshua.

Her eyes were covered by a cloth around her head. "Master, I have been blind for many years. When I was young, my cousins flung heavy stones from our roof to see whose stone would travel farthest. One stone did not fly but dropped onto my head. I was knocked senseless. When I awoke, my world was shrouded in darkness."

Yeshua stepped toward her. "Have you forgiven the cousin whose sin stole your sight?"

"Yes, Lord." She knelt, reached out, and clung to the fringes of his prayer shawl. "Have You not taught us to pray that our trespasses will be forgiven just as we forgive those who have trespassed against us?"

Theo turned to Barid. "I do not remember my name, my tribe, my former life. How can I repent of sins I do not recall?"

Barid gazed at Theo with a look he could not read. "You cannot recall one sin, during your last ten years as servant at my inn, of which you should repent? Even I, an unclean pagan, know that no man lives a perfect life."

Yeshua looked up toward Theo with eyes that seemed to say *Come. Forgive and be healed of your hate.*

Yeshua released the cloth covering the young woman's eyes. "My Father in Heaven has heard your prayers. Go and serve the Lord."

She gasped. "I can see." Her voice faltered and her face glowed. "Lord, for what sin was my sight snuffed? For I would never repeat it."

"Just as with our forefather Job, neither you nor your house had sinned. Your blindness was the work of the evil one. Out of your darkness, your faith and forgiving spirit have given great glory to the Lord."

Theo shrank back from his place before Yeshua. Hate snaked around his heart, choking the hope he had allowed to rise within. The crowd pressed close, and Theo moved farther away.

Barid followed and grabbed his arm. "Where are you going? Healing power abides in Yeshua's hands. You were closest. Your miracle was at your feet."

"You well know that I do not remember those who beat me. What you do not know is that for ten years I have studied every face, be he Roman or Jew or pagan, wondering if he could be one of the men who crippled me. And my mind is consumed with ceaseless hate."

"Are you delighted with your crutch and pain as constant companions? Content to live out your life a cripple?" Barid's face filled with undisguised disgust. "You are yet a young man."

Theo shook Barid off. Worry wormed into Theo's stomach. "I will not forgive those I do not remember, nor those I do—the priest and Levite who passed by and left me to die." His worry cramped into an angry stone. "To beg Yeshua for healing, then be spurned because I refuse to forgive, would be beyond bearing."

Two Temple guards thrust past Theo, dragging a woman between them. She clutched a cloak and sheet around her to cover her nakedness. Theo could not see her face beneath her long dark curls. But as she passed, he could almost smell her fear. Almost hear her heart pounding. Three Pharisees followed, the tails of their black turbans and hems of their robes billowing behind them.

"Wait," Theo whispered, then turned to follow them. Barid came alongside him. The Temple guards threw the woman to the ground at Yeshua's feet.

The head Pharisee pointed his staff at the cowering woman. "She was caught in the very act of adultery. The Law of Moses commands us to stone adulterers. What say you, Yeshua of Nazareth?"

The woman crawled up onto her knees, bowing low, her face to the ground. A picture of abject shame and humiliation.

Several onlookers had picked up stones along the way. One man held jagged stones in both hands. Barid closed his hand over the hilt of his short sword. "They would stone her? Here? In the Temple?"

Theo's palm hovered over Barid's sword hand. "No. They would not defile the Temple."

"Why bring her to Yeshua for judgment?" Barid released his grip.

"It is a cunning trap. If Yeshua condemns her to death, He usurps Roman authority and contradicts His teaching that the merciful will inherit the earth. If He grants mercy, He breaks the Law of Moses. If He forgives her sins, He claims to be HaShem."

"Whether this woman lives or dies means nothing? These Pharisees only feign righteousness?" Barid's tone was laden with scorn.

"The Pharisees seek ways to accuse Him." Theo looked toward Yeshua. "Hypocrisy or blasphemy. Either charge will satisfy."

Yeshua stooped before the woman.

She pushed up, raised her eyes to His.

Theo studied her face. A lancing jolt raced through him. He did not remember where, he did not remember when, but he knew at some place, at some time, he had seen this woman's eyes ... both amber, one a glittering gem, the other a glinting cat eye.

Chapter Six

Theo grabbed Barid's arm. "I know this woman."

Barid pulled Theo to the side, away from others. "Who is she to you?"

Theo's heart thrashed in his chest. "I do not know, but I know those eyes." His voice shook. "I have not seen her at your inn or on the Jericho Road."

"I, too, would have remembered those arresting eyes. Think. Where else could you have seen this doomed woman?"

Realization struck Theo like a hammer hitting a nail. "She must be someone from the empty tablet of my life before I was beaten. She could be the key that unlocks the secrets of my past."

"Could she have been your wife?"

"Look at her. Ten years ago, she would have been a young girl, not of an age to be married."

"Study her face again."

The woman looked desperate. Without hope. So afraid. So alone. "I am sure she was someone close to me."

Theo had never sensed even the slightest vestige of his

former life. But now the sight of this woman had sparked something. He stared at her eyes and tried to sift vague impressions —wheat from chaff—truth from imaginings.

A sudden icy chill spread from his center and raced down his arms and legs. Would this frightened, forlorn woman be stoned to death? Would he be left forever in a fog of buried memories?

Theo looked from the woman on her knees to the crowd surrounding her. Some hung back, wringing their hands, worry etched on their faces. But others, rocks in their hands, lunged forward. A pack of wild dogs, bloodlust in their eyes.

Theo's breaths came heavy, as if a grinding stone had been laid upon his chest. He looked toward Yeshua. *HaShem, speak to Your prophet. Grant this woman undeserved mercy.*

Yeshua bent down and wrote with His finger on the ground where only the woman could see.

"Come, Rabbi, what say you about this adulteress?" The head Pharisee's jeer pierced the gathering.

The people muttered. Now some raised their hands, praying for clemency. Others raised their rocks, urging condemnation. An uneasy silence loomed. A wordless battle for the life of this hapless woman raged.

Yeshua did not look up. He crouched and continued writing.

Barid nudged Theo. "What is He doing? Is He writing His judgment?"

"He is writing downside-up, from left to right, so only the adulteress can read his words."

"Can she, a woman, read?"

Theo's mind was filled with the memory of teaching a little girl to read, but in his mind's eye, the girl's head was bent toward the parchment, and he could not see her eyes.

"I do not know how I know, but I believe I taught this woman to read."

"Could she be a daughter?" Barid's deep, excited voice crackled with hope.

Theo put his hands on his head, then lifted them as if opening his skull. "Your wits have left you. Look at us. We are too close in age to be father and daughter."

The youngest Pharisee moved toward Yeshua and stopped at his side. "Rabbi, are you so filled with mercy that you fear pronouncing the punishment demanded by the Law of Moses?" The Pharisee's mouth tightened into a mocking line.

Yeshua finished writing.

The adulteress pulled her cloak tighter. Her face softened, changing from fear to something else. Perhaps acceptance. Perhaps courage.

Yeshua straightened and met the eyes of each onlooker, His gaze seeming to encompass an eternity. Finally, His gaze came to rest on the eldest Pharisee. "Let anyone among you who is without sin be the first to cast a stone."

Yeshua stooped and wrote on the ground again.

The woman studied the second message. Her shoulders shook, silent tears streamed down her cheeks, and she prostrated herself on the ground before Him in an attitude of worship.

Theo held his breath, afraid to break the sanctity of the moment.

The eldest Pharisee tossed his rock from one hand to the other as if his hands were two sides of a scale.

All eyes were turned to the Pharisee. The people's murmurs quieted. The children settled into a surprising silence. Even the birds of the air halted their morning song.

It seemed all of creation held its breath with Theo.

The eldest Pharisee flashed a look of begrudging defeat

toward Yeshua. He moved through the curious crowd, and they parted like the Red Sea. At the gate, the Pharisee laid his rock on the ground and left the Temple.

Theo waved toward the remaining men holding rocks. "Yeshua has cut the snare the Pharisees set for Him." An almost silent laugh escaped Theo's lips. "They are caught in a trap of their own making."

"Tell me what this means."

Theo motioned Barid to lean close and whispered. "The Pharisees brought no witnesses. There was no Accuser. The Law of Moses requires both. Anyone who lifts a hand against this woman has broken the Law they so rigorously uphold." Theo waved his crutch toward the remaining Pharisees. "It is they who should be stoned."

Barid smiled, with a look of relief mixed with growing belief. "Yeshua knows every letter of the Law. Every stroke of the quill. It is as if He wrote it Himself."

The crowd's mood seemed to shift against the Pharisees. Rumblings became grumblings, and grumblings became shouts. The Pharisees' faces turned ashen.

Barid clapped Theo on the shoulder. "Every ember of evil intent against this woman has been doused."

"Doused by the living water Yeshua offers those who follow Him." Theo's words had spilled from deep within.

"The battle for her life is already won." Barid rapped his knuckles on Theo's arm.

The next Pharisee left, placing his rock beside the first. Then each man in turn, from oldest to youngest, put their rock upon the pile.

Praise HaShem. Not one soul was left who would dare stone her.

A Certain Mercy

Zara

Zara, on her knees, body and mind numb, stared at the Temple courtyard floor and the growing pile of rocks. The last man spat, then threw his rock on the pile.

Zara's hands trembled, her legs shook, her heart quaked. She lay down on her side, hugging her knees.

She would not be stoned. She would not suffer the bruising, cutting blows of rocks hurled at her. This day, she would not watch her lifeblood seep away. Would this prophet proclaim some other punishment, some other penance?

Breathe, just Breathe.

Again, that still, small voice spoke to her soul.

Zara wanted to sink into the ground, hide from the weight of her sin. She had been sure she would die a slow, horrific death. She wanted to cry. Cry out her dead lover's name. But she would live. Live with the guilt and the shame. For Auri's death, she alone bore the blame.

Breathe, just Breathe.

She gasped but could not draw in air. She gazed at the hem of Yeshua's robe, gathering the courage to look upon his face.

Breathe, just Breathe.

Peace washed over her. The heaviness lifted and Zara drew in a deep breath.

Mere moments ago, she had stared Death in the face. Now, she sought the eyes of Yeshua —calm and filled with abounding grace.

Three trumpet blasts sounded. The signal for the Temple gates to open for the morning sacrifice.

Zara shivered. Like the sacrificial lamb, her blood had almost been spilt too. But Yeshua had redeemed her from the clutches of Death.

He gestured for her to stand.

She rose, clutching Joanna's cloak, covering her nakedness.

"Woman. Where are they? Has not one man condemned you?"

"Not one, sir."

"Then neither do I condemn you." His face was full of compassion, no trace of judgment.

Heat rushed through her veins—a cleansing fire of forgiveness.

"Go. Leave your life of sin."

The fire in her veins settled to a warmth that cradled her heart.

She studied what Yeshua had written on the ground. *Fear not.* A promise of hope.

The second time, He wrote just one word, *Zera*, not Zara. Zera meant seed. A new beginning.

Yeshua had given her a new life. A new name.

Chapter Seven

From Temple Mount To Bethany
Same day, mid-morning

Zera (Zara)

J oanna approached, her arm linked with another woman. Following just behind them was a big man walking beside a man with a crutch.

Zera looked down. "Kinswoman, I have brought such dishonor upon our family."

Joanna's arms enfolded her. "Praise HaShem for His mercy. I feared you were lost to us." She held Zera as snug as the swaddling clothes wrapped around a newborn babe.

Zera settled into Joanna's forgiving embrace, surprised but thankful for her undeserved love.

"Zara, these are my friends. Mary of Bethany, Barid the innkeeper, and his servant, Theo."

Zara forced herself to look up. "I am now called Zera."

A question flickered across Joanna's face, but she held her tongue.

Mary of Bethany, as small, dark, and delicate as Barid was big, blond, and brawny, took off her own cloak and held it up. "Put your arms in and wear this front-to-back over the other one."

"Here, take this." Theo removed his rope belt and handed it to Mary. She used the belt over both cloaks to gird Zera's waist. "Now, you are well covered."

A boy on the cusp of manhood ran up to her and took off his sandals. "You have need of these, I do not. My feet are not so tender as yours." He scampered away.

"A thousand thanks. I am overcome by your many kindnesses."

Barid knelt and began to put the sandals on her battered feet.

Mary offered Zera an arm and steadied her. "You cannot return home, not to your humiliated husband. Who knows what wrath he may wreak?"

"Do you know that boy? I want to return these sandals."

"Keep them. Emet is a servant in our household, and we will replace them."

Joanna took Zera's other arm. "We will go with Mary of Bethany to her brother's home, the House of Lazarus."

They started across Solomon's Portico but stopped when Emet ran in front of them chasing a wild dove. "Look, these stacked stones look like a pillar of remembrance."

Remembrance. Auri was dead.

She stepped away from Joanna, walked to the pile of stones, and chose a small, sharp one. She clenched her hand, a jagged edge digging into her skin, her shame. *Auri.* A stone of remembrance of her sin.

She had succumbed to temptation. Auri was dead, yet her

life had been spared. Her sin forgiven. But she could never forgive herself.

Mary of Bethany joined her and put an arm around her waist. "We must leave this place. Your husband may be on his way here."

Barid gestured to Theo. "We will escort the women home."

Zera's legs shook so badly she dared not take a step. "I was within a hairsbreadth of being stoned."

Mary squeezed her tighter. "Can you walk?"

"I will try ... but I am suddenly undone."

Joanna rushed forward and supported Zera from the other side. "We will help you."

"Theo, you walk in front and scout for any sign of trouble." The big man's stern tone sounded like a soldier.

They walked for too long a time, too great a distance. Steeply downhill. It was all Zera could do to take the next step through the mindless fog that seemed to enshroud her. All she wanted to do was stop moving and sleep, but she pictured hands holding rocks raised to stone her, and her legs gave way.

The women kept her from sinking to her knees and moved her to sit on a nearby boulder. The lame man helped her drink a cup of water. She could not recall any names. Except her new one. *Zera. New beginning.*

She must survive. Yeshua had defied the powerful Pharisees and put Himself at risk. His mercy to her must not be in vain.

The big man joined them. "It is yet another mile to Bethany."

Zera looked at the road now rising steeply uphill. She tried to stand, but her legs failed her again. "Forgive me. I can go no farther."

His face took on a look of understanding, a gentleness she

had never seen on Joram's face. "Allow me." He lifted her into his arms.

Zera settled into his strong embrace. She was safe. She was not alone. Zera's tears flowed freely, silently. She had been forgiven by a prophet of the Lord. The innkeeper's long strides lulled her to sleep.

After some time, she roused to what seemed part dream and part wakefulness.

"Barid. Zera most needs sleep." A woman's voice. "A place under this tree will serve."

Zera did not want to leave the warmth and peace of the big man's arms.

He lowered her to the ground onto something soft.

"I will keep watch over her." The lame man said.

Someone covered her with a cloak, and she pulled it close.

Sleep rolled over her, and she succumbed to oblivion.

After what seemed hours, Zera startled awake—heart racing, breaths coming fast and hard, drenched in sweat. She sat, wiped her brow, and leaned against the trunk of a tree by a fallow field. She was not in a stoning pit, not surrounded by black-robed Pharisees, not looking into the all-seeing eyes of Yeshua.

She took a deep breath and fought to settle her fear. But her legs still trembled, and she struggled to stand.

Theo helped her to her feet. "Zera, move slowly."

A fount of gratitude welled up within her. This lame man knew what a burden it was to move slowly. After a few moments, she gathered some strength and walked toward Mary, who stood by the cookfire. "I would help with the work."

"Yeshua is joining us for a meal." Mary looked past Zera, a faraway look in her eyes. The sound of awe in her voice. "It is not work, but an honor to prepare food for Him, our teacher, our Lord."

"Then, please, let me be so honored."

Mary took Zera's arm. "You still seem overwrought. You must sleep longer, regain your strength."

"Please, give me a task. Any task." Zera shuddered. "If I sleep, the terrors of the stoning pit will torment me again."

"May your night terrors be banished."

Zera placed her hands over her heart. "How is it that you are so tender with me, a fallen woman? Your loving-kindness astounds me."

Mary brushed a lock of hair away from Zera's face. "Yeshua teaches us that He came to redeem the sinners, not the righteous. I strive to be as merciful and forgiving as He."

"He would be pleased with you. Now, tell me, how may I help?"

"Very well. Stay here. I will go to Martha, my sister, at the house just up the hill. See what she would have us do now."

Martha was directing servants who prepared a long, low table in the outer courtyard, under a cluster of olive trees. Mary spoke with her and returned with leeks and garlic, which Zera added to the pot.

Martha looked toward Zera, scowled, and headed her way.

A flash of fear ran through Zera's veins. Had she done something to displease her?

Martha walked right past Zera to Mary. "Sister, do you mean to leave this woman in this shameful state of dress?"

"She has just awakened. Forgive me. I will make all things right."

"Humph." Martha left, shaking her head.

Mary laughed, a light musical sound, and there was amusement in her eyes that made Zera smile.

"Would you care to share what has tickled your spirit?"

"My sister is like our toothless sheepdog, Samson. Her *humph* is like his growl—never followed by a bite. But she was right, you will want to wash." Mary led Zera toward the house into a small chamber. "There is a basin of water and a linen towel." She opened a wooden chest. "Here are clean garments." She laid a clean head covering, long tunic, and cloak, on the raised sleeping pallet and left.

Zera washed and dressed quickly, grateful to be clean. She rushed back to Mary.

"You seem remarkably revived."

"I feel much stronger now. How many guests are expected?"

"We never know how many sheep will follow their Shepherd here." Mary lifted the stir paddle, tasted the stew, and added salt. "More and more of Yeshua's followers set up camp and sleep in the field we have left fallow."

Could she bear to face Yeshua? He had told her to go and sin no more. If Auri was not surely dead, she might well run straight back into his arms. Would Yeshua somehow read her heart and know of her weakness? "When will Yeshua come?"

"We never know the hour of His coming." Mary wiped her brow. "If He is delayed past nightfall, our handmaids will fill and trim all the oil lamps."

Handmaid. Rhea. Zera had been blinded to all things beyond herself. Her faithful handmaid had been left in Joram's greedy clutches.

Chapter Eight

Bethany, House of Lazarus
The next day

Zera

At first light, Zera found Mary of Bethany. "I must go to Joram's house before he sells my handmaid at the midday slave market."

Mary searched Zera's eyes and nodded. "You cannot face your furious husband alone." Mary called for Emet, who was climbing a nearby tree. "Find Theo and Barid."

Emet ran to the house and emerged a few moments later with Theo hobbling and Barid striding behind him.

Mary lifted her hands to them. "Zera plans to return to the House of Joram."

"You have both been so kind." Zera's voice hitched over her worry and gratitude. "Though I have no right to ask for your help, my husband Joram is cruel and desperate for money. I fear he may sell my defenseless handmaid this very day."

Theo tucked his crutch closer, so he stood taller. "I assure you I am of sound mind, but somehow, I know in my bones, I am entrusted with your safety."

"I do not understand." Zera sent a questioning look toward Barid.

"Since Theo was beaten and crippled ten years past, he remembers nothing of his former life."

Theo's eyes studied Zera's face, not with the look of a lover, not with the look of a husband, but with the desperate look of a man who is lost, unable to find his way home. "I do not remember you, but I know I have seen your eyes. Tell me. Do you know me?"

Zera studied Theo from face to feet. She did not know anyone who was lame, yet there was something about him that seemed to call from her past. And at the Temple, he did not flinch when he first met her eyes, as if her cat eye was familiar to him. Theo's face was filled with hope for answers. But she would not offer false assurance. "In truth, I cannot say that I know you."

"Nevertheless, Zera, I sense you are someone of import to me and I must offer my protection."

The sincerity in Theo's voice brought a quiver to Zera's lip. She looked from Theo to Barid. "I must make haste to save my handmaid, but I do not know what dangers we may encounter."

Barid touched the hilt of the gladius at his waist. "If you are determined to return to the house of your husband, we will go with you. His anger may know no bounds, and under your law, I cannot be a witness."

Theo turned to Emet. "Are you of age? Bar mitzvah?"

The boy stopped squirming and puffed out his chest. "Yes."

Zera smiled at his lowered pitch and his effort to seem manly.

Theo waved him forward. "Go tell mistress Martha we may have need of you as a second witness, then catch up to us."

They rushed to Jerusalem, entered through the gates, and went up the winding streets to the upper city and the mansions of the wealthy. Zera tucked her veil so only her eyes could be seen. Her fear for Reah flooded her with a newfound strength and vigor. Joram's house came into view.

Zera glanced toward her chambers at the corner of the mansion where she had been pulled from her peaceful sleep next to Auri. The memory set her insides skittering.

Barid signalled for the group to halt. "We must not rush in before we know who and what awaits. What may oppose us."

Zera could picture Barid with the shield and sword of a centurion, ready for battle. "There is a side entrance for servants."

"Stay in the shadows. Show us the way." Barid rounded on Emet. "And not even the squeak of a mouse from you."

Emet, wide-eyed, covered his mouth with his fingers and nodded his head.

Zera stepped through the gate into the courtyard. "Look, the servant door is ajar."

Barid turned and leaned close to Theo. "Wait here and keep watch so our way of escape will not be blocked."

Barid crossed his arms and inspected Emet. "If you would go with me to the front lines, you must follow my orders, without pause, without question, without distraction."

Emet brought his fist to his chest.

Barid stroked his chin. "How can we cross the courtyard without attracting notice?"

"We must pretend we are travelers." Zera's whisper was quiet but sure. "A family willing to work for shelter and food. Each day, people come to that door begging for help."

"Every day?" Theo looked toward the door.

"They know the lady of the house will never turn them away." At the last setting sun, she was mistress here. Now, mere hours from the next sunset, she was hiding as a beggar woman. "Let us find my handmaid." Zera put her arm around Emet's shoulders and hunched forward, pretending she was a much older woman. She shuffled across the courtyard, Barid close at her side.

When they reached the servant's door, Zera and Emet pressed into the shadows of the fig trees that shaded the threshold. Barid stood guard behind the nearest tree.

Another couple waited nearby. The man grinned at Barid. "They say the mistress comes to the door morning and night. This morning she did not come."

Tears blurred Zera's sight. Praise HaShem. They had not borne witness to her humiliation.

"Please. Please. Take my part. Plead for me." Reah's frantic cry carried from the servant quarters.

Joram's personal manservant led Reah, hands bound by a rope, through the courtyard. The two black kittens crept up, pounced, and clawed at her hem.

"Please beg the master not to whip me." She pulled back, dug in her heels. The kittens scurried away.

The manservant yanked her forward, spat on the ground. His mouth slitted into a cruel grin. "The master would never whip you."

A look of relief dawned on Reah's face.

"That would mark you. And ruin your price on the auction block." He grabbed her shoulders and shoved her forward. The manservant headed straight toward Zera. She shrank back and looked down, but she heard her handmaid trip across the threshold.

Zera did not dare move, did not dare breathe. But her heart broke over Reah's pain.

The man seeking work motioned toward the door. "They say the master here is as greedy and cruel as the mistress is generous and kind."

"You have spoken true." Barid reached up and picked figs, which he shared with the others.

Murmurs drew Zera's attention back to the gate. Ira and his son were in deep conversation, oblivious to their surroundings. Zera held her breath when they reached the doorway and prayed she would go unnoticed.

At the threshold, Ira's profile was outlined by the sun. "Joram, your summons took me from my work. What could you possibly want from me?"

Ira's son was now at his shoulder.

Zera moved, well behind him but where she could see into the room.

Rhea threw herself at Ira's feet. "Save me. I am heartbeats from being carted away to the auction block."

Fury darkened Ira's face. "I see I have arrived none too soon." He unbound Reah's wrists. "You cannot sell this woman. She is not your slave to sell."

"My wife is dead. I am her sole heir." Joram tucked his thumbs into the embroidered edges of his robe. "You will turn Zara's holdings over to me. And her slave will go to the auction block this very hour."

"Your wife is not dead."

Joram crossed his arms, a smug snarl crossed his lips. "By now, she has been stoned for adultery."

Without doubt, her husband would take every advantage of her untimely death.

"You must be the only man in all Jerusalem who has not heard the news." Disgust colored Ira's tone.

"What news?" Joram's face tightened and his voice broke.

"Yeshua of Nazareth challenged the Pharisees. There was

no Accuser, no partner in the adultery. And there were no witnesses. Thus, if anyone had cast a stone, he would have broken the Law. Zara lives. She has been set free."

Ira's son moved Rhea behind them.

Joram's eyes turned black as pitch, his face changed to that of a demon. He grabbed Ira and shook him. "You lie. She must be dead. I want her dead." Joram's hands cinched Ira's throat. "I need her dead."

Ira's son drew his sword.

Joram grabbed Ira from behind, pulled a knife, and laid the blade against Ira's throat. "When Zara's steward dies, no one will stand between me and her fortune."

"If you kill my father, you will be stoned."

"You have no second witness. My slave cannot and would not testify against me."

Emet rushed through the door. "I overheard the evil you have spoken. I am a witness."

Joram released Ira.

He rubbed his throat. "If you murdered me, it would have done you no good. When you became possessed by the demon of casting dice, Zara's father appointed my son, upon my death, the steward of all Zara's wealth."

Ira faced Rhea. "Come. I will safeguard you until we can reunite you with your mistress."

Rhea fell to her knees. "Praise HaShem, you saved me from the slave auction."

Zera moved into the shade.

Ira and his son helped Rhea to her feet, left the mansion, and walked slowly across the courtyard.

Emet followed them outside but lingered near the doorpost. Joram's manservant strode outside, heading toward the servant quarters.

Barid pulled Zera farther away from the door. "Do not try to speak to Rhea now."

Emet came near and spoke into Zera's ear. "Joram paid his manservant to follow your steward. Be wary. See how he hides near that tree and sneaks behind them out the gate."

Loud thuds and the crash of shattering pottery made Zera start. Joram must be casting everything in reach against the unforgiving stone walls. Casting pottery in place of his beloved dice. Joram was well named. *One who casts.*

At least Rhea had not suffered for the sins of her mistress.

Auri. Zara tugged at Barid's sleeve. "I must speak with Ira and assure that the man caught with me is buried with honor."

Barid looked at her with an expression beyond astonishment. "My lady, have you lost your wits? You must hide. Your husband has every temptation to plot your death."

"Both of you are blind. You have missed the mark." Emet edged between Barid and Zera and looked from one to the other. "No one notices a servant boy, and secrets are spilled. I heard Joram speak freely to his manservant. Everything that has befallen you has been a plot conceived by your cunning husband. He set a trap to catch you in adultery. Only if you were dead could he call Ira and demand your inheritance. An inheritance he desperately needs to pay his gambling debts."

A fire raced through Zera's veins. Not fear. Not shame. But a blaze of fury. Her husband had neglected her. Left her lonely and alone with Auri. For many days. And many nights. Her husband had woven a web of temptation. A temptation he meant to be fatal.

"Joram meant to murder me by stoning."

Chapter Nine

Zera edged her back along the wall and moved farther away from the servant door of the mansion. This place was no longer home, but a death trap. "Hear Joram raging on? He wants my riches. He wants me dead."

Barid moved next to Zera, shielding her from the view of those coming and going through the door. "Danger lurks in every corner. We must leave."

The beggar couple looked at each other with wide eyes. "Even though we are faint with hunger, this is not the time to ask anything of the master." The husband put his arm around the wife, and they started across the courtyard. The beggar woman's eyes searched the branches of the plucked fig tree. "Even the high branches are empty. We will not eat tonight."

Emet pulled a round of bread from his waist sack.

Barid playfully jabbed Emet in the side. "Your boyish frolics are pardoned by your manly charity. Give them the bread and take Zera with you. Traveling with them will keep you and Zera safe from prying eyes. Warn our friends in Bethany that Zera is in danger."

Emet ran up to the couple and offered them his bread. The woman hugged him. The man raised his hand in blessing. Both tore into the loaf, ravenous as wolves. Emet looked back, waiting for Zera to join him.

Barid turned to Zera. "Do not delay. Make haste. You must leave with the boy. Now that Joram knows you live, he will seek to take your life by some other means."

A wave of fatigue and fear washed over Zera. She slowly slid down the wall.

Barid signalled Emet to go. Once again, he scooped Zera into his arms. The strong, steady thrum in his chest coaxed her unbridled heartbeat to settle.

At the courtyard gate, Barid stopped at Theo's side. "We must keep Zera out of sight." She nestled closer into Barid's hold. She wanted nothing more than to stop her panicked thoughts and vanish.

"Traveling with me, a cripple, and carrying Zera in your arms, will draw the attention of each one you pass."

"You go ahead to Bethany. Zera is overwrought. We may need to stop along the way."

"I have a plan." Theo's voice was pressed with purpose. "Cover Zera's face completely and call out loudly as you go— *unclean ... unclean ... unclean.* The people will assume you are carrying a dying woman to the Valley of the Lepers. None will look closely, most will turn their heads, all will keep their distance."

Zera covered her face and studied Theo as he hobbled away. Something in the timbre of his voice seemed familiar, comforting. But she had never known any man who was lame.

Barid called out in his deep, commanding voice, "Leper. Unclean." He took long strides down the hill away from the houses in the upper quarter. "Leper. Unclean." From within the folds of her head covering, Zera watched the crowds on the road scatter. They left Jerusalem and turned onto the steep road up to Bethany.

"Take her to Yeshua of Nazareth." One woman's cry broke through. "He sleeps in Bethany this night. The lepers hoping for healing will camp beyond the fallow field, far away from those who are well."

"Bless you." Barid's voice seemed to blanket Zera in safety.

"You need not carry me farther. My strength has recovered."

"I cannot put you down when I was just calling out *leper*, but we are nearing the branch in the road that leads to Bethany. There will be fewer travelers there."

Barid's stride shortened, and he moved off the road. "Here are some boulders. We will stop to rest and drink water." He set Zera on the largest boulder.

She studied the faces of a few others who had stopped with them. None had been near at Barid's last warning shout.

Barid handed her a cup and poured from his waterskin.

Zera slid the cup beneath her face veil and drank deeply. "Many thanks for all you have done for me."

"In truth, it was Theo, my servant and friend, who felt compelled to help you." Barid's cheeks reddened. "Though I, too, feel it is the will of the Lord."

Zera knew she had not masked the surprise in her eyes. "You look and dress like a pagan—are you a worshiper of our one true God?"

"My closest friends are a Samaritan and a Jew. Both worship the One God from different mountains. Both believe Yeshua is the long-awaited Messiah." Barid's face shifted from earnest to amused. "I would not be the first gentile to become a God-fearer, but you are the first to ask."

Barid took the empty cup from Zera and put it in his sack.

"What think you of Yeshua, who rescued you from certain death?"

"Before this morning, I only heard rumors of Him. Herod Antipas fears Yeshua of Nazareth may be John the Baptizer come back from the grave."

"Zera, Herod's fears are unfounded. Yeshua and the Baptizer were kinsmen. Both walked the earth together."

"At Solomon's Portico, Yeshua spoke and acted with the authority of a prophet. And our prophets have been silent for four hundred years. Even the Pharisees accepted His judgment. What think you of this Yeshua?"

"I watched Him heal. His miracles confirm the truth of His every word."

"Barid, your face shines with the light of a certain faith."

"Yeshua says He has been sent by the One God. And I believe He can only speak truth—no matter how hard to hear. He can only do good works and love others, for there is no evil in Him."

Surely, her savior, Yeshua of Nazareth, was as holy as Joram of Jerusalem was heinous. "You speak as if you are a close disciple, and you live by His words."

"My tongue moved of its own accord, but my mind and heart rejoice in agreement."

Sorrow and guilt settled like an ox yoke around Zera's neck. "One day, my heart may rejoice again. But for now, I am content that my life was spared." Zera rose. "If we are to reach Bethany before nightfall, we must leave now."

They climbed the steep road. The sun was low, golden rays breaking through the clouds. It reminded her of the Belenus sun-god image emblazoned on Auri's chariot.

Auri.

Zera pulled her cloak close. Her sinful desires had caused his death. She must make sure no one else suffered for her sins.

They walked into the village of Bethany and turned down a path lined with fig trees. After close to one hundred paces, they rounded a bend, and the house of Lazarus came into view. The nearby field was filled with Yeshua's followers who lit campfires, for the nights were growing colder. The flickering fires in the dark night reminded Zera of stars shining across the heavens.

They returned to the tree where Zera had slept. She turned toward Barid, but Emet appeared at her shoulder, seemingly out of nothingness. "Come with me. Theo and Joanna have supper waiting away from any others."

"Thank you, Emet."

Barid tousled Emet's hair. "Well done. You made good time. You must have been watching for us."

Emet grinned and scampered ahead. Barid and Zera followed him into the field and approached the campfire. Theo stood and guided Zera to a fallen tree trunk. She sat next to Joanna, facing away from the light of the other fires.

Joanna took Zera's hand. "Theo has told us Joram wanted you dead."

"I cannot ever return home. I must hide from Joram. Seek a new life ... a new family. A new home."

Emet cupped his hands, whispering to Joanna. "Let me tell her. Let me tell her." The boy's whisper was dancing across the air.

"You may show her."

Zera looked to Joanna. "What is this?"

"A happy surprise, but be still."

Emet brought a woman out from the darkness, into the shadows of the firelight.

Reah.

"Praise HaShem." Zera ran to Reah, took her hands, and began to skip a feast day dance. She stopped and hugged her.

Joanna's eye sparkled, but she put a warning finger to her lips.

Zera quieted. "Reah, you are safe. We came to rescue you and watched from the shadows when Ira saved you from the slave auction."

Reah sat by Zera. "You came for me? At the risk of Joram's rage?"

Zera pulled Reah close. "Because of my weakness, you were almost sold. How could I have lived with that guilt?"

"Oh, my lady, I watched your husband treat you worse than he treated me, a slave. While Joram had set you aside, another made you feel worthy of love."

Barid crouched in front of them. "Reah, how did you come to be here so quickly?"

Reah turned to Barid. "Emet was—"

"Let me tell it." Emet set his shoulders and stood tall. "I caught sight of Joram's spy following Ira, his son, and Reah. I followed them to Ira's house. When the spy left to report to Joram, I gave Ira warning." Emet shuffled from foot to foot. "Reah and I made haste to Bethany."

Barid clapped Emet on the shoulder, almost toppling the boy. "You are a clever soldier."

A hallowed hush fell over the field. Zera looked up. Several guests arrived and were led toward the low table. Martha rushed to wash the feet of a tall man with the strong presence of a leader.

Zera whispered to Joanna, "Well-intended but high-handed Martha may have met her equal."

Joanna laughed under her breath. "He is the big fisherman, Simon. Now called Peter."

Emet ran to help. He washed the feet of a much smaller man, with the semblance of a gentle, faithful follower.

Joanna gestured toward the smaller man. "John, the soft-spoken disciple who is quick to grasp the fine points of the teachings of Yeshua."

"He is come." A vigorous, mature man entered. He so resembled Mary that he could only be her older brother, Lazarus. He ushered Yeshua to the place of honor.

Some called out soft greetings. Others waved and nodded. Emet washed Yeshua's feet, and He placed His hand on Emet's head, blessing him.

What could she say to her redeemer? A forgiver of sins. One who many hoped was a future king. Zera sighed her relief. She was down the hill at the cookfire, where she could hear and watch, but not so close she would need to say or do anything.

Mary served Yeshua. He blessed the bread and the wine. "Master, this day your hands have healed the masses, your lips have offered forgiveness and hope. Now let us offer you sustenance and peace and rest."

Yeshua looked weary. Weary to the bone. His shoulders slumped as if He carried the sorrows of the whole world. The people gathered in groups around cook fires. They devoured their food like starving sheep.

Mary reached for a nearby harp, placed the kinnor in her lap, and strummed softly.

Zera's heart lightened. "Such a singular soothing sound. Such unusual workmanship."

Theo used his crutch to lower himself onto the log next to Reah. "My Samaritan friend Samuel, who rescued me from sure death, carved that harp for Mary. One day, you may meet him and his wife, Shamara."

"You call a Samaritan friend? I hope, in time, you will share how this came to be."

A young voice began to sing a psalm of Ascent. One of the beloved psalms sung when going up to a feast in Jerusalem. Emet—his captivating, high voice pure and sure.

One by one, others joined the praise. One song would end and within a few breaths, someone else would begin another.

Barid's deep, rich voice often joined the music-making.

Zera smiled, unable to hide her admiration. "You, a pagan, know more of the melodies and words than I, a Jewess in the line of Herod."

"For many years, countless caravans camped near my inn, and I learned the shared songs of the land. Though Theo remembers nothing of his life before the beating, strangely, he has never forgotten the songs of his people."

The music faded, and Yeshua stood to sing. His face lifted to the brilliant starry heavens.

He began singing an ancient melody, a *tehilah*. This one, by tradition, sung only by men.

"Hava nashira, hal ... le ... lujah. *Let us sing together. Praise the Lord.*"

Words from before the exile to Babylon. Before the rule of Judges and Kings. Before the time of Moses.

Yeshua's tenor—part sorrow, part joy—carried across the field scattered with cookfires. Emet's lilting soprano joined in, creating a haunting harmony.

"Hava nashira, hal ... le ... lu ... jah."

After the next phrase, Barid added his resonant bass, a new layer to the harmony.

"Hava nashira, hal ... le ... lu ... jah."

Zera's soul took flight. This was a song she had oft heard her father sing.

These people, this place, this night felt like home. Like family. Her family.

Theo pushed himself up with his crutch and joined the worship. His gentle, baritone voice seemed to surround her, carrying her back on a sea of memory to another place and time. A beautiful chord lingered in the air. Harmony reigned until the last note waned.

And a thrill sparked through Zera. Her heart went still. Stuttered then fluttered and trilled.

Theo's speaking voice had pricked at Zera's memory, but his singing voice had opened the floodgates. Zera had heard Theo sing before. More than once. Long ago, when she was a young girl.

She rose, took Theo's hands, and kissed them. She gazed into his eyes. Eyes filled with questions. "I do know you. I know you well."

Zera hugged Theo and felt a shudder run through him. She stepped back, and bewilderment flickered across his face.

"You say you know me?" Theo's chin trembled, and his face turned the gray white of oncoming storm clouds.

The big man took Theo's crutch and offered his arm. "My friend, you should sit."

When Theo was seated on the log, Zera dropped to his side.

Theo stared at her. "I know your amber eyes, your cat eye, but nothing more." Disappointment dragged the pitch of his voice lower. "Who am I to you?"

Joanna looked to Rhea and Barid. "We will take our leave so Zera and Theo may speak without other ears to hear."

"Please stay." Theo gestured to a nearby log. "I would have our friends with us when I learn of my past. Barid, draw that log close so each may sit."

Barid placed the log, sat, and cleared his throat. His face filled with worry. "My lady Zera, take care to uncover Theo's past in small sips."

"Why?" Theo's voice faltered.

"One of my soldiers lost all memory after a horrific blow to the head. His friends sought to spur his memory by flooding his mind with stories of his past. When he still had no recall, he became distraught and disbelieving."

Zera touched Theo's hand. "Do not push your mind past the point of peace."

Theo shook both fists in the air, his face red as a pomegranate and warped with emotion. "Peace has abandoned me for ten torturous years. I will not wait one blink of an eye longer. Zera, tell me. Who am I to you?"

"We are cousins. My sweet, loving, departed *ima* was your mother's younger sister."

Theo's look of shock was etched with uncertainty. "Ten years past, you were a young girl, yet you seem so sure you know me."

"You oft sang to me. From feast to feast and year to year, I grew ever fonder of your voice in my ear."

Theo turned to Joanna. "You are Zera's kinswoman, too, yet you do not know me?"

Joanna moved to sit on Theo's other side. "Our fathers, not our mothers, were brethren in the house of Herod the Great. But Zera's memories tickled mine. I do know your singing voice." She leaned past him to look at Zera. "But my memory cannot trace his face."

Zera fought to keep the pity she felt from showing in her eyes. "Theo was badly beaten, and he has aged ten years. Of course, his countenance is not the same as when we were young girls. Before, he was known as—"

"Do not speak my name." Theo covered his ears. "I do not want to be called by a name to which I am a stranger." He sighed as if he could blow away all his misery. "The man you believe me to be ... What manner of man was he?"

"You were a righteous man apprenticed to my father, the overseer in the winter palace in Jericho."

Barid gestured to Theo. "My friend, that rings true, for you have managed my inn with skills I did not teach you."

Joanna touched Theo's sleeve. "My husband, Chuza, is head steward over all the holdings of Herod Antipas. He spoke highly of you as a man of wisdom beyond his years. A youth who held onto worldly goods lightly and loved ones tightly."

"And I remember nothing of this." Theo's tone took on notes of anger and chords of doubt. "Would that there was iron-clad proof I am truly this man you remember."

Zera clasped her hands together. "Some of our past seems to interweave. The man of whom I speak was lost to us the second week after the feast of Shavuot. Though we searched and offered rewards, no sign of him was ever found."

Barid jumped up. "That is the same week Samuel found you on the road and carried you to my inn. I thought he had brought me a corpse to bury."

Zera touched Theo's cheek. "The very same week you left my life, leaving no trace, you entered Barid's life having no past."

Theo pushed Zera's hand away from his face. "I could be some other man. This could all be merely happenstance."

Zera picked up a rake leaning against the tree and spread the embers in the fire. She stared into the orange and yellow waning flames. *HaShem, please grant Theo a glimmer of memory to assure him my recall shares truth.*

An ember sparked and spat a hot speck toward her. Zera leapt back, bumping into Barid, her throat tightening around a knotted scream.

Barid steadied her. "Your eyes are as wide as those of an owl. Why be afraid of a spark?"

Zera raised her sleeve and pointed to a scar near the crook of her elbow. "When I was very young, I was running and tripped by the fire. I could have been badly burned. I still remember the pain. And then, somehow ..."

Zera knelt in front of Theo. "You have a scar. A brand from a metal rake on the bottom of one of your feet. Which foot is it?"

"I do not know. Who gives the soles of their feet any notice?"

Barid laughed. "It is his right foot. I cared for him for weeks. Theo had so many wounds, I never considered that small scar would be the key to unlock his past."

Zera used water from Barid's waterskin to soak the hem of her tunic. She washed Theo's foot, then lifted it to check the sole. "Look, here is the scar. It is a brand from two tines of a rake."

Theo traced the scar. "Praise HaShem. I am this honorable man you say I am." His hands shook and his voice broke. "Could it be that the One God marked me then, for such a time as this? To offer proof I am your kinsman?"

Zera stood and put a hand to her lurching heart. "Even then, the One God sent you to save me. I remember tripping, facing the fire, screaming. I could have burned my hands, my face. I could have been marked, ruined for life. You snatched me away and kept me from falling into the flames. But you lost your footing and stepped back onto a red-hot rake."

"Praise HaShem, at that time I was not crippled and could move quickly. You speak of my past with such clarity, but for me, my past remains a black cave. A cave where I may be trapped forever. None of your tale has sparked any remembrance." Theo's face was flat—without joy, without sadness, without hope.

Barid brought Theo a cup from his wineskin. "Zera has given you much new knowledge, but it does not yet ring true. If it is the will of your One God, in His time, He will awaken your mind to the past."

"But I must know ..." Theo's anxious face seemed haunted. "Have I a wife? A child?"

Zera gentled her voice to soften the truth to come. "You were betrothed."

Theo's eyes glistened in the starlight. "Tell me. Where is this woman now?"

"The tale of your betrothed is long, and I am overcome by weariness. Yesterday, I was nearly stoned to death. At midday, I learned my husband wanted me dead. And now, my cousin, who was lost and is found, does not remember me. Let us speak of these things in the morning."

HaShem, give me the strength and the words to tell Theo the sorrowful fate of the woman he had loved beyond life.

Chapter Ten

House of Lazarus
The next morning

Theo

Theo woke and sat on his sleeping mat, rubbing his eyes. Where was Zera? He had to know what had happened to his beloved. But Rhea and Zera's sleeping mats were already rolled up. They must be helping with the morning meal. Joanna was moving near the fire, a towel girded around her waist. Barid still slept.

Daybreak silvered the hills of Jerusalem to the north. The golden roof of the Temple was out of sight from Bethany. Though the sky lightened, Theo's memory remained dark. Hearing of his unremembered past had unsettled him.

He grabbed his crutch and pushed to his feet. A fierce cramp sent a bolt of pain pulsing through his leg. Theo forced himself to walk and the cramp eased—only to return after a few more steps.

Barid roused and met Theo's eyes. "My friend, are you in pain?"

"Pain is my merciless jailor. And mornings are the worst."

Barid rushed to help and began massaging Theo's calf.

"Cursed be the men who beat my memory from my mind and the strength from my limbs."

"Hate devours you from within."

"If I give up my vengeance, to what else should I cling?"

"You have kinswomen now."

"Kinswomen I do not recall. Because those men beat me and left me to die."

"Why suffer one hour longer? Yeshua is here. Ask Him for healing of your pain-wracked body."

Joanna stirred the fire back to life. "I have been traveling with Yeshua nigh on two years. He not only restores the body, but also the mind and spirit."

Zera and Reah brought their morning meal, platters of bread and figs, from the table near the house.

"I do not see Yeshua and His disciples. Have they already left for the Temple?" Disappointment drained Barid's booming voice to almost a whisper.

Zera handed him a round of bread. "No. He is teaching in the courtyard at the house."

Theo turned to Zera. "Tell me what has become of my betrothed. Though I have no memory of her, I still must fulfill my promises to her."

Zera gasped, then coughed, unable to hide that something was amiss.

"Since my body was never found, she has been left *aguna* —unable to marry another. She must have been more despondent than a widow."

Zera took Theo's hand. "Your beloved grieved for your loss, but she was not forever forlorn. John, the prophet, baptized her near Jericho on the same day he baptized Yeshua. She was one of Yeshua's earliest followers and brought Joanna to Him."

Theo covered Zera's hand with both of his. "I must marry her if she will have a cripple. Or I will give her a *get* of divorce."

The tears in Zera's eyes made Theo brace for bad news.

"Your beloved succumbed to a summer fever, but—"

"My betrothed is dead. And I am left numb. I should shed true, tender tears. Grieve that we never shared a wedded life. But how can I mourn with no memory of her?"

"But your beloved came to believe in Yeshua's promise of the resurrection to eternal life. Her last words in this life were a pledge to meet you in the next one."

He had never considered such a hope. The earth seemed to quake through Theo's core. "Resurrection? Are not those here of the House of Lazarus, Sadducees who reject the teaching of resurrection?"

Lazarus walked toward them, bringing a pitcher of water. "Before Yeshua came to us, we did not believe in demons. Then, we saw Him cast them out. Whomever we were in the past and whatever beliefs we held matters not one whit. We are now followers of the Messiah who offers the gift of eternal life." Lazarus raised his hand in blessing over the group. "Yeshua is so much more than we understood, expected, or dared hope for. He has raised the dead to a longer life in this world, but He teaches that when the Lord comes to judge, all the dead will be raised to eternal life."

Joanna turned to Theo. "For those who gain eternal life, there will be no more tears, no more pain, no more deformity of mind or body. You will be whole. And you will know your beloved when you see her."

"I pray one day I may come to a place of such hope. Such faith. But I must confess, the will to forgive my enemies eludes me. So how can I be forgiven? Or healed? Or gain eternal life?"

Lazarus stroked his beard like a rabbi considering a challenge from a student. "The Lord's ways are a mystery. Often hidden from mere men. Sometimes revealed to the greatest prophets. Yet sometimes spoken by the lips of children." Lazarus poured a cup of water for Theo. "We are meant to wait for the fulfilment of every prophecy in scripture."

Zera raised her cup, and Lazarus filled it. "Thank you, sir, for your kindnesses to a frightened, hunted woman."

"Mary has told me of your narrow escape at the Temple, and Emet has told me your husband still seeks to murder you."

Theo pushed to his feet and put an arm around Zera. "We would not bring trouble to your household. My kinswoman and I will leave."

Barid stepped to Theo's side. "They will come with me to my inn."

"There will be no immediate trouble. Word was brought to me this morning about your husband. Hours ago, he won a large wager. He has the lucre to fund a feast for a week."

"We can stay and hear Yeshua teach." Joy and relief flooded Zera's tone.

Lazarus turned to Barid. "Yeshua will remain here two more days. You are welcome."

Theo's hope surged. He may yet muster the courage to ask for healing. "What say you, Barid?"

"You stay with Zera and Reah. I must return to the inn. My hired man expects me today." The wariness of a warrior flickered in Barid's eyes. "Take heed. Joram's good fortune and Zera's safety may both be short-lived."

Lazarus clasped Barid's forearm. "On the third day, I will send a donkey cart with Zera and Reah hidden under the straw. Theo will drive."

"Many thanks. Zera should not stay at my inn. It is often teeming with travelers." The wariness in Barid's eyes had now invaded his tone. "Joram's spies may track Reah, believing she will lead them to Zera. I will send Zera to our friends at the forge."

Reah's chin quivered. "My lady, we will be parted. Me at the inn, you at the forge."

Zera touched Reah's cheek. "Take heart. We are together now. And we will hear Yeshua teach for two more days."

Two more days. Theo would see Yeshua perform wonders beyond belief. If only he could find the will to forgive his trespassers, then he would dare ask for his miracle.

Chapter Eleven

Forge at Jericho
Heshvan (November), four weeks later

Zera

*Z*era fed the doves, soothed by their calm cooing. The dovecote at the back of the forge had been Zera's refuge since Theo brought her to Jericho four weeks past. Well hidden from Joram's spies, she felt safe, but she missed Reah. The circular tower was open to the sky, the stones rising well above her head. The steady ring of hammer striking anvil assured her that Dex, the blacksmith, was near and on guard.

Sophia, his wife, joined her. The tall raven-haired beauty held a gray messenger dove and gently removed the royal silver tube from the bird's leg. "He just flew in."

Zera took the dove from Sophia's hands and placed it in a nesting box.

"Now where has Gaius gone?" Sophia tucked the message in her waist sash and fisted her hands on her hips.

"He is behind the dovecote, slinging rocks like a warrior at an unarmed tree."

"Who made him the sling?"

"Your husband. After Theo told your son about our hero King David and his victory over the giant Goliath, Gaius begged his father to make him a sling. Then the boy hung a helmet high in a tree he dubbed Goliath. Gaius, of course, is David."

Sophia peeked through a gap between stones. She turned back to Zera with wide eyes. "Gaius strikes the tree every time he spins and releases a stone, even though he has not yet seen his fifth winter."

Zera joined Sophia and watched through the chink in the dovecote wall. "That tree does not stand a chance against your son's repeated blows." She turned to Sophia. "I hope Barid will deem it safe to bring Reah this evening. Will many people come to the forge today?"

"On the eve of the Jewish Sabbath, it will be simple to keep Reah hidden. Though we are Romans, all know Dex and I do not work the forge from sundown unless the work is urgent."

"Why would you keep the Sabbath?"

"Talk of Yeshua spreads with the speed of a desert sandstorm, and we desire to follow His ways." Sophia gestured to the back of the house. "Come, let us prepare the evening meal." They walked to the cookfire. Sophia poured water and lentils into the pot. "Many of Yeshua's teachings are simple and clear. Yet others are a difficult puzzle."

Zera hugged herself. "In Bethany, Yeshua often challenged our previous understanding of HaShem." She touched the sharp stone of remembrance tucked at her waist. "Since my brush with death, I have no certainty of anything. Except that Yeshua is merciful. Sophia, I will stir the stew."

"And I will tend to the rest of the meal." Sophia went inside.

Zera stoked the fire and listened to the rhythm of Dex's hammer hitting the anvil and his son's stones hitting the tree. She stared at the stew pot, lost in her thoughts, lost in time.

The ring of the hammer had ceased.

Dex walked toward her. "My mother used to say that staring into a steaming pot will hinder the boil."

"And my nurse, Reah's mother, used to claim if you worry well enough, the trouble will never come to pass." She stood and added cumin and salt to the stew. "Have you any news of Joram?"

"Joram continues to cast dice and win more than he loses. When I last traveled to the inn, Barid had not caught even a sniff in the wind of anyone looking for you or your handmaid."

"Though I would never wish good fortune on Joram, his greed and winning wagers keep him from the need to plot my death."

"We are glad to hide you here. It is such a blessing for Sophia to have the company of another woman. She tells me—" Dex jerked his head toward the road. "Look, Barid has come. And Reah too."

At the sight of her beloved handmaid, Zera smiled, but her stomach twisted with shame. Not for the space of even one breath had she considered what her adultery would cost her innocent, faithful handmaid.

Reah jumped down before the cart had fully stopped.

Zera ran to her. "I have sorely missed you."

Reah's face was calm, but her eyes were brimming with something unsettled, unreadable. She hugged Zera close and spoke in her ear. "I have news for your ears alone."

"After the meal, go to the dovecote where we will not be overheard."

"Reah, you are welcome here." Sophia approached, holding her son's hand. "I am Sophia, wife of Dex. Zera speaks of you with great regard."

"Barid has told me of his long friendship with you and Dex." Reah bent toward the boy. "And who is this?"

He straightened and threw his shoulders back. "I am Gaius, only son of my father."

Zera laughed along with the others.

Gaius stomped his foot, his eyes brimming with tears. "Why do you mock me?"

Sophia knelt and looked him in the eyes. "We do not mock you. We are pleased at how quickly you have become a flawless copy of your father."

Dex waved to Barid. "Come. We will settle the donkey and bank the fire in the forge."

Zera and Reah entered the house and helped Sophia finish setting out a simple supper of bread, honey, olives, and lentil stew. Gaius stuffed his mouth with bread and honey, then ran toward the door. "There is still some light for slinging." He turned back to Sophia, a pleading look on his face.

"You may go. But when it is dark, you must spread your mat in the back room and go to sleep."

"Yes, Mother." He bolted through the door, almost colliding with Barid and Dex.

Sophia brought a pitcher of barley beer and cups to the table. "Let us enjoy our supper."

Barid wiped his brow and sat. "Queen Herodias sent a message to the inn that you and I are to meet her in Caesarea."

"Why Caesarea, not Shechem? Dex sat next to Barid. Shechem is so much closer to my forge here in Jericho."

Barid dipped his bread in the lentil stew. "There will be

great crowds there for the gladiator games sponsored by Pontius Pilate. Many places to hide from prying eyes."

Sophia passed the basket of bread. "The queen is attending the games? Will that not give even more offense to the Jews who already hate her?"

"The queen will attend the chariot race, not the gladiator games." Barid jabbed an elbow into Dex's side. "We may have a chance to attend the grand chariot race Herod Antipas is hosting in the hippodrome."

Zera's chest tightened as if it had been placed in an olive press. Herod had always wanted to win or buy Auri back from Joram. Now that Auri was dead, the Judeans would not have their famed charioteer to cheer.

Dex's eyes flashed. "I have a friend who is a farrier caring for the Blues horse team. Before he left for Rome, he was my apprentice here at the forge. If we find him, perhaps we can watch the teams practice before we place wagers."

Sophia took Dex's hand. "What will you wager?"

"Set aside all worry. Neither Barid nor I ever wager more than the cost of an evening's entertainment. We both have watched foolish men throw away the blessings of their hard labor chasing a fortune that can be lost as quickly as it was won."

Zera swallowed against the tight lump in her throat. Joram. She had almost lost her life at the hands of such a fool.

"Travelers at my inn could speak of nothing but the upcoming race. King Herod has spared no expense to curry favor with Pontius Pilate. He has brought not one, but three champion quadriga horse teams and veteran charioteers from the Circus Maximus in Rome. They are arch-rival teams called the Greens, the Blues, and the Whites."

Gaius came through the door, dragging his feet and folding his sling. "It is dark, but I am not yet tired."

Sophia put her arm around Gaius and pulled him close for a hug. "You must sleep now. You gave your word." Gaius trudged off into the back room.

Dex pointed to the message tube tucked at Sophia's waist. "Is that message for me? It bears the stamp of Herodias."

"Yes. The dove flew in just before supper and it slipped my mind." She opened the tube and handed the scroll to Dex.

He unrolled the scroll and glanced at it. "This message is for me and Barid." Dex began to read.

Bring the women staying at the inn and the forge to Caesarea. I will meet with them and hear your reports at the chariot races.

Zera's palms slicked and her mouth went dry. "Herodias knows where we stay. We are doomed. Her husband, Herod, is kinsman to Joram. My murderous husband has found me." Zera stood. "Reah, we must run, hide, pray."

Reah came near and Zera pulled her close. "My lady, if Joram knew where you were, he would already be here."

Zera looked to Barid. "Will you help us hide?"

"Hiding from Herodias when she has sent for you is foolish. Be at peace. Herodias never shares all she knows with anyone." Barid's steady tone quieted Zera's runaway fear. "But her little bees, as she calls her spies, have clearly been humming to her about you."

Zera stepped away from Reah and looked to Dex and Barid. "You are blacksmith and innkeeper, but you give reports to Queen Herodias?"

Dex tapped his cheek. "Always face-to-face. Nothing is ever written."

Barid took a deep draught from his cup. "We are the keepers of the queen's secrets. Secrets we dare not share."

"Secrets in Shechem?" Zera could not keep the worry from her voice.

Sophia motioned for them all to sit. "Do not ask and we will not lie. It is for the safekeeping of others."

"Safekeeping?" Reah's raspy whisper was more unsettling than an eerie scream.

"What you do not know can never be tortured from you." Sophia put a gentle hand on Reah's back.

Reah reached for Zera. "What could Queen Herodias want with us?"

Zera gathered her courage. "We must trust HaShem."

Dex gulped his barley beer. "Herodias has never asked us to do anything other than protect and hide innocents."

"And do you always follow her orders without question?"

"Herodias is a powerful woman." Dex laughed and wagged a finger at Barid. "But once, our friend Samuel ignored her direct order."

Barid's gentle smile twisted into a smirk. "Samuel saved the queen's life. But ..."

Zera wondered what Barid was holding back. "Was the queen not grateful?"

Dex pushed up from the table. "Herodias richly rewarded Barid and me the next day. And richly ignored Samuel. But that is his story to finish."

Sophia rose and began to clear the table. "Remember, you leave at first light for Caesarea."

"To the races." Barid raised his cup.

Dex grinned, pulled out a coin, and rolled it across his fingers. "I will wager on the Blues in honor of my former apprentice."

Auri would never race again. Her desire had caused his death. Burning shame rode up from Zera's stomach, stabbing her heart from deep within.

Barid pushed back from the table. "Even though I loathe Joram, unless I see something worrisome in the practice runs, my wager will be placed on Joram's unflinching charioteer. The famed charioteer with ice in his veins. Auriga Maximus."

Zera's heart stuttered, and her mind skittered like a stone skipping on water. "But Auriga is dead." Zera bit her lip.

Barid looked up sharply. "Why would Auriga be dead?"

"There were rumors he was killed." Zera clasped her shaking hands. No one save Reah knew the name of her lover.

Sophia poured Zera a cup of water. "Your face is as white as washed wool."

"I am too warm." Zera downed the cup.

"My lady, fresh air will revive you. You promised to show me the dovecote."

Reah rushed Zera into the privacy of the dovecote and took Zera's hands. "It is true. Auriga is racing five days hence."

Auri was *alive*.

Zera's short and shallow breaths took off at a gallop. She was pulled back to the terrifying morning she and Auri were caught together. Brutal men had rushed in and dragged her from her chamber. But behind her, there were no sounds of struggle, no fleeing footsteps, and no sickly-sweet smell of shed blood. Now she knew why. Joram let Auriga live because he was the only source of gold for Joram's next gamble.

Zera's view tunnelled. The earth seemed to fall away from her feet.

Reah caught her around the waist. "My lady, sit here on the stool and take your air in and out slowly."

Zera's heartbeat and life's-breath entwined in a rhythm that thrummed her lover's name.

Auri ...

Auri ...

Auri ...

She must see Auri. No matter the cost.

Chapter Twelve

Caesarea

Four days later

Zera

Zera took a deep breath of the fresh salt air and smiled at Reah, who dozed beside her in the donkey cart. Barid and Dex walked alongside, leading the donkey in turn, as they had for the last three days' journeying toward Caesarea.

She had never been so near the Great Sea. Its cresting waves, soaring sea birds, and sandy shore stretching to the horizon. Since she heard Auri was challenging ruthless Roman charioteers here at the famed hippodrome tomorrow, her stomach burned and churned. The rhythm of the waves soothed Zera's bewilderment at the news that Auri was alive. News she still could not quite fathom.

Barid stopped the donkey cart at the imposing entry arch to Caesarea.

Rhea roused, rubbed her eyes. "I never dreamed I would see a city with so many Greek and Roman temples."

"One would never believe that Jews live here." Zera checked to make sure the men were paying them no heed. "I must devise a way to see Auri alone."

"Alone? Yeshua bade you go and sin no more. Would you grind your foot into His mercy?"

"You misunderstand my intentions. I will not fall into sin. Joram threatened Auri with death if he ever betrayed him. I could use my wealth to protect him."

"Leave Auriga's protection to HaShem. You lie to yourself. How will you resist Auri's charms?" Reah's brows pulled down into a fierce frown Zera had never seen. "Remember the wisdom of the prophets of old. The heart is deceitful above all things."

Barid called out to Dex. "Herodias left word of the inn where she made provisions for us to stay, but nothing more."

"Let us search for the inn later." Dex sounded so eager. "I would go first to the stables and see my former apprentice. He will help us gain entry to the races tomorrow."

Zera stood and stretched her arms. "I have been riding for so long. I need to walk."

"My lady, I would walk by your side."

Barid helped them down. "Reah, you must take care. Zera is dressed and living as a commoner. To all who would see you and Zera, they should regard you as equals. Take care not to call her 'my lady' before others."

Reah looked at Zera with fear in her eyes. "I would never wish to reveal your true person."

"Be at peace. The longer we maintain this ruse, the less burden it will be to treat me as an equal."

Barid waved toward the sea. "I never cease to wonder at the

sheer size of this harbor. It was made from imported volcanic ash that hardens in water."

Zera gazed at the monumental city towering around her. "I have never been to Caesarea, but my late father spoke of this place with such awe."

Barid led them past a theatre. "There, commanding that promontory jutting out onto the Great Sea, is King Herod's palace." They walked along the seashore. "On our right hand is the hippodrome."

Reah came beside her and nodded toward men sitting in a row on stone seats, their garments arranged around them, talking with great zeal. "They look like a flock of crows lined up on a roof."

Zera glanced at them and laughed.

Dex grinned and shot an amused look toward Barid. "And I would guess they are arguing politics or discussing the races." The races. Soon she would see Auri from the stands in the hippodrome.

Zera held Reah's hand and hurried after Dex and Barid, who led them behind the end of the hippodrome that held the barred starting gates called *carceres*. They continued into the stables, a maze of horse stalls for the Blues, Greens, and Whites —the famous factions who sponsored horse racing teams that had traveled from Rome.

"Hear the cheers and jeers of the crowd at the gladiator games?" Reah stopped. "The amphitheatre must be near."

Zera shuddered. "And the shouts of joy in victory and the cries of agony in defeat assault my ears."

Dex and Barid both seemed oblivious to the noise of the crowd. For the entire journey from Jericho, the men spoke of nothing other than the races tomorrow.

And from the moment she heard Auri was alive, Zera

thought only of her chance to see with her own eyes that he still drew breath.

Dex's pace quickened and his stride lengthened. "My apprentice told me to meet him at the stalls of the Blues faction."

Barid, big man that he was, barely kept pace with his eager friend.

Dex hurried through the open doors of the brick stables and looked back. "Barid, wait for the women."

Zera and Reah hurried to catch up to the men.

Zera stepped inside and breathed in the scent of the sweet straw heaped over the paving stone floor. "I did not expect the stables to be so spacious and smell so clean."

"We Romans treasure our horses." Dex stepped around a mucking rake. "These stables are owned and managed by the racing factions from Rome. No expense is spared. The stalls are mucked twice a day. The horses are brushed after every run. And their manes and tails are rubbed with aromatic oils each morning."

Reah opened her arms and turned slowly. "The stables are so big, with so many rows of stalls."

Dex looked around. "It can be a maze. The first time I saw it, I, too, was in awe. This splendid stable was built to board only racehorses."

Zera pointed down the row. "Look, a blue banner hangs from the rafters over several stalls. You said your former apprentice cares for the Blues. He may well be there."

In one stall, a young man spoke softly and patted the withers of a restless stallion. He slowly ran his hand down a foreleg and picked up the hoof.

Zera tripped, and Barid gently caught her arm. "Careful." His tone was so tender.

Barid's manner was light as day when set against Joram's dark-as-night demeanor.

The young man looked up. "Dex. Greetings, my friend. Come take a look at my *introiugus* stallion. This fearless lead horse is the only one capable of anchoring the tight turns from the inside rein."

Dex opened the door and edged into the stall. The stallion eyed him and snorted. Dex murmured about nothing, gentling the horse. He joined his friend and bent down to look over the hoof.

"See ... there is a small red spot. Several weeks ago, I lanced a boil and drained pus from this same spot. It healed completely, but now ... What do you think?"

Zera eased closer and raised up on her toes to see over the top rail.

Dex pushed a finger into the soft portion of the foot. "I think I can feel the edge of a trapped stone. We must remove it before the affliction worsens. And we must be quick about it."

Dex pushed on the stallion's foot with both thumbs. The stallion did not flinch or snort or rear. "Good. He is not too tender yet. But we must soak the foot in warm salt water."

"I will send a stable boy to fetch some." The apprentice whistled, and a young boy came running.

Zera pulled a piece of straw from his curly hair. "You were so close, yet so quiet."

"Quiet, I am not." The boy grinned, not at all shy that he had lost two front teeth. "Just ask my master."

"And who is your master?" Barid moved toward the boy.

"My master is the master of all these stables."

"Tell me true, boy. You were too quiet just now. Were you spying on someone?" Mistrust weighted Barid's tone.

The boy's eyes went wide, and he shook his head. "No. No.

No. I was staring at the shield of a golden-faced god, tacked to the wall of a stall around the corner."

Surely it must be Auri's Belenus god. Auri. So near. She would bury her feelings and keep her face still as a death mask.

Barid walked toward the boy. "Evil tricks to undermine opponents can come from any quarter."

"I am no spy."

Reah moved closer to the boy. "Is no one guarding the horses for the team from Jerusalem?"

Zera put her hand on Reah's shoulder. She was such a blessing. She knew Zera would want to find Auri.

The boy stood tall. "The new *horator* is on guard. Auriga Maximus says this horator is the best outrider ever to race as part of his team. Auriga trusts his new man to protect him and his chariot. The man's daring and tactics on the tight turns steal my breath."

"Enough about another team. My Blues stallion needs care. Boy, bring some sea water for the horse's hoof and do not dally."

The boy nodded and hastened away.

Dex studied the stallion. "He stands evenly on all fours, but we must remove the stone before the practice laps. Then we will watch him run. If his run is hindered, you may need to move him to an outer rein or replace him with one of the spares."

The apprentice reached up to a high shelf lined with bowls and jars. He set a bowl on the wide top rail and chose two jars filled with herbs. "I will make a salve to apply as soon as the stone is removed."

Barid turned to Zera and Reah. "Dex will be tending the stallion for some time. Perhaps we could walk for a bit."

Zera wagged a finger at Barid. "I know your true intent. You want to see the Jerusalem team and judge if they are worthy of your wager." Zera's breath quickened. Barid may walk them past Auri's stall.

"You have unmasked me." He tilted his head and studied them both. "The new horator would not know you, but keep your heads and lower faces covered, and do not speak."

The boy rushed back with a bucket of sloshing seawater. He handed it to Dex. "I left a second bucket of seawater over a cookfire. Perhaps a hotter soak will better serve."

Dex flipped him a bronze mite. "Boy, you did well."

The boy caught the coin, grinned, and tucked it away.

Barid waved to Dex, who was already soaking the stallion's foot. "The women want to walk."

"My friend, we will need your strength to help hold the stallion if he decides to take offense at our proddings."

Barid met Zera's eyes. "You must stay here." Though his face was unchanged and his voice steady, there was a flicker of something in his eyes. "I would be forever saddened ..." He seemed to hitch over the word. "... shamed if some ill fate were to befall you."

"Hmm..." Reah looked from Barid to Zera. "Or ill fate befalls me." A knowing smile lifted Rhea's lips.

Barid blushed the color of new sweet wine. "You serve at my inn, so it is presumed that you are under my protection." He turned back toward the stall.

Zera nudged Reah and whispered. "Offer a pretext for us to take our leave." Her tone was a command, not a request.

Reah covered her eyes with the back of her hand. "I would not watch the stallion's suffering or even a drop of the poor beast's blood spilt."

Zera linked arms with Reah and began to move away. "We will stay close."

Barid lifted the latch and moved into the stall. "Stay in sight."

Zera laughed lightly. "We will stay in hearing. This row is short, and we can only go a few paces before we must turn. You will readily find us."

After a few steps, Reah spoke in her ear. "My la ... Zera, you must not see Auriga. Would you risk placing him in more danger?"

"He is not here now, the new outrider has never seen me, and I am dressed in common garments." Something pecked at Zera's mind. "When Auri and I were caught together, Joram seemed consumed with rage. Perhaps his humiliation and fury were merely feigned? Perhaps he plotted for many months to have others mete out my death."

"It may well be true. Your husband is both cruel and cunning."

They turned the corner, moving toward the Jerusalem team.

"Now that I have had time to mull on it, Joram would never kill the man who laid chariots full of gold at his feet. I had lost the last ember of Joram's love for me, but Auri's victories still stoked the raging fire of Joram's love of money."

"My lady, is it not strange that Auriga's name was not spread abroad as the man who seduced Joram's wife?"

A fount of fury welled in Zera's chest, speeding her breath and spurring her heartbeat. "It would not pay for Joram to besmirch the name of his prize charioteer. It mattered not a whit to Joram which man he used to seduce me. I see now how that snake, Joram, contrived to fan my affections, my desires, and my downfall."

"Zera, your eyes glint daggers of hate."

Anger lit a fire in her chest, rose, and seared her cheeks. "May HaShem blot Joram's name from the Book of Life and free me from the snares of his murderous mind."

Chapter Thirteen

Zera spied the golden Belenus shield and stopped. She pulled Reah close and whispered, "Auri's team must be the Yellows. The Jerusalem stalls are draped with golden yellow banners."

They crept close to a middle stall where an outrider snored softly in the straw. Two black kittens slept curled in the corner.

Zera's heart thrilled. "Reah, those must be the same kittens."

"Auriga must have taken them to the stables when I fled the mansion."

The stallion snorted and seemed to regard her with a wary eye.

Zera stepped onto the first rail and peered into the stall. She looked up to the rafters and was startled to meet amber eyes that matched her own.

"An owl." Reah's voice was as haunting as a spectre. "A portent of death."

Zera's stomach twisted into a tangled knot.

The stallion snorted and lowered his head into the feed

bucket. Something was tucked into the crevice between the boards. The knot in her stomach twisted tighter. She climbed to the second rail and leaned in. "Whatever is secreted here is meant to stay hidden."

Reah tugged Zera's cloak. "Take care, or you will fall in with that skittish stallion. For what do you reach?"

"I do not know, but it caught my eye." Zera stretched until she could barely pinch the small flat packet between her longest fingers. "I have it." She pushed back with one arm, and Reah helped her down. Something was wrapped in a layer of parchment, pierced with a nail and tied with a long lock of hair. Long golden hair. Auri's hair. An evil foreboding shuddered up Zera's arms and bristled on the back of her neck.

Reah stepped back, her face frozen in a grimace of fear. "Surely, this is a curse tablet."

Zera opened the parchment with shaking fingers. A thin lead sheet with an etching of an overturned chariot. Latin words sprawled in many directions. But Zera could only decipher one word. *Auriga.*

"HaShem, hide us under Your wings." Reah tugged at Zera's sleeve. "We must go."

"I will not leave with sorcerer's curses called down upon Auri's head. There may be more curse tablets. I must search every stall."

Reah lifted her hands. "HaShem, only You can vanquish the powers of darkness."

In the next four stalls, Zera was able to readily reach the curse tablets. At the final stall, the curse tablet was not where she had found the others. The Belenus image on the far wall glinted in the sun. "Something low in the beard is flawed. The final curse packet is tucked into the rays of the god's beard."

"My lady, the most spirited stallion blocks any safe path."

"Auri's life depends upon revoking the powers of darkness."

Zera turned to Reah, handed her the curse tablets, and whispered. "Because it is set in the Belenus shield, this curse is meant to kill the god's power to protect Auri. This most potent curse must be removed."

"My lady, wait for the stable boy. He knows these stallions and they know him."

"I must fetch the curse before the outrider in the next stall wakens and thinks I am the sorceress."

"I wish he still snored. If you are caught, you will be dragged before Joram."

"If I am caught, run to Barid." Zera lifted the latch on the stall. The door creaked and Zera flinched. But the outrider did not stir. "Hold the door in place, but do not latch it."

The stallion picked up his feet. And his nostrils flared. Zera murmured, hoping to gentle the stallion. After what seemed an hour and a day, he settled.

If she went behind the stallion, she could be caught too close to his hooves. Hooves that could strike like lightning. Hooves that could kill. If she went in front, he might bite or knock her from her feet with his head.

Zera took a deep breath and held it. She was small. She eased to her hands and knees and crawled slowly underneath the stallion's belly. The stallion stepped back, barely missing her hand.

Zera did not cry out.

Did not breathe.

The stallion seemed to settle and drank from his water bucket. His slurping covered her next deep breath. She stood, snatched the curse tablet, and put it between her teeth. She eased back down on her hands and knees. Once clear of the stallion's belly, she rose again.

The stallion stopped drinking. He turned to her, snorted, and reared high, hooves punching toward her head.

Zera was yanked from behind and thrown from the stall.

Reah broke her fall. Zera stared up at Barid's broad back in front of the rearing stallion.

He held up both hands and spoke, his deep voice finally settling the stallion.

The stable boy, so quiet on his feet, was suddenly beside the stallion in the stall. He pulled an apple from his sack and offered it to the horse.

The stallion whinnied, his ears pointed forward. Then, he took the apple and chewed.

Both man and boy backed out of the stall.

Barid turned on Zera, his face furious, eyes flashing. He opened his mouth, but she lifted the curse tablet in her hand before he could speak. "Look. I had to gather them all."

Reah showed him the remaining curses.

Barid's face changed from fury to revulsion and disgust. "We must destroy them."

The boy backed away, his eyes wide and worried.

"Shh ... we are fortunate the outrider sleeps deeply." Zera pointed at him.

Barid moved and peered into the next stall. He looked back, his eyes scanning. "The outrider has fallen into the sleep of death."

Reah took Zera's arm. "The curses killed him." Her voice was a whispered screech.

"No. White foam bubbles from his mouth. The outrider was poisoned."

"This may weaken the power of the curse." Zera pulled a nail from her curse tablet. "We must warn the Yellows and Auriga Maximus."

Barid took the tablet from her. "No. We must let those who hid the curses believe they are still in place." He unwrapped the parchment and read the tablet. His face turned the color of a white-washed tomb.

"Auriga Maximus is in danger." Zera clenched her fists so tightly, her hands hurt. "Read the curse."

Barid took the nail and scratched through the words. "We dare not. Words spoken aloud are given more power."

"You Romans are most superstitious ... Your priests study the livers of sacrifices to determine your fates."

"You chanced crawling under the belly of a stallion to remove a curse. Tell me you are not equally superstitious." Barid held up the tablet and shook it in front of Zera's face. "Would you chance that my reading the curse aloud will add to its power?"

"Never." Zera's mind flooded with evil imaginings of what horrors the curses invoked.

Screee. Screee. Screee.

The owl in the rafters took flight, flapping so close to her, she ducked and covered her face with an arm. The owl flew down the long row and out the open doors.

Dex came running toward them. "Was that an owl?"

"We have problems more grave than an owl." Barid held up a curse tablet. "If we are discovered here, we will be blamed not only for the curses, but also for the poisoning of the Yellows' most skilled outrider."

"Come quickly." Dex's voice brooked no protest. "Boy, you come too. You should not be here when the dead man is discovered."

Barid took Zera and Reah by the arms and hurried them along. The boy ran behind them.

Dex left the stables, waved them on, and headed toward the sea, leading them away from travelers who were raising tents and tending cook fires. When their group was gathered on the sandy shore, Barid turned to the boy. "Go back to your master, but stay well away from that cursed Yellows stall. And tell no one what you have seen." The boy ran as if he were being chased by demons.

The waves slapped near Zera's feet.

Reah held up the curse packets. "I will throw these in the sea."

"Nooo ..."

"No." Dex's shout was the frantic echo of Barid's bellow.

Dex took the packets from Reah's raised hand. "They must be destroyed by fire so the lead will melt and the written curse rendered powerless."

Zera's hand moved to her heart. "Auriga's Yellows will be saved."

Barid shielded his eyes from the sun and looked toward the gate where they had left the donkey and cart. "We must find the inn where Herodias has reserved us a place. We can destroy the curses there."

"How will we know what she will have us do next?" Dex sounded worried.

"My friend, I know you prefer to plan. But surely you know by now, Herodias prefers to keep everyone unsure and in the dark." Barid clapped Dex on the shoulder. "I know only the name of the inn we seek, and the sign posted above the door."

Zera joined them. "For what place do we search?"

"I have never heard of it, but it is called Auriga's Folly."

Terror seethed through Zera's veins like steam seeping up from a hot spring. "And the sign?"

"A drawing of an auriga—a charioteer caught in reins wrapped around his waist—dragged behind an overturned chariot."

Zera's fear for Auri rolled to a boil that burned with every swallow, every breath, every beat of her heart.

A Certain Mercy

The sinking sun lit the Great Sea on fire. She prayed Auri's heart would still beat when the sun next set.

Chapter Fourteen

Caesarea

Day of the Chariot Races

Zera

The lull of the ocean waves did nothing to calm Zera's spirit. Barid and Dex made their way forth from their night's stay at the seaside inn. Zera and Reah trailed behind.

"The men move too quickly." Zera balked at the peevish tone in her voice. "Reah, forgive my ill humor. I did not sleep." They hurried past the Roman baths, the marble columns glowing in the rays of the rising sun.

"Your restlessness was not lost on me. My lady, the straw in our pallet rustled each time you stirred. Would you care to share the burden of your worries?"

Zera matched Reah's whisper. "The innkeeper confided to Barid that mere days past, Herodias bought the inn and changed the name to *Auriga's Folly*. Why? Did Joram share the name of my lover with her husband?"

Reah bit her lip and tilted her head. "Men would not concern themselves with the lovers of other men's wives. Not unless they could exploit that knowledge for gain."

Zera studied her surroundings. Barid and Dex, paces ahead, paid them no mind. A few early merchants carted their wares on the path to the hippodrome. "Why would the queen concern herself with the lover of a woman like me? What is that cunning woman's gambit?"

"Who knows the twisted workings of the queen's mind?"

"Was the inn's new name and new sign meant to taunt me, haunt me? A sign that raised visions of Auri defeated—crippled for life or mortally wounded." Zera's stomach wrenched like a foot caught on uneven stones.

"Perhaps Herodias, Jerusalem's most ill-famed adulteress, is intrigued by the mercy Yeshua offered you, also an adulteress."

"Yeshua commanded me to cease from my trespasses. In truth, I do not wish to fall into sin, but if I am ever to have peace, I must speak with Auri one last time."

"I beg you. Let me be your shield from sin. Do not meet with Auriga alone." Reah sounded desperate, as if she would shackle herself to Zera hand-to-hand and foot-to-foot.

Zera gestured up the road. "Look, the hippodrome. Even more magnificent up close."

"The hippodrome in Jerusalem seems a child's toy when compared with this splendid structure."

Barid turned and walked toward them. "Wait here. Herodias commanded Dex and me to meet a man who holds a forked staff and sits on a stone seat between two vacant ones. I see him ahead."

Zera faced the long row of raised seats. "It looks like a dais with thrones for a council of kings, but here poor men sit alongside the rich."

Barid's hands went to his belly, but he could not hold back his deep booming laugh. "It is surely a seat where all men are equal."

Dex nudged Barid's side. "And given enough time, all men will report here."

Zera's cheeks warmed with a discomfort she could not name. "This is clearly a place reserved for men, but you speak in riddles I cannot unravel. Speak plain words to us women."

Barid's face matched the rose color of the dawn. "You speak true. We Romans are not so overmodest as you Jews. These are latrines."

Zera crossed her arms and tried not to smile. "We cannot stay here waiting for your *consensus ad idem,* your meeting of the ... minds."

Dex and Barid burst into roars of laughter.

Reah flashed Zera a mortified look and took her arm. "We will go on to the hippodrome and find seats among the women."

Barid's face darkened, creased with worry. "Remember, choose places in accord with your station, not among the rich, but also do not stand among the rabble. Amidst the rabble, bets won or lost spark even the women to brawl and sometimes wield knives."

Dex turned to Zera. "We have yet to be told when Herodias will see you and Reah. You must watch for us in the crowd. We will take places at the boundary between my Blues faction and Barid's Yellows."

Barid shrugged. "I have yet to place my bet. I may change from the Yellows to the Blues. The Yellows have lost their best outrider. But, then again, the Blues' lead horse has a tender foot. Who is to know how it will endure the pounding of a seven-lap race?"

Zera waved a quick farewell. Auri was so close. The crowd heading for the hippodrome grew thicker. "We must go now, if we are to have any choice where we sit."

Reah clung to her arm as they entered the swift current of the crowd, sweeping close from all sides. Tokens were passed out in the streets, tessares that allowed entrance to the races. Whiffs of strong perfumes and sweat rancid from too much garlic and wine blended into a sickening smell. Zera held her breath.

"My la ... Zera, take this. It will help." Reah handed her a small cloth.

Zera put it to her nose. Rose-water perfume. "Bless you."

The long oval hippodrome with three levels of arches loomed over them. At the ground level, each faction had its colors draped over the entrances for its allies. At the gateway, a man with a yellow shawl draped over his shoulders studied them, then held out his hand. "You will want mid-level. Two tessares for each of you."

"Sir, how many will be allowed in?"

"They say it seats twenty thousand strong." He rubbed his thumb across his fingers. "But we always manage to pack in more for the right price."

Rhea paid the man and linked arms tightly with Zera. "We must let no one between us or we may be lost to one another."

Zera wended her way through each small gap in the crowd.

"Why move so quickly? We will all sit in the hippodrome."

"We have middle section seats, but I want to be in the closest row allowed to us." She could not confess to Reah that she longed for Auriga to spot her, to know she would witness his victory in the most anticipated race ever run in Caesarea. "We will keep our head coverings up, but to keep our faces veiled would attract notice. The other women do not remain covered."

Reah stared at her with knowing eyes. "Do you hold onto the dream that somehow he will know you from such a distance in such a crowd?"

Zera felt her cheeks heat and looked away.

They climbed the stone stairs and wedged onto the first stone bench in their section.

The large woman next to Zera jammed her with an elbow hard enough to make her fall against Reah. "Good thing neither of you is bigger than a sand flea. Or I would have had to banish you to the bench behind me."

Zera smiled a tight smile that only thinly veiled her offense at the woman's rough treatment.

"And you sand fleas are in good time. The opening trumpets have not yet sounded."

Reah leaned forward to speak around Zera. "We have never before been to Caesarea and would be grateful for any wisdom you could share."

"You have planted your buttocks in a charmed place, for I am called Fortuna. I know these races well, and for a small fee, I will share my vast knowledge of the horses and the aurigas. Then, I will tell you the wisest wagers for each race today."

Zera leaned close and spoke into Reah's ear. "Talking with this commoner will make it seem that she is with us and hide us from the prying eyes of Joram's spies." She turned to the large woman, taking care to keep her cat eye well shaded by her head covering. "Our men will handle our wagers, but your insights will add spice and enjoyment to a long day that could have grown tiresome." Zera threw Reah a lost look. "How much should I offer the woman?"

Reah reached across Zera's lap and handed Fortuna three bronze mites. "Bless you for relieving our tedium with the lesser races."

A blast of trumpets. The sound spurred Zera's heart to a

gallop. She turned and caught sight of four Roman soldiers on the bridge above the starting gates, each with a team color pennant hanging from their trumpet.

Zera took her cup from her waist sack. "Reah, could I have some water?"

She opened the waterskin and poured a cup for Zera and herself.

Zera swallowed slowly. "We must portion our water. The day will be long and hot."

Fortuna elbowed Zara again. "Do not fret." She pointed toward the north. "Look, the Roman aqueduct is not far, and there are places to fill a waterskin."

Reah spoke around Zera. "Our men forbade us to leave the hippodrome."

"When I go to fill my waterskin, I will take yours and bring back water for us all."

"If we drink too much water ..." Zera's mind could not escape the modesty of her privileged upbringing.

"Have neither of you ever been to the races?"

"Only once in Jerusalem." Zera had seen Auri race once long ago when she was a young, contented bride. As much as Joram had been allured, she had been appalled. The pagan rites, the noise, and the risk to men and horses had left her sickened.

"If you do not drink enough, you will faint before the final race." Fortuna smirked. "I will take you to a place in the shadows of the arches where women water the stones. But you must never go there alone. And you must always carry a small knife at your waist and place this in your hair." She pulled out one of her hair combs. It was fixed with a needle-like blade.

The trumpets sounded again. Fortuna lumbered to her feet. "Pontius Pilate has arrived with Herod Antipas and his kinsman, Joram of Jerusalem. They are the sponsors who have funded the races today."

Joram. Was her husband in league with Herod? Zera looked toward the high viewing box built into the seating area. Joram sat with the ruling class. He had risen so high, and she had fallen so low.

Reah shielded her eyes and squinted. "Fortuna, who else sits in the cushioned seats under the shade of the *pulvinar,* in the shrine to Caesar Augustus?"

Fortuna pointed toward the viewing box. "Pilate's wife wears a long white tunic hemmed in purple and a matching purple stola. Herodias is in a golden tunic as a sign of favor and fortune for the Yellows. And Joram's wife would have been seated with them." Fortuna sniggered and wiped her running nose with her sleeve. "But she was caught with a lover." Her tone was snide, laced with scorn.

Zera trembled. She wanted to stop her ears and close her eyes and blot out her shameful past. She pressed her hand against the stone of remembrance she kept bound at her waist.

Reah squeezed Zera's hand. "What happened to her?"

"Word is she somehow found *favor* with one of the Jews' prophets." Fortuna raised her brows, a suggestive look on her face. She elbowed Zera again, but this time, catching her under the ribs.

Zera turned away so Fortuna would not see her neck and cheeks redden.

"Oh." Reah managed to keep her voice steady and her face calm.

Fortuna grinned, revealing blackened teeth. "Joram's wife has vanished like a rat running down a dark alley."

A cry of welcome and worship arose from the crowd. The *pompa circensis,* the elaborate opening procession, had begun. Statues of the Roman gods and emperors were carried in through the triumphal arch and placed in the middle of the track. Musicians played flutes and lyres, and boys dressed as Roman warriors danced before the rulers. An unending line of officials entered the hippodrome, chests held proud, chins lifted high, revelling in the adulation of the crowd. Each man climbed the stairs to their proper rank, bowed to Pontius Pilate, and took their place beneath the viewing box.

Zera stretched to better see the procession. "Surely the charioteers will come next."

Fortuna turned to Zera. "First, an ox will be sacrificed in the temple and its liver read by a priest. See? The fire for the burnt offering is already blazing."

"It is one thing to hear about readings of the liver ..." Reah's whisper betrayed her revulsion. "And quite another matter to witness such a grisly sight with one's own eyes."

"I am grateful"—Zera leaned close to Reah—"that the bloody pagan rite will be performed in the temple, far from us."

The priest came forth from the temple and reported a fortuitous reading of the liver and entrails. The crowd rejoiced.

Fortuna took a swig from her wineskin, and blood-red wine dribbled onto her chin. "If the priest had announced a troublesome reading, the races would have been cancelled." She wiped her mouth with her sleeve.

Zera pointed to the center *spina*. "Fortuna, see that row of seven dolphin sculptures on high poles? Are they meant to call to mind the dolphins that helped Moses and our people cross the parted Red Sea?"

"The Herodians who built this hippodrome only feign worship of the One God. If you are so innocent as to believe the fanciful tale that dolphins helped when the Red Sea opened, you are ripe for the picking by some deceitful man with only one thing in mind."

Zera's cheeks burned. She had been the one to tempt Auri into sin.

Reah tilted her head. "Why, then, are the dolphins mounted in such a prominent place?"

"They are a symbol of Neptune, god of the sea, but he is also the god of horses and horsemen."

Rhea's eyes were wide. "Somehow, the dolphins moved. They were all nose down, but they were just turned nose up."

Fortuna laughed, leaned across Zera, and flicked Reah on the nose. "They are ready for the races. A dolphin is turned nose down when each of seven laps is completed."

"But why? Can the people not reckon to seven?"

"My little sand flea, after the first race, you tell me if you can reckon to seven." Fortuna took another swig of wine. "Not only those who have downed more than one wineskin may lose count. Amid the battle of chariots, the charioteer and his outriders face many threats to their limbs and lives. Even the champions admit they lose all sense of reckoning."

The starting gates opened and Zera's hope plummeted. All twelve Blue bannered chariots moved onto the track. "Fortuna, I expected to see only the teams for each race. How can you judge the teams when the teams for the entire day are clumped together?"

"If we are placing a small bet, we watch for only two-horse teams. For larger bets, we watch for the four-horse teams. Some horses have markings that make a team easy to spot."

"How can you put a name to the charioteer? Each is clothed in a leather helmet, a leather tunic banded around the chest, and leather trunks to cover the thighs."

"Some have special designs on their chariots, others you can tell by their unusual stance or horse team."

The Belenus emblem. Zera would look for it. When each team reached the turn marker, the next entered the track.

The Yellows, Auri's team, entered the hippodrome. Zera's mouth went dry, and her breaths came fast.

The crowd exploded with cheers. These were their Judean heroes. The team that dared challenge the champions of Rome. The charioteers' heads and reins were held high, the horses kept to a slow trot.

"Reah, watch the four-horse teams. Tell me as soon as you see him."

"The chariots are in close formation. I cannot single one out."

Zera could not spot the Belenus god emblazoned on Auri's chariot. Only at the final race would she know Auri by his Yellow chariot banner. Her sight clouded with tears.

Fortuna droned on, sharing details of every race, none of which interested Zera. But when Fortuna spoke of Auri, Zera listened.

"Auriga Maximus trained in Rome. And I have heard that the Roman races are more brutal and fatal than those in Jerusalem. But our favored Judean charioteer has never raced against Rome's seasoned champions. To win, he will need skill and cunning and Neptune at his side."

The day was already sweltering, but Zera was suddenly chilled. She drew her cloak tight.

HaShem, I beg You, do not allow the final race of this day to become the final race of Auri's life.

Chapter Fifteen

The Final Chariot Race

Zera

Zera stared at the devastation the eleventh chariot race had left in its wake. Auri's race was next. Her stomach twisted like tangled reins. She did not want to gape at the track, but found she could not look away from the broken chariots, broken horses, broken men.

Fortuna looked at Zera, a gleam of bloodlust in her eyes. "That last *naufragia*, the shipwreck of three of the four chariots, was the greatest thrill thus far."

Reah squeezed Zera's hand. "HaShem is merciful. All three injured charioteers were able to walk away. Is it just here near the Great Sea that the chariot crashes are called *shipwrecks?*"

"Bah." Fortuna sat down next to Zera and waved her hand, seeming put off by Reah's ignorance. "The Romans thought chariot crashes looked like broken ships bashed against unforgiving rocks." Fortuna held out her hand. "Give me your money. We agreed on a denarius, a one-day wage, to be bet on the Yellows, same as everyone around us. We did not yet discuss the odds."

"What odds would you suggest?" After all the havoc that Joram's wagers had wrought, who would have thought she would be brought so low as to wager too? But betting would help her be taken for a commoner.

Fortuna patted her belly and belched. "I can cover three-to-one odds, though if I lose, I will not eat for a week."

"Agreed." Reah reached around Zera's back and handed Fortuna a denarius. "This is all we can risk."

Reah moved her hand to Zera's shoulder and pulled her close. "Auri will race next, the final contest of the day."

Zera fought back the queasy feeling that crept up into her throat.

Fortuna eyed Zera. "You look as if you would be sick. Are you so soft-hearted?" Some new notion seemed to flicker across the big woman's face, and she squinted and peered at Zera. "Or perhaps you are with child?"

Jolts of wonder, fear, and disbelief raced through Zera's veins. She reached for the waterskin and took a sip, pushing down her queasiness and her shock. It could not be. She had never considered that she might be with child.

Reah glanced at Zera, an uneasy light in her eyes, then leaned around her. "No, Fortuna. We are just worried that if we lose our wager, our husbands will be angry for a week."

Fortuna threw back her head and laughed. "Have you two no cunning in you? Just tell them that after you bought some food, pickpockets stole your coin purse." She clutched the money and trudged away to place the wager.

"Are you with child?" Reah's face mirrored the worry that unsettled Zera.

Zera checked those nearby paid them no heed. "We spent less than one night-watch together more than five weeks past. And I did not conceive in the full three years when my husband oft visited my chambers."

"That matters not at all. Has your moonblood come upon you since the day you were discovered together?"

"No, but you know there have been times of great distress when my moonblood has departed for months." Zera wrung her hands, her mind and heart divided. She had longed for a child to love. A child to love her.

"Be still." Reah covered Zera's restless hands with her own. "We must watch and wait. The coming months will reveal the truth of the matter."

"Thankfully, if I am with child, the baby would not be declared bastard-born even though all Jerusalem might suspect the child was seed of my sin."

Reah turned back to the track and drew Zera close. "You are not divorced. Under the Law, any child would be reckoned a child of Joram."

"But both Joram and I would know that the child could not have been fathered by him." Zera gasped at the new thought. "I ascribed my sick feelings to distress. That I am with child now seems more certain." Her voice trembled, but she gathered her courage. "This child will be my only rightful heir and must be shielded from Joram's evil plots."

The trumpets announcing the last race sounded. Fortuna returned and sat next to Zera again. "The charioteers are casting lots for their positions. We want the inside, the gods willing."

Zera stared at the gates where horses snorted and whinnied and reared. Above the inside gate, a green flag was raised.

Fortuna clenched her fists. "May the Greens be cursed and the inside lane be slick and rutted."

"The Romans are despised overlords." Reah's voice was soft and low. "Even their sports are perverse and cruel."

Zera closed her eyes. This day, she had witnessed the deaths of horses and men. More than enough for one lifespan. *HaShem, let Auri live—whole in body, mind, and spirit, even if he is not the victor of the race.*

Reah grabbed Zera's arm, and she opened her eyes. "The next inside lane will serve."

"Baal's blood." Fortuna pounded a fist on her knee. "Without the inside lane to gain the victory, Auriga Maximus will have to drive with the strength of Hercules."

The old woman behind Fortuna leaned forward, shaking a scrap of yellow cloth. "Auriga Maximus will also need the wisdom of Jupiter and the daring of Mars."

The trumpets blew a fanfare, and the four teams pulled up to the gates. The parade circuit was about to begin. The crowd roared and jumped to their feet as one. Many waved flags or scarves in the color of their favorite team. Others waved palm branches.

First, the Greens charioteer on the inside lane cracked his whip over his team of black stallions and drove past the viewing box. His two outriders rode matching mounts behind them.

Next, the Whites and their outriders pranced by. An image of Pegasus, the winged white horse, was fashioned on the chariot, and their horses' coats shimmered like alabaster.

"Here are the Blues." Reah clapped her hands. "The team of Dex's apprentice."

Auri will be next.

Fortuna elbowed Zera. "Rumors fly. The Blues are our biggest threat. They have more money than Plutus, the god of wealth. Look at those magnificent, gray-blue stallions."

The growing noise filled Zera with dread. She craved

silence. A silence in which to pray for Auri. A silence in which to examine her soul.

Suddenly, the roar of the crowd soared. A rumbling thunder Zera could feel in her chest. Auri's Yellows entered the hippodrome.

Auri. Helmet tucked under one arm. Golden hair flying in the wind. He looked to be the embodiment of the Belenus god. And his exotic four-horse team of goldens matched his glow. One mare and her three-stallion offspring.

Fortuna shook triumphant fists over her head. "Auriga Maximus, our Judean champion, is the only driver who dares to run a mare."

The stench coming from under Fortuna's raised arms made Zera angle away.

Reah handed Zera a perfumed cloth. "A mare surely is not as strong as a stallion."

Auri had once shared his tactics with Zera. "Word is that Auriga Maximus counts the mare as most sharp of mind. When she runs on the inside, she steadies her three stallion sons, so the team races as one."

As each chariot completed the circuit, it halted and faced the viewing box.

Pontius Pilate stepped forward and raised his hand.

The crowd went silent.

Zera drew in a deep breath, trying to steady the spinning in her head.

"Herod Antipas, Joram of Jerusalem, and I, Pontius Pilate, have narrowed the final race to four chariots, only the three best Roman teams and the challenging team from Judea. In Rome, our four factions ran races to determine which would compete here. The Reds proved to be our weakest team and were left behind." Pontius Pilate, his sneering face smug and proud, turned to Herod. "Now we will see if the Judeans are fit to tie the sandals of our Roman champions from the Circus Maximus."

The crowd grumbled at the poorly cloaked insult. An undercurrent of unrest swarmed through the hippodrome.

Fortuna began to shout "Max-i-mus. Max-i-mus. Au-ri-ga Max-i-mus." She raised her fist and punched it in rhythm. The chant spread around the hippodrome like rolling thunder. Much of the crowd raised fists against Rome.

Zera wobbled, and Reah helped her sit down. Now the race was not only a battle of charioteers, but it had taken on the passion of a political protest. "A win or a loss could bode trouble for Auri. If he wins, Pontius Pilate may view him as a provincial hero who could incite unrest."

Reah nodded, her face lit with understanding. "And if Auri loses, the disillusioned Judean crowd may turn and rise against him."

Chapter Sixteen

Zera

The crowd took their seats, waiting for the teams to enter the starting gates. The last race would pit the experience and skill of the champion Roman teams against the cleverness and courage of the lone Judean team. The Roman charioteers wrapped their reins around their waists. Auri did not.

Zera turned to Fortuna. "Why would a charioteer wrap the reins around himself?"

"Wrapped, he can use his entire weight to control the horses, and he is less likely to be thrown from the chariot."

Horses reared. Their driver and footmen settled them.

"But if the chariot tips ..." Reah's voice was tight and her eyes wide. "He cannot jump free."

"And if a wrapped charioteer is thrown, he will be dragged." Zera did not know if she should be relieved or fearful that Auri had not wrapped his reins.

Pontius Pilate raised a purple cloth, and the crowd rose.

Zera held her breath. Men standing on the *spina* in the center raised starting flags, watching for Pilate's signal. He dropped the cloth, and the flagmen dropped their flags.

The chariots lurched forward and were off on the first of a seven-lap race. The Greens took an early one-length lead. The others raced within a nose of each other. The second dolphin at the top of the *spina* turned down. The start of the second lap. At the first turn, the Greens pulled in even tighter to the inside.

Fortuna wagged a fat finger at the track. "The Greens will never hold that turn."

Zera looked back in time to see the Green chariot flip and crash into the *spina* wall.

Auri's Yellow chariot raced around the wreck, and now the inside lane was open. The attendants ran in and cleared the driver, horses, and wrecked chariot away—barely escaping before the three remaining chariots rounded the track again.

Coming into the first turn of the third lap, Auri reined his horses toward the inside, but the Blue team cut in front of him, pushing him to the outside. The Whites stole the inside lane.

"Thieving Romans." Fortuna clamped her hand on Zera's shoulder and lumbered up to stand on the stone bench. "Sons of harlots. We are not blind. We see the Blues and Whites conspire together to destroy our Yellows."

The Whites raced ahead. Auri cut to the inside, his horses racing half a length behind the Blues for the entire fourth lap. Midway during the fifth lap, the lead Blue horse stumbled, throwing the Blue driver to the floor of his chariot. His feet dangled from the back. He grabbed the side rails, but the ill-fated charioteer could not reach for the knife at his chest to cut the reins and save his own life.

Every few paces he slid farther down. Closer and closer toward a death-drag.

Zera buried her face in Reah's shoulder. "I cannot watch."

Fortuna pounded on Zera's back. "Our crazed Auriga Maximus has waved his outrider to the far side of the Blue chariot. What in the name of Jupiter is Auriga Maximus doing?"

Zera straightened and stared at the track. The Yellow outrider leaned down, grabbed the fallen charioteer's arm, and shouted something to him.

Auri positioned his chariot closer to the Blues and pulled his knife. He nodded to his outrider and leaned over the rail of his chariot. Auri's chariot tipped onto one wheel.

Zera swallowed hard past a lump of terror that filled her throat. "Auri's chariot is going to overturn." Her heart raced away with her breath. She would watch her Auri crash and die.

Reah pulled her close and shouted. "Pray. Pray for HaShem to shelter Auriga under His wing."

Auri grabbed the Blues' reins, cut them, then centered himself, righting his racing chariot. His outrider held onto the fallen charioteer, keeping him on his feet. He ran alongside the horse until he was able to scramble up and sit behind the man who helped save him.

Fortuna jumped up and down. Her face was scarlet as the oxblood offering. "You fool. Why sacrifice time and strength to save an enemy? If you lose, do not dream the people will ever forgive you."

The Blues faction leaped to their feet and roared at the daring rescue of their charioteer. They took up the chant, "Maxi-i-mus. Max-i-mus. Aur-i-ga Max-i-mus."

Reah took Zera's hand and lifted it toward the heavens. "The Lord has answered our prayer for protection."

Zera brought their hands down. "Yes. But I feel a sword has cleft my heart in two. One half is well-pleased with Auri's courage, the other half is enraged at his foolhardy gamble." The

Blues stallions continued to run in their lane, pulling the empty chariot. "The risk Auri took was a hundred-fold worse than any of Joram's wagers. Auriga cast the dice where the prize to be won or lost was not merely lucre but his life."

"The last lap. The last lap." Fortuna stamped her feet on the stone bench. "Run, Yellows. Run like the wind. Catch those White cheaters."

Fortuna's loud voice seemed far off. Zera's mind had gone numb—taken leave of her body. Zera found herself looking down on the track like an eagle hovering over the scene. Only the warmth of Reah's hand kept her tethered to this place.

The Blue outrider spurred his horse ahead and began to dart in and out near the Whites' team, breaking their stride and rhythm. He was now in league with the Yellows.

The Yellow horses lengthened their strides and steadily began to close the three-length gap. Finally, Auri's Yellows drew even on the outside of the Whites' charioteer. The Blues, pulling an empty chariot, easily kept pace to the outside of the Yellows.

The Whites' charioteer whipped his team, but they were lathered and could give no more. He turned and viciously whipped Auri's Yellows, flicking the whip near their eyes, cracking it near their ears.

Zera muttered to herself. "Auri never whips his horses. The goldens run for him, not from fear but from love."

The Yellow team startled, half-reared, but pulled forward. The White charioteer began to whip Auri.

Zera watched in a daze. She could not cry. She could not shout. She was beyond feeling, beyond hope.

The crowd jeered.

Auri lifted his arm to protect his head from the cutting whip. Then he grabbed it and yanked the White charioteer. The man lost his footing and was dragged on the ground. The

White chariot crashed along the inside wall and the horses broke away.

The White outrider herded his team of horses well out of the way. The race attendants took the White charioteer off on a litter.

Reah tugged on Zera's tunic. "If the Yellows do not move to the outside, when they come around on the final lap, they will crash into the Whites' chariot."

Fortuna shook her head, her face a picture of despair. "The Yellows cannot move. The Blues horses are well-trained. They will stay in their lane and force the Yellows to stay on the inside."

Zera suddenly seemed to come back to herself. "A part of the White chariot is still in Auri's path."

Zera and Reah wrapped their arms around one another, their cheeks touching to see through a gap in the crowd in front of them.

Auri's chariot was a quarter circuit away from the downed White chariot, yet his team did not slow. He raised his reins and let them go slack.

Fortuna jumped up and down. "Brilliant. Watch. His only chance is to keep the horses running full on and in stride."

A tense quiet fell over the crowd. It seemed no one took their next breath. As Auri's horses approached the broken chariot, Auri bent his knees and the horses leapt, landing in perfect harmony. The chariot bounced hard but remained upright. Auri was thrown forward in the air and flipped—his heels flew over his head, he landed facing backward with his legs across the front chariot rail. His legs were at risk of being crushed against the center *spina* wall at the upcoming tight turn. In the nick of time, Auri scrambled and wrested his legs back into the cart.

Zera's waves of terror were replaced by waves of relief.

The crowd exploded with cheers and applause.

Auri's Yellows pulled ahead of the Blues and crossed the finish line first. The Yellow trumpeter stepped forward and sounded the victory. The other trumpeters joined in.

The Yellows' fans shouted at their good fortune. The Judean Champion had won the race, and they had won their wagers.

The Blues' fans at the far end suddenly cheered.

Reah pointed. "Look, the Blues' horses are so well trained, they finished without their charioteer."

Auri slowed his team to a trot, tucked his helmet under his arm, and waved to the crowd. He stopped before the viewing box, stepped out of his chariot, and climbed the stairs to the Roman Prefect Pontius Pilate. The Prefect crowned him with a wreath of laurel, and Herod Antipas handed him a palm branch. Auri stood with his hands lightly clasped behind his back. Pontius Pilate lifted the prize purse, and the crowd shouted. Before Auri reached for it, Joram took the leather pouch and placed it in his robe.

The crowd hollered and growled their rage.

It was Joram's right as slave-owner to take the entire purse, but it was not the accepted custom.

The crowd hissed. A pulsing hiss. A throbbing hiss, naming Joram a snake.

Pilate and Herod both scowled and leaned close to speak with Joram. He nodded, patted his robe, and waved toward Auriga, suggesting the victor's purse would be shared.

Pontius Pilate's and Herod's faces relaxed. Pilate raised his hands appeasing the crowd, but Auri's hands pulled apart and he fisted them behind his back. He turned, came down the stairs, climbed into his chariot, and began his victory lap. A groundswell of the Max-i-mus chant grew to the pitch of rolling thunder.

A Certain Mercy

Auri completed the circuit and drove out of the hippo-drome. And out of Zera's sight. She must speak with him. Ask forgiveness for her sin of leading him into temptation. For her seduction. A seduction that put his precious life at risk.

Chapter Seventeen

Hippodrome

After the Final Race

Zera

The crowd lingered in their seats, reliving the twists of fate in Auri's race that had quickened their blood. Zera looked beyond the crowd in the hippodrome to the Great Sea. The sun sank into a crimson-clouded sky, and she sighed her relief. A red sky at night was a portent of calm weather and mayhap a calmer path for her life.

Fortuna handed Zera two stones painted yellow. "Take these to claim your winnings."

"Many thanks. If not for you, Fortuna, we would have made no wager."

"I am well named. Your fortunes were bettered the day you met me." She waved and grinned a black-toothed farewell.

Zera pulled Reah past Fortuna, who stood gossiping on the stairs. "To the stables. Now. Before Auri's overjoyed faction hoists him upon their shoulders and carries him to the nearest tavern."

Reah stopped. "Wait. Joram may come straight to the stables."

"Soon night will fall and we will not be so readily seen. We will take care." Zera tightened her grip on Reah's hand and hurried down the stairs.

"Move slowly, or you may rush into Joram's presence unawares."

They neared the stable, deserted of all horses and men save the Yellows team. Just inside the door, Zera turned to Reah and whispered. "Stay here deep in the shadows and watch for Joram."

"And if I see him?"

"Coo loudly like a mourning dove. Then run and seek Barid."

Zera crept along the path to the Yellows stalls. To Auri. He murmured to his horse, his deep voice so gentle, so alluring.

She shrank into a dark corner next to the stall where Auri brushed the golden mare, his trailing hand stroking her coat.

How she longed for Auri's strong, comforting embrace. His forbidden touch. His lingering lips.

The loud cooing of a mourning dove warned her to hide. Nearby, a bale of hay was piled high with horse blankets. She crouched behind it and tucked her robe close.

Joram strode past her, mere paces away. "Auriga?" His tone was one of vexation and something else she could not name.

A cold chill crawled up Zera's back and pebbled the skin on her arms.

Joram should have been overjoyed at Auri's victory, yet he was not.

"You do not answer me." Joram's tone was an ugly taunt. "You pout and think you deserve the entire purse."

Zera peered around the edge of the blankets.

Auri tossed the brush from his stall. "I won. This time, keep your word. Call a scribe and give me my freedom."

Freedom? Why would Joram offer Auri, his wife's lover, freedom? It was madness, beyond reason.

"I will not give you either the purse or your freedom." Joram pounded the stall rail, and the mare stomped and whinnied. "I drown in my debts."

"You lie. You hoard your gold for your next wager. Pay your debts with the victor's purse and this day's winning bets."

"Slave, you know nothing. You presume that I bet on you."

"Why would you not?" As soon as the words left Auri's lips, his face changed to a look of loathing. He lunged for Joram, the same look on his face when he spoke of his father's fatal contract with Herod Antipas.

Terror twisted knots in Zera's stomach.

At the last moment, Auri reined in his anger and clutched the top rail of the stall. "You bribed the Whites and Blues to work together to take me out of the race. Tell me. Who was slotted to win?"

"The Whites. I bet everything on the Whites."

"You did not trust that I would win?" Auri pounded the rail with a violence that Zera had never seen. "No matter what you threaten, I will never race for you again."

Joram laughed. An ugly snort of a laugh. "I do not need you to race. I need my wife's fortune. For the second time, you have been the spider in a web of my making, a web my wife cannot resist."

Zera's breath caught.

"May you be cursed forever. You are a liar and a would-be murderer." Auri's face burned crimson, and his voice was as sharp as an assassin's blade. "You promised me freedom if I won this race against Rome. But you entered me in a rigged race that could have been my death."

"Auriga Maximus." Herod Antipas stood outlined in the light at the stable door. "That you won and lived through this day's war-on-wheels is my two-fold gain."

Joram turned, his face uncertain. "What is your meaning?"

"I am calling in your debt. This very day. I bet on the Yellows, our Judean team. Your secret bet was against me." Herod strutted toward Joram. "At long last, I have won back my prized charioteer."

Joram sank to his knees. His face went gray. "I cannot pay. Give me time."

"Oh, but you can. You must. You may keep the victor's purse, but I will take Auriga Maximus, your outriders, your footmen, and your team of goldens as payment in full." Herod swung his embroidered cloak over his shoulder and looked at Auri. "Prepare to leave for Jerusalem in the morning." Herod waved for his horse, mounted, and rode off.

"Joram." Even from the side, Zera could read the anguish that creased Auri's face. "I have lost, but Joram, you have lost more. The fates have turned against you. Twice you have lied to me. Today, and more than a year past. When you promised me freedom in exchange for my seduction of Zara."

Auri feigned his love for her? Seduced her to gain his freedom?

Zera's heart slammed against her ribs and swelled to bursting, like new wine in old wineskins. Surely her ears had played her false. Her chest tightened around shallow sips of air. And then, her mind shattered—her thoughts scattering in all directions.

Zera's mind was at war with her heart. Her heart clung to her desperate need for Auri's love. He was a kind man, not cunning and cruel like Joram. Auri had just risked his life for a fallen charioteer.

But when Zera sifted her thoughts, she knew her deceiving heart was the author of her confusion. Her mind could never blot out Auriga's confession of his deception. His words rang true. Zera's heart turned to stone. She would forever be alone.

Joram laughed, but his cruel laugh had taken on a new timbre. The otherworldly timbre of a demon. "You say I have lost, but I have won. I made sure tidings of this race were cast far and wide. I knew Zara would come. You were the enticing bait in my snare. And, with her death, her fortune will pass to me, her only heir."

She had flown into a trap. She took a calming breath and gathered her wits. Was it safer to run or to stay hidden?

Zera was grabbed 'round the shoulders from behind, her head pulled back, her neck laid bare to a blade raised high in the air.

She screamed, and Auri charged toward the stall door, but Joram blocked him.

A big hand grabbed the wrist of the assassin holding the knife. But he wrestled free, shoved Zera out of his way, and stabbed her savior.

Her savior, Barid.

Barid lowered his head and plowed into the assassin, knocking him to the ground and the blade from the man's grip. He scrambled to his feet and fled from the stable. Joram ran close behind.

Barid clutched his shoulder, his wound spurting blood. He grabbed a rub-down cloth and pushed against his wound.

"You took a blade in my stead." Zera helped Barid sit on the bale of hay.

Barid pulled his arm from his robe. "A blade I took willingly and would take again."

Auriga brought a linen towel and ripped it into strips. "Zara, we must stem the fast flow."

"Tell me how to help."

"I will bind a strip around his shoulder, and you must press with both hands with all your strength over the fount of blood."

Auriga guided Zera's hand. "Press here with all your strength."

Auriga's touch no longer ignited any spark of desire. His betrayal made her skin crawl with shame. She had almost been killed while chasing after her desire for him.

Zera pressed with all her might, yet a river of blood still bubbled through her fingers.

Barid put his hand over hers and pressed. "Auriga, the wound is too deep. It must be packed. Get a long, thin cloth strip ready. When I bare the wound, use a finger to push the linen in as far as you can and keep pushing in the next bit until it will take no more."

Barid winced with every push of the cloth into his wound. The flow slowed, and Zera helped Auri bind Barid's wound. "Reah found you none too soon."

"Reah did not find me. Herodias sent her man to warn me that Joram's spy followed you."

The memory of the blade raised high reminded her of the stones raised high. A great trembling seized Zera, leaving her weak and spent. Her life had been spared yet again. But why? Why did she still draw breath?

"Zera, I did not know." Auriga looked down from her glare. "I did not know ... all."

"Never speak of this to me." Zera did not understand Auri's denial, but she did know that every vestige of Auri's flattery and caring had been a sham. Her lover was an imposter.

Dex came running through the stable door. "What has happened here?"

"An assassin." Barid looked at Auriga. "Go tell the queen. Tell her all. Leave no remnant unspoken."

Blood soaked through Barid's dressing. "My mind is mud. Help me down before my strength fails me."

Dex eased the big man to the floor. "Auriga, tell the queen to send a physician. Without delay."

Zera knelt next to Barid. His stab wound was her fault. He had been willing to die for her—a fool of a woman, a wanton woman. A deceived woman who dared believe she was worthy of love, even if only the love of a slave.

Auri stood looking down at her. Zera could not meet the eyes of her traitorous lover. She would cast Auri from her mind and cast him from her heart. And she would never confess the truth to him, the truth that he had fathered her child.

Chapter Eighteen

Caesarea

Auriga's Folly Inn

Zera

Since Barid had been stabbed, Zera, Reah, and Dex had kept an all-night vigil. They sat in subdued silence around the table in the common room of their inn at Caesarea. In a back room, the physician sent by Herodias fought to save Barid's life.

Near daybreak, Reah and Dex dozed at the table, their heads resting on their crossed arms. Zera walked to a sailor's window and stared through a porthole with a view of the restless sea. *HaShem, please preserve Barid's life. I am the one who deserved death.*

Herodias swept silently into the inn.

Zera roused Dex and Reah, who both rose as soon as they realized they were in the presence of Queen Herodias.

The queen's owl-like eyes met Zera's, then looked to the others. "I trust my inn has been a comfortable refuge, adequate for your needs."

"My lady ..." Dex's voice faltered. "I am forever in your debt. Thank the gods you sent your man to warn us of Joram's assassin and your physician to tend to Barid."

Herodias straightened. She had a way of seeming to tower over those of much greater stature. "You and your friend once saved my life and have continued to be of great service to me. I never forget those deserving of reward, just as I never forgive those who betray me."

Dex's face paled. "My lady, how may I serve you now?"

"You and Reah, go help my physician tend to Barid. Zera and I will join you in due time."

Reah headed for the back room. Dex nodded and walked behind Herodias. He put a finger to his lips, and his eyes flashed an unmistakable warning for Zera to guard her words.

"And Dex, there is no need to signal from a blind spot at my back."

The queen sounded more amused than annoyed, as if she scolded a child.

Dex dropped his hand, a sheepish look crossed his face, and he hurried away.

Zera could not keep the question from her eyes or her voice. "My lady, it would seem there *is* no blind spot at your back."

Herodias smiled. A smile that offered to share a secret. "There are no hidden eyes in my hair or sorceries at work. I simply caught a flicker of something in your face—the face that was before me, not the one at my back."

Worry simmered in Zera's veins. Worry that floated atop her ever-present queasiness like scum in a stagnant puddle. If she and Herodias ever came to cross purposes, Zera would rue the day.

She looked away from the queen whose probing eyes seemed to scratch at Zera's thoughts.

"Do you not think my name for the inn, *Auriga's Folly*, is quite clever?"

Zera wiped away tears that threatened her dignity. "In truth, the inn should have been named *Zera's Folly*, for I trusted an imposter, a man who played me false."

The queen sat at the table and gestured for Zera to take a place across from her.

Footsteps at the courtyard door drew their attention. The innkeeper nodded to Herodias and carried a pitcher to the serving counter. He poured a sweet-smelling drink into cups and brought them to the table. "Warmed watered wine, just as you prefer."

"Good. But bring the pitcher and leave us to ourselves."

He placed the pitcher and a small brass bell at the queen's hand. "At the slightest ring, I will come quickly."

The queen's eyes darkened and her face hardened. "If you are within earshot of this bell and can come quickly, you have not truly left us. Have you not heard how harshly I deal with spies not my own? No bribe is worth the risk."

The man's face was as fixed as the Roman concrete that had formed the bottom of Caesarea's Harbor, but his hand trembled when he took the bell and tucked it in his waist. "By your leave, I will retire to the tavern next door." The innkeeper sidled toward the threshold.

Herodias was a cat clawing a mouse, her lips twisting into a cruel smile. "Innkeeper, you forget ..."

Confusion clouded the innkeeper's flustered face. He moved his feet as if he would curtsey, then shifted into an awkward bow.

The queen's smile settled into a sneer. "You forget your wife." The queen's voice carried power and privilege.

The innkeeper's red-faced wife crept from her hiding place behind the courtyard door. She rushed across the room, and her husband pushed her out the door.

Herodias studied Zera's face. Zera met her gaze, sensing the queen would tolerate nothing less. A tense silence blanketed the room.

"Zera, you have usurped me."

Zera curled her lips under and bit back her question.

The queen's face flickered back to the look of the taunting cat. "Yes. It is true. You have usurped my place as the most scandalous adulteress in Jerusalem. Perhaps in all of Judea. Though none of us Judean women could hold a candle to the libertine women of Rome. I am pleased that mouths no longer murmur about me. Instead, they besmirch your name."

Zera said nothing. What could she say? She wanted to hide the blush that heated her cheeks.

"Come, girl, what say you?"

Zera could not read the queen's face, so she would speak only the obvious. "I am glad my abject humiliation has served some practical purpose."

"Oh, it has, and I would repay you. That is why I ordered Barid and Dex to bring you and your handmaid here to Caesarea, where I could protect you. I needed to hear their latest reports of other matters, but my little bees told me Joram plotted to kill you."

"Little bees?"

"My spies are little bees, ever-present, never noticed." She tilted her head. "The innkeeper and his wife will never know that if they have remained near, my little bees will buzz, and I will hear."

"My queen, your little bees have served you well."

Hate aged the queen's face. "I have great disdain for a man

who sets aside his wife and seeks to take her life. You may well have heard of my loss of favor with Herod. Salome, my daughter, was forced to tempt Herod with a dance of seven veils. She danced to preserve her life and mine."

"And now you have saved my life from a murderous husband."

The queen leaned forward and took Zera's hand. "That this new prophet, this Nazarene, refused to pass judgment on you, an adulteress, has tied the tongues of those who would depose me."

"Yeshua did not declare me innocent."

"But you were spared from death in the stoning pit."

"Even still, Yeshua confronted my accusers. Each was forced to admit that they themselves were not without sin. They left the Temple Mount with their sins unforgiven. Yeshua turned to me and declared that since no one was left to accuse me, neither would He accuse me." Zera's voice had faded to a soft confession. "I left the Temple Mount assured my sins were forgiven."

"Even the Baptizer did not forgive sins. Does this Yeshua claim to be a god, equal to our emperor?"

"Before that fateful morning when I was cast at Yeshua's feet, I had never seen Him. I only know He speaks with the authority of our One God. He commanded me to go and sin no more."

Herodias threw back her head and laughed. A harsh, mocking laugh. "But only weeks later, my little sand flea flits to the hippodrome in search of her lover." Herodias smiled and wiped tears from her eyes. "Your commitment to *sin no more* was very short-lived."

"Sand flea?" A wave of frightful understanding set Zera's thoughts afire. "Fortuna was one of your little bees."

"She sent word the moment you and your handmaid broke away from her at the end of the races. She was sure you went to find your lover."

"I only wanted to talk with him. Ask his forgiveness."

Herodias slammed her fist on the table, making the cups wobble. "Liar."

Zera's chin quivered, her hands trembled. She brought the cup of wine to her lips. Perhaps the wine would serve to calm her.

"I cannot and will not safeguard you if you persist in deceiving yourself." The queen's voice was soft but carried the weight of death. "Such deception will place those you love, as well as those who love you, in harm's way." She moved her face even closer to Zera's, almost nose to nose. "Including the babe you may carry."

Zera jerked back, dropping the cup. Wine splattered and the cup shattered against the stone floor.

"Fortuna suspected. Now your slip with the cup leaves no doubt that you believe you are with child. As for Auriga Maximus, what say you now?"

Zera gathered the courage to admit that she had lied to herself. "Though I knew it was unwise and unlikely, I had hoped to see Auri alone in the stables. I wanted him to take me in his arms, assure me of his caring."

"Now that rings true to my ear."

"You may trust from this moment forward, I will not deceive myself, or you."

"I trust no one upon whom I do not have a death grip."

"You have no death grip on me."

"Think again, my little sand flea. I have a two-fisted hold on you." Herodias grabbed Zera's wrists. "Joanna, your kinswoman, is very much within my powerful reach. For reward or retribution."

"Yes." Zera could hardly croak her answer.

"And ..." Something flickered across her face. A threat more ominous than Zera could fathom. "Of course, your precious Auriga Maximus is once again my husband Herod's slave."

Zera's heart felt trapped inside an iron fist. Then her heart pounded a relentless war drum in her ears. "Auriga played me false and left me to Joram's revenge. I care not one whit about the fate of Auriga Maximus. I hate him with an abiding hate. A hate that springs from the depths of my soul."

Herodias flashed her a wry smile. "You are young. You have not yet learned that an abiding hate is merely an abiding love turned on its head."

The truth of those words pierced her like a lance thrust in her side. She must tread carefully. Though the queen had not mentioned them, there were others within her reach that Zera had come to love—Reah, Dex, Sophia, Barid, and her cousin Theo.

"I will not endanger my friends. I dare not return to the forge. And Reah cannot stay with me. Together we are more readily noticed."

Herodias put her elbows on the table and pressed her fingertips together into a pyramid. "My spies will follow Joram and his men, but until he is utterly ruined and can no longer threaten your life, you cannot rest your head in one place for more than a few nights."

Zera drew in a sharp breath. The words of another echoed in her mind. "A wise man once said that foxes have holes and birds of the air have nests, but the Son of Man has nowhere to lay His head."

"And who is this Son of Man?"

"Yeshua of Nazareth."

Herodias remained unmoved, fingertips still touching. "Years ago, Joanna became captivated by Yeshua's teaching and wanted to follow him. I convinced Herod she could be a useful spy. Joanna came and went for many months. Then, stricken by a sudden wasting disease and nigh onto death she could barely breathe and no longer walk."

"But she is not weak. She has walked far with me."

"Joanna's husband, Chuza, brought her to the would-be prophet, and he healed her of her devastating wasting disease. Now she rarely returns. She is loath to leave Yeshua even for a day. And I am loath to deny his miraculous power. What more does this rabbi teach?"

"Yeshua promised rest for those who come to Him. Those who labor and are heavy laden." Zera's voice lifted with hope.

"I have heard the man speaks in riddles."

Yeshua's words in Bethany flooded back to Zera. *Take My yoke upon you ... and you will find rest for your souls. For My yoke is easy and My burden is light.*

Zera was one of the heavy-laden. She was burdened with fear that Joram would find her. She despised herself for being duped by her lover.

A lover whose child might be growing in her womb this very moment.

Her mind sifted through that fateful day when Joram flung her into the street. Joanna had been just outside her door. Was she out early spying for Herodias? A shiver of revelation ran through Zera. Joanna's presence was the hand of HaShem.

HaShem, what am I, a miserable sinner, to do?

That still, small voice spoke to her spirit. *Follow Me.*

The peace of new hope descended upon Zera, and she smiled at Herodias. "I will seek and find Yeshua of Nazareth. And follow Him wherever He may go."

"Yeshua never stays in one place for many days. Even his disciples do not know where he will next rest his head. Hiding as a commoner amongst the many women who travel with him may help make you as difficult to track as the wind. But you still must beware of Joram's spies."

"Yeshua once saved my life. And I know in my bones, He is the only man who walks the earth who can truly keep me safe from all manner of evil."

Chapter Nineteen

Inn on Jericho Road

Kislev (December), two weeks later

Theo

Constant busyness was the only way Theo knew to settle his anxious stomach and slow his worried heart. Barid and the others had not returned to the inn from the races. Two Sabbaths had passed. No word had come.

Theo limped, clearing the clay bowls left from the morning meal. Last night, Herod and Herodias had arrived at the inn unannounced. Thankfully, they stayed outside in the king's opulent tent. But the inn was overfull—rooms strewn with extra sleeping pallets and a slave had slept in the stable.

Theo hobbled toward the stable. The slave would need help readying the mounts for Herod and his guards. He passed the queen's litter where the king helped Herodias into her nest of pillows for their trip to Jericho.

"*Shalom*, my lady." Theo dared not ask after his friends. He had heard that the queen's plans were often kept from Herod.

The king turned to Theo. "Tell my slave to make haste. The sun is up. We would be off."

"Yes, my lord." Theo fought to keep the exhaustion from his voice. When the king's retinue stayed for the night, tending the inn for Barid without another pair of hands was beyond Theo.

Theo entered the stable. The strong slave groomed Herod's black stallion. The light behind his golden hair and beard made him look like a gilded statue. "I have come to help. Herod is eager to return to Jericho."

Theo started toward the stall of a golden mare.

The slave looked up sharply. "Halt. Only I tend to those four goldens." His voice, though low and soothing, seethed with something else.

Theo quickly moved to do the slave's bidding, his crutch rustling the straw with every hobbling step. "I am called Theo."

The man studied him. The same look dawned on his face that Yeshua had when he first saw Theo. Compassion without pity. A comforting look that allowed him his dignity. "Theo, calm yourself. When my quadriga team senses your quick moves and tense bearing, they become skittish."

Theo took a deep breath and let it out slowly. "Ahh. You are Auriga Maximus, hero of all Judea. Travelers have spoken of nothing else since the great race in Caesarea." Words rushed from his mouth, his tone betraying his restlessness. "I have heard hundreds of recountings of your daring rescue of your fallen opponent and—"

A raised brow from Auriga Maximus cut off Theo's words like an axe blow. He returned to his grooming.

Theo's cheeks burned. "Forgive my chittering. My master Barid and my friends have not returned from the races."

Auriga's grooming brush stopped. "Barid ... big pagan with fair hair and eyes like mine?"

"Yes. That is my friend. I have had no word."

Auriga turned, his eyes dimmed, and he hesitated over his next words.

Herod barged into the stable. "Auriga. Where is my mount?" His words were impatient, but his tone was playful. "It is well past the hour I would have left, but how can I be angry with my new-won and winning charioteer?"

"New-won?" Theo blurted and cringed. It was not his place to speak.

Herod clapped Auriga on the shoulder. "I won Auriga Maximus when his master was foolish enough to try to rig the race and bet against him."

Auriga smiled at the king. An unreadable smile, but one that was surely false.

"My new goldens are not readied. Hasten to bridle them."

Auriga's face turned to stone. His eyes darkened to the color of a storm-brewing sky. "My lord, the goldens must follow slowly on lead ropes. The journey from here is steep and narrow. It has rightly been called the Ascent of Blood. Would you risk a twisted foot, or worse, a fall?"

Herod nodded. "Your counsel is sound. Follow in your own time with the goldens."

A flash from Theo's past made him shudder. He could almost feel the pain. "My lord, forgive me. You see before you a cripple. But I was not always thus. I was beaten by bandits and left for dead near here on the very road you travel. Though Auriga is a big man, he is but one man. Your goldens and he would be a ripe plum dangling before a band of robbers."

Herod frowned, and Theo feared he would strike him. But the king's face did not cloud with rage, only deep thought.

"You were wise to warn me. I will send two guards with

him." The king flipped a gold coin to Theo. "An aureus for ensuring the safety of my golden slave and horses."

Theo held in his hand a month's wage for a legionnaire. He bowed his thanks.

Theo and Auriga readied the horses for those who were departing. The two guards stationed themselves at the turnoff on Jericho Road and waited.

Auriga returned to his grooming of the goldens. Theo watched him, spellbound. Something about Auriga's long fingers and the way his hands moved as he groomed the horses poked at Theo's mind. Had he seen this man before, or was it a figment of fancy?

"Auriga. Stop at the inn before you leave. I will pack food-stuffs for you and the guards."

"Many thanks. We must leave before the sun reaches its peak to make Jericho before dark."

"I remember nothing from before I was beaten. But just now, your manner seemed known to me. Am I known to you?"

Auriga barely looked his way. "Since I was enslaved, brought to Rome then Judea, I have had but one friend. And he is long dead." His voice carried notes of deep sorrow.

Theo sensed there was nothing he could say that would offer comfort. He went to the inn and prepared the food. The clopping of hooves drew his attention, and he finished tying up the sack. He looked from the low window and saw Auriga guiding his goldens on lead ropes.

Theo ran outside and handed him the sack. "*Shalom.* Peace be with you."

"And also with you." Auriga walked away.

As the charioteer left, the feeling of familiarity stayed with Theo.

He hobbled back inside, set his crutch in the corner, and forced himself to stumble about the room. Despite the discomfort, Theo followed Barid's advice that moving without the crutch would keep the deformed leg from further weakening.

Herod's hunters had brought down an enormous stag and left the meat in payment. Theo went out to the cookfire and added venison to the stew pot.

The rumble of a nearby cart sent Theo scurrying out front to meet the guests.

He spotted Dex driving the donkey cart at the turnoff from the main road. Reah sat beside him. Barid, the color of goat milk, sat propped up in the bed of the cart.

Theo's worry spiked and his spirit sank. Barid looked weak. He must be ill or injured. And Zera ... where was Zera? Had Joram murdered her? *If HaShem wills, let her be safely asleep in the cart.*

The cart stopped, and Theo peered over the side. "Tell me true. Is Zera dead?"

Barid gave Theo's hand a feeble squeeze. "She lives. And praise your One God, she is strong in body. But with all that has come to pass, she is heavy of heart."

Dex stepped over the seat and into the cart in front of Barid. "It is a long tale. Help me get Barid inside."

Reah climbed down. "I will prepare a meal."

Theo gestured toward the back of the inn. "In the court-yard, there is a venison stew simmering on the cookfire."

Reah reached for her bundle of belongings and headed to the cookfire.

Theo looked at Barid. "You would be proud that King Herod was well served when he stayed here last night."

"And I am well pleased, my faithful servant." Barid was breathing hard and looked spent.

"On the road from Caesarea, we ate no meat." Dex licked his lips. "My mouth waters for the venison. And it will restore Barid's strength and help him heal."

"Was your shoulder injured by man or beast?"

"A knife wound to my shoulder, and much life's-blood drained from me." Barid leaned on Dex and eased himself slowly out of the cart.

Theo took Barid's arm. "You were a *malak*, an angel, ministering to me through my darkest nights, in keeping with the meaning of your name. Now, it falls to me to be an angel for you."

"This HaShem of yours, he creates peevish angels?"

Barid's jibe was unexpected. And rang so true. Theo erupted with laughter. "I must concede that some days the pain in my leg makes me more burdensome than merely peevish. There is a saying among our wisest men, that the Lord's ways are truly mysterious." Theo grinned at Barid. "Perhaps, as punishment for some past sin, you are well deserving of a peevish angel."

Dex opened the door to the inn. "May I never commit that same sin for which I would be so amply rewarded."

Theo helped Dex bring Barid inside and over to a table. "I will feed and water the donkey so she can continue on after our meal." Dex steadied Barid as he sat.

"Theo, I would sit and tell you of Caesarea." Barid's voice was breathy after the short walk.

"Sit back and rest. I will not be long." Theo quickly tended to the donkey. Barid was a broken shell of the vigorous man who had left the inn weeks ago. *HaShem, I beg You, restore this good man to health. Though a pagan, my friend seeks to live by the words of Your prophet, Yeshua.*

Dex poured cups of barley beer. "Theo, come sit with us." Sophia and Gaius must think some ill fate has befallen me."

"I have been worried. I sent messages to Sophia with travelers to Jericho that I had no news of you."

Over the supper of venison stew, Dex and Barid told Theo

of the warning from the queen's spies, the horrific attempt on Zera's life, and the near-mortal wounding of Barid. Reah was strangely silent. There must be something more. Something she dare not speak.

Theo's worry eased with the assurance that Zera still drew breath. "Bless you for taking the blade meant for Zera. And praise HaShem that the blade was not poisoned."

Barid's hand moved to his wounded shoulder. "Both the assassin and Joram fled, so Zera cannot come here. She is still in danger."

"Where is she? Who will be her safeguard?" Theo's voice quaked under the weight of his qualms.

Barid touched Theo's arm. "Peace. Herodias has her spies watching for Joram, but we all are in agreement. Zera must not stay in one place for long."

Dex rose. "She travels with the women who follow Yeshua. Disguised as a commoner from Galilee, she will go unnoticed. Joanna will be amongst them. I must take my leave and travel to the forge while it is yet light." Dex walked to the door.

"Wait." Reah fetched a waterskin and bundle from the counter. "Bread and figs for your trip."

Dex took the provisions. "You are a brave woman and a faithful friend. It heartens me to know you will help Theo and Barid run the Inn."

Reah sniffled and looked down. "I miss Zera. I have been at her side my entire life. Though I know it is best we are parted."

"Your parting will not be for eternity."

"May the gods go with you, my friend," Barid called from the table.

Reah followed Dex out through the open door, and she called back. "I will settle the donkey and cart in the stable. And when I return, I will cleanse and dress your wound."

Theo flinched, remembering the racking pain of changing a

dressing. He filled their cups with barley beer. "You said Zera is heavy of heart?"

"She was grateful to be rescued from Joram's evil plots and offered the queen's protection, but knowing Joram will persist in his attempts to kill her weighs on her."

"It greatly saddens me that she must see an ever-present assassin at her heels, behind each door, and hovering over her when she sleeps."

"Neither Dex nor I could discern why Zera would ever go to the Yellows' stalls after the race. A place Joram would surely visit after the victory of his quadriga team."

Theo's thoughts tumbled one over the other. "Perhaps she sought to accuse her husband with his sins against her. Or come to an agreed price in exchange for a *get* of divorce."

"Her reasons for the foolhardy choice to visit the stables remain unspoken. But in the days before Zera left to follow Yeshua, she barely ate."

"Was she fasting as a form of repentance?" Suspicion hammered a sharp nail into Theo's mind. "Or did she fear poison?"

Barid glanced at Theo with a look of shock. "I never considered that she might be worried about poison. But we all ate from the same pot, even Herodias. So Zera had little reason to fear poison."

"Fear does not always follow reason." Theo tugged at his beard. "Fearful thoughts can take possession of one's mind. All-consuming thoughts can leave one's mind running a dangerous, never-ending chariot race. A race that chases away all other feelings of peace or joy or safety."

Theo looked over Barid's shoulder and saw Reah return.

"At the sight or smell of food …" Barid pushed his bowl away. "Zera looked as if she would be sick. I never saw such a thing, except when Sophia—"

Reah stamped her foot, cutting Barid off. "Zera is not wasting away. Her lost desire for food can be put down to a spirit of melancholia." Reah busied herself clearing the meal. "She has had such spells before." Reah's movements were sharp twitches like a rabbit that senses a hound nearby. She was holding something back.

Theo tried to draw out from Reah what she was loath to divulge. "How long since you last saw your lady?"

"Ten days past, since she left to find Yeshua."

"Alone?" Theo blurted his alarm.

"She was in the company of a woman named Fortuna. A woman trusted by Herodias." Reah turned to Barid. "You must rest."

He pushed down on the table to stand. "Each morning, I am stronger, but my endurance quickly wanes." He moved forward on tottering legs.

Theo hurried to the corner and brought his crutch to Barid. "This may be just what is needed."

Barid took the crutch and hobbled to the back room. Theo watched him go, struck by the notion that they had traded places. A shiver ran through Theo. He sensed the hand of HaShem shaping his new life. Barid needed him. Sophia and Dex had befriended him. Reah relied on him. And Zera had remembered her love for him, her kinsman. He had been lost, and now he was found.

HaShem, You weave an intricate tapestry with the threads of our lives.

Chapter Twenty

Inn at Jericho Road
Adar (March), three months later

Theo

After three months, they had fallen into a comfortable pattern of days. Work began at dawn. Reah tended to the needs of the inn and the guests. Theo tended the beasts in the barn. Barid oversaw everything and helped them both.

Theo handed Barid a rake, picked up another and mucked a stall. "Barid, it gladdens me to see that your strength has fully returned."

"The mending of my shoulder has been so slow. One month more and I would have gone to Yeshua for healing. Our guests speak more and more of His unfathomable miracles." Barid's smile was honest, but there was an edge of challenge in his tone. "Why will you not turn from vengeance? Why will you not dare ask for your miracle? You could live sound of body and healed of heart."

Theo's swallowed hard against a brick of dread. "Last night, a guest said Yeshua was healing many near the place of His baptism by John. In Perea, the place where His calling began. The guest wondered if Yeshua had returned there because He knows His calling is near its end."

"If He is this Messiah your people await, how can His calling be near its end? He is yet a young man with years of good works before Him. Teaching. Healing. Forgiving sins."

Theo's dread was now the size of the Temple cornerstone. "Yeshua speaks in parables, but there are murmurings that He has prophesied His own death."

"HaShem will protect Him."

Theo spread fresh straw in the stall. "This guest warned that the Pharisees are determined to kill Yeshua."

Barid's eyes turned as icy as a mountain stream. He grabbed Theo by the shoulders and leaned close. "My friend, *carpe diem,* seize the day. Do you not see you must ask for your healing without delay?"

"I do sense an urgency I cannot name. Last spring, I first wondered if this Yeshua was the Messiah when He told a parable that revealed His intimate knowledge of the attack that left me crippled. Then, Zera and I sat at His feet for two days in Bethany. Now I am sure He is Messiah, but His ways and words are steeped in mystery."

"Must we understand every jot and tittle to believe?"

Like the unrolling of a Torah scroll, a flash of revelation opened Theo's mind. "Now I understand what Lazarus meant when he said it is in the droughts of our understanding—the mysteries—that the living water of faith is poured out."

A peaceful silence rested upon them. A silence mixed with something hallowed.

"Barid, Theo, Rhea," a frantic young voice shouted from the road. Theo and Barid hurried to the front of the inn and met Reah coming from the back. Emet ran down from the main road, waving his arms.

"You must find Yeshua." Emet bent over and dragged in ragged breaths. "Lazarus is at the brink of death."

Theo stared at Emet sitting on the road, still sucking in breath. The boy was spent from bringing them news that Lazarus was nigh unto death.

"The boy must rest before he goes any farther." Reah brought Emet a cup of water, which he grabbed and downed.

Barid waved toward the road. "Travelers are arriving. They must be hosted, but one of us must go to Yeshua."

"Send me." Theo thrust his hand into the air. "Mary and Martha rely on us to carry their message swiftly. I know the very spot in Perea where Yeshua is teaching."

"Take the donkey cart. You should reach Him by nightfall. Reah and I will tend the inn."

Reah directed the travelers toward the door and looked back. "I will make ready for the coming of Yeshua. He will pass by the inn when He goes to Bethany."

Emet struggled to stand. "I should be the one to go to Perea. The message was sent with me."

Barid steadied him. "You have done well. And you may trust Theo will deliver the word without delay. Stay for a meal, then return to Martha and Mary. You may well be needed for other tasks."

Theo hurried to the stable, hitched the donkey to the cart, and stopped at the front of the inn.

Barid brought Theo his crutch. "You may need this in the throngs that surround Yeshua." He clasped Theo's arm his fingers pressing hard . "Be bold. Ask for your miracle. May your return be free of any further need of a crutch."

A wave of sorrow crashed through Theo. "It's not a lack of courage. I have carried this hate so long, it has become a constant companion, as needed as my crutch. I do not know how to set aside my hate."

"But consider, you rely on your crutch less each day."

As Theo drove the cart to Jericho, he was drawn into a sandstorm of memory. Memory of his life since the near-mortal attack. Theo thought of how many times he had refused to leave the inn, afraid he would miss catching the Levite and priest who had left him to die. But after ten years of brewing hate that had turned the wine in his life to vinegar, Theo had spotted the holy hypocrites.

He and Samuel had tracked the priest and Levite to where Yeshua was teaching a crowd. He shared a parable that spoke of the holy men and their sin of abandonment. The priest had been remorseful and forgiven. The Levite strode away, unforgiven, wallowing in his pride. After hearing the parable, Theo was finally able to leave the judgment for their sin at the feet of Yeshua.

Theo snapped the reins, urging the slow donkey forward. They rounded the last bend, and the forge came into view. Theo pulled up and waved both arms at Dex.

Dex was hammering at a fiery anvil and would not hear a call. He looked up, spotted Theo, and came at a run. "My friend, you look distraught. Is a life in the balance?"

"Lazarus of Bethany stands at the door of Death. I must get word to Yeshua."

Dex was quickly at Theo's side, unhitching the donkey.

Sophia and Gaius came out from the house. She took the reins. "I was within hearing and will bring a well-rested donkey." Sophia headed toward the stable. "Gaius, come help me pour water into the trough for this thirsty beast."

Theo shifted on the hard bench of the cart and stretched

out his legs. "A morning on the road has left my legs cramped and my throat parched." He reached for his waterskin and drank.

Dex rested his arm on the cart. "What other tidings have you?"

"That Lazarus was taken ill, the physicians were called, and he seemed to improve, but then took a sudden turn. The physicians say that a cure is beyond their skills, but they will stay and ease his pain."

Sophia returned leading a fresh donkey, and Dex hitched him to the cart. "What more do you need?"

"If I find Yeshua quickly, I may bring Him here for the night. We will not be able to travel as far as the inn before nightfall."

"We would be honored to host the prophet. Like us, many of our friends have come to believe He is the Promised One awaited by the Samaritans and the Jews." Sophia handed him a full waterskin.

Dex turned the donkey to face the road. "May your journey be swift and safe."

Theo made a clicking sound and flicked the reins. The donkey clopped toward Perea. The cart lurched, and Theo's thoughts thrust back to the men who ambushed him. How could he forgive faceless enemies when he was left with recurring terrors in the night and a maimed body?

His heart wanted revenge. His mind wanted justice. But his soul knew that coddling his hatred was like drinking poison.

He shook himself from his runaway rage. Now was not the time to think of himself. His friends were in need of him. Theo's chest was a vise of fear that stole his breath. Fear that he might reach Yeshua too late for Lazarus to be healed.

Along the way, Theo saw few passersby. But each one

confirmed he was on the right path. Theo rounded a bend and spotted a crowd scattered around Yeshua.

Several of them quietly rose, walked to the Jordan River, and stood waiting with others. Theo could hear the soft ripples of the river. Two disciples baptized those who came to repent.

Theo climbed down from the cart, tethered the donkey to a fig tree, and picked up his crutch. He stared at Yeshua for a few moments, blanketed by a sense of awe. The sense that he walked on hallowed ground.

"... though you die, yet will you live."

Yeshua's words reawakened Theo to his purpose. Lazarus. He started picking his way through the crowd. The going was fraught with many well-meaning followers who did not move aside. They assured Theo that Yeshua would begin healing after He finished teaching His lesson.

"You do not understand. I come with a message for Him."

The people either did not believe the urgency of his plight or would not give way to another. Theo's frustration became a simmering cauldron. He was stuck fifteen paces away from Yeshua. He tried to shout, but the people hushed him and closed ranks. He had expected to come close to Yeshua and deliver a message for His ears only. But that was not to be.

"I am the Way, the Truth, and the Life. No one comes to the Father, but through Me." Yeshua's words carried like a resonant voice hovering over still water.

How would Yeshua respond to a rude interruption?

HaShem, Father in Heaven, show me the way.

Theo was reminded of the tale Lazarus told of a paralyzed man in Capernaum. He was let down through a hole in a roof and placed at Yeshua's feet. The prophet had not been offended but had healed the man. Surely, he would want the needs of his friend Lazarus brought before him.

Theo pushed closer and was jostled by those seeking to

silence him. His boiling frustration erupted into outright anger. He lifted his crutch and, with all his might, flung it high in the air toward Yeshua. "Look up," he shouted. The crutch flew into the air, parting the crowd between Theo and Yeshua. Theo's crutch came down and thudded on the ground merely a pace from Yeshua's feet.

The crowd went silent—watching, waiting for Yeshua's response. The prophet turned to Theo, His eyes sparking with something that was not anger, but mayhap admiration, even amusement. Theo rushed forward and stumbled in front of Yeshua.

He bent, picked up the crutch, and held it out for Theo, looking at him with keen compassion. A look that seemed to invite Theo to ask for healing.

"Master, Mary and Martha of Bethany have sent word to You, saying, *Lord, behold, he whom You love is sick.*"

Murmurs streaked through the crowd.

"Lazarus, as close as a brother to Yeshua."

"A loyal friend."

"See what Yeshua will do."

"He will go to him now."

"Perhaps He will heal here—by only the word of His mouth."

Yeshua raised His hand, and the people stilled. "This sickness is not unto death, but for the glory of God, that the Son of God may be glorified through it." Yeshua's eyes dimmed, His face overcome with sadness, and He handed the crutch back to Theo.

Was Yeshua sad for Lazarus? Disappointed Theo had not asked for healing? Mayhap both? Yeshua withdrew with some of His disciples without another word.

What was Theo meant to do? Would Yeshua give His disciples guidance before He traveled to Bethany with him? Theo waited, and so did many others. Over time, the crowd began to slowly dwindle. Theo was left alone with his crutch and his confusion.

The sun set, and the disciples who had been baptizing at the Jordan River returned. Several women were with them. Zera, dripping streams of water from her long tunic, wrung her long hair and wound it into a braided knot at the nape of her neck. She had been baptized.

Joanna ran up to Zera, spoke, and pointed toward Theo. Zera turned and waved, a smile of pleasure eclipsing her look of surprise. She lifted the hem of her robe and ran to him. "*Shalom*, kinsman, why are you here? You look troubled. Is all well at the inn?"

"Trouble haunts Bethany. I was sent to tell Yeshua that Lazarus is nigh unto death."

"Will He go with you now?"

"Yeshua said something about glory, but He speaks in riddles. And He said the sickness was not unto death. He left me without a word. That was hours ago. I thought we would surely be well on our way to Bethany by now. But it is too late to go—even to the forge."

"It is a warm, clear night. Many will sleep under the stars. Stay, and we will decide what should be our part in this matter in the morning." Zera turned toward the women's tents. She stopped and looked back. "Be at peace. If Yeshua says this sickness is not unto death, then Lazarus will not die."

Faith raced against doubt through Theo's veins. "Zera."

"Yes."

"Yeshua called Himself the Son of God."

A Certain Mercy

Zera

At first light the next morning, Zera found Theo among the many men sleeping on the ground. She shook his arm, and he sat up and rubbed his eyes. She waited, though it was an effort to contain the urgency that kindled in her spirit. When he seemed awake enough, she began her story. "It came to me in a dream. Yeshua said He will tarry here. I asked, *Why, Lord?* He smiled and answered, *My Ways are not your ways.* As soon as the words left His lips, I was overcome with the sense that both you and I are needed in Bethany."

Theo looked at her for a long moment.

She waited in patient silence and prayed for HaShem to give her kinsman wisdom.

Theo took a long, deep breath, seemed to come back to her, and met her eyes. "It is the Hand of HaShem. Yeshua has delayed his journey to Bethany, but we are meant to be there, to be a comfort."

Zera shivered under the morning chill and the ponderous weight of their calling to Bethany. For she did not dare share with Theo that in her dream, Yeshua had said she would be needed to help prepare the body of Lazarus for burial—*as you will one day help prepare Mine.* Was her dream a revelation from the Lord or a deception from a demon?

Watch and wait.

The voice in her head sounded like the voice of Yeshua. His words were a mantle of comfort.

Theo and Zera left in the donkey cart, a day's travel ahead of them. A glorious sunrise with slashes of Tyrian purple broke across the eastern sky. "Look, Theo. The colors of royalty."

"Just last night, Yeshua claimed He was the Son of God."

"Then He, the humble carpenter's son from Nazareth, is royalty. I have followed Him, heard Him teach Truth for weeks. That this is true, I have no doubt, for He has no guile in Him."

"How can this be?"

"My bewilderment is sure, yet my faith that it is true is unwavering."

"My beloved kinswoman, you mirror Yeshua. You have learned to speak in riddles."

They stopped at the forge for water and hitched up Barid's donkey. After exchanging blessings with Sophia and Dex, they continued their journey.

"Zera, Dex shared with me that your heart was troubled. You may always come to me and share your burdens."

She stole a glance at Theo. "Only Reah knows these things, but you are my kinsman, and it is right that I confide in you." Zera's voice quivered, and her sigh was as bottomless as a deep well that springs from a bed of rock.

"What things are these?" Theo seemed to tense, but he kept his eyes on the road before them.

Such a blessing. Zera did not want to read the shame in Theo's eyes for her sin. A sin that was a disgrace to any kinsman. "Only Reah knows that Auriga Maximus, the charioteer, was for one night my lover."

"Was he not Joram's slave?" Theo's calm voice seethed with undercurrents of fury.

"How is it that he still lives?"

"He lives because he made a bargain with Joram to seduce me in exchange for his freedom." Shame flooded Zera's soul. Rivulets of tears streamed down her face.

Theo covered her hand with his. "Take comfort. Your sin has been forgiven by the Son of God."

"And I have forgiven Auriga."

"How can you forgive any man who would dishonor you, tarnish your virtue?"

"You do not know of the guilt that should be heaped upon me. I was not a flawless wife. I flaunted my desire for Auriga in the face of my husband, hoping jealousy would rekindle his passion for me." She girded her heart so she could speak the truth she had never spoken. "If I had not revealed my lust for Auriga, Joram would never have thought to tempt Auriga with his freedom."

"It is not all your doing. Both Joram and Auriga played a part in your tragedy." Theo's voice was as gentle as his spirit. "Would that I could so readily forgive such a grievous offense."

"Yeshua teaches that we must forgive our enemies, as well as those who spitefully use us." Zera gently moved her hand to cover the child not yet born. "And I choose to forgive Auriga, the father of my child. But myself I will never forgive."

Chapter Twenty-One

To Bethany

Theo

Just outside Jerusalem, Theo drove the donkey cart along the base of the Mount of Olives. He pointed to the Temple. "Zera, see how the low sun glints from the roof and all things near are infused with a golden glow?"

She nodded.

Zera had been strangely silent since her confessions. "We will be in Bethany well before the sun sets. Something spurs me onward."

Theo clicked his tongue, urging the donkey to a faster pace. "About a mile ahead is the turn toward Bethany. Then we will be close to the home of Lazarus."

Now the road was filled with travelers and their carts, shepherds and their flocks. The daily bustle was broken by a crescendo of high-pitched trilling. A gathering of paid mourners rounded the bend.

"My dream ..." Zera grabbed Theo's arm.

Theo's hand shook with the certain fear that he was too late and Lazarus was dead. He called out, "For whom do you mourn?"

The mourners parted and walked around the cart in the failing light. All were barefoot. Not one broke stride or slowed to answer.

He looked at Zera. Her face, etched with grief, was softened by one glistening tear.

"It must be Lazarus."

"Your dream?"

She nodded, choking back a sob. "Look up the road."

Mary and Martha walked alongside a litter carrying the wrapped body of Lazarus.

Emet ran up to them. "How far off is Yeshua?"

Theo's palms slicked and his mouth went dry. What could he say about Yeshua's absence? Nothing that would be of comfort.

Martha hurried up just behind Emet and stopped beside the cart. "You told Yeshua of our plight?"

Theo nodded, his tongue thick, overwhelmed by the death of Lazarus.

"Then He knows." Martha's voice was edged with a hope Theo could not fathom. "When Yeshua heard my brother was ill, what did He say?"

"In truth, He spoke in riddles as He is wont to do." Theo shot a warning look at Zera. How could they possibly tell these loving sisters that Yeshua had announced to His disciples that Lazarus would not die?

Zera removed her sandals, climbed down, and hugged her, then Mary, as she joined them.

"Though we do not understand all He said or all He

intends, we do know He said that in this matter, the Son of God would be glorified."

Martha looked up quickly. "Zera, you meant to say Son of Man."

Theo raised a hand calling Martha's attention. "No. He said Son of God." Something fluttered in Theo's chest and sent ripples of excitement through him. "And I am sure He was speaking of Himself."

"The Son of God?" Martha's look of uncertainty changed to a look of wonder. "Come with us to the mouth of the cave that is to be my brother's grave."

Theo removed his sandals, tethered the donkey, and hobbled alongside the bier with Zera and the sisters.

They came to the near side of the Mount of Olives, scattered with burial caves. Many were closed with heavy stones. Many others had open mouths, waiting to swallow the dead. Mourners blanketed the hillside, for Lazarus was much known for his good works and much loved for his wisdom and laughter.

At the opening to the cave, the bier was lowered. Mary lifted the burial facecloth that lay folded to the side. "The sun now sets. All who would gaze upon my brother's face for one last time, come forward before I cover it."

Theo stepped forward. That Lazarus was gone, there was no doubt. His face was white, and the breath of life had left him.

Zera took the jar of myrrh from Martha and held it while she anointed her brother's face. "We will await the coming of our Master. Only at the last streak of light will we surrender our beloved brother to a final goodnight."

Theo looked toward the road, praying for the coming of the Promised One. The Worker of Miracles. The One Who Had Raised the Dead.

The face of Lazarus was covered, and an agonized silence spread over the gathering. A silence that took on weight when his body was covered with a shroud and tied with linen strips at the hands and feet. A silence that seemed to slay all hope when the stone was rolled into place, sealing Lazarus into an unending night.

A lone man's voice began a prayer for the dead.

Martha stepped toward him. "Please. We will not say the prayer for the dead until Yeshua comes."

Grumblings of dismay and rumblings of disapproval from the crowd hissed toward Theo's ear. But Martha and Mary did not seem to hear.

The sisters held fast to one another, bent under the burden of their sorrow. Oil lamps lit the path at their feet. Mary touched Martha's cheek. "Come with me to face each day still numbered to us in this life. A life bereft of the laughter and love of our brother, Lazarus."

Theo and Zera joined the mourners walking the mile to the house of Lazarus. Mary turned when she reached the threshold. "Sister, remember this but marks the end of the first day. Perhaps the soul of Lazarus abides nearby. And Yeshua has raised the dead."

Martha took both Mary's hands. "Yes." A kernel of hope slipped into Matha's voice. "Perhaps Yeshua will arrive before the third setting of the sun."

Theo took Zera's arm and led her to the field where cookfires were already burning. "Many believe that the soul stays near the body for three days. It seems grief has blurred reason. Mary and Martha may cling to a shred of hope that Life may still vanquish Death." Theo could barely voice the staggering thought.

Zera turned to Theo. "Do they hope for a raising of the dead after the sun has set upon the sealed burial cave?" Zera's voice faltered, her eyes brimming with questions and fear. "Who can read the heart of another?" Zera gestured to the cookfire and fallen log where they had slept before and unrolled a blanket near some of the women. "Has anyone been raised from death to life beyond the hours of one day?"

The woman known as Magdalena looked up. "The other raisings by Yeshua were shortly after the victim had fallen into a sleep of death. And it was the same with the raisings by the prophets of old."

Zera turned to Theo. "Then they wait for a miracle beyond all miracles."

Magdalena spread her sleeping pallet next to Zera. "We will mourn with them and count each sunset waiting for Messiah to come."

Theo stared into the fire, his mind struggling to grasp what Yeshua meant when He had said He was the Son of God.

Third sunset since the death of Lazarus looms

Zera

Zera patted the log by the cookfire. "Magdalena, we have been serving the mourners all day. Come sit with me."

Magdalena checked the sun low in the west. "We have little more than an hour before the third sunset since the death of Lazarus."

"Yeshua has not come, and I do not want to wait alone."

"Call me Lenah."

"Lenah? Hope for the future? We are surely sisters in both faith and name, as Zera means new beginning."

Magdalena stood. "Let us walk to the well. Our water jars

are near empty." They balanced their jars, one on a shoulder, the other on the opposite hip.

Zera picked her way through the field around other cookfires. "I was surprised to find you here."

"Yes, Zera, I travel with Yeshua, but He sent me here, saying Martha and Mary would have need of me. Praise HaShem, I visited with Lazarus before he suddenly took sick and died. He never judged me for my scarlet past."

Zera had heard the rumors of Magdalena's demons.

"Your silence teems with questions." Lenah looked at her with such kindness.

"May I ask you something, though it may cut close to the bone?" They followed the path to the well.

"There are no forbidden questions when they are asked with a heart that seeks truth."

"Tell me, after your deliverance from a plague of seven demons, did you ever long for sinful things in your past?" Zera felt her cheeks warm.

"Mercifully, I was baptized into a sea of forgetfulness. I had no memory of my demonic deeds or desires, so they had no foothold on my soul. I sense it is not the same for you."

Lenah's kind eyes and voice coaxed Zera to confess all—her adultery, Yeshua's forgiveness, how she had chased after Auri despite Yeshua's command to sin no more.

And her wretched humiliation when she learned Auri had been bribed to seduce her.

They reached the well, and Lenah wound the crank that lowered the leather bucket from the crossbar. "You say you have forgiven this man. Now you must cast off all thoughts of him."

"Banishing all reminders of Auri is not possible." Zera placed a hand on her rounded stomach. "Each morning, I am more certain I carry his child. My torment will be to live with a constant reminder of my lover."

"You are not the first woman to suffer such a plight." Lenah's face softened, eyes full of compassion. "You must love Auriga as the father of your child. And sweep away any other love from the most hidden corners of your heart." Lenah swung the bucket toward Zera.

Zera filled the jars on the ground, then sent the bucket back down the well. "My heart has deceived me more than once. In truth, I do not know how to banish all forbidden thoughts of him."

Lenah drew up the next full bucket. "You are not alone. I had to learn to exchange one form of love for another."

"But I thought you were not lured by your past."

"After my deliverance from demons, I was not lured by my past, but by a very real and intriguing present."

Zera could not keep a question from her face.

"The Master looked upon me as a fully redeemed, cleansed woman. I began to harbor hope."

Zera filled the remaining water jars. "Hope?"

"Even though many of the disciples were married, Yeshua had taken no wife." Lenah's face flickered with shifting emotions. "I began to hope that Yeshua might consider me as a possible wife."

"You hoped to become His wife?" Zera could not dampen the shock in her tone.

"Yes." Lenah sighed out a breath. "But He never once looked upon me with the eyes of a lover, but always with those of a brother. One day, Yeshua asked me to walk with Him, and I confessed my hope for a husband."

"What did He say?"

"That He and I were called to love one another with a love the Greeks call *agape*. A chaste love without condition—both selfless and sacrificial. *Agape* is the love your heart must bear for the father of your child."

"Do you believe Yeshua will ever marry?" Zera balanced her water jars and waited for Lenah to do the same.

"He told me that from before the beginning of time, He has been the Bridegroom of His Bride, the people of Israel."

"Another of His riddles." Zera pondered these new notions as she and Lenah returned to the house at Bethany and set the water jars on the portico.

"Let us sit with the mourners on the ashes and keep silent unless Mary or Martha is moved to speak."

"I have heard of this tradition but never seen it."

"Some sit on a heap of ashes, rip their clothes, wear sackcloth, even sprinkle ashes on their heads. All are signs of deep mourning and repentance for any sins." Lenah led Zera to the courtyard where the sisters grieved on top of the ash heap.

Zera and Lenah sat in the ankle-deep ashes at the edge of the mound.

Zera sifted the ashes from long-ago cookfires through her fingers. Shards of broken pottery pricked her palms. *We all die and return to dust. To ash. Even so, Yeshua promised His followers living water and eternal life.*

"Sister, we are near the third sunset." Martha's tone swelled with fretfulness. "Yeshua should be here by now."

"He has the heart of a healer." Mary pressed her hands together, moving them up and down, lending weight to each word. "He will have tarried to help others along the way."

Martha shook her head, a flicker of anger crossing her face. "And the ember of hope to which I foolishly clung has been snuffed out." Now her voice weakened, choked with fresh tears.

The sun sank, its flame smothered behind dark clouds.

Mary rose and gathered Martha into her arms. "What now, sister, what now?"

Martha's anguished cry tore Zera's heart asunder.

Mary straightened Martha's head covering. "Lazarus is dead. We must surrender our hope and our will to the ways and the will of the Lord."

Martha pushed away and turned her back on Mary. "We have sheltered, fed, and clothed Yeshua and His disciples. Why does He ignore our prayers and leave us sitting on an ash heap of sorrow?"

Lenah stood and faced Martha. "We must remember, prayers are not demands, but humble requests lifted up to the Lord." Lenah's gentle voice quivered.

The last streak of light faded in the west. Out of the darkness, Mary began to sing a soft psalm of praise. Lenah joined her, and one by one, the other women also lifted their voices.

Zera stared at the growing number of stars, the windows of heaven unshuttered. Her thoughts drifted back to what Yeshua had told Theo. How the illness of Lazarus would bring greater glory to Him, the Son of God.

How could death ever bring glory?

At the first streak of light on the fourth day since the death of Lazarus, the women took up their places in the ashes.

"The crowd has dwindled." Lenah gestured toward the road.

Zera sighed her discontent. "Most would not linger among the caves of the dead to console the living."

Mary's face was downcast. A stone mask set in sadness for all eternity.

"He did not come." Martha's voice bristled with rage.

Zera could not tell if Martha's rage was with Yeshua, that He had done nothing, or with herself, because she could do nothing more.

"Martha, He will come, though not when we expected. We must be ready for His coming." Mary took Martha's hand. "I know you would not allow the prayer for the dead to be said, but now that the third day has passed, should the *kaddish* not be offered?"

Martha stood, picked up an oil lamp, and walked in the direction of the grave. "Yeshua has tarried at least two days. Let Him meet you in the ashes and say the prayer for His dead friend when He comes." Her tone was as dead as her brother.

Zera trailed behind Martha in the dim light. Creeping dread fed the snake of doubt that slithered through Zera's veins.

Lenah came alongside Zera. "Have faith."

"I traveled with Yeshua for weeks. And I was so sure He was a righteous man, a prophet, even the Son of God. But He did not come." Zera would carry the deeply sown disappointment and doubt that Martha and Mary would not shoulder.

"He will come in His own time." The stillness in Lenah's tone sparked Zera's frustration.

"How can you be so calm? Have you no compassion?" Zera's voice was loud, laden with fury.

Lenah gazed upon her with the same look of acceptance that shone in Yeshua's eyes when He had offered her mercy. "Consider, what is the true root of your anger? Is it not fear?"

Zera gasped, so taken aback at the gentle admonishment. Her mind faltered over the question. What did she fear? Memories drifted across her mind's eye. "Where men are concerned, my heart has misled me twice before. I will never again seek passionate love. Then my unworthy heart will be shielded from the piercing pain of lost love and betrayal."

"My *ima* used to say ..." Lenah's eyes dimmed, pulled into

the past. "We make plans and HaShem laughs. He reaches down with a loving hand and stirs, muddling the pot of our best laid plans."

"Both Joram and Auri rejected and betrayed me."

"Yeshua has not rejected nor betrayed you. Nor Mary, nor Martha. Faith that does not withstand the crucible of a test is no faith at all."

"Now I have put my trust in another man. Yeshua." A tremor of trepidation turned Zera's knees to water. She reached out for a nearby boulder.

Lenah helped her sit. "Yeshua is not like other men." Her whisper was soft, but sure.

"But now, I am a witness to the anguish of Mary and Martha, His loyal disciples." Zera braced against the shudder that ran through her. "And I am afraid, truly terrified, that He has abandoned them. Afraid my foolish heart has betrayed me yet again. Terrified I may have put my trust in another man of deceit."

Chapter Twenty-Two

Bethany

Adar (March), three weeks before Pesach (Passover)

Theo

Theo watched light vanquish darkness in the eastern sky. Lazarus was dead, four days in the tomb.

Emet passed by the fire, now burned down to ash.

"Boy, please go look for Yeshua. I sense He is near."

"At once." Emet sprinted away.

A thought plucked at Theo's mind. Was not Lazarus now in deep darkness? Did not Yeshua teach He was the Light of the World?

Theo knelt in the field facing the morning sun, head bowed. He fervently prayed for a miracle, one he dared not speak. Not for himself, but for Lazarus.

Theo sensed someone coming and looked up. Just as

Martha, Magdalena, and Zera were moving to kneel beside him, Emet burst upon them, breathless from running.

"The Master ... Jerusalem." Emet dragged in several breaths. "Told Him ... Lazarus four days dead." Emet caught his breath again. "He is at the crossroads to Bethany."

Martha hurried onto the road and set out to meet Yeshua. The others caught up with her.

Yeshua came over the rise in the road. A lone figure in white. He stopped and opened His arms wide.

Martha stepped close to Him. "Lord, if You had been here, my brother would not have died."

Theo heard no anger, no reproach in Martha's tone. Her words were a confession of complete faith in His power.

Those who traveled with Him came up the road behind Him.

Yeshua's eyes glistened and He tilted His head, waiting in patient silence.

"But even now, I know that whatever You ask of the Lord, He will give You."

Yeshua welcomed Martha into His arms.

Martha's words stunned Theo, and his thoughts raced in every direction.

Some onlookers whispered to each other.

"Has Martha's sadness lured her into the sinking sands of madness?"

"What could Martha possibly want Yeshua to ask of HaShem?"

Theo beckoned Zera and Magdalena to draw near. They stood where they could hear Yeshua's disciples whisper amongst themselves.

"Yeshua knew Lazarus was dead and waited two more days."

"Then, without warning, He started for Jerusalem."

"Even though when He was last in Jerusalem, the Jews sought to stone Him."

Thomas stepped out from the group and leaned close to Theo. "Yeshua told us He has come to wake Lazarus."

Magdalena gasped. Her hand went to her mouth as if to stifle her cry, then her hand moved to her heart as if she hoped His words would come to pass.

"His riddles are often beyond our understanding." Thomas looked at each one in turn. "Even so, we came to Jerusalem knowing we may be stoned with our Master." Each disciple confirmed with a nod their willingness to die with Yeshua.

Theo turned back to face Yeshua. Martha remained in His comforting arms.

Yeshua looked over her shoulder, met every eye, studied each face.

A quiet descended upon them. A holy quiet. A quiet brimming with expectation.

Yeshua released Martha and she stepped back.

Yeshua's eyes locked on Martha's face. "Your brother will rise again."

"I know that he will rise in the resurrection at the Last Day."

Yeshua once again opened His arms wide. A cloud hovered over the sun and a dark shadow shrouded Him.

Theo trembled—for the briefest moment he thought he had seen the outline of a man crucified on a cross.

"I Am—"

As one, the gathering drew in a shocked breath. And Theo's chest tightened until he could barely breathe.

Yeshua had spoken aloud the Name never spoken. The Name of HaShem. The Name HaShem had revealed to Moses at the burning bush. Yeshua had claimed to be the One True God.

"I Am—the resurrection and the life. He who believes in Me, though he may die, he shall live. And whoever lives and believes in Me shall never die." Yeshua looked at Martha. "Do you believe this?"

Martha drew in a deep breath, her face shining with hope. "Yes, Lord, I believe that You are the Christ, the Son of God who is to come into the world." Her voice was soft, but laden with conviction.

Yeshua smiled as if pleased with her new depth of understanding. "Where is Mary? Go tell your sister I ask for her."

A stream of travelers on the way to Jerusalem passed by. Several slowed, glancing at them with undisguised curiosity.

Theo drew Martha aside. "We must not attract notice. Someone may report to the Pharisees. Yeshua's life is still in danger."

"I will go to Mary in secret." Martha pulled her cloak around her. "For everywhere Yeshua goes, vast crowds gather. Crowds that may harbor spies or assassins."

Zera spoke to Theo. "Martha will want to make ready for our guest's coming. But she is not meant to wash or work during her week of mourning. And look, with her feet bare, she must pick her way across the stones in the road. I am going with her. She needs my help, for she is even more tender of foot than I."

Yeshua moved under a fig tree and sat on a boulder, sharing bread and water with His disciples. The Son of God. Yeshua seemed such an ordinary man—fully human. He thirsted, felt hunger, and weariness. Yet somehow, He seemed so much more.

Theo strove to sift his beliefs, the kernels of truth from the chaff of falsehoods. He believed HaShem was the One True God. But Yeshua claimed He was the Son of God. And He claimed He and the Father were One.

Theo's soul swelled with joy, sure Yeshua spoke the truth.

But his mind was overrun with swirling doubts that shouted. How was Yeshua's claim not blasphemy? Blasphemy deserving of death.

Zera

Zera steadied Martha, who winced with every mincing step. But when they arrived at her home, she pulled Zera straight through the gate and into the courtyard.

Mary sat alone on the ash heap, a cluster of women on the ground at a distance. Martha led Zera amidst the ashes and spoke into Mary's ear. "The Teacher is come and is calling for you."

Rapture flickered across Mary's face. But within the space of a breath, she quickly secreted her joy, rose, and left.

"She must be going to the tomb to weep." One of the women stood and started to follow after Mary.

Martha lifted her hand, stopping the woman. "After I have rested, I would welcome your company on the way to the tomb." Martha beckoned Zera close. "Show only Mary the spot where Yeshua waits."

Zera ran to Mary and took her arm, guiding her around the rocks that jutted up in the road. Zera patted the girdle at her waist. The stone of remembrance was still there, still sharp, still accusing. It dug into her side, reminding her of her undeserved forgiveness and her utter unworthiness.

When they reached the crossroads, Zera led Mary to a small clearing where Yeshua sat under a fig tree.

As soon as Mary saw Yeshua, she ran forward and fell at His feet. "Lord, if You had been here, my brother would not have died." She echoed the words and faith of her sister.

Even so, she wept, wailing high-pitched trills of unabashed grief.

Yeshua's face changed from one of peace to one of mourning. He groaned from deep within Himself. A groan of such pain that it slashed Zera's soul. When His cry died to nothingness, Yeshua wept.

Theo whispered. "See how He loved him."

Yeshua stood and helped Mary rise. "Where have you laid him?"

Theo stepped out from the group of men, his crutch tucked under one arm. "Lord, come and see." He hobbled down the road to Bethany.

Mary of Bethany and Zera followed them. Zera could not conceive of a depth of love and trust that asked no questions, expected no answers. But Mary's unwavering trust did not bind the tongues of the naysayers. Those who followed them buzzed like stinging wasps.

"Why did he not come in time to save Lazarus?"

"He could not be moved to work a miracle for his friend?"

"He even healed a servant at the request of a pagan centurion."

Each barb was louder than the last.

"Could not Yeshua, who has opened the eyes of the blind, also have kept this man from dying?"

They wended their way through a large gathering at the place of the burial caves hewn into the Mount of Olives near Bethany. Martha waited just down the slope from the tomb of Lazarus. Lenah stood a few paces off with some of the other women. Zera joined them. Mary and Yeshua went to Martha. The sisters held each other around the waist as if bracing themselves to stand against a great storm.

Yeshua turned His tear-streaked face toward the tomb, raised His hands to heaven, and groaned again. This groan was the frightening snort of an angry stallion. A groan that thundered and echoed—sounding as if even the rocks cried out.

Zera trembled and turned to Lenah. "Yeshua sounds angry. Surely He is not angry with Martha or Mary."

"I know well this righteous anger." Lenah pulled Zera close to her side. "Yeshua is angry, but not with any one person. He is angry with all sin, all disease, all death. Angry with the darkness that came into the world when Adam and Eve fell."

Zera took Lenah's hands. "Yeshua has promised His followers eternal life. See how He stands before the tomb of Lazarus and groans like a gladiator ready to battle in an arena where Life is pitted against Death?"

Yeshua slowly dropped His hands. "Take away the stone."

Martha turned to Yeshua. "Lord, by this time there is a stench, for he has been dead four days." A look of revulsion crossed her face.

In truth, when Zera had helped anoint the body with fragrant spices, a slight off-putting odor had already been present.

Yeshua gazed at Martha with a piercing intensity. "Did I not say to you that if you would believe, you would see the glory of God?"

Martha stared at Him, her face moving from revulsion to acceptance. She motioned to the men to remove the stone.

The men looked to one another. Horror and terror and dread overtook their faces.

A fervent look flickered across Theo's face, and he tugged on another man's sleeve. The other man arranged his head covering over his nose and mouth. Theo did not.

Zera watched Theo and the other man strain to roll the stone up the channel in the rock. Two more men came to add their strength. Finally, the tomb was open.

Yeshua raised His hands, eyes looking toward heaven.

"Father, I thank You that You have heard Me. And I know that You always hear Me, but because of the people who are standing by, I spoke this aloud. That they may believe that You sent Me."

Zera's spirit soared like an eagle on the wing. "None seemed to balk at a stench."

"New life has no stench." Lenah sniffed, then cupped her hand, wafting the air toward her nose. "Renewed life carries the sweet fragrance of a newly born babe."

"Lazarus, come forth." Yeshua's booming voice thundered in Zera's chest and seemed to shake the heavens.

All eyes and ears and hopes were nailed to the opening of the cave. A silence filled with awe charged the air. All of creation seemed to hold its breath waiting to hear the first gasp of life from the risen Lazarus.

The wait stretched beyond bearing. At last, the hint of a shadow appeared at the mouth of the cave.

Zera sank to her knees, trembling, quaking. "The shadow has moved, now given greater form in the light."

Lazarus shuffled slowly out of the cave, bound hand and foot by the graveclothes. His face still covered with the cloth. A captive of Death now set free.

"Yeshua has miraculous power—even over death." Zera's quiet murmur was overwhelmed by cries of horror and amazement.

At the sight of the risen corpse, many followers fell to their knees. Some even fainted.

"Is it a spectre?"

"A walking dead man?"

"Yeshua, the Messiah, has defied death."

Yeshua raised His right hand. "Loose him, let him go."

Theo removed the facecloth. The face of Lazarus shone with life. His eyes searched for Yeshua. When he found Him,

Lazarus returned Yeshua's brilliant smile.

Zera leapt to her feet, hugged Lenah, and whispered. "Tonight we will dance and sing praises."

The men who rolled the stone away unbound Lazarus from his graveclothes.

Yeshua had called forth a miracle beyond all other miracles. Zera's heartbeat quickened. Yeshua had the power to keep her safe. Like Lenah, Zera would love Yeshua with *agape*. Like Lazarus, she would earn eternal life.

Lazarus stood in his seamless *kitel*, his white burial garment, and looked toward his sisters.

"Our brother lives." Martha took two steps forward, faltered. Mary caught her, easing her sister to the ground.

Mary looked from Yeshua to Lazarus, her face filled with unbridled joy. "Yeshua, our long-awaited Messiah, brought you back to us."

Martha got up to her knees, raised her arms high. "Hallelujah, The Name of the Lord be praised."

Lazarus took small, timid steps up to Yeshua. His shoulders shook and his hands trembled. "I heard Your voice, and it shepherded me back to life."

"I Am the good shepherd." Yeshua opened his arms, encompassing the growing crowd. "My sheep hear My voice, and they know Me."

Zera watched scores of onlookers come close to Yeshua and kneel. "Lenah, see how many now believe in Him?"

"It is always thus after a miracle."

Zera's soul spilled over with joy. "Now no one can deny a belief in resurrection. The Sadducees have been shown to be in error and will take great offense."

A soft laugh escaped Lenah's lips, and her eyes gleamed with great gladness. "Many will come to faith in Yeshua."

Zera stared at the slope scattered with burial caves.

"Yeshua called the Pharisees white-washed tombs. On the outside, clean and seemingly righteous. But inside, unclean and filthy and evil. Full of dead bones."

"No one can deny the divine power of Yeshua. The Pharisees will be furious."

Zera's eye caught movement, and she pointed to the west side of the Mount of Olives. "Look, some rush to report to the priests and Pharisees."

Lenah wrung her hands. "Yeshua is in great danger."

A shudder of fear ran through Zera. "Yeshua's raising of Lazarus after four days in the grave has poked at a nest of hissing snakes. And unleashed a brood of angry vipers."

Chapter Twenty-Three

Bethany

Morning after the Raising of Lazarus

Theo

The morning chill wakened Theo, his mind alive with thoughts of the awe-inspiring raising of Lazarus. Last night, Yeshua had withdrawn into the house with Lazarus and his sisters. Mary and Martha looked overjoyed but spent. Lazarus looked radiant and renewed.

Before dawn, Theo rose from his blanket and crept around the others sleeping by the cold cookfire. He walked to a nearby grove of fig trees and leaned against a tree trunk, awaiting the rising sun. Sensing someone at his side, he turned and saw Yeshua.

"*Shalom*, Theo. You are troubled. Be at peace."

"Teacher, my sleep was haunted by memories from so many years past. Fear-filled memories of my beating by bandits."

"Yes, I know." Sympathy softened Yeshua's face.

Theo was sure Yeshua knew every thread of his crippling terror, his seething anger, and his unflagging hatred.

"You see all of my pain and all of my shame."

"Theo, what would you have Me do?" Yeshua's tone was a balm for Theo's wounded soul.

"I have heard You teach that to be forgiven, I must forgive my enemies. Even those enemies I do not recall."

"Do you believe this?"

"You have said it, so it is truth." Theo's heart swelled with certainty that he must forgive and sorrow that he did not know the way. "My most fervent wish is to learn to forgive so that I may gain eternal life too. But I am as Lazarus was when he emerged from the burial cave. My heart is bound in the grave-clothes of hate, and I need help to be loosed and set free."

"Beloved Theo, the mind plows the path that the heart will follow. Pray for your enemies, those who persecuted you."

"Lord, I will pray. What more must I do?"

Yeshua lifted His hands over Theo's head, fingers spread as a High Priest bestows a blessing. "I will show you the way of forgiveness. The way that leads to eternal life where there is no pain, or sickness, or death."

A fire of faith sparked in Theo's mind, spread warmth through his limbs, and settled around his heart. "Amen, Lord. Let it be so." Theo clung to the promise of eternal life from the Promised One. In eternal life, his body would be healed and whole. Forevermore.

"I will leave you to your prayers and enter into Mine." Yeshua strolled away, the rising sun crowning His form as He disappeared into the blinding light.

Theo knelt under the fig tree and prayed as Yeshua asked. He prayed that his enemies would be blessed. And his burden of hate seemed lighter.

Over the next two days, crowds swarmed to Bethany. Gawkers, to catch a glimpse of a walking dead man. Faithful followers, to rejoice with Lazarus and the Lord. And seekers of Truth, who never seemed to tire of the testimony of the man returned from the grave.

Each morning, Theo forced his mouth to speak prayers for his enemies aloud. Each morning his spirit seemed a bit less encased in stone. He was learning that it is hard to hold onto hate when you hear yourself pray aloud for a man.

At midday on the third day, Barid and Reah arrived by donkey cart and stopped by the cookfire. Zera welcomed Reah with a close embrace. "I have missed you." She stepped back and took Barid's arm. "And you as well."

His neck reddened at her touch.

She rushed back to the cookfire. "We will serve you a simple meal." Zera rubbed her lower back and leaned toward the pot to ladle stew. Her robe swung near the fire, and she smoothed it, holding it close over her middle.

For the first time, Theo saw that she was surely with child. A child she had carried nigh on five months.

The red splotches on Barid's neck spread up onto his face. He quickly covered his surprise and greeted Theo out of hearing of the women. "Joram must not hear Zera is with child. He would be within his rights to sell the child into slavery, regardless whether the babe is his son or that of a lover."

Theo walked around the cookfire, unhitched the donkey, and held the reins. "Walking throughout Judea with the women who follow Yeshua, Zera would be difficult for Joram's spies to find. And she told me Herodias has sworn to protect her."

"The name of Yeshua is on the tongue of every guest at my inn. The truth or falsehood of His miracles is the fodder of every conversation. Reah and I came to see, with our own eyes, the wondrous work of Yeshua."

Theo glanced up toward the house. "Yeshua and a few disciples seemed to be offering signs of leave-taking to Lazarus and his sisters."

Joanna broke away from the women and ran to Theo. "High Priest Caiaphas—a Sadducee who rebukes any belief in the resurrection of the dead—is said to be furious. A trusted friend told us that Caiaphas called a secret meeting with members of the high council. They plot all manner of evil against Yeshua. We must depart without delay. But the Master asks that you and Zera come away with Him into the wilderness, to the hill country."

"Where?" Zera gathered her things.

"A small village of which we must not speak." Joanna glanced around, intoning in a low voice. "Martha has already readied provisions for you and Theo for the journey." Joanna hurried back to the other women.

Barid crossed to the cart and clasped Theo's shoulder. "Take my donkey. I would spare Zera the walking. Her feet are already swollen."

"Many thanks. You will understand that I may not return immediately to the inn."

"The Lord has His reasons. Reah and I can walk back and will manage the inn."

Reah came close and hugged Zera. "We had so little time together."

"It will not always be so. We will pray for the day when any danger from Joram is past."

Barid took Zera and Theo's blankets and folded them for a saddle. He beckoned Zera and spoke so quietly to her that Theo couldn't hear his words.

Her shoulders slumped and she looked down, shamefaced.

Barid gently lifted her chin, met her eyes, and spoke again. He said something more and swept her up into his arms, ready to lift her onto the donkey's back. Zera placed her arms around his neck. For a moment, it seemed to Theo that their lips were so close—Zera's last breath was Barid's next.

The moment passed quickly, and they moved their heads back.

Barid settled Zera on the donkey and arranged her cloak to cover her legs.

A jolt of new knowing ran through Theo's mind. He picked up a lead rope and headed toward them. They had been a picture of a man and his wife. Barid cared deeply for Zera. He had taken a knife for her. Been willing to die for her.

But Theo was sure Zera never had any inkling of Barid's feelings. Not until this moment, when he had gazed upon her with such unabashed caring. Theo was worried for Barid. And worried for his kinswoman. For Zera was still another man's wife.

He attached the rope and led the donkey and Zera away from Barid and his forbidden feelings. He doubted distance would snuff Barid's increasing affection.

On the way into the wilderness, Theo followed Yeshua and his disciples, those few who had been asked to withdraw with Him. Theo prayed that Yeshua would be blessed and His purposes fulfilled. But Theo still struggled to pray for his enemies. The words came more easily, but his raw feelings of hate ofttimes taunted him.

The road dwindled to a rough path that took them up steep and rocky hills. They stopped twice to rest and draw water at wells. After yet another hour of travel, he saw a village perched on a high hill.

When the villagers spotted Yeshua, they shouted out greetings, and He waved, opening His arms. The children spilled down the hill, racing ahead of their elders.

Zera laughed. "They surround Him like herd-dog pups flock to their shepherd, hungry pups vying for crumbs and affection."

"And He blesses each one." Theo looked up at Zera. "You seem in good spirits. I pray the journey has not been too taxing."

"I am grateful Barid provided the donkey to carry me." Zera then called to the children, "What is this place named?"

"Ephraim." The cry was a chorus of proud, loud voices.

It was the cool of the day when they reached the village, Theo stopped the cart and reveled in the view spread out before them. "Look toward the west and you can see Jerusalem. And to the east are more rolling hills of wilderness."

Zera pointed. "What is that hazy blue?"

"The sky is so clear, I believe we can see as far as the Salt Sea." Something tugged at Theo's mind. A vision of walking along a beach of sand with clumps of glistening white salt. "It seems to me I have walked its shores." His tone was laced with excitement, and he hoped that his vision was true.

"Yes, many years past, we were there together. My father took us with him to meet a ship laden with bitumen. Are threads of memory coming to you?"

"Little threads of memory come to me more often, but I have no way to know if they are truth or dream. It is a corner of a tapestry. I cannot yet make sense of the whole pattern of my past."

"Theo, when you have these moments, ask me. I may be able to confirm some of your snippets as truth."

Her words sparked another image of a ship coming in on the shore of the Salt Sea.

Perhaps one day he would remember all his past life, all his lost years.

Joanna called to them. "Come, Zera, I will show you where the women will set up camp."

Theo helped her down, tethered the donkey, and joined the men by the well. Yeshua was not there. He must have gone off by himself to pray. They gathered to listen to a messenger who had just arrived.

"The men of the Jerusalem Council were in a state of great turmoil. They were sure that Yeshua's signs and wonders would cause everyone to believe in Him. They worried that the Romans would take away both the Temple and their positions."

Theo stepped forward. "What more did you hear?"

"Caiaphas, the high priest, argued that it was wise that one man should die for the people, so that the whole nation would not perish. The Council agreed with him and plotted to put Yeshua to death."

Yeshua was suddenly in their midst. "Both the chief priests and the Pharisees have given a command that if anyone knows My whereabouts, he should report it, that they might seize Me."

Some of the men looked around, faces filled with alarm. Others jumped to their feet reaching for short swords, ready for an ambush.

Yeshua raised His arms. "Peace. I have told you that I must suffer many things. But My time is not yet come. It is dark. Let us retire to rest and pray and sleep."

Yeshua's voice was as calm as still waters, while Theo's mind was as turbulent as a storm at sea. With every faction looking for Yeshua, it would be more difficult to hide Zera. One of Joram's spies was sure to recognize her.

What if Yeshua were captured? Though His disciples

refused to speak of it, He had predicted his own death. How could Theo keep Zera safe without Yeshua or Barid?

And now Theo had a new worry. He was having more and more flashes that may be scenes from his past. And they were not all pleasant. Zera had said he was a good man, but what if he remembered a secret sin? Or a loathsome deed? Perhaps the blank slate of his past was, in truth, an unsung blessing.

Chapter Twenty-Four

Ephraim

The next day

Zera

Zera stood on the high hill in Ephraim near the small dovecote and stared toward the Salt Sea in the distance. Throughout the morning, seven messenger doves had flown into the dovecote. Something foreboding unsettled Zera's stomach, and it was not the child within. This was a small village. Even the dovecote at Jericho did not often have so many messages.

Theo hurried toward her. "Zera, we have need of you. The dovekeeper of Ephraim has gone to bury her mother."

A man rushed up to them. "I am the village elder. With so many messages, we should not wait for our dovekeeper."

"Something of import must have happened. I told him you worked with the dovekeeper in Jericho and could safely retrieve the messages." Theo took her arm and walked toward the dovecote.

Zera went to the first nesting box. "This place must be cleaned."

The elder shrugged. "My wife has been feeding and watering the birds, but did not know what more was needed. The dovekeeper will be back soon."

"This bird has nothing tied to the leg." She moved to the next box and lifted the dove. A royal message tube. A jab of surprise made Zera draw a quick breath. "Theo, I will gentle the doves. There is a small knife just there. Help me cut free each message we find."

Zera moved through all the nesting boxes. "We have found seven messages. Two are rolled in royal tubes of brass. Three are from Jerusalem. And the other two are from Jericho."

Worry creased the elder's face. "Something is greatly amiss."

She opened the tubes with shaking hands and sorted the sealed parchment rolls. "This one is sent to you." She handed it to the elder.

He read the message. "A receipt for our taxes."

"Two are meant for Joanna. Two are sent to Thomas, the Twin. I will deliver them straight away." She placed them in her waistband and turned to Theo. "And these last two are marked for you." The surprise in her voice matched the look on his face when she handed them to him.

"Who knows I am here?"

"I do not know."

Theo nodded to Zera. "I will find you after I have read them."

The elder turned to leave. "We are grateful for your help."

"I will show your wife how to care for the doves."

He nodded and left.

Zera found Joanna at the well and waved her away from the other women drawing water. "I have four messages to deliver, but I wanted to give these two royal ones to you first."

Joanna took the scrolls. "Herodias often sends me missives by dove."

"You do not seem alarmed."

"It is only mildly surprising that her spies know so quickly we went to Ephraim."

"I will wait to see if you must reply."

Joanna sat on a boulder and opened the first scroll. As was the tradition of all dovekeepers, Zera withdrew a few paces and turned away, allowing the one who received the message privacy.

A stifled cry made Zera turn back. Joanna looked up, her face now composed and unreadable. "When you have delivered your other messages, please return to me."

The earlier foreboding that unsettled Zera's stomach now soured. The burning bile that crept upward felt like an awl boring holes deep within her chest.

She hurried to find Thomas, the Twin. He was sitting with Yeshua. They both looked up together. She could not keep the gasp from her lips nor the surprise from her face. How had she not noticed before? Thomas was a double of Yeshua. A Twin. Both men grinned, amused as if her response was quite common. "Forgive me, Thomas. I ... I ... just always assumed 'twin' meant you had a birth brother or sister."

"And I do, a sister. She and I are kinsmen to Mary, mother of Yeshua."

Yeshua gestured toward Thomas. "Our friends thought it clever to call Thomas a Twin. A double meaning—referring to his birth sister and Me, his twin in appearance."

Thomas nudged Yeshua with his elbow. "When I was

young, I would pretend I was Yeshua and cause our mothers no end of vexation."

"But now, our mothers never mistake us, one for the other." Yeshua laughed, and the cares on his face seemed to lighten. "Zera, you have forgotten. You have messages for the Twin."

Zera handed them to Thomas. "I will return soon to see if I am needed to send a dove with your reply."

She went back to Joanna and sat on the boulder next to her. Joanna took both of Zera's hands. "Joram is dead."

"Should I feel loss or relief at such news? Joram was not young, but not old." Memories of their early life together flooded in. She had loved Joram once, and he had loved her. But those thoughts were swept away by her fear of his cruelty. Now she was safe from his murderous intents. "Was it too much strong drink?"

"No. Joram was tortured and his body left before his house for all to see. Some of his creditors were convinced he had a hidden stash of riches for which he was foolishly willing to go to the grave."

Something jabbed Zera from within, and she whimpered.

Joanna put her arm around Zera. "It is too soon. Has the shocking news startled the child to an early birth?"

"No. But I am quite sure the babe kicked. Until now, I have felt only fleeting stirrings." Her hands wandered across her belly. "I felt another smaller one." She took Joanna's hand and placed it on the spot, covering it with her own.

"Wait ..." After a moment, another strong kick.

Joanna laughed. "This child will be an athlete."

Auri was an athlete. Zera smiled a half-smile but said nothing, pricked by the painful memory of her lover. Had Herodias told Joanna the name of the child's father?

Joanna glanced at Zera. "Regardless of the child's strength

of body, he or she will be of strong courage and faith like the mother."

"I am glad I felt the quickening of life just after hearing I am a widow. My child is freed from the demon who would have been his father under the Law."

"And I am thankful that you and the child are freed from Joram's spiderweb of spies."

Theo hobbled toward them. Everything about his face, his speed, his burdened breaths, suggested he must share some matter of great import.

Zera braced for bad tidings.

Joanna stood and motioned for Theo to sit. The last women were leaving the well, water jars balanced on their hips and shoulders.

Theo took a few breaths and gathered himself. "Barid marked the messages for me, but they were surely meant for Zera."

"How did Barid know we were here?"

"He went to Herodias."

A light wind stirred, and Joanna lifted the hood of her cloak to cover her hair. "We have just learned from Herodias that Joram is dead."

"I am glad I was not the one to deliver such news." Theo's tone was filled with relief, yet his countenance was brimming with compassion. "But there is more that I regret to share."

"Please tell me that Barid has suffered no further harm from Joram's spies." Zera's worry for Barid was a fishhook snagged deep within her. Yet she had sworn she would never give her heart to another man.

Theo took both of Zera's hands. "Our friend, Barid, is still as strong and stubborn as his ox."

A feeling of peace settled over Zera. "I never thought I

would be glad to hear of Barid's willful nature. What further tidings have you for me?"

"Ira, your steward, went to the inn hoping to get word to you." Theo's face darkened, and he took a deep breath. "Creditors have seized all that was deemed Joram's property. Joram's mansion, your home, what should have been your rightful inheritance, is forfeit." Theo glanced at Joanna, and something flickered across his face.

"I will leave you." Joanna took a step away.

"No. Stay." Zera looked at Theo. "I would trust Joanna with my life."

"Ira secreted a remnant of your wealth, but you must speak of it to no one else. Now that you do not have to move about, ever in fear of Joram, Barid offers a place with Reah at the Inn. You need no longer walk the land with no place to call home."

"Barid is a good man, but I cannot leave Yeshua, a righteous man. He is the Promised One, our Messiah. And He has said He will not always be with us."

Sadness drifted onto Theo's face. "The end of Yeshua's time with us may be fast approaching."

Zera looked from Theo to Joanna. "The Passover is near. Do you think the Teacher will go up to Jerusalem for the Feast?"

Joanna turned one palm upward like a rabbi beginning a lesson. "Passover is a pilgrimage feast. The Law requires Jews to travel to Jerusalem for Passover. And Yeshua has taught us He comes to fulfill the Law."

Thomas strode toward them, his messages clutched in his hand. "Make ready, tomorrow we leave Ephraim."

Zera rose, rubbing her back. "Yeshua has been warned that cunning men with gravitas, such great power, plot His death. Will He dare to go to Jerusalem?"

"I do not know." Thomas gestured to the wide view from

Ephraim. "I only know that we go first to Perea, then to Jericho."

Theo turned to Zera. "Think of the child. We could go straight to Barid's inn and wait for Yeshua to pass by. It would ease your weariness from the road."

Joanna took Zera's arm. "Please listen to Theo's counsel."

Zera looked to Thomas. "I want to hear Yeshua teach and follow faithfully while He is still with us ..." Her words were spirited, but her tone betrayed her. Zera was tired to the bone.

Thomas looked from Zera to Theo. "If she were my wife, I would insist that she rest for the sake of our babe."

Theo's breath caught and his neck reddened. "We are not man and wife."

Thomas remained silent, but surprise swept into his eyes.

Zera's cheeks burned hot with shame. She looked at Joanna.

"Zera is a widow." Joanna's voice was calm, steady, but her eyes flashed like a lioness protecting her cub.

May Joanna be blessed. Her quick thinking had spared Zera more humiliation.

"Thomas, can you not reason with Yeshua? Plead with Him to stay far from the Passover feast?" Theo turned to Zera. "And it will be dangerous for His followers too."

"Theo speaks true." Thomas waved the messages in his hand. "Yeshua left word with Lazarus where we were going. The first message was from him. He delights in telling the curious crowds his raising from the dead is proof our Messiah has come. Lazarus pokes the Pharisees in the eye, and they will surely seek to silence him."

"And Yeshua is not there to protect him." Theo rose and leaned on his crutch. "Are you able to share the other message?"

"The second message reports that Pontius Pilate has

brought Roman reinforcements from Caesarea. A larger force than ever before."

"It is as I feared." Joanna wrung her hands. "My lady Herodias says such an imposing presence of Roman soldiers will only serve to feed Herod's well-known hatred of Pontius Pilate."

Thomas turned to Zera, his face stern yet his eyes soft with concern. "Woman, you must consider your child. The soldiers will put down the slightest sign of unrest or rebellion. They will be swift and brutal. Guilty and innocent alike will perish."

A stubborn courage settled in Zera's center. "Enough talk of future troubles we cannot know and cannot change. Any worry I harbor for my safety is eclipsed by my faith in Yeshua. I will go to Barid's inn, but when Yeshua goes to Jerusalem for Passover, I will follow Him."

Chapter Twenty-Five

Inn on Jericho Road

Adar (mid-March), two weeks before Passover

Zera

Zera walked into the back courtyard of the Jericho Inn and turned her face to the sky, savoring the warmth of the sun. The week of rest here had renewed her strength and spirit. Bracing her rounded belly, she eased onto the bench. Even though it would be many moons until the birth, she felt as wide and weighted as a millstone.

Reah took a long robe from her mending basket then handed Zera a short tunic with a gaping seam. Reah settled on the bench and put the basket at her feet.

Zera leaned close. "Show me, yet again, how to tie the knot so it lies flat inside the seam. My lack of patience with the wait for my child seems to goad an impatience with my mistakes." Foolish tears sprang to her eyes.

"My lady, do not be such a harsh judge of your beginnings. You were never trained for the tasks I have done all my life."

"Forgive my senseless tears."

Reah laughed and patted Zera's hand. "There is naught to forgive. Everything and nothing brings tears spilling down your cheeks. It is the way of women heavy with child."

Zera wiped her tears with the tunic she was mending. "I can no longer sleep on my stomach. My stormy nights leave me short of sleep and short of temper."

"In time, this too will pass."

Barid walked through the courtyard door and stoked the cookfire, then walked toward them.

At the sight of him, Zera almost pricked herself with the needle coming up through the seam. Barid's cheerful nature always dampened her temper and lightened her temperament.

Barid feigned a look of surprise. "My lady is mending." His voice was a gentle jibe.

Reah held up a hand. "Do not utter one word more, or you and I will be showered with tears."

Barid's face changed from one of jest to one of confusion. His face was ever open. There was no deceit in her champion.

"I stay at your inn with the promise that I will work as all of you do. But my efforts are so child-like and useless." Zera's lip quivered. She lifted her mending. "I am the worst needle-worker in the whole of creation."

Barid made a great show of inspecting it. He flashed her a grin that would set any woman's heart aflutter. "Your handiwork is by no means the worst in creation." His eyes sparked with mirth. "But it may well be the worst in all of Judea."

Reah snapped her mending at him and giggled. Her giggle was as catching as the spread of good news.

Zera sputtered, then gave in to a deep-seated laugh. "You have lifted my spirits."

"And I, Barid the Wise, will improve your mending." He bowed so deeply he almost toppled. "Please stand, and I will enlighten you."

They rose, and Zera flashed a questioning look to Reah, who answered with a shrug.

Barid lifted the bench, moved it a few paces away. "You were sitting under a darkening shadow. This spot will stay bright. You will not lose light 'til fall of night." With a bow and a flourish, he motioned for them to sit.

Zera brushed her loose, long hair back over her shoulders, suddenly aware of her disheveled appearance. "We are in your debt for enlightening us."

Barid turned to go, but he looked back at Zera with a disarming grin. "Maybe now you will sew faster than the slowest of snails."

Zera watched him leave, yet she could not help but wish he would stay.

Reah and Zera worked in comfortable quiet for some time. Zera shifted, and Reah looked up. "My lady, the sun has kissed your face. It is the color of a pink Jerusalem rose."

"But the sun has made me thirst."

"We will rest inside."

Reah and Zera entered the common room of the inn.

"We are wilting." Zera sat at the table, facing the front door.

Barid brought two cups of water. "Fresh from the cold stream." His gaze lingered on Zera.

Reah tugged at his sleeve. "Your sunlight has burned our wilting rose."

Barid poured for Reah. "And here I was hoping it was merely a blush at the sight of me."

Zera's hands went to her hot cheeks, her mouth pressing

back a smile. She turned to Reah. "Tell me. Do all men flatter themselves so brazenly?"

"Most certainly do." Reah wagged a finger at Barid.

"I do not. Ever." Barid's tone was flat, his face a puzzle. He went to the counter and brought back a basket of bread.

"But you have reason to be proud. You own a well-known, profitable inn. And, you were a greatly admired centurion who has seen much acclaim." Had she caused offense? Just as she was about to ask, Theo returned from the stable and joined them.

An awkward quiet seemed to share a place with them at the table. Theo looked around. "What has happened?"

"It is nothing." The cheer in Barid's voice sounded false. "My early life was not one of privilege and honor but one of want and shame."

A wisp of worry flitted through Zera. She must make things right. "Forgive my sharp words and harsh spirit. I spoke in jest."

Barid turned to Zera. "You could not have known. In truth, your strength of spirit is compelling, not unlike that of my mother."

"Tell me of her." Zera motioned for Barid to sit.

He poured a pitcher of barley beer then brought it to the table. "I will need more than water if I am to share this tale."

Theo dropped his face into his hand. "And it is a long one."

Reah turned to Theo. "Since you have heard it, perhaps I can help you muck the stalls."

"But I—"

Reah delivered an obvious elbow jab, worthy of Fortuna, into Theo's side.

"Uffh."

Tugging at Theo's sleeve, Reah stood.

He followed Reah to the door and glanced back, rubbing his side.

When their voices faded, Zera turned to Barid.

"Like you, my mother carried a child but had no husband to protect her. But there is more ..." He stopped and swallowed hard as if a stone were stuck in his throat. "I am a child of war."

An unmistakable pain overtook this good man's face. But there was something else too. Something sown deep. She would wait in calm quiet, inviting him to continue in his own time.

"My mother was a captive slave of Rome's army. And captive women are ravaged by many conquerors. I am the child of many fathers and no father."

"Your mother and I ..." Zera's hand went to the lump forming in her throat. "We share a bed of pain."

"She did what was needed to survive. With courage and cunning equal to any Roman commander, she seduced men of station who could and would protect us."

"But how did you rise from slave to centurion?"

"My mother was faithful and caring to each of our protectors until they were transferred to the next campaign or passed away. But I saw her loneliness, her sorrow. She longed for someone who would merit her love and value her love above all others."

"Every woman yearns for such a man. Was she blessed to find him?"

"A patrician, whose wife was failing, bought my mother as a companion for his wife. My mother was deeply indebted that the man agreed to buy me as well. She saw how he truly loved his ailing wife. And he saw how my mother befriended her."

"Your mother was not only a strong woman, but an honorable one."

"After the wife passed, the other servants begged their master not to sell my mother. It was not a difficult choice, for he had come to love my mother. And she him. Though they did not marry, they lived quietly as faithful husband and wife."

"But how came you to be free? You, the son of a slave."

"This patrician was not an ordinary man. He taught me to read and write, celebrating each of my victories. I grew tall and strong, and I was agile and fleet of foot. When he deemed me an adult, he freed me. He had no heirs, so with my mother's blessing, he adopted me."

"But why would you choose a military life?"

"To honor the life of the brave centurion son he had lost."

"You are not just a good man, but a loving man. Did you never love a woman as the man who adopted you loved your mother?"

Barid's face darkened and he took a deep draught of his barley beer.

"Forgive me. I must learn not to pry."

He met her eyes. "When I was a new centurion, the woman I loved was wed against her will. Her father married her to another, more wealthy than I. Her husband took her to a distant province, and I never saw her again."

Zera shuddered and touched Barid's hand. "How horrible for your love to be stolen from your arms. And you from hers."

"We both have suffered that plight." Barid placed a gentle hand on her shoulder. "I know your husband was cruel and neglectful. I do not judge you for craving comfort and love with another."

Zera could not contain her wrenching sobs. Barid did not know the whole of her folly.

Perhaps it was Barid's forbearing words or his soothing way, but Zera found herself confiding everything—even her lover's name and the way he traded her life for his freedom. "And worst of all, when I gave myself to him, I knew he desired and admired me. But I sensed he did not love me."

When she had finished, he took both of her hands, and his

face filled with understanding and compassion and mercy. "And what have you learned in this valley of pain?"

"I was using Auriga Maximus to fill a vast hole in my own heart. My love was a false love. Serving of self. Not sacrificing for another. Now Auriga is a slave of Herod and will never be free. And it is my doing."

"Auriga charged to help you when the assassin raised his blade, but Joram blocked him. Auriga also helped stem the blood that flowed from my wound. And I saw his selfless courage in his harrowing chariot race ..." Barid's voice faded to nothing.

"What is it you wish to say that you are so sure I will not wish to hear?"

"Over my many years as a centurion, I have learned to take the true measure of a man. Surely there is a piece of Auriga's story that we are missing."

"Regardless, I have forgiven Auriga, but I oft chide myself for my own foolishness. I will never again trust my deceitful heart."

"One day, you will find a man worthy of your love. Then, you must learn to trust not your heart, but his."

Zera could see the love on Barid's face. A love that frightened her. A love she was not worthy to accept. She warned herself to stay far from temptation and gently withdrew her hand from his. She set her tone to be light, untroubled. "Now you speak in riddles. You are beginning to sound like Yeshua."

Chapter Twenty-Six

Inn on Jericho Road

Nisan (late March), one week before Passover

Theo

Theo stood next to Reah by the sign for Barid's inn and offered water to the crush of Passover pilgrims. They hurried to arrive in Jerusalem before the oncoming Sabbath sunset.

Barid and Zera approached. Barid bringing water jars, Zera bringing a basket piled high with bread.

Theo could see that something had changed between them. There was a distance, an awkwardness that had not been there before. He called to Barid. "You have come in good time. Our water has just run out."

"Reah, where do you want me to set these down?" Barid carried the heavy water jars as if they were empty.

Zera handed out the bread. "Theo, the Passover is not for a week. Why do the pilgrims rush tonight to Jerusalem?"

"They must make proper preparations." Theo did not hide the surprise in his voice.

"I know nothing of this." Zera sat on a flat rock. "Though we were Jews in Herod's house and observed the Feast, we were not as strictly observant as other sects. The preparations were always carried out by the servants. What must be done tonight?"

"Tonight, they will observe the Sabbath from sunset to sunset. It is the next day that is of great meaning."

"What meaning?"

"It is Lamb Selection Day. A lamb is inspected and, if found to be perfect, selected for the sacrifice."

"I remember a little of this from when I was a girl. The lamb lived with the family and was watched for days so all could see that it was without fault and an acceptable sacrifice. My father and Chuza chose the lambs for Herod's house."

Theo's spirit sank. "I was your father's apprentice, but I have no memory of going with them to choose a lamb. Yet I remember the skills of stewardship and the rituals of Passover."

"If the Lord is willing, your memory will return in His good time." Zera bent to pick up an empty water jar.

"Stop." Barid rushed to her side and lifted the stone jar onto his shoulder. "We agreed you would leave off the heavy tasks until after the babe is born."

"No. You agreed with yourself." Zera's tone was a mixture of annoyance and amusement. "Many women with child do these tasks for as long as they are able."

Theo watched Zera fist her hands on her hips and his skin prickled. In that moment, Zera reminded him of someone else. Someone he did not remember.

Reah moved closer to Zera. "Women who do heavy tasks until childbirth are commoners, not wealthy women. We commoners are accustomed to heavy labor and have built up our strength."

"I will do my share of the work." The stubbornness in Zera's voice was familiar. She was as stubborn as her mother had been.

Theo drew in a sharp breath. The unexpected shard of memory sent a chill creeping up his spine. The face of Zera's mother took form in his mind's eye.

"Theo."

He ignored Barid's call, not wanting to be snatched from a memory that may continue.

"Theo."

Again, Theo tried to hold onto the vision, but Barid stepped in front of him, and the face of Zera's mother faded.

"Did you not hear me call?" Barid's tone was gentle, not angry.

Theo glanced toward Zera. "I was caught up in the past."

Wide-eyed surprise flickered across her face.

A smile overtook Barid's face. "You have remembered something?"

"Zera's willfulness reminded me of her mother. And I saw her face."

Reah laughed. "Theo remembers well. Zera's mother was strong-willed. Some would say she was stubborn. You, Barid, have met your match in Zera."

Both Barid and Zera turned as red-faced as a field of poppies.

"Bah. My stubborn nature serves me well." Zera waved a hand and walked away.

Theo watched Zera hurry away in a huff. He struggled to keep his grin hidden. Each day, Zera's gait was more like a waddling goose.

The crowds had passed by and now the occasional straggler

stopped for water. Theo looked down the road toward Jericho. Coming around the bend was a cluster of pilgrims. Some of the men spoke loudly and gestured with their hands in what seemed to be a deep debate. One tall, slender man looked his way. Yeshua.

Theo pointed. "Look. Yeshua is almost here. Reah, go fetch Zera."

Barid stepped onto the road. "Looks to be about ten of them. We must prepare a meal."

"No, there is not time. They will only want the water and bread we have here. They must walk with great speed if they are to arrive in Bethany before Sabbath sunset."

Within moments, Yeshua's disciples were drinking water and eating bread.

Yeshua clasped Theo's arms. "You have been praying for your enemies."

It was not a question. It seemed as if He knew every word of Theo's prayers.

"I see the light of forgiveness dawning in your eyes."

Theo fumbled pouring water for Yeshua. "There is a new serenity within me."

Yeshua lifted His hand. "May you be blessed the eve of this Passover when you will fast with the firstborn."

Theo suddenly remembered keeping the traditional fast with Zera's father and all of the firstborn sons of the house of Herod on the eve of Passover. And how Herod Antipas, a grown man yet the youngest son, sat before them gorging on rich food while the firstborn sons ate nothing.

"Rabbi."

At the sound of Zera's excited voice, Theo turned and saw her running to greet Yeshua. Reah ran alongside holding Zera's arm.

"Rabbi." Zera broke away and stumbled to her knees before

Yeshua. A stone fell from her waistband and settled between Yeshua's feet.

Once again, Zera was on her knees before Yeshua.

With one hand Yeshua picked up the stone. The other hand He offered to Zera and helped her stand.

"Master, I wanted to greet You properly, but I stumbled like a child."

"Your joy has moved My heart." Yeshua held out His palm, offering her the stone.

Theo saw Zera take the stone. Why would she keep a stone?

"Daughter, look at Me. One day, you will be freed from the memories and shame that torment you. When you have forgiven yourself, you will surrender this stone of remembrance."

Zera tucked the stone back into her waistband. "I will pray for the day when I forget my sin and throw this into the sea."

Theo was filled with sadness. Zera had carried this stone and her shame since the day she had been caught in adultery. He took Zera's arm and led her toward the group of disciples.

Joanna ran to Zera and embraced her. "I have missed you. You look well."

Zera led Joanna to the flat rock. "I am well. But I am worried there will be trouble when Yeshua goes up to Jerusalem for the feast."

"Some close to Him believe He will be crowned King. And they quibble and vie for the places at His side." Joanne's voice was laden with disapproval and disgust.

Thomas stood, facing the disciples. "This has been a most needed rest, but we cannot linger. We must go."

Yeshua walked up to Theo, rested His hands on Theo's shoulders and seemed to gaze deep into his soul. "This year in Jerusalem."

Theo's befuddled mind could not sort Yeshua's words. There were so many ways to decipher His declaration of "this year in Jerusalem."

"*Next* year in Jerusalem" was a phrase some secretly prayed at the end of the Passover meal. A prayer of hope for the coming of Messiah. And a prayer that Messiah would overthrow their cruel oppressors.

Theo wanted to run after Yeshua and ask if He would bring in His kingdom. The kingdom awaited by so many for so long. Theo's hands seemed to lift of their own accord. But a dark thought brought his spirit low and his arms down. Jerusalem may be a deadly dangerous place for Yeshua. The thought of His death wound like an iron chain around Theo's chest and shackled his breath.

Chapter Twenty-Seven

Inn on Jericho Road

Nisan (end of March), Sunday, five days before Passover

Lamb Selection Day

Theo

The rumble of a fast-moving cart broke into Theo's musings and he rushed from the stable. Dex, his face intense, drove his donkey cart up to Theo. Sophia sat next to him, her arm linked with their son.

Dex got down and handed Theo the reins. "Please hitch a fresh donkey to my cart." His words were polite, but his tone signaled he would brook no delay. He turned and helped Sophia and Gaius down.

Theo unhitched the donkey and led her to a trough of water.

"Husband, I will tell Zera and Reah the good news." Sophia walked toward the inn.

Theo stopped and looked at Dex. "What news?"

"A messenger dove flew in early this morning." Dex looked about. "Where is Barid?"

Barid came around the corner of the inn, smiling a welcome. "My friend, I am here."

Dex turned, and Barid seemed to register the fervent look on his friend's face. "What has happened?"

"A message came to the forge. Two disciples have borrowed a donkey and her colt and taken them to Yeshua, Who goes up to Jerusalem today. Word has spread, and people gather waiting to greet Him. Some hope He will declare himself Messiah and bring in His kingdom."

Barid turned to Theo. "Is your Messiah meant to be a king?"

A bolt of lightning burned through Theo's veins. "Yes, Yeshua has called us to repent and proclaimed the kingdom of Heaven is at hand. At the very gates."

Zera hurried toward them, carrying blankets. "Sophia shared that Yeshua must be about to ride into Jerusalem."

"May we all be witnesses of this triumph." Excitement gilded Barid's deep voice.

Dex nodded and clapped Theo on the shoulder. "We also want to meet Lazarus, the man you and Zera saw raised after four days in the grave."

Sophia and Reah joined them with baskets of provisions. Sophia reached into her waistband and handed a message to Theo.

Theo broke the blue wax seal that signified urgency. With fingers trembling, he unrolled the message. "It is from Thomas. I am needed in Jerusalem."

"We will travel with all speed." Barid took the blankets from Zera. His eyes narrowed and his lips pursed. "Will there be a place for Gentiles in the Messiah's kingdom?"

All eyes turned to Theo. "Our prophet Isaiah said our

people must be a light to the Gentiles and offer salvation to the ends of the earth."

Barid slapped Dex on the back. "Perhaps we may attain a place and gain honor in this new kingdom."

Dex grinned at Barid. "Yes, but now we cannot delay. Do we have need of a second donkey cart?"

Theo surveyed the traveling party and their goods. "I will hitch a fresh donkey to our larger cart. That should serve."

"If Yeshua is crowned king, we may be away for more than one day." Sophia leaned toward Barid. "I hope you are pleased. Before we left, I asked our apprentice to mind the forge and send his brother to stay and oversee your inn."

"Bless you. You have thought of everything."

Dex reached up and touched Sophia's cheek. "*Wisdom.* Your deeds live up to your name."

Barid helped Theo onto the seat and brought him his crutch. "Your leg is much stronger, but for moving through the crowds, you will need this."

Theo took the crutch and stored it in the back of the cart. He studied Dex and Barid—two muscular men, former centurions, dressed as Romans—and his stomach lurched. "I mean no offense, but is it not foolish to dress as Romans in a crowd of Jews welcoming their king?"

Barid looked up at Theo. "No offense is taken. We must consider your words."

Dex crossed his arms. "It is hard to know. In the past, false Messiahs have enticed crowds to riot. Our Roman garments may be an advantage."

Sophia gestured toward a basket. "You need not decide now. I have packed Judean garments for you both."

Barid laughed. "Sophia, you plan for every outcome. You surpass any Roman commander I have known, including your husband."

"Let us be on our way without delay." The quiet purpose in Zera's voice sent a whisper of foreboding through Theo. She sat unmoving in the cart, her eyes already fixed toward Jerusalem. She had been so still, Theo had forgotten she was there.

Theo looked to the sky. "The sun has not reached its peak. We will be in Jerusalem well before the time of the afternoon sacrifice. In good time to find our friends from Bethany."

The way up to Jerusalem was pleasant. Theo drove the cart carrying the women and Gaius. Barid and Dex walked beside them. Since most pilgrims were already there, the roads were clear. Those who came today would have no place to stay within Jerusalem.

As they neared the Mount of Olives, people rushed past them, removing their cloaks and head coverings. Theo drove around the final bend and Gaius stood up in the cart. "Look, the path down the Mount of Olives is covered with garments all the way down the hill."

"Yeshua has been received as The Messiah." Zera cried out, her voice a sound of unrestrained joy. She pointed toward the peak of the mount. "He is here."

Yeshua crested the hill riding on a donkey. Her colt bridled to her, shoulder-to-shoulder, plodded alongside.

Theo's spirit wanted to sing at this first glimpse of his Messiah as his King.

Yeshua got down from the donkey and stood by the colt. Some cloaks had been placed on his back. Yeshua moved from the donkey to mount her colt.

"The message said that colt has never been ridden. He may bolt." Theo heard the misgivings in his voice.

Dex looked up at Theo. "Must He ride an unbroken colt?"

"To ride an unbroken colt that is obedient to Yeshua's commands shows the crowd His power over creation. To ride a donkey rather than a horse shows He comes in peace, the most humble of kings."

Yeshua started riding down the Mount of Olives. The colt, still bridled to the donkey, obeyed His every cue. Surely this colt had been born for this moment, to serve this humble king.

Barid and Dex helped the others down from the cart, for in this jubilant crowd, they could only move forward on foot. Theo tethered his donkey under a nearby tree. They walked slowly, steadily into the current of the crowd.

Yeshua rode farther down the slope, and the multitude began to rejoice and sing. They praised God with loud voices.

"Blessed is the King who comes in the name of the Lord!"

"I was mute, now I speak."

"I was deaf, now I hear."

"I was blind, now I see."

Other followers shouted. "Peace in heaven and glory in the highest."

"I was dead, and now I am alive." The voice of Lazarus rang forth. "My graveclothes bear witness."

Theo's group was now beside the path. Yeshua would pass by within arm's reach. Theo turned to see Lazarus lift his graveclothes and curious onlookers flock to him.

Pharisees shunned Lazarus in the same way they would a leper. The tallest Pharisee, fury distorting his face, called to Yeshua. "Teacher, rebuke Your disciples."

Near Theo, Yeshua halted the colt and turned to face the Pharisee who challenged Him.

The crowd went silent as a sepulcher. All looked from that Pharisee to Yeshua, anger seething on the faces of His disciples.

Yeshua's countenance was calm, His smile confident. "I tell you that if these, my disciples, should keep silent ..." Yeshua's hand moved across the crowd, tracing the path of the sun moving from sunrise to sunset. "The stones would suddenly cry out."

The people shook their fists at the Pharisees and shouted with a great roar. A roar rumbling of war. The roar of the ancient battle cry of the lions of Judah.

The Pharisees withdrew and slunk away.

The people thundered with renewed praises and shouts of triumph. Passover pilgrims waving and sharing cut palm branches streamed out from Jerusalem to meet Yeshua.

"Hosanna. Save us now." The chant spread through the frenzied crowd.

Yeshua urged his donkey forward.

Zera and Reah, Sophia and Gaius, waved palm branches, shouted, and walked amidst the throng, ushering Yeshua toward Jerusalem.

Dex and Barid moved with them, one on each side of their group, keeping them together.

Theo looked over the jubilant crowd. He would remember this moment all the days of his life.

Yeshua rode down where He could see the entire city of Jerusalem laid out before Him. Yeshua wept, but Theo could not hear His words.

Gaius went up on his toes, then jumped up and down. "Look, I see the Eastern Gate."

Dex came closer to Theo. Barid joined them. "We must keep moving, but be prepared to protect the women if the crowd turns dangerous."

Dread prickled Theo's arms. "Why would the crowd turn violent? Yeshua comes dressed as a humble man riding the colt of a donkey. He is not wearing kingly robes or riding a white warhorse."

Barid surveyed the scene. "Some of the factions—the Pharisees, the Sadducees, the Zealots—may turn on each other, or on Yeshua and His disciples."

Dex spoke in Theo's ear. "Waving palm branches has long been a sign of victorious defiance."

Barid put his arm around Theo's shoulder. "Even we Romans know the cry *hosanna*, save us, is more than a prayer to Hashem. Listen, the crowd calls for Yeshua to be crowned king."

"Blessed is He who comes in the name of the Lord."

"He is the Promised King of Israel."

Barid pointed across the city. "Today, Roman soldiers will enter through the Western gate. It is fortunate Yeshua the Messiah will enter through the Eastern Gate. Let us pray no one reports a growing insurrection to the soldiers."

Theo studied the crowd. Fear knotted his stomach, but joy tugged at his heart. "The crowd may try to crown Yeshua."

Zera came up to them. "I think Yeshua comes offering Himself as the Lamb for selection, not as a warrior king."

A shiver of dread ran through Theo's veins. "But the lamb that is selected is sacrificed."

"I pray Yeshua will choose to take His rightful place as king, not lay down His life." Barid's voice dropped to a worried whisper.

A look Theo did not understand passed between Zera and Barid, and she touched his arm. "Yeshua also said He would take up His life again."

"Yet another one of His riddles." A heaviness settled over Theo. "We may not understand now, but I trust He will unveil this mystery one day."

Dex lifted Gaius and swung him onto his shoulders. "We enter at the gate. It will be difficult to stay together."

The thick crowd hemmed them in. "We women will link

arms." Sophia pulled Zera and Reah close. "Zera, stay between us, so you are not jostled. We will protect you and the babe within. If we are divided, go away from the crowd to the House of Lazarus."

Gaius, from his perch, pointed back to the gate. "Here is Yeshua."

He passed by so close to Theo and his friends that they patted the colt or touched His robe.

Theo looked from Barid to Dex. "Yeshua has ridden the same path into Jerusalem the Messiah was foretold to follow. Truly, He has come." Wonder and awe raced through Theo's veins. But his wonder soon turned to worry.

Barid clasped his shoulder. "My friend, what is wrong? Your Messiah is here."

"In all the furor, I have just remembered Thomas sent for me. Now I must find him in the midst of this throng."

Chapter Twenty-Eight

Zera

At the Eastern Gate, the crowd crushed in on every side so Zera could barely breathe. Theo was still hobbling beside her. Rhea clung to Zera, and she clung to Sophia. She glanced back. Barid and Dex, with Gaius perched on his shoulders, kept close to them.

People swarmed the road, all reaching for Yeshua. The singing of hosannas and hallelujahs blanketed them with a heavenly sound.

Ahead, Thomas shouldered through the crowd. Zera tapped Theo's arm and waved toward the Twin.

Thomas finally broke through the last line of followers and stepped in front of Zera and Theo. "Praise HaShem. Theo, you have come while there is still time."

"Your message said you had need of me, and I left the inn straightaway."

Thomas looked at Zera. "In this clamor, only you and Theo can hear most of my words. Share my warning with the others later. Last night, I learned that the Pharisees have been plotting to kill Lazarus. But now I know, the Pharisees plan to take hold of Lazarus this very day."

"Thomas, what must I do?" Courage strengthened Theo's tone.

"Lazarus must be taken from Jerusalem and hidden."

Fear overtook Zera's mind. "Must I risk losing Theo again? Why choose my lame kinsman to protect Lazarus, rather than a more able man?"

"Theo is not one of The Twelve. He is not known to the Pharisees." Thomas sounded patient, but firm. "I once asked Yeshua about Theo's reputation."

"What did Yeshua say of me?"

"He said you have kept both people and secrets safe. And He added that each day your hardened heart softens, moving closer to the will of HaShem."

Theo smiled and stood as tall as he could. "Where would you have me take Lazarus?"

"You must decide where Lazarus should hide. Never reveal the place to any of The Twelve disciples. Then his where-abouts can never be forced from our lips."

Zera shuddered at the thought of what the disciples might have to endure to keep Lazarus safe. And what more might they willingly suffer to protect Yeshua?

Barid stepped forward. "Dex and I will help."

"Barid." Zera touched his arm. He met her eyes. "How did you hear Thomas from behind us when I could barely hear him over the noise of the crowd?"

"I did not hear Thomas. He was facing me." Barid touched Zera's lips. "My mother taught me how to read the movements of the mouth." Barid looked back to Thomas. "Dex and I could escort Theo and Lazarus until he is safely secreted away."

"No. Both you and Dex tower over me. You must not go.

Neither of you could ever travel anywhere unnoticed or unremembered." Thomas touched Theo's sleeve. "May you and Lazarus travel under the wing of HaShem." Thomas barged into the crowd.

Gaius, still perched high, rested his chin on Dex's head. "Is Lazarus the man who said he was raised from the dead? The one with the strips of cloth?"

Zera looked up. "Yes. Yeshua raised him from the dead. I was there."

"And Lazarus is there." Gaius pointed across the road. Lazarus was less than thirty paces away. People had stopped to watch as he smiled broadly, lifted his graveclothes, and motioned toward Yeshua.

Zera stared at him, caught up in the memory of Lazarus shuffling out of his burial cave. But movement around him caught her attention. Zera had seen these men earlier on the hillside. Like a pack of wild dogs, servants of the Pharisees surrounded Lazarus. A knot of fear made Zera's heart pound. "Barid, Lazarus—"

"We see." Barid plowed his way into the crowd. Dex handed Gaius to Sophia and followed Barid.

The servants laid hold of Lazarus and shoved him toward the Temple. Barid and Dex each took two servants by the back of their robes and flung the men off like dolls made of straw. Then they hurried Lazarus back through the Eastern Gate.

Theo used his crutch to push himself onto his toes. "I have lost sight of them. But we agreed to meet in Bethany if we were separated."

The pounding in Zera's chest gave life to a tight ball of fear. "They cannot go to Bethany. The house of Lazarus is the first place the Pharisees will search."

Sophia set Gaius down and took his hand. "Barid and Dex

were soldiers. They know taking Lazarus to Bethany would be foolish."

Zera looked about. "Much of the crowd has gone on with Yeshua. Let us also go back through the Eastern Gate and we may find them."

Sophia put her son's hand in Reah's. "Please take Gaius to Bethany. And Gaius, you must not speak of Lazarus to anyone."

"Yes, Mother."

Zera hugged Reah. "Warn Mary and Martha of what has happened and assure them we will keep their brother from harm."

When Reah and Gaius had left, Zera turned to Theo and Sophia. "If not Bethany, where will they go?"

Something dawned in Sophia's eyes. "To the Third Centurion Inn."

Theo grinned. "Yes, I have heard many tales of the feats of the three centurions."

"My husband and Barid served in the Roman army with the innkeeper. The tales of their deeds become more dramatic with each passing year." Sophia led them through the Eastern Gate and along the towering city wall.

"But what if they are not there? How will we find them?"

Sophia turned back, her face a picture of calm. "They will be there. I would stake my life on it."

They continued until they entered the city through the Western gate and came to a tavern built within the courtyard of a large inn. Sophia waved to the innkeeper, another Roman. Carrying three pitchers, he wended his way through the outdoor tables, stopping to pour drinks for his guests.

A Roman centurion grabbed a full pitcher.

"Longinus, share that with the others."

"No. I have need of it." Longinus lifted the pitcher and

drank deeply. "For the next week, I am centurion of the unit charged with carrying out floggings and executions."

Sophia shrank back. "Let us wait here, in the corner, until the innkeeper has time for us."

"Yes, far from that soldier." Zera pulled Sophia farther back. "What an odd name."

"That is not his name. Dex has told me about him. He is called Longinus because he is a head taller than most soldiers and carries a long spear. He is a fierce fighter but despises the prolonged brutality of a crucifixion."

Theo set aside his crutch and took a pitcher from the innkeeper. "You must be Marcus."

"How do you know me?"

"For the last ten years, I have been Barid's servant at the Jericho Inn. And who has not heard of the three centurions who saved each other's lives? Centurions who all became innkeepers with their spoils of war and retirements from Rome?"

"I could use your help." The innkeeper slung a towel over Theo's shoulder. "We are more well-known among the new soldiers now than we were in our youth."

Theo poured a round for the next table and swept the coins into his hand. "That is because you keep the soldiers well-watered." Theo flashed a sly smile and dropped the coins into the innkeeper's waist-sack. "Yes, Sophia brought us to you."

Marcus looked up and Sophia crossed the room to him. "Are they here?"

The innkeeper nodded and jerked his chin toward the outdoor stairs. "Take the first room on the second floor and you will find all you need."

Theo and Zera hurried up the stairs behind Sophia. They stood behind her to keep anyone from a happenstance glimpse of Lazarus from the courtyard below. Zera knocked lightly on the first door.

Dex opened the door a crack then pulled her through and hugged her. Zera and Theo squeezed through behind her. Barid sat across from Lazarus at a table along the wall.

A worried look crossed Dex's face. "Where is Gaius?"

"Gaius is with Reah on the way to Bethany. They will take news to Mary and Martha."

Dex stroked Sophia's cheek, and Zera longed for such love and tenderness. She could not help but steal a glance toward Barid. He smiled at her and Zera's spirits lifted. She forced herself to look away.

Lazarus crossed his arms and leaned back in his chair. "Bethany. That is where I should be. Awaiting the coming of Yeshua and His disciples. Martha and Mary were told He would stay with us for several nights, until the Night of Preparation for Passover."

Theo rapped his crutch sharply against the stone floor and Lazarus looked his way. "If not for Dex and Barid, you may have been robbed of all breath to complain."

"What are you saying?" An anxious look flicked across the face of Lazarus.

"Thomas learned from a friend, a member of the Sanhedrin Council, that the Pharisees plot to kill you."

Lazarus stood, his face suddenly distorted with shock, then fear. "I thought they meant to arrest me, banish me from the city."

Zera went to Lazarus and took both his hands. "Already this morning, Thomas sent for Theo at the Jericho Inn."

"Thomas has asked me to hide you from your enemies."

"But Yeshua is not hiding from His enemies." Lazarus seemed to gather stubborn strength.

Barid moved closer, towering over Lazarus. "And you, my

friend, are not Yeshua." Barid's deep tone echoed with the challenge of truth.

"Come, let us reason together." Zera kept her voice gentle, soothing. "Lazarus, you are not called to the work of the Messiah. Nor to a place among The Twelve."

"But I must go to Yeshua. He has called me to be a steadfast friend, to stay at His side, not cower in an inn."

Theo pounded a fist on the table. "You must not put yourself in danger. Would not Yeshua want you to remain alive?"

"But I am troubled. He may have need of me. I must go to Him."

"Yeshua raised you from the four days in the grave Lazarus." Zera squeezed his hands. It would be a small thing for Him to call you back from any place you are hiding." She looked intently into, a face so full of life. "Lazarus, we are called to keep you safe. You are a living and breathing testimony to Yeshua's power over Death."

Chapter Twenty-Nine

Sunday near sunset

Theo

Theo drove the cart back toward Jerusalem. His mind churned over the task of keeping Lazarus hidden from those who plotted his murder. *HaShem, show me where Lazarus will be best hidden from the eyes of his enemies.*

Why had he been chosen to protect Lazarus? Yeshua said Theo was trustworthy. He was not known to the Pharisees and priests. And no one would take notice of a cripple and an old man.

Theo entered the Western gate and drove back to the inn.

It was true, he had helped hide women from evil men at Barid's inn, the forge in Jericho, and in Shechem. But Barid's inn and the forge at Jericho were too close to the disciples in Bethany, too close to the priests and Pharisees in Jerusalem. Shechem was farther away, a two-day journey from Jerusalem.

Theo neared The Third Centurion Inn. From the road, he could hear the talk in the courtyard had become loud and lewd. He drove to the back, where the innkeeper lived with his family. Theo tossed the reins over the seat, still mulling over where he should take Lazarus.

A voice seemed to whisper to Theo's soul. *Samuel, a Samaritan, hid among the Jews in Jericho for years. Why not hide Lazarus, a Jew, among the Samaritans at Shechem?*

Theo climbed down from the cart. When his foot touched the ground, Dex and Barid were suddenly at his side.

Theo spoke in an urgent whisper. "We must fill the bed of the cart with something more than straw."

Barid rolled a large barrel forward. "I have purchased three barrels of barley beer you can bring back to my inn once you have our friend safely secreted."

Dex helped Barid lift and place the barrels so that the cart was well balanced.

Sophia brought them a pile of robes and cloaks. "Downstairs in the tavern courtyard, I was able to trade the large Judean robes meant for Dex and Barid for smaller ones. Our fugitive will need something more humble and common, for he is a wealthy man whose unique robe is known to many."

Zera slipped from the back door and approached them. "I was praying for guidance and was prompted to buy this from a merchant passing by the tavern." She shook out a cloak with a distinctly Samaritan pattern. "I hope our guest will not take offense."

Theo whispered in her ear. "I, too, was praying. Your purchase of a Samaritan cloak is an answer to my prayer. Remember the Lord will meet all of your needs."

Zera glanced toward Barid, and a flush spread up from her neck and set her cheeks on fire. When Barid met her eyes, she looked down, but not before Theo caught a deep sadness overtaking her face.

Something had happened between Zera and Barid—their friendly banter was traded for short answers and awkward silences. Perhaps Theo could help heal the rift between them upon his return.

"Dex, help me bring the large basket from the kitchen." Barid headed back to the inn.

After a few moments, they returned carrying a large four-handled basket filled with round loaves of bread. They manhandled the unwieldy basket into place in the bed of the cart.

Theo took hold of his crutch and his courage and settled himself onto the seat for the long trip ahead.

Barid reached out and slipped a gold aureus into Theo's palm. "No matter which direction you are headed, take the Western Gate. If the guard decides to search your cart, grin broadly and say Marcus sends his greetings. Wait for the guard to return the greetings. When he does, slide the gold coin into his hand."

"Does this guard not care about the security of Jerusalem?" Theo's voice betrayed his own anxious doubt.

Barid smirked. "Of course, but an aureus equals his monthly wage and is a great temptation. The guard trusts that Marcus smuggles for advantage in trade, never in politics."

Zera ran out from the kitchen and handed Theo a piece of honey cake. "To satisfy your sweet tooth. Go now with the blessings of the Lord."

Theo took a bite and spoke around the crumbs clinging to his mouth. "Are we not forgetting our fugitive?"

Zera patted the side of the large basket. "Let us pray that this *perfectly risen* bread will be kept safe from the dust and dangers of the road." She covered the bread in the basket with a cloth.

Lazarus must have somehow crammed himself into the basket.

"Hunger haunts me, and I need to take some bread from the basket. Soon."

Barid nodded and patted the donkey. He had understood Theo was speaking of Lazarus. "As soon as you have cleared Jerusalem's gate, you may take some bread for yourself and store it in a blanket under the straw."

Theo flicked the reins. For once, the donkey seemed as ready to move as he and plodded along at a good pace. He caught himself drawing in bulging breaths as if he somehow could breathe for Lazarus. *HaShem, please hide us from the eyes of evil Pharisees and spies.*

The donkey broke into a trot. Perhaps she sensed Theo's rising worry. The Western Gate came into view and the sun slung low, sinking quickly behind the horizon. The gate would be closed at sunset.

When Theo was within paces of the gate, he set his face and voice to mask his worry and seem untroubled.

A Roman guard strode in front of Theo's cart and held up a hand.

Theo grinned. The broad, dramatic grin of a Hypocrite, a famed actor playing in Herod's court. "Marcus sends his greetings."

The guard said nothing, but stared intently at Theo. His mouth went dry, but he said nothing, offered nothing. This guard must not be the friend of Marcus.

After what seemed an entire night's watch, the guard sneered and moved to search the cart.

Something stirred in Theo's gut. A warning to keep silent.

The guard grabbed the end of the seat and hoisted himself

nose to nose with Theo. "Though I am not the man Marcus expected at the gate, I know his friend." The guard opened and closed his palm. "I will happily share any greetings with him." Theo took a deep breath and a big risk. He placed the aureus in the guard's open palm.

The guard moved his hand up and down checking the weight, then bit the coin to assure it was soft gold. "It is my bad fortune I can no longer wager this on Auriga Maximus. He will never race again."

Theo's stomach lurched. Had the father of the child Zera carried been killed in the hippodrome?

The guard tucked the gold coin in his leather satchel and stared at Theo.

Theo prayed his bribe would be enough. He would distract him with talk. "I, too, wager on Auriga Maximus. What has befallen him?"

"You have not heard?" The guard's tone quickened, and his face brightened at the chance to share fresh gossip.

Theo shook his head, his heartbeat racing like Auriga's quadriga chariot.

"Brave man that he is, Auriga leaned out of his chariot and grabbed the arm of his fallen outrider running alongside him. He pulled the man out of the path of an oncoming chariot and into his. But Auriga's right shoulder was wrenched from its joint."

"And the shoulder will not heal?"

"It has healed, but at times, his joint gives way. Even though Auriga won the race, Herod was furious. Now, Auriga is stableboy to Herod's stallion."

Theo slowly lifted his reins partway, praying the guard would take his subtle cue and let him leave. "We must find a new favorite charioteer."

"There is always a new favorite just outside the starting

gates." The guard climbed down and waved Theo forward as the last sliver of sun set into a crimson sky. The heavy, looming West Gate closed behind them. Theo's cart was the last allowed to leave this night until the break of morning's first light.

Theo urged the donkey to trot. Should he tell Zera about Auriga's accident? Would she hear of it from another? He continued around the city. Theo could not stifle the feeling that he knew Auriga in his forgotten past. And the famed charioteer seemed to be a man of honor—not a man who would plot a murder. Especially the murder of a woman. Theo drove the cart onto the Roman road north toward Shechem.

He forced himself to wait until the first mile marker, then called to Lazarus. "Are you well?"

"Still risen." His words and laugh were muffled.

"I will drive two miles farther north, where there is a clearing off to the side of the road. There I will release you, away from prying eyes."

"It will be such a blessing to rise again."

Theo could not help but smile. "My friend, have you always had such a lively wit?"

"Mary claimed I was too serious. And Martha, that I was not serious enough." Lazarus dragged in a breath and his voice sounded weak. "So, I jested with Mary and spoke with great reason with Martha."

"Do not speak more. I hear a wheezing in your words. Soon you will have water and a rest." Theo clicked his tongue to the donkey, and she picked up her pace.

At the second mile marker, Theo called to Lazarus and strained to hear his answer. At the third mile marker, Lazarus did not answer Theo's call. Swerving to the side of the road, he stopped and scrambled into the back of the cart. He removed the loaves of bread from around the ashen face of Lazarus. His brow was beaded with sweat, his eyes were closed.

Theo braced against the back of the seat and tipped the basket onto its side. He pulled his knife, ready to cut the basket and free Lazarus, but that would take time. Praise HaShem, Lazarus began to rouse.

Theo heaved the bottom of the basket as high as he could. But this was a job for two men. He crawled under the bottom of the basket and Lazarus slid down so his chest was freed.

Theo crawled out from under the basket and grabbed Lazarus under the arms. The basket spat Lazarus out like a stopper from a flask of wine. He landed on top of Theo's legs, leaving him sprawled on his back.

Theo stared up at the stars and the nearly full moon and smiled. "The Romans believe the full moon is a time of lunacy, but for us Jews it marks festivals of deliverance."

Lazarus rolled off of Theo's legs. "Tonight, it has been both a time of madness and of escape. Have I hurt you?"

Theo moved both legs without pain. "I am as whole as I ever am. And you?"

"I cannot complain. You have raised me from a basket that for a moment I thought would become my second tomb."

"It is well known, the finest bread is risen twice." Theo's smile turned into a laugh.

Lazarus echoed Theo's deep laugh. "How many men can claim they are twice risen?"

Theo wiped tears from his eyes. "Tell me, how many men since the beginning of time can claim they have been even once risen?"

"I would think fewer than the fingers on one hand." Lazarus reached into the basket and pulled out his grave-clothes. "I keep these with me as witness to my death."

"Do you not see that your graveclothes stole space, pressed on your chest, and smothered you?"

"Praise HaShem. He protected me from my own foolishness."

"We will climb down and stretch our legs. Then be on our way. But first, put on the Samaritan garments Sophia bought for you."

"Where are they?"

"Here, folded under the straw."

Lazarus touched the new cloak, then drew back his hand.

"You have been raised from the grave and almost captured by Pharisees. What could possibly trouble you?"

Lazarus climbed down from the cart and frowned, his mouth seeming to fight off a sneer. "I never thought I would don a Samaritan robe." He changed garments. "Never would I have foreseen my death, my raising, or my running from danger. Especially to Samaria."

"Do you believe Yeshua would have us hate Samaritans?" Theo climbed down and gave the donkey water.

"Yeshua teaches us to love those who hate us. But I confess, I struggle with loving the Samaritans who have been our mortal enemies for generation upon generation."

"Out of my obedience to Yeshua, I force myself to speak blessings aloud and pray for the men who made me lame."

"Shh." Lazarus cupped an ear with his hand. "A rider on horseback is coming fast upon us."

Theo led Lazarus farther off the road out of the moonlight and stepped in front of him. The rider, a royal messenger, flew past. He did not slow or even glance in their direction.

Theo climbed up onto the seat and offered his hand to Lazarus. "Ride beside me. If you keep your cloak draped over your head as a hood, your face will remain in shadow. You should be safe."

Lazarus arranged himself on the seat beside Theo. "It would seem we travel to Samaria."

"Yes. To the house of my good friend for these ten years past, my most beloved enemy."

Chapter Thirty

Theo kept the donkey at a slow, steady pace but held his breath, listening. "I hear the hoofbeats of many riders coming from Jerusalem. And within the same hour that the royal messenger sped past."

"Surely the Pharisees have not found us so quickly and sent Temple guards to arrest us." Lazarus tugged at his beard.Worry etched creases around his eyes and ploughed furrows across his brow.

Theo looked back, squinting into the distance. The cloud-covered moon was suddenly freed from its shroud. "A small unit of Roman soldiers rides toward us at a fast trot." He reined the donkey to a stop.

"Theo, wait at the side of the road for the soldiers to pass. To move farther away would cause suspicion."

"And you must try not to speak or draw attention."

Lazarus placed his hand over Theo's. "Put your reins in your lap and rest your hands as I have done."

"Why?"

Lazarus smiled, his look patient, reassuring. "That way, they will not see you tremble."

The unit of soldiers rode up and their commander signaled them to halt. "Have you seen any riders on the road tonight?"

Theo lowered his tone to keep his voice from breaking. "We have seen one man riding fast who passed us by."

"Samaritan, was he a Jew?"

For a moment, Lazarus did not respond. Theo held his breath. Lazarus had forgotten he was dressed as a Samaritan.

"Forgive me. I do not hear well." Lazarus turned toward the commander. "The rider was a royal messenger. But we will report anyone else we see. Who should we look for? Are they dangerous?"

"We are chasing a group of three bandits. These bandits are the most brazen of Zealots. They plot to steal gold and goods to support their next rebellion."

"Why would bandits molest poor commoners?" Theo's ambush flashed through his mind.

"Large shipments have just come into Caesarea. To avoid ambush, some of the wealthy dress as commoners. More than one caravan travels from that port toward Jerusalem. Merchants will sell their wares at the Passover a few days hence. You would be wise to pay one of the caravan masters for protection."

Theo lifted a hand toward the commander. "A thousand blessings for your warning."

The soldiers rode off. Theo and Lazarus watched until they were out of sight. Theo snapped the reins, and the donkey responded with a trot. Theo grinned. He could not help himself. "For all your aversion to that cloak and our neighbors in Samaria, you play a good Samaritan."

"Tell me about this Samaritan, this beloved enemy of yours."

"Do you remember the parable Yeshua taught that has come to be known as The Good Samaritan?"

"Yes. That parable has been oft repeated amongst the followers of Yeshua. The Samaritan is portrayed as the good neighbor and righteous. And the priest and Levite are pictured as unfeeling and unrighteous."

"Think back." Theo's tone changed as if his fervor could cause Lazarus to better remember. "With what words did Yeshua begin the parable?"

"There was a certain man ..."

Theo held up a palm. "What did those first words mean to those gathered?"

"That Yeshua was about to teach a tale of people who truly walked the earth. A story based in fact, not fantasy."

Theo stopped the cart and turned to Lazarus. "My friend and I both heard Yeshua teach the story in Bethany, exactly as *we* had lived it ten years before." The precious memory made Theo's eyes brim with tears.

"What are you saying? The man is you?"

"We must travel on." Theo gently flicked the reins. "Lazarus, tell me the parable as you heard it that night."

"There was a certain man ... a man going down from Jerusalem to Jericho. But robbers stripped him of his clothes, beat him, and left him half-dead."

Theo patted Lazarus on the knee. "Yes. That man was me. Years had passed, but at once I knew Yeshua was telling my story and I cried out."

"But many men travel the road from Jerusalem to Jericho. The road is known to be a haven for robbers."

"Those were the words of my friend Samuel. At first." Theo glanced at Lazarus. "Continue with the parable."

Lazarus put a hand to his head and closed his eyes as if he read a scroll written on his mind's eye. "A priest and a

Levite saw the man and passed him by on the other side of the road."

Theo clutched the sleeve of Lazarus. "The face of that Levite and priest were the only things I remembered. My past life was blotted out." Theo's voice hitched over the hate he had kept alive. "For ten years, I searched every face that traveled past Barid's inn. Earlier that day, I finally saw both men and rushed after them in a rage." Theo swallowed hard and drew in a long, shuddering breath.

Lazarus sighed. "The remnants of your wounded body and mind haunt you to this day."His deep, rich tone was as soothing as the healing balm of Gilead.

"Samuel followed me, afraid of what I might do to these men. Afraid of what punishment I may rain down upon myself."

"Did you confront them?"

"No. But I spotted them just ahead in the crowd, snaked my way behind the priest, and raised my crutch to crush his head."

Lazarus gasped. "Lord, deliver us from evil."

"Just as I brought the crutch down with all my strength, my steadfast friend Samuel stepped between us and took the blow meant for the wicked priest. The priest never knew his life had been saved. But I knew that, once again, I had been rescued by my beloved enemy."

"How did you come to be at Bethany?"

"Samuel and I thought the priest and Levite were going up to Jerusalem for their allotted time to serve at the Temple. Samuel convinced me I should confront them there before the high priest. But they turned toward Bethany and followed the crowds to a place where Yeshua was teaching." Theo blew out a long breath, wishing he could cleanse all the hate from his heart. "That priest and that Levite were there, sitting near Yeshua."

"Did they recognize themselves in the parable?"

"Surely they did, for the Levite stood, spat, and left, but the priest sitting on a boulder, buried his face in his hands in a posture of shame."

"Did you still seek revenge?" Lazarus looked at Theo with a face full of compassion. "Would that I could lighten your burden of hate."

"Yeshua had humiliated the priest and Levite with their hypocrisy before a great gathering. Finally, their evil had been brought into the light. Even though I did not forgive them, I was content to leave their judgment with HaShem."

"The next part of the parable ..." A look of revelation shone upon the face of Lazarus. "A Samaritan came upon the man and took pity on him. He went to the man and bandaged his wounds, pouring on oil and wine."

"Yes. Yes. That was just as I lived it." Theo's excitement welled up within him and words rushed from his lips. "When Yeshua spoke of the Samaritan, I glanced at Samuel. He was trembling, his face pale, his eyes wide with awe. He made me swear I had never spoken of these things to any man, woman, or child."

"And of course, you had not."

"How could I speak of what I never knew? I reminded Samuel that I was left for dead and many of the details of the story that Yeshua spoke, I had never known."

"But the parable does not end there. The Samaritan brought the beaten man to an inn on a donkey and paid the innkeeper to care for him." Lazarus slapped the seat and laughed. "The innkeeper can only be our trusted friend, Barid."

"Yes. He cared for me for months with a tenderness that belies his size and past as a Roman centurion. But ..." Theo grinned and elbowed Lazarus. "You have not recognized one character in the parable."

Lazarus stroked his beard and smiled an uncertain smile. "I miss your meaning."

"Today we are pulled by the very same donkey who carried me to Barid's inn. Samuel believes I was riding her when I was ambushed. When Samuel found me, he came upon her, trapped in a nearby thicket, crying great tears."

"I, too, have once seen a donkey spill tears when it was gravely wounded. You do seem fond of this beast beyond all the others under your care."

"Yes, it is true." Theo stopped the cart. He climbed down and offered the donkey water which she slurped, looking at him with grateful eyes. "I know, it has been many miles, and you thirst." Theo turned back to Lazarus. "And after Samuel and I heard Yeshua teach the parable that spoke of our own lives, we both came to believe Yeshua of Nazareth was the Promised One. The long-awaited Messiah. That was the night I first met you, Lazarus. It was nearing sunset, and we shared a Sabbath meal."

"Now I recall. Yeshua requested that I host both you and your friend."

"Lazarus, tell me. You, the man who was called back from Death, what think you of the mystery of our Messiah?"

"When I heard Yeshua shout, *Lazarus, come out,* I knew that call carried all the authority and power of HaShem. If Yeshua had not called me by name, but simply called, *Come out,* I believe every soul with me in *Sheol,* the place of the dead, would have come out of their burial caves."

Theo trembled, and a warm thrill ran through his veins. "The vision you have called to mind is unfathomable. But in the depths of my being, I know I have heard truth."

Lazarus reached into the basket, took a bread round, and

handed part to Theo. "And I await the day when He brings forth the resurrection of the dead to eternal life."

"My risen friend, what a momentous day that will be. To meet our departed loved ones and family from generations past."

"And the patriarchs and prophets of old."

Theo and Lazarus resumed their travel and continued to share stories—Lazarus of his whole life—Theo of the last ten years.

"Lazarus, do you know how far we have traveled?"

"I see the Roman marker. We have traveled close to fifteen miles since the North Gate. You have not yet told me where within Samaria we are going."

"HaShem has laid it upon my heart to take you to Shechem."

"An interesting choice. The place of Jacob's well. Yeshua speaks of meeting a woman there some three years past who recognized him as Messiah. She brought her whole village to hear him teach. Many came to accept He was the long-awaited Promised One."

"Lazarus, that woman, of whom you speak, is Shamara, wife of Samuel, the man who saved me and supped with us that Sabbath eve."

"I do not remember hosting a man called Samuel. But my sisters and I have hosted so many, particularly since Yeshua called The Twelve."

Why would Lazarus not remember Samuel? He had been in deep conversation with Yeshua and quite near Lazarus. Theo thought back to the scene at the Sabbath meal and suddenly understood the confusion. "Samuel was disguised as a Greek."

"Ah, now I recall him. I am sure there is much more to his story."

"A story for another time. Thankfully, you did not balk at hosting a cripple and a man you presumed to be a pagan Greek at your Sabbath meal."

"Now I must wear a disguise. And you take me, a Jew, for refuge to the Good Samaritan."

Theo shrugged. "Yeshua's deeds and teachings turn all expectation regarding the promised Messiah on its head."

Chapter Thirty-One

Caravan camp near Ramah

Later that night

Theo

Theo slowed the cart and peered into the dark. "Ahead, there is a large caravan camp. A village of tents. Camels, horses, and oxen are corralled within a circle of carts."

"All is still. The fires have burned down to embers." Lazarus stood in the moving cart, taking a wide stance, and put a hand on Theo's shoulder. "A wealthy caravan master must abide in that large tent. He has hired guards to watch on all sides."

"It was my plan to travel farther, but if we stop here, we will be in the safe shadow of the caravan." Theo stopped the cart.

"The moonlight gilds a city in the distance."

"We must be near the crossroads of Ramah." Lazarus stepped down from the cart.

"Wait, my friend, remember you are no longer a wealthy Jew, but a lowly Samaritan who may not be welcome here." Theo climbed down. "Let me speak with the guards."

"The caravan master could be a foreigner. And you, a Jew, also may not be welcome." Lazarus slung a bundle over his shoulder and joined him. "We will go together."

The nearest guard was looking away. Theo set his tone to be calm and peaceful. "Guard."

The man turned, his hand already on the hilt of his sword.

Theo raised his arms so the guard could see he was harmless.

Lazarus glanced toward Theo and did the same.

"What brings you here?" The guards on either side of him watched them with the sharp stares of eagles.

"We merely seek to camp in the shadow of your caravan. We are easy prey for bandits."

"You would have us guard you too?" A nearby guard snarled. "For nothing?" He spat on the ground.

"Of course, not for nothing." Lazarus wheedled, his voice an invitation to bargain.

"For what then?" The guard on the other side sounded tempted.

"We could part with half a barrel of barley beer. But of course, you must not drink until a time when you are not on watch."

The three guards looked to one another and the center guard crossed his arms. "Make it the whole barrel. We will unload it in the morning when our watch ends."

A laugh from behind the guards startled them all. "I am thankful you do not wish to distract from the watchfulness of my guards."

260

The guards turned to face the caravan merchant, a man with a long, silver-streaked beard styled in the way of the Jews. But he wore an exotic black robe woven with golden threads and a silk turban. He waved the guards back to their posts. "Is that the voice of my friend Lazarus?"

Theo cringed. It could be fatal to have attention called to the presence of Lazarus.

"Lazarus? No. I am not he. But oft mistaken for him. And it becomes a point of embarrassment, because he is a wealthy Jew and as you can see, I am a lowly Samaritan."

Theo had been told Lazarus was a brilliant man, and now he had seen his quick mind give answer to keep his name concealed from the guards.

"And you are?" Lazarus moved close to the caravan merchant.

"Yosef of Arimathea."

Yosef took Lazarus by the arm and motioned for Theo to follow. "Come. You are my guests and under the protection of my guards and their barrel of barley beer."

"Kind sir, though you may not recognize a servant, I remember you from the few times your caravan stopped at the Jericho Inn."

"Ah, yes. And your name?"

"I am called Theo."

The center guard stepped forward. "Sir, please, we meant no offense with our side bargain."

"No offense was taken. You did not compromise your watch. And a merchant always rejoices when a good bargain is struck." The admiration in Yosef's tone made Theo smile.

They passed clusters of small tents where servants and slaves slept outside. Yosef led them toward his towering tent, its brass fittings gleaming in the bright night. Two torch stands lit the entrance. Yosef lifted the leather tent flap and ushered them into a room partitioned with sheer silks. A sea of exotic rugs was spread across the floor. He warmed his hands over a central brazier, then took his place on a high-backed chair. "Sit, my friends."

Lazarus sat upon a chair at Yosef's right hand.

Theo brought a camel saddle closer and sat by an open trunk filled with scrolls.

Yosef put his hands on his knees and leaned forward. "Lazarus, tell me, my friend, why are you in disguise?"

"Have you not heard?"

"These three weeks past, I sailed home from Rome. Then, my caravan has journeyed from Caesarea. What has happened?"

"Without warning, I was overcome with a mysterious malady and within the space of two sunsets, I was dead. But Yeshua of Nazareth—"

Yosef grinned and slapped his knee. "Yeshua must have been near. He raised you back to life as He has done for others."

Theo stood and rubbed his hands together. "No, Yeshua was far away in Perea, and He did not come quickly."

"Yeshua raised me from the grave after I had been four days dead."

"I saw Lazarus walk out from the burial cave." Theo's voice picked up pace. "With my own eyes. There was a multitude of witnesses."

"Your very life confirms what I have believed since He was a boy. Yeshua is our Messiah." Yosef raised his hands to heaven. "But I received a message in Caesarea saying that Yeshua is in danger and has even spoken of His death."

Lazarus shook a fist. "Caiaphas and a group of Pharisees plot to kill Him. And me."

"But why would they not welcome their Messiah?" Yosef pulled his cloak closer and shivered.

"A cauldron of evil simmers in Jerusalem." Theo added fresh coals to the brazier, and the sweet smoke of incense wafted toward him. "Men of power fear Yeshua will start a rebellion that will bring the iron fist of Rome down upon our people."

Yosef stood and warmed his hands over the brazier. "I do not believe Yeshua would ever call for violence or revolt. When He was asked if we should pay taxes to Rome, He said to render unto Caesar what is Caesar's and to HaShem what is His."

Lazarus crossed his arms and smiled. "Of course, we Jews know everything truly belongs to HaShem, Creator of the heavens and the earth."

Theo picked up bellows and fanned the embers. "A day and night have not passed since the people wanted to crown Yeshua king. His coronation would usurp the power of the Pharisees and Caiaphas. The evil men Yeshua has named a brood of vipers."

"They claim Yeshua's miracles come from Satan because they fear they will lose their influence." Lazarus reached into his bundle and pulled out his graveclothes.

Yosef's face paled and he looked sickened. "Why would you keep unclean graveclothes to which Death clings?"

Lazarus lifted them up toward heaven. "These graveclothes do not hold even a whiff of Death, but the sweet smell of myrrh and spikenard. They are evidence I was fully wrapped for burial."

Yosef clapped Lazarus on the shoulder. "My friend, for those set against belief, your graveclothes may mean nothing."

Lazarus smiled an unreadable smile that at the same time was somehow arresting. A smile that seemed to hold a deep wisdom. "You speak truth, but there have been rumors that I would never see death again or that I could not be killed. I kept my graveclothes to show others that I know I will have need of them again." Lazarus returned the graveclothes to his bundle.

Theo looked at Yosef's darkened face, aged with creases of worry and woe. "What says Yeshua about His kingdom?"

Theo opened one palm. "On the one hand, He says He goes to Jerusalem to lay down His life, and we are to pick up our cross and follow." Theo opened the other palm. "On the other hand, He says the kingdom is come and He will pick up His life again."

Lazarus lowered his head, his hand on his brow. "With each season, His riddles become tighter knots, more difficult to unravel."

The three men lapsed into a contemplative quiet. A quiet that allows one's mind to reason. A quiet that allows the ears of one's heart to hear. A quiet that, in time, prompts one's soul to speak.

Lazarus lifted his head. "Perhaps we are not meant to solve this riddle, this mystery. Rather, we are called to bear witness when the mystery is revealed."

Yosef moved to Lazarus and lifted his sleeve. "You dress as a Samaritan now. Near here, ten years past, I met a young Samaritan who was running for his life from an Avenger of Blood."

Something pricked at Theo's mind. "What became of this Samaritan?"

"Yeshua was with me and told him to trade his green-threaded robe for a Samaritan one. Beyond that, I do not know, but have oft prayed and wondered what became of him. I sent him to seek refuge from Herod." Yosef wrung the fringes of his prayer shawl.

A tranquil warmth blanketed Theo. "I was written into the

next verses on the scroll of Samuel's life. HaShem stirred his Samaritan heart to take pity on a Jew left to die by brutal bandits. On the road to Jericho, Samuel stopped and saved my life even though he was desperate and running to save his own. After many years hidden among the Jews in Jericho, Samuel was finally able to appeal to Herod."

"Theo, did Herod set him free?"

"It is a long tale with many interwoven threads, but the hand of HaShem reaches far into the future. Now, my friend Samuel, this same righteous Samaritan from so long ago, will safeguard Lazarus in Shechem."

Yosef lifted his hands. "Praise HaShem who protects righteous men, be they Jew or Samaritan."

"Life has curled back on itself, for now I, Lazarus, will be a Jew hidden among the Samaritans. Do you not think, at times, HaShem looks down upon us and laughs?"

"How could He not?" Yosef smiled, rose, and opened a gilded chest. "I do not know why, but I felt compelled to buy Samuel's robe from my servant and kept it these many years." Yosef handed the robe to Theo.

"Samuel and his Beloved will be overjoyed to have it returned." Theo studied the unique green thread along the hem. "Yeshua spoke of this very robe the first night I met Him. He said that this robe, lost to Samuel many years ago, would become woven into my story as well. Yeshua seems to know every jot of our lives past, present, and future."

Yosef turned pale and trembled.

"Forgive us if we have troubled you." Lazarus returned to his chair.

"I was just now reminded of the day Samuel and Yeshua met in my caravan camp. He suggested I purchase a tomb in a garden on the Mount of Olives." Yosef wiped his sweat-beaded lip. "At first, I took great offense. I was not an old man, but I feared Yeshua foretold my death was at hand."

Lazarus looked toward Yosef, his face forlorn. "Did Yeshua say more about the tomb?"

"He hugged me and said every man will need a tomb, even the Messiah. Then He looked at me, His eyes deep wells of sadness and something else I could not discern. Now I am filled with dread for Him."

"Here." Lazarus poured a cup of water for Yosef. "Some scriptures foretell of a suffering Messiah, while others describe His triumph and kingship. Some of our greatest rabbis have proposed that there will be two Messiahs."

Yosef took a sip of water, his hand quivering. "When I told my kinswoman, Miriam, I had purchased the garden tomb, I asked her if she believed her son was the suffering Messiah or the triumphant Messiah."

Theo's tongue tripped ahead of Yosef. "How did Miriam reply?"

"She looked up at me, her face glowing with a fervor of faith, and said it was a great mystery she had often pondered in her heart. She has determined to watch and wait and pray. And I vowed to Miriam that I would not abandon her—be her coming days filled with great triumph or great sorrow."

Theo lowered himself back onto the camel saddle seat. "Thomas has told me powerful men plot to kill Yeshua." A great sadness washed over Theo. "I fear Yeshua may be dead before the sun sets for Passover."

Tears spilled down Yosef's cheeks into his beard. "If His death comes to pass, then the garden tomb I bought so long ago will be used for Him.

The skin on Theo's neck slithered with the feel of a snake encircling his shoulders. "Evil will come against Him, but we must hold fast to our faith that Yeshua is the Lord's Messiah."

Chapter Thirty-Two

Outside Shechem

Monday

Theo

Theo lay in the back of the cart heading to Shechem, glad for the rest after the long talk with Yosef late last night. When they left at daybreak, Lazarus insisted he drive the cart. Now the sun was up and judging by its place in the sky, it must be late morning.

Theo sat up, brushed the straw from his hair and beard. "Let us stop, stretch our legs, and water the donkey." He looked to Mount Ebal, the barren, rocky mountain of curses to the east, and then to Mount Gerizim, the lush, fertile mountain of blessings to the west.

Lazarus drove the cart through the bend and stopped near Jacob's well at the crossroads. No one was drawing water at midday. Behind the well, the village of Shechem seemed quiet.

Theo filled their waterskins. "When we enter Shechem, we

267

will soon come upon a cluster of huts. One is the home of Samuel and Shamara."

"I will need their help to learn to pass as a Samaritan, so I do not bring danger to their door."

"Do not fear. Samuel has experience hiding in disguise." Theo drove them into the village past the huts. All was as Samuel had oft described to him.

Yonah, the young woman Herodias was hiding from Herod, waved from a small garden and ran to greet him. Praise HaShem. She seemed to be in her right mind. Shamara, Samuel's wife, carried a wriggling, red-faced, squalling baby. She hurried to them, her eyes as full of life as her arms.

Theo stopped the cart. "*Shalom*, Shamara. I see you have much news since we last saw one another at the inn."

Lazarus laughed. "That strong son of yours has a set of bellows in his chest. If it were possible, he could wake the dead."

"Yes. Well, Shechem is on fire with reports that Yeshua has awakened a man after four days in the grave. Do you have news of this?"

"I—"

Theo used his foot to nudge Lazarus at the ankle. He must not give himself away. "Before we stop here, I must go directly to the High Priest of Shechem, then we will return."

Shamara patted the infant's back, and he brought forth a loud burp and stopped crying. "You are welcome to stay with us. When we married, Samuel added rooms to this house, and my father lives next door, so we have room for you both."

A little girl about the age of Gaius ran from the garden and poked her head between the skirts of Shamara and Yonah.

Theo leaned toward her and raised the pitch of his voice. "And who might you be?"

"Lyra."

Of course. The baby girl he had helped save from overwhelming heat, more than three years past. The baby Sophia had nursed alongside Gaius. The baby Yonah cared for as if she were her own.

Lyra took Yonah's hand and led her back to the garden. "I want you to see the row of lentils I have planted."

Theo lifted the reins.

"Wait." Shamara raised a hand. "Johakim is no longer the high priest."

Creeping fear threatened Theo's calm. Johakim had come to believe Yeshua was the Promised One. Who knew what the new high priest might accept or understand. "Is Johakim dead?"

"No. Praise HaShem. But without an heir, it was time to choose and train a successor. The village agreed that Johakim would train Jonathan, the heir of his wife's kinsman Seth, as the next high priest. He is from the priestly line of Aaron. This Passover will be the first for High Priest Jonathan."

Theo readied the reins. "My errand will not wait. But I will return, and we will have time for a proper visit."

"We will expect you and your friend for supper."

After Theo pulled away from the huts, he turned to Lazarus. "You must hide now."

Lazarus scrambled to the back. "I will hide under the straw."

Theo leaned back as the cart climbed the hill to the House of the High Priest. "My friend, you must stay hidden until I am sure who can be trusted here." Theo stopped at the iron gate.

A servant came running. "Who goes there?"

"Theo, from the inn on Jericho Road and a friend of Samuel, humbly requests to speak with Johakim."

The man hurried inside. Within a few moments, a man in

long black robes came out from the mansion. "I am Johakim." The servant opened the gate and left.

"And I am Theo. Where may we speak unobserved and unheard?"

Johakim took hold of the donkey's bridle and led her under an arch into an inner courtyard. "Here are my private quarters." He clapped his hands, and every servant and slave scurried away. "Steadfast friend of Samuel, what brings you to me?"

"The answer lies not with what, but who. The disciple Thomas believed Yeshua would want the man He so recently raised from the dead to be kept safe." Theo climbed down from the cart and whispered. "I was charged with hiding him from those who would see him harmed or killed."

"Even in Samaria, we have heard of this miracle. But we were not sure if it was an outrageous rumor or an undeniable victory over Death." Johakim glanced about. "Where is this man now?"

Lazarus sat up suddenly in the back of the cart. Theo jumped. Johakim gasped and stepped back.

"I am the risen one." Lazarus flashed a mischievous smile.

Johakim waved to Lazarus. "Hasten inside."

Lazarus climbed down while Theo tethered the donkey.

They followed Johakim to his private chambers. He gestured for them to enter. "My library."

The room was filled with shelves of scrolls, inkwells, and standing oil lamps. Johakim sat at the only chair in the room, an ornate high-backed chair, at a large table. "You will forgive if an elder sits and you are left standing."

Lazarus smiled. "I have been sitting for hours. Standing is a relief."

Theo merely nodded, anxious to continue. "Samuel told me you believe Yeshua is the Messiah, but I was not sure of the sympathies of your new high priest."

"The new High Priest Jonathan believes that Yeshua is the Messiah, as do most in Shechem. Even so, we must keep the true name of our fugitive from others—not only for his safety, but for theirs." Johakim turned to Lazarus. "Come closer, let me look at you."

Lazarus stepped forward. Johakim smiled. "A piece of straw hides in your beard." He drew it out. "After a few more days' growth, we will trim your beard into a more squared-off Samaritan shape."

Theo moved next to Lazarus. "We must keep this hiding place from Herod. I feel sure if Queen Herodias learns of Shechem's role in sheltering Lazarus, she will keep silent, for we also hide her secrets." Did Johakim know that Samuel and Lyra and Yonah were all secrets Herodias kept from Herod? Theo would take care to say nothing that would give them away.

Johakim placed his hands on the table and stood. "Theo, only you and I and the new high priest Jonathan will know the name of Lazarus."

"The Pharisees feared Lazarus would foment a rebellion. But they will no longer search far for him, since he has been removed from the eyes and ears of Jerusalem."

"Even so, we should not call this man Lazarus." Johakim opened a scroll and ran his finger right to left searching the text. "Let us call him Amon, which means trustworthy or one who confirms."

"A fitting choice, for my breathing body confirms the truth of the resurrection of the dead."

"Yeshua has warned of a time when He will no longer be with us." Theo's spirit sagged. "Soon, I fear the testimony of Lazarus will be needed to confirm the hope of eternal life."

Three soft taps on the door of Johakim's study brought a smile to his lips. "I know that knock." He threw the door and his arms open wide. "It is my favorite little girl in all of Shechem."

Lyra giggled and gently lifted a messenger dove. "There is a message from Jerusalem for you."

Yonah stood behind Lyra and guided her into the room.

Lazarus stood and bowed to Lyra as he would to a princess. "I am called Amon."

Lyra giggled at his game.

Yonah stood tall, regal. "*Shalom*, Amon. Lyra learns the ways of a dovekeeper from me."

Theo worried for Yonah, for her secret. Even in her common garb, Yonah's singular beauty could not be concealed. She exuded the presence of royalty.

Lazarus looked up and peered searchingly at Yonah, then at Theo. He knew he must keep his face as blank as a new clay tablet.

Lyra brought the dove to Johakim. "This is the first time I am trusted to take a message from the dove's leg." Excitement bubbled in Lyra's voice. "I wanted you to watch."

"And I am glad to bear witness to this moment."

Yonah took the dove from Lyra. "If we may, I will place the dove on your table and gentle her, so she stays still."

Johakim nodded.

Lyra took a small needle-like blade from Yonah's waist girdle and moved the dove's leg out from under its body. "I slip the blade under the binding cord with the sharp edge pointing away from the bird and me."

Yonah made cooing sounds and soothed the dove. "That is just right."

Lyra slowly cut the brass tube free.

Theo drew a deep breath, only now aware he had not taken one while little Lyra wielded the knife.

Lyra's face pinked as bright as a morning sunrise. She

handed Johakim the message and moved away. "A dovekeeper waits several paces back to learn if there is to be a reply." Lyra spoke each word with great sincerity.

He opened the brass tube and slid out a small scroll.

Yonah pointed to the seal. "The message bears the seal of Prima, the dovekeeper in Jerusalem."

Johakim unrolled the scroll. "Warn the believers in Shechem that Yeshua drove out the buyers and sellers from the Temple courts. He overturned the tables of the moneychangers." Worry flooded Johakim's face. "Yeshua said the Temple has become a den of robbers. I worry for His life."

Johakim looked up at Theo and Lazarus. "Does Yeshua mean to create such chaos? Does He mean to shut down the Jewish Temple at Passover?"

"Yeshua's ways are a mystery to us, but not to Him." Lazarus lifted his hands like balancing scales in the marketplace. "Crowds of commoners have come to love and follow Yeshua. But on the other hand, many hate and fear Him. He rushes headlong into a snare."

Fear born of confusion spurred Theo's heartbeat to race. He took a calming breath. "We must trust that Yeshua directs His destiny, even if it is one we would not choose."

Lazarus put his arm across Theo's shoulders. "Let it be so."

Yonah lifted her hands toward the heavens. "I have found that Hashem is with us—even through the dark valleys we did not choose to enter."

Johakim turned to Yonah. "HaShem mourns and rejoices with us. Shares our tears of joy and tears of sorrow." He leaned down to face Lyra. "Thank you for delivering this message. I will send no reply."

"Come, Lyra. We will place the dove back in her nesting box and walk back to your *abba's* house." Yonah guided Lyra, holding the dove, past Lazarus and they left.

Johakim returned to his chair. "Theo, I am glad that you chose to bring Amon here. The new High Priest Jonathan and I will be honored to hear more of his friendship with Yeshua."

Lazarus bowed to Johakim. "I am grateful for your shelter in Shechem. Peace be with you." He lifted the top of his cloak as a hood and walked to the door.

Theo joined Lazarus. "We will both stay with Samuel tonight, but at first light, I must return to Jerusalem. For surely, The Twelve may have need of me. Yeshua has challenged the authorities. Men with power seek to murder Him."

Chapter Thirty-Three

Theo stood at the door of Samuel's small stone home. Shamara had proudly led Theo through the courtyard and backrooms Samuel added when he brought her here as his bride. Shamara, Yonah, and Lyra readied a simple supper. The nutty, pungent smell of cumin made his mouth water.

Snores drifted to him from the inner courtyard where he had left Lazarus dozing in a chair near the cookfire.

Lyra giggled and covered her mouth. "That man snorts in his sleep."

"Shh." Yonah gently tapped Lyra on the head. "Amon needs a good rest, so take care not to wake him until the meal is served."

Theo's friends could never conceive of the miraculous awakening of the man who slept in their courtyard. He looked around the doorpost, spotted Samuel walking up the path, and hobbled out the door.

Samuel came closer, carrying a covered harp under each

arm. "*Shalom,* old friend. It has been almost a full turn of seasons since I have laid eyes upon your face."

"*Shalom,* Samuel. I have brought Amon, a friend in great need of refuge."

"He is welcome. Few know better than I the desperate quest for refuge."

"I would embrace you if your arms were not so full. Are those harps for me to take to Prima to sell in Jerusalem?"

"Yes. We are so grateful she has found buyers for my hand-crafted kinnors."

"To my ear, your harps have an exquisite tone. Prima is such a clever woman. She has found more than buyers for you, but also a market for herself."

"I am pleased for her. Tell me more."

Theo turned and fell in step with Samuel's gait. "As first harpist in the famed kinnor choir of Herodias, she has been allowed to offer music lessons to the young royals at court. And she has spread the word far and wide that the harps of Didymus the Greek are the only harps Herodias will play or allow in her kinnor choir."

"How shrewdly she protects my true name by selling my harps under the name I used when I was disguised at King Herod's court." Samuel's voice held notes of relief.

Turning to Theo, he nodded, his eyes glinting with humor. "Prima's brilliant strategy is also self-serving. Any merchant who would seek to compete with her will never find the harp-maker called Didymus the Greek."

"Let us sit here for a moment." Theo waved toward some nearby boulders. "My leg throbs after so many hours in the cart and I came away from the house without my crutch." He sat, and Samuel leaned against the side of a tall boulder.

Samuel's face filled with sympathy, then took on some

other emotion. "Have you never asked Yeshua for healing?" His tone held a draught of impatience.

"No. I asked Him to teach me to forgive. Rather than be given an able body in this life, I would choose to learn forgiveness and gain an eternal life in paradise, a place of everlasting healing."

"Yeshua takes great delight in teaching all who seek wisdom. What did He say to you?"

"To pray for my enemies each day. I compel myself to do so, and with each prayer, my desire for revenge seems to soften." Theo patted his leg. "And my leg seems to straighten. Perhaps the changes are all the imaginings of a hapless cripple."

"In Shechem, we have witnessed those who have been healed slowly. I will pray that this miracle will come to pass for you."

Theo stood, clapped Samuel on the shoulder, and laughed. "Is it not enough of a miracle that a Samaritan prays for a Jew?"

Samuel grinned and his eyes sparked with amusement. "Miracles are placed along our path just as seeds are planted in a field. Who is to know the manifold harvest they will yield?"

They continued walking and entered Samuel's home, and he rested both harps against the wall.

Yonah set plates on the table. "Samuel, which harp do you favor over the other?"

Shamara came in from the cookfire, a sleepy infant in her arms. "Do not tell us. Yonah, you must play them both for us after the meal. Then, we will decide which we prefer."

"Yes. Yes. Play for us." Lyra placed a basket of bread on the table.

"Come, little one. It is time to help me stir the pot." Yonah stepped outside and Lyra followed.

Samuel took his sleepy son from Shamara and turned to

Theo. "Have you met my son?" He tousled the baby's curly copper-colored hair.

"I have." Theo sent a wry smile to Samuel. "But when we first met, he was not so happy."

Shamara took Samuel's arm. "My son is like his father. Most content when he is well fed."

"Our meal is nearly ready?" Samuel's tone was a hopeful plea.

"We will serve as soon as our guest wakes. He has fallen asleep in the courtyard." Shamara took the infant from Samuel's arms. "I will settle our son for the night." She went into a room at the back.

"Shamara is such a doting mother." Theo could not keep the joy from his tone.

Samuel motioned Theo to sit at the table. "Of course she dotes on him. She has waited for this son through many years of trials and troubles and many husbands not of her choice." Samuel sat beside Theo. "She had come to believe she was forever barren, but I clung to my *ima*'s deathbed prophesy." Samuel's voice faltered. "The promise to which my *abba* also clung. The promise that Shamara would one day bear my son."

"What is his name?"

"His name is Abram." Samuel's voice broke and he gripped Theo's hand.

Abram. Samuel's father must be gone. Samuel and Shamara would not name a child for a kinsman who still drew breath. "I did not hear of your *abba*'s passing. It saddens me that he did not see his long-awaited grandson."

"HaShem is gracious, and His timing is perfect. My *abba* cradled our son until the seventh day of his life. Then, speaking of a vision of his beloved Ruth reaching out for him, my *abba* passed peacefully. The next day, our son was circumcised and named Abram following the Law that commands a son be named on the eighth day of his life."

"I am glad for you, my friend. A son, an heir, is a new beginning for your bloodline, your House."

"Yes. And my son was born on Shemini Atzeret, the feast of new beginnings."

"The season of your son's birth also marked a new beginning for me. I met a woman whose eyes haunted me. And somehow, I was certain, without a shred of doubt, she was part of my murky past." A fount of gratitude welled up in Theo. "Yeshua offered her a new beginning. Later, she recognized me as her lost kinsman from years past."

Samuel leapt to his feet, overturning his chair. "You know who you are?"

"She told me I was a good man. Kind and caring. I did not wish to know my name or other details that elude me."

"Why remain blind to your past?"

"Knowledge of things I cannot recall sets my spirit teetering on a cliff's edge."

"Who is this woman to you?"

"My mother was sister to Zera's mother. Her father was the former overseer at Herod's Winter Palace in Jericho. I was apprenticed to him."

Samuel's ruddy cheeks faded to the color of milk. "The former overseer was your uncle?" Samuel's voice was shaky and weak. "He hired me to work in the royal garden. This overseer was a righteous man. When I was arrested by overzealous holy men, he never abandoned me in prison. And he made sure Herod heard straightaway of my plight."

"It gladdens me to learn that my uncle was honorable. My uncle rescued you many years after you rescued me. He had given me up for dead years before."

Samuel's face filled with awe and utter surprise. "All this time, we never knew of that virtuous man's kinship with you."

"And all this talk of my past prods me to strive to remember. But somehow, striving to remember seems to bury the memories deeper. Only when my mind is calm do pictures from my past seem to come at the most unexpected moments."

Lazarus came through the back door. He stretched and yawned.

Shamara returned. "The babe is asleep. Come, let us enjoy the meal."

Lyra and Yonah joined them. Yonah carried a pot of savory stew, Lyra carried a long ladle.

During the meal, each spoke of how or when they came to know Yeshua was the Messiah. Theo looked at Lazarus when it was his turn to share. His face was so elated. Theo was sure it took every bit of self-control Lazarus could muster not to tell the story of his raising. But Lazarus told of Yeshua's many healings of the blind, the deaf, the lepers.

Lazarus turned to Yonah. "You have not spoken. What think you of Yeshua of Nazareth?"

"Though I have never heard Him speak, each time I hear of His miracles, more shards of my shattered soul seem to heal. For me, the surety that Yeshua is the Promised One was a gradual awakening."

"Tell me, Yonah, did you ever hear John the Baptizer teach?" Lazarus spoke with rising zeal. Theo thought he heard an edge of accusation.

Yonah looked at Lazarus as if she heard nothing but respect in his voice. "Anyone at Herod's court during the Baptizer's imprisonment heard him call the people to repent and announce the coming king."

Lazarus leaned toward Yonah. "Then tell me ..."

Samuel stood so quickly that he knocked over his cup,

spilling wine on Lazarus. "Forgive my clumsy wave of the hand." He wiped the table, and Lazarus blotted at his wine-stained sleeve.

Theo studied Samuel's face. He knew that look—dread. Well-disguised dread, but nevertheless dread. If Theo were a man to gamble, he would wager that Samuel had spilled the wine as a distraction. But a distraction from what?

"Do not be troubled. I will wash your sleeve in the morning." Yonah refilled the cups.

Lazarus offered her a curt nod. For the remainder of the meal, Lazarus stole glances at Yonah, catching her unawares. His jaw was tight, but apart from that, his face was a sealed scroll.

Theo gestured to Lyra. "The day has outlived the little one's wakefulness."

Lyra's eyes drifted shut, her head drooped, and her face almost fell into her bowl.

"Come, child, it is time to sleep." Yonah lifted Lyra onto her hip.

Lyra leaned her head on Yonah's shoulder. "But I want to hear you play the harps."

Yonah kissed her brow. "We will settle you in a dove nest of blankets and I will play a lullaby."

Shamara rose. "I will fetch the blankets."

"Wait." Theo could not contain his broad smile. "I have something special to cover her."

"Hurry, this little girl is growing heavy." Yonah boosted Lyra, who had slipped down from her hip.

Samuel took Lyra from Yonah. "Please, play them both. We want to hear how they sing."

Theo rushed to the cart and found the green-threaded garment Samuel had worn when he was forced to flee Shechem. Theo returned and spread the garment over Lyra.

Shamara rushed to Samuel and ran her fingers over the cloth. "I cannot believe the testimony of my own eyes." Then she turned and lifted an edge of the cloth before Samuel's face. "Look. The green thread, the special dye. Long ago, your mother and I wove this for you."

"How did you come by this?" Joy rang in Samuel's voice and shone on his face.

"Yosef of Arimathea kept it and prayed over it for Samuel through all these years." A lump formed in Theo's throat. "Imagine a Jew praying for a Samaritan, so faithfully." The voice of Yeshua echoed in Theo's ears. *Pray for your enemies.*

"But how did you come to meet Yosef?" Samuel settled Lyra beside Yonah.

Theo's voice was blocked by tears. He glanced at Lazarus and gestured for him to answer.

"We stopped at a caravan camp near Ramah. Yosef has been a close friend of mine for many years. When he saw my Samaritan robe, he was reminded of you, Samuel. He had no news of what befell you after you parted ways."

Theo regained his composure and his voice. "When I saw the cloak with the green thread, I knew Yosef could only have been speaking of you. I told him our story and how we came to believe Yeshua was the Messiah."

"Lazarus, how fares Yosef?"

"Just as you remember him. Yosef never seems to age. He sends a thousand blessings to the House of Samuel."

Yonah strummed gently on the harp in her lap.

Lyra tugged on Yonah's sleeve. "*Ima*, play the song I love most."

Theo startled. He did not expect Lyra to speak of Yonah as her mother.

Lyra seemed to catch his look of surprise and sat up. "I am a little girl with four *imas*." Lyra crossed her arms and sealed her announcement with a nod of her head. "My birth-*ima* died, but she kissed me first." Lyra lifted a finger and then a second one. "Next, there is my milk-*ima*, Sophia. She has a son named Gaius. My milk brother."

Lyra touched Yonah's cheek. "She is my always-*ima*. Yonah has always been with me."

"And the fourth *ima*?" Theo's heart swelled with love for this little girl. Samuel's firstborn.

"Shamara is my wife-*ima*. Shamara is my *abba*'s wife, so that also makes her my *ima*."

Samuel settled Lyra into her woven nest, his hand lingering on the cloth.

Yonah strummed a chord. "Lyra, you are four-times blessed. But now the moon is well-risen and you must listen while I play your song." Yonah sang of a dove and his lost love.

Theo remembered the melody. It was the same song Yonah had sung at Barid's inn when she was fleeing from Herod.

Samuel and Shamara held one another, their tear-filled eyes shining like moonlight on water. The song faded, leaving a soft stillness in its wake.

"Please play one more." Lyra's lulled voice drifted toward sleep.

Yonah began plucking softly. Her fingers were flickering fireflies dancing across the strings.

Theo squirmed at the fierce intensity with which Lazarus stared at Yonah. Theo knew that she was in hiding and that Yonah was not the name given her at birth. He could not help but wonder about her past. Samuel and Dex knew, but they had kept it from everyone else. Much as Theo now kept the knowledge of Lazarus from the people in Shechem.

Yonah let the last chord ring. When it had faded, she rose and crept away from Lyra. She moved to put the harp against the wall, but Lazarus suddenly blocked her way, causing her to look up, directly into his angry face.

"Yonah, is it?" Lazarus spoke her name with suspicion. "You play with the skill of the queen." His tone was more accusation than admiration.

"Herodias taught Prima to play the harp, and she teaches many of the handmaids to play even to this day." Yonah started to step around Lazarus, but he moved in front of her again.

Theo's belly cramped around a fist of fear. Lazarus might uncover Yonah's secret.

He looked like a donkey that would not budge. "But the song of the harp in your hands sounds very different from when Prima plays."

"Yonah was a handmaid of the queen at court who Prima also taught to be a dovekeeper." Samuel shot a look of alarm at Theo. "Yonah was sent here to care for the dovecote at the House of the High Priest."

"Amon?" Now Yonah echoed the tone of Lazarus and spoke his name as if she knew it was not his name. "My mother taught me to play, and Herodias taught my mother."

"As she did mine." Theo blurted the truth without forethought, but a vision was burned into his mind. A vision of Herodias sitting with a woman and placing her fingers in position on harp strings.

Theo wanted to linger with the memory of his mother, but there was a more pressing problem. Though he did not know why, he knew Yonah must stay hidden. Lazarus might wreak great trouble if he divulged her true name. Just as she could if she unearthed his.

Chapter Thirty-Four

A taut thread of discord still threatened the harmony in the room after Yonah took Lyra to her sleeping pallet.

Something about Yonah had left Samuel greatly unsettled.

Shamara lit the oil lamps while Lazarus sat at the table whittling. He showed her his work. "I am making a whistle for Abram."

Shamara laughed. "Though every mother thinks her child brilliant, Abram is but a babe. It will be some time before he can enjoy a whistle. But I will keep it for him."

Yonah returned and began to clear the table.

"Time passes ever more quickly than one expects." Lazarus glanced toward Yonah. "A son or daughter can become unrecognizable."

Theo flinched and watched Yonah. For the blink of an eye, she stopped moving, then resumed her work as if she had not heard.

Theo picked up his crutch and went to Samuel. "Let us walk. I would hear more of your life here in Shechem."

"Yes, it is a warm night." Samuel opened the door into the face of a flustered royal runner who stepped back and clutched a leather-wrapped scroll close.

Theo spotted the seal of Herodias, and his supper turned to vinegar. Had the queen's spies found Lazarus so quickly? Would her husband, King Herod, use the whereabouts of Lazarus as leverage to pacify the priests and Pharisees?

The runner took a deep breath. "A message for the woman called Yonah. Dovekeeper of Shechem."

Yonah came forward, worry flickering across her face. Her hand shaking, she took the message. "My beloved has gone to Jericho. I pray no ill fate has befallen him." She unrolled the scroll and read. Her face lit with unabashed joy. "The queen sent word ahead of Ozri's return. She granted him permission to marry me. She asks that the new High Priest Jonathan have us sign the *ketubah*, the wedding contract she has already signed and sent with Ozri." Yonah turned to Shamara and waved the message in the air.

Shamara ran to the blushing Yonah and hugged her. Both women laughed through their tears. Yonah wiped her cheeks and looked back at the message. "We are to proceed with the marriage on the earliest day that the Law allows."

Yonah dismissed the royal runner with a wave of her hand. "There will be no reply."

Samuel smiled and threw an arm over Theo's shoulder. "You must take word back to Sophia, Dex, and Barid. They will share in our joy."

"The queen knows of our friendship. She wrote that she would send them with my dowry and her wedding gift."

"The queen is over-generous with her handmaid." The stare Lazarus gave Yonah was sharp enough to cut through bone.

Yonah did not flinch. She did not look away. "The queen has often said I reminded her of a child she once lost."

"Wife, we must celebrate with a glass of sweet wine." Samuel's tone was merry, but Theo could still hear a note of concern.

Shamara brought a flask of wine and cups to the table and motioned for them to gather round.

Shamara glanced toward Theo, a puzzled look on her face, then poured the first cup for Yonah and the others. Judging by the look on Shamara's face, she also knew nothing of Yonah's past. The pointed remarks and probing questions by Lazarus had sparked Theo's speculations.

Samuel raised his cup. "May the Lord bless you and Ozri. And shelter you under His wing."

Shamara raised her cup. "May the Lord show you His favor and give you His peace."

Theo raised his cup. "May the Lord smile upon this union and be gracious to you." Theo rejoiced for Ozri and Yonah, but he was pricked by a twinge of loss. What woman would ever marry a lame man who did not know his own name?

"Shamara, do you think Yeshua would bless the union between a Samaritan and a Jew?"

Shamara took Yonah's hand. "Perhaps it is more important that you both believe Yeshua is the Promised One."

Yonah raised her cup and sipped. The others joined her.

Lazarus lifted his cup but offered no blessing and did not drink.

Yonah looked around the table. "I am grateful for all your many kindnesses to me." She turned to Lazarus. "The home of Samuel and Shamara has been a safe haven for many, and I trust it will continue to be so."

Theo's stomach roiled as if it held a thousand scurrying

scorpions. Yonah's words suggested she knew Amon was also in hiding.

Lazarus rose and strode out the door.

Theo followed. What was Lazarus thinking?

Lazarus turned on Theo. "Do you know the wicked woman your friend harbors?"

Theo ushered Lazarus away from the house. "Samuel knows. I only know Herodias wants her protected." The scorpions scuttled from Theo's stomach up into his chest.

Lazarus fisted his hands. "She is the harlot who danced so seductively she captured the attention of Herod." Lazarus spewed his words, his face furrowed with fury. "When Herod offered her a prize, she demanded the head of John the Baptizer."

"All of Jerusalem knows of this calamity. But how do you know Yonah and the harlot are one?"

Lazarus quickened his pace. "I was at court the day my friend Yosef of Arimathea sold that young temptress exotic silks in the seven colors of the rainbow. The same silks that were made into veils she shed as she danced for Herod."

Theo could not keep up and stopped. "You claim she is the daughter of Herodias?"

Lazarus turned and shook his fist. "I know. Without a speck of doubt, that woman is Salome."

"Yet Yonah claims another mother. She said Herodias taught her mother to play the harp."

"A very cunning, clever parsing of the truth. Herodias is her mother, and she taught herself to play the harp." Lazarus sounded more hate-filled with each word he spoke. "And Salome is the child that Herodias lost."

"Samuel has always known who she is, and he brought her here to his home. I trust his reasons and his reckonings." Theo felt as if one of the scorpions had stung his throat and left a growing lump of fear.

"But can you not see? Both Salome and Herodias hated John the Baptizer, cousin of Yeshua. How much more must they hate Yeshua and his followers? You must warn Samuel. If it suits the queen's purposes, she will betray us to Herod." Lazarus looked over Theo's shoulder. "Here is Samuel now."

Samuel came up the path behind them. "I thought I would join you on your walk."

"Samuel, my friend, I trust you with my life, but we both know Herodias is self-serving and without scruples." Theo hoped his words would not offend Samuel. "I fear the queen has loosed her daughter, Salome, as a she-wolf among the lambs that follow Yeshua."

Samuel took Theo's hands in his. "No, Theo. Heed my words. Yonah was as much a victim of evildoers as were you. She was the victim of Herodias and Herod, you were the victim of bandits. She was broken of mind, you were broken of body. She strives to forget, you strive to remember."

Lazarus, the fury receding from his face, looked at Samuel. "How can you be so sure Yonah is a true believer and not a spy for Herodias?"

"Yonah was a mad woman. Now she is of sound mind. She has heard the teachings of Yeshua and chosen to forgive those who used her. She has repented and knows she is forgiven of her sins. Her mind is at peace because she has forgiven and forgotten."

Theo's knees weakened and he grabbed the arms of Lazarus and Samuel.

They helped him sit on a nearby boulder. "What is it, my friend?"

"I am a true follower of Yeshua, suddenly convicted by your words. Yonah has a greater faith and purer heart than mine. For I know in my mind I must forgive and forget, but my stubborn soul is slow to follow. I have neither forgiven nor forgotten those who beat me and left me for dead."

"I see now that I was too quick to judge Yonah. And you, Samuel." Lazarus put his hands together. "I would ask your forgiveness."

"You have it." Samuel turned away from Lazarus and put his hand on Theo's shoulder. "I will pray for your struggle to forgive."

"Yeshua has told me to watch Him. To do so, I must be with Him. For I fear His time with us is short. At daybreak, I will return to Jerusalem." Theo took some calming breaths and stood. "I must trust Yeshua will show me the path to forgiveness of my enemies."

Chapter Thirty-Five

Bethany, House of Lazarus
Tuesday morning

Zera

Zera and Reah served the morning meal to the growing number of people who had slept under the stars. They had come to the House of Lazarus to feed their growing curiosity about the walking dead man. But when they discovered Lazarus was not there, they stayed to hear Yeshua of Nazareth feed their starving souls.

"My lady, I miss the days when Barid and Theo were staying here with us."

"I slept poorly last night. I, too, wish Barid were here."

"You speak of him with fondness more and more of late." Reah tucked a loose strand of Zera's hair behind her ear.

"Barid must tend his inn, and the disciples had need of Theo."

Martha wended around the cookfires in the field and

encouraged the women to ready their camp for the day. She glanced toward the low table outside the house where Yeshua and his close disciples were eating. "Zera. Reah. Please serve more water to the Master, and make sure that He and those at the table with Him have had their fill."

Zera hurried toward the table, and the child within kicked. She did not slow. This was a chance to serve Yeshua with her own hands. She filled a pitcher from the tall stone jars and poured water for each man, working her way to the center and Yeshua. Some nodded their thanks, some offered a quick *shalom*. Judas Iscariot never acknowledged the women who served. Joanna said he ignored her unless she had a donation of gold in her hand.

Zera turned and watched Reah pour water for Yeshua. She could not help but smile. Reah was as awe-struck as she.

A man grabbed Reah around the waist from behind, lifting her feet from the ground. She cried out, her face terror-stricken.

Zera opened her mouth to protest, but she, too, was clutched from behind. A big foul-smelling man started to carry her off. Her heart raged against her ribs. And she fought to free herself from his iron-clad hold and reached toward the disciples.

They rose as one.

Peter's hand was already on his sword. He looked to Yeshua.

Every eye turned to Him.

HaShem, keep us from bloodshed.

Yeshua stood and held up His hand. A command for order. His face was calm, but His eyes flashed lightning. "You dare manhandle these women and disturb the peace of this house?"

The man holding Zera leaned toward Yeshua. She gagged at his rancid breath. "This woman, widow of Joram, and her slave are to be sold this afternoon to cover a large debt he left at his death."

"Release them. The debt will be covered." Yeshua's steady tone settled the cresting wave of panic that crashed over Zera.

Judas Iscariot clutched the money bag tightly as if his heart would seize if Yeshua asked him to part with even a widow's mite from the disciples' shared purse.

The men let go of them but did not move away.

Yeshua pointed to the road.

Zera's eyes followed Yeshua's finger. Ira, her faithful steward, drove up in his donkey cart, stopped, and climbed down. "Praise HaShem, I am not too late." His whole demeanor frenzied, he took several hurried steps forward. Then he looked up and met Yeshua's eyes. He seemed to take on Yeshua's calm and slowed to a sedate pace. When Ira reached Yeshua, He motioned for him to speak.

Ira turned to Zera. "My lady, forgive me, but I was just notified of a new debt and have brought the funds to redeem you."

Zera's horror settled, but then she looked into Reah's hopeless eyes, and a great fear overcame her. "There must be funds to also redeem Reah." Zera heard her tone teeter toward panic.

"My lady, if you redeem Reah, you will have nothing left."

Reah gasped and her sad eyes brimmed with tears.

"I will have a treasure beyond compare. I will have Reah."

Ira's face was overtaken by a proud smile. "I knew that would be your choice. Your *abba* and *ima* were people of honor. As is their daughter."

Ira paid the debt collectors. Yeshua stood and spoke to the rough men. "Go now in peace."

Bewilderment and surprise filled their faces and they hastened away.

"Daughter of Jerusalem, you have chosen to cherish a

person over your purse." Yeshua glanced toward Judas, who still clutched the money bag, his knuckles white as shark's teeth.

Zera's spirit lifted. She had pleased the Master. "Is it not as You have taught? Do unto others as you would have them do unto you."

"Zera, you have chosen well and will be blessed for it."

Yeshua had called her Zera. The name he wrote in the dirt. Trembling, she bowed her head and drew Ira and Reah aside. Zera whispered. "Ira, my only regret is that you and your son will have nothing further to manage of my holdings and will no longer earn your share of the profits."

"My lady, let not your heart be troubled. We are skilled stewards. We have not only managed your inheritance well, but also our own share."

Zera clasped his hands. "I have been blessed with a kind and faithful steward. Though I cannot pay, I would ask one final task of you."

"Anything, my lady."

"Have manumission documents drawn for Reah. If she is free, she will never again be at risk of being sold."

Reah knelt and hugged Zera around her knees. "I do not wish to leave my lady. Please do not send me away."

"Never." Zera helped Reah to her feet and gathered her into an embrace. "Together, we must ask HaShem to guide our way."

Martha waved at them. "Reah, please come. I have need of you." Martha hurried away and Reah followed.

Zera walked back to the cart with Ira. He climbed up onto the seat and lifted the reins. "I will send the document for Reah to Barid at the Jericho Inn, along with the womanly things from your dressing table."

"Many thanks."

"Oh. Stay a moment. With all the furor, this flew from my mind." Ira reached into his waist sack and removed a small linen-wrapped packet. "This was taken from one of the secret nooks in your chambers. It was never part of the estate of Joram."

Zera took it and unwrapped the packet to reveal a small alabaster ampule of precious perfume attached to a leather cord. She ran a finger over the smooth, cool marble. "This belonged to my *ima*. My father would take this precious ampule from a locked chest on his study table and hold it in his palm when he would tell me stories of my mother." Zera placed the leather cord around her neck and let the ampule fall under her robe, next to her heart. "Ira, blessings on your house for your steadfast service and many kindnesses to me."

"May the Lord go before you, my good lady." Ira flicked the reins and drove off.

Zera's ear clung to the word "good." Ira had called her "good" even though he knew of her shame. Yeshua had blessed her choice to redeem Reah. Zera touched the rock of remembrance tucked at her waist. It did not feel quite so sharp. Perhaps the path to forgiving herself was lined with days filled with righteous choices.

Reah returned, a small bundle slung over her shoulder. "Yeshua is going to the Temple. I have brought provisions so we may go with the others and find a place where we can hear every word He speaks."

They joined the disciples and the other women. The morning walk to the Temple was quiet. Zera enjoyed the warmth of the sun, the soft breeze, and the nearness of Yeshua.

With each passing day since Yeshua's kingly entry into Jerusalem, the disciples seemed more subdued. It was as if they suddenly had ears to hear Yeshua's dire warnings and were left steeping in worries of what may come.

They came upon a withered fig tree. Zera shuddered and took Reah's hand. "Look, here is the fig tree that the disciples saw Yeshua curse. Last morning, the tree was alive, but fruitless. This morning, the barren fig tree is utterly dead, withered from the roots."

A little way ahead, Yeshua and the disciples had stopped.

"Shh." Reah drew Zera farther along the path. "Yeshua is teaching The Twelve. We, too, can hear His words from here."

"Therefore, I tell you, whatever you ask for in prayer, believe that you have received it, and it will be yours. And when you stand praying, if you hold anything against anyone, forgive them, so that your Father in heaven may forgive you your sins." Yeshua moved down the road toward the Temple.

Zera and Reah followed Him at a distance. Thoughts of Theo came to her mind. "We must pray for Theo. Pray that he will find forgiveness for those who maimed him. Even if he never learns who they were."

"My lady, when you stand praying for Theo, I will pray for you. Yeshua just said when you pray, if you hold anything against anyone, you must forgive them." Rhea enclosed both of Zera's hands in hers. "Even though you have repented and been baptized, you still hold your own sin of adultery against yourself."

The truth of Rhea's insight stabbed Zera deeply. "Yes, I had never considered that I must forgive myself." Tears of conviction blurred Zera's sight. "You are a loyal friend who dares to speak truth to me. The damning voices in my head grow weaker the longer I am near Yeshua."

Zera considered these things as they approached the Temple. Reah, who read her so well, kept quiet, giving Zera the silence in which to search her heart.

Yeshua paused outside the Temple to speak with His disciples. The other followers gathered near Him. He looked around like a shepherd counting his sheep. Assured each one was present, He entered the Portico of Solomon and sat in the place He was known to teach.

They all followed him in. Zera and Reah spread their cloaks under a large, twisted column. Zera looked to the spot where she had been flung before Yeshua. Her stomach thrashed like a sudden storm at sea. The pile of rocks that had been raised against her had been completely cleared.

She touched the rock at her waist, the only rock that remained from that dreadful day. For months, she had pondered the words Yeshua said to her in this place. But somehow, here in the Temple again, with the accusing rocks gone, a new understanding came to her. Those who would have stoned her shared her humiliation and shame in equal portion. They were no less sinners than she. The storm in her stomach was becalmed.

The Pharisees and scribes pushed their way forward. Much of the morning was wasted with debates over questions that did not seek truth but were designed to trap Yeshua. To lure Him to speak words that would incriminate Him with Rome—or discredit Him with the crowd.

Much to the delight of the common people, Yeshua responded with clever answers and parables that exposed the hypocrisy and evil of those who tried to ensnare Him.

When the sun was high overhead, Yeshua finished His lesson and withdrew with the disciples to a quiet corner.

Reah stood. "When the shade has shifted, Yeshua will move to His usual place across from the Temple treasury."

Zera picked up their cloaks. "Let us find places now. The numbers of new followers who come each day to hear Him rise like leavened bread. Some are here searching for their true Messiah. Some are merely onlookers waiting for a moment of dissent or drama. And some are spies for the Pharisees and Herod and even Pontius Pilate."

Reah led the way to a large column where they again spread their cloaks. They sat and shared a small round of bread, dried figs, and water. "My lady, eat some more, for the babe you carry."

Zera's stomach was a little queasy, but she ate another fig. Her lids grew heavy, and she leaned against the column. "Reah, please wake me when Yeshua returns." Zera knew Reah would never leave her unguarded in a public place. For years, it had been her handmaid's duty to remain ever vigilant, protecting her mistress and herself.

The warmth of the afternoon sun and the low hum of the passersby lulled Zera to sleep. She dreamed of Reah's mother applying perfume to her *ima*'s hair. Perfume from an alabaster ampule, like the one Ira had given her.

Something in the bustling around her changed, and she awakened. She startled and saw Reah, asleep beside her. Where were their bundles? She did not see them. The ampule. Zera's throat tightened. She felt for the leather cord at her neck. The ampule of perfume was still there. She shifted to look around Reah, and the rock dug at her waist.

Lenah leaned over from Reah's other side. "I have your bundles and have been keeping watch, so Reah might rest. Poor child is bone weary from the ghastly threat of being sold into slavery this morning."

"Your careful watch over us was a great blessing, a *mitzvah*. For Reah would never have slept had I offered to watch."

"Reah said your eyes were heavy with sleep even before Yeshua withdrew."

Zera stood and stretched. "Look, Yeshua stands a little off from His usual place, and His disciples spread their cloaks before Him. We must move closer to hear—but Reah is so tired, it would not be kind to wake her."

Lenah sat in Zera's place. "You move closer, I will stay with Reah. In the aftermath of your fright today, Yeshua's teaching may calm your spirit."

"Many blessings be upon you, Lenah."

Zera slowly shouldered through the crowd. How much easier it would be if Barid were here to plow the way. She came through an opening, and Joanna waved to her. Wending her way over, she sat down beside her kinswoman. Miriam, the mother of Yeshua, sat at Joanna's right hand.

Miriam leaned forward. "*Shalom*, Zera. What a harrowing day. I am filled with joy and relief that your steward arrived in due time this morning. What madness to think that you could have been sold into slavery."

Heat rose to Zera's cheeks, and a burning wave of shame ran through her veins. Overcome with shyness, her tongue thickened, and her eyes misted. She could think of no reply. She had seen the mother of Yeshua but never spoken with her.

Joanna stood and traded places with Miriam.

Miriam took Zera's hand. "My sweet young woman, let your tears fall, like living water. You are among friends."

Zera's flowing tears seemed to free her tongue. "How can you call me sweet? Surely you must have heard why I was thrown at Yeshua's feet. Even though He granted me mercy, many still look upon me as an adulteress."

Miriam took a cloth from her waist and gently wiped Zera's tears. "I well remember those same looks when I carried Yeshua within my womb. Many decided I must be an adulteress whom my husband forgave for love of me. Only my husband knew of my visitation by an angel, who promised I would fulfill prophecy and conceive, though yet a virgin."

An angel had come to Miriam? Yeshua was born of a

virgin? His birth was a miracle of miracles. Awe filled Zera. She met Miriam's gentle eyes. "Your kindness soothes me. Those hateful, condemning looks have been a torment for me to bear. Unlike you, I was guilty of the sin. How much more a burden it must have been for you to bear the shame of a sin of which you were innocent."

"None of us is without sin. We each need a sacrifice to pay the price for our sins."

Joanna leaned forward. "Yes, we need a sacrifice. I saw the prophet, John the Baptizer, standing on the banks of the Jordan. And he pointed to Yeshua—*Behold the lamb of God who takes away the sins of the world.*"

A shiver ran through Zera's soul.

Chapter Thirty-Six

Three trumpet blasts sounded outside the Nicanor gate near where Joanna and Miriam sat with Zera, across from the Temple treasury.

A flurry of worry slicked Zera's palms. "The trumpets blare. Has something dire befallen us?" She clutched Joanna's arm.

Joanna glanced toward the gate with a look of annoyance, not alarm. She patted Zera's hand. "It is merely some puffed-up Pharisee. The trumpets call the people to witness his extravagant donation to the Temple."

"I have never seen such a thing."

A pompous Pharisee walked slowly through the gate, leading a donkey laden with bulging burlap sacks. The top of one sack had been left open, and Tyrian shekels glinted silver as brightly as the Temple roof glinted gold.

His servants walked behind the donkey, prodding the hapless beast of burden to keep moving. It shook its head and brayed pitifully but plodded on.

Joanna glared toward the Pharisee. "He has overburdened

his poor donkey for show. Next, he will go to one of the thirteen bronze donation boxes."

The Pharisee stopped at the donation box directly across from where Yeshua stood and shot Him an arrogant look, full of challenge. Without breaking his stare with Yeshua, he reached into the open bag, grabbed a handful of shekels and dropped them one by one into the box.

"The clink of each coin can be heard from here. How can this be?" Zera turned to Joanna.

"The top of each box is a funnel, a trumpet that magnifies the sound and the pride of each rich donor and further humbles the poor when they bring their meager offerings." Joanna's lip curled, and her face changed into a grimace of disgust. "See?"

The Pharisee signalled his servant to cup his hands around the mouth of the box and dropped coins more quickly. The clatter surged to a sound that broke off all talk. The echo lasted well beyond the offering of the last coin. When silence returned, the Pharisee stepped aside and directed his servants to continue to drop coins into all thirteen boxes.

"This is not the first time those men have delayed my son's teaching." Miriam's face was calm, but her voice was edged with the iron strength of a loving, vigilant mother.

Joanna put her hands on her hips. "See how each servant leaves with a haughty lift of his chin aimed at Yeshua and His disciples."

Then, a poor woman wearing a threadbare cloak slowly approached a donation box. She looked around, her face creased by weariness and hunger. She kissed her clasped hands, looked to heaven. Then, she lifted her hands over the donation box. Two sharp tinks quickly died.

When she turned to leave, Zera noticed her face had softened—her worry replaced with a look of peace only the Lord could provide.

Joanna rose. "Zera, stay. Listen. I will come back for you soon."

A disciple brought a stool, and Yeshua sat and looked over the crowd.

His followers watched the woman leave through the gate, then settled to listen to Yeshua teach.

"Beware of the scribes who want to wear long robes and be greeted with respect in the marketplaces ... yet they devour widows' houses ..."

Zera's ears pricked, for she too was a widow whose house had been taken by the scribes to pay a debt.

"You have witnessed many wealthy men put large sums into the treasury. Then a poor widow came and put in two mites, the smallest of copper coins."

The babe inside her kicked. With all her riches gone, how would she provide for her little one? She was left with nothing but the ampule of perfume hanging next to her heart.

"Truly I tell you, this poor widow has put more into the donation box than all those others. For they have given out of their abundance, but she gave out of her poverty. She has withheld nothing and given all she had to live on." Yeshua rose and dismissed the crowd with a blessing.

Zera stood, shook out her cloak, and turned to Miriam. "What trust. That poor widow surrendered her means of survival. May HaShem shelter her under His wings." She helped Miriam to stand.

"Did you not do the same this very morning when you paid the debt for Reah?"

"It is not the same. I gave my last coin to save Reah. And I have Reah with me." The child within kicked again, and Zera's hand went to meet it. "And, I have Barid."

Miriam looked toward Zera's hand. "Oh? And who is Barid?" Her tone held no judgment, only love.

"He is not the father." Zera's heart churned, and her cheeks burned. "I meant to say we have Barid. Reah and I. He has told us we will always have a place to stay and work at his inn."

Something flickered across Miriam's face. She bent and picked up her cloak. "What a caring innkeeper to take in a woman carrying a child. A child not his own." She looked up, a smile in her eyes.

"My kinsman, Theo, has served Barid faithfully for years." Zera's excuse sounded weak even to her. Barid did care for her and she for him, but their love could not be. She must not let her heart deceive her. She was an adulteress. She did not deserve Barid, and he did not deserve to carry her shame. Or the burden of another man's child.

Joanna slipped up beside them, a secretive smile on her face. "Let us return to Bethany without delay. Mary and Martha will need our help serving."

Miriam put her cloak over her shoulders. "In recent years, I enjoy the warmth of a cloak in the late afternoon."

Zera laughed and folded her cloak over her arm. "And the child I carry makes me feel as if I am next to an oven of baking bread."

Joanna took Zera's arm. "Let me help you keep your footing as we make our way down the Temple steps."

After they walked down several steps, Zera turned to Joanna. "I just noticed, you have left your cloak, we must turn back and find it."

"Do not be troubled about my cloak."

Zera gave Joanna a questioning look but said nothing more.

The wind picked up as the three women walked along the road. They came to the withered fig tree Yeshua had cursed and Zera could not help but shudder.

"The tree died so quickly." Joanna's quivering voice made Zera turn.

Joanna was shivering, shaking. Zera placed her cloak over Joanna's shoulders. "Please take this. You must not catch a spring chill. I am still warm, and you are cold."

"I am glad for the child that warms you so well." Joanna pulled the cloak close. "When we arrive in Bethany, I will return your cloak. I have another there."

They reached the road that turned off to Bethany. The widow from the Temple sat off to the side, a beggar's cup in her hand. Many men slowed and dropped coins into it. And women offered her food. The widow nodded and called out a blessing to each one.

Miriam gestured to those who took pity on the woman. "I see my son's teaching has helped one poor widow."

An evil foreboding sent a chill through Zera's veins. Miriam was a widow. If Yeshua were to die soon, who would support her? Yeshua's brethren had all disavowed Him.

Joanna put her arm around Miriam's waist. "Yes, she has food and money, for now."

Zera's spirit lifted. "Yeshua taught us to pray, *Lord, give us this day our daily bread.*"

"And He has provided." Miriam turned and hugged Joanna. "I see that widow has a fine new cloak."

Dusk was descending quickly. In the dim light, Zera only now realized that the widow wore Joanna's finely woven cloak. "Joanna, you saw a need and filled it. It is a gift to see needs beyond your own. I am sure Yeshua is pleased, and I am proud to be your kinswoman." *HaShem, show me what Yeshua has need of and how to best serve Him from my poverty.*

Miriam moved to a patch of grass at the side of the road. "Let us stop here for a moment. Zera. For the child's sake, you must not weary yourself."

The three women sat and drank water. Reah approached,

carrying a small oil lamp. "Lenah and I will go ahead and help the sisters serve. There is no need to hurry."

Lenah joined them and handed Miriam a lamp. "Here, this will be a lamp unto your feet."

"As is every word that proceeds from the mouth of the Lord." Miriam cupped her hand to shelter the flame.

"I have another." Joanna took a lamp from her bundle and lit it from the one in Miriam's hands.

Reah came near. "Does my lady have any other need of me?"

"You must learn to call me Zera, for you are now to be a free woman."

"Slave or free, you will always be 'my lady' to me."

"And you will be a friend forever ... no ... a sister, to me." Zera stood and hugged Reah. "We will come in our own time."

Oil lamps flickered to life all along the road as did the first stars. Zera savored the still of the oncoming night.

"Yeshua and the disciples are coming." Miriam rose. "Let us walk just ahead of the men so we will be protected by their presence."

Zera straightened and the ampule swung and tapped against her heart. Her one thing of value left. Should she sell it? *Watch and wait.* Something within her spirit seemed to speak to her. All the way back to Bethany, Zera sensed the rise and fall of the ampule with each breath she drew.

They arrived at the House of Lazarus, and Lenah brought Miriam to a place of honor at the table of women. Joanna and Zera retired to their usual cookfire where Reah had kept the meal warm for them. They ate quickly.

Zera yawned. "Sleep comes fast upon me."

"I am weary." Joanna spread out their bedrolls and they settled side by side.

"Joanna, may I ask you about your gifts to the work of Yeshua?"

"Of course. Though my husband and I take care not to make a show of our gifts."

"I do not mean to pry. Do you give your offerings to Yeshua or to Judas Iscariot, since he is the one who handles the purse for the disciples?"

Joanna turned to face her. "Though I am not ready to accuse him openly, I am quite sure I saw him once take coins from the common purse and pocket them." The tone of Joanna's whisper was filled with misgiving. "The next time I give an offering, I will not give it into the hand of Judas Iscariot."

"He is not to be trusted. I sense that Judas Iscariot harbors a love of money. The look on his face when he clutches the money sack mirrors Joram's greedy look when he would take jewelry to wager."

"Oh, I am sorry." Joanna's soft murmur faded into sleep.

Zera closed her eyes. *HaShem, You know I am a widow who would give my all. Show me Your will.* She rolled onto her side. With one hand, she caressed the child within and with the other cradled the ampule of perfume.

She drifted to sleep, into a place of dreams. Dreams that were so vivid they feigned wakefulness. To a place where Yeshua stood holding an open scroll, his hair and beard white. He resembled a prophet of old, but He wore no mantle, held no staff.

Zera came close. "Lord, I know You are a prophet sent by HaShem. Where is Your mantle? Your staff?"

"My head has not been anointed before the eyes of men."

The scene shifted, and Yeshua sat on a blazing white throne dressed in a simple white kitel, a finely woven seamless garment. A magnificent white stallion pawed the ground nearby.

"My Lord, I know You are to be a king. You have said Your kingdom is come, but You wear no crown and have not mounted the victor's stallion that awaits You."

"My head has not been anointed before the eyes of men."

The scene shifted once again. Yeshua stood before an altar, dressed in the garments of a High Priest.

"Lord, I do not understand. Are you also to be a High Priest?"

"Have faith. One day, you will come to understand."

"But You have no knife with which to slay the sacrifice. Nor basin to catch its blood."

"My head has not been anointed before men."

"Lord, what am I to do?"

"Watch and wait. And in My Time, you will know."

Zera started awake, her mind haunted with the thought that Yeshua's head had never been anointed as a prophet, priest, or king. If Yeshua were to die, the Pharisees might turn on The Twelve and the women who traveled with Him. Then they may be hunted, imprisoned, or even sentenced to death.

HaShem, please do not let the life of my babe end before it has drawn its first breath.

Chapter Thirty-Seven

Bethany, House of Lazarus

Nisan 12, (April), Wednesday morning

Zera

Zera sat up in the dark, her heart pounding as hard and as fast as the feet of a royal runner. She wiped her face, hoping she could clear the remnants of fear left by her dream. By the soft light from the embers in the cookfire, she could see Joanna sleeping peacefully. Zera wished for such untroubled slumber, untouched by terror.

Zera's vivid dream still plucked at her mind. A dream that she knew had been of great import, but her memory of it had vanished. Was this the same feeling that pestered Theo each day? A single fragment came back to her ear. Yeshua calmly saying, "My head has not been anointed."

Another mystery to ponder. Another riddle to solve. But not now. It was hours until dawn. She closed her eyes and drifted into inconstant sleep.

"Zera. Morning breaks." It was Joanna who shook her shoulder and woke her.

Zera rolled over. These last dreams had been scattered shards of what may have come before. She stood and stretched, then shook her arms and legs. "Why are you in such high spirits?"

"It is two days before the Passover and the Feast of Unleavened Bread. Yeshua and The Twelve are invited to sup with Simon the Leper. His wife invited some of the women to the women's banquet table so she may learn more of Him from us."

"Be still for a moment." Zera shook her head to clear the lingering fog of sleep. "Did I hear you rightly? Simon the Leper? How can a leper host a banquet? Who would come?"

"Yeshua healed Simon a year ago today." Joanna's joy-filled smile took Zera's thoughts from her bothersome dreams. "He celebrates the anniversary of his miraculous healing with Yeshua as his honored guest."

"We have witnessed countless miracles, yet how often are we present to share in the joy of the aftermath?"

Joanna turned to go. "I will tell Martha we will not be here this evening."

"Wait. If people still call him Simon, the Leper?" Zera tried to still the quiver in her voice. "Shall I be forever known as Zera, the adulteress?"

Joanna hugged Zera, stroked her hair, and let her cry on her shoulder. "Be at peace. I have never heard a single soul call you by that name of shame."

Zera stepped back. "Truly?"

"Truly. But Simon wants to be called 'the Leper.' He wants to remind everyone of the miraculous healing Yeshua has bestowed upon him. For twelve years, Simon dwelt as an outcast in the Valley of the Lepers, cut off from the land of the living. Now he lives in a land of abundance. He rejoices with friends at a banquet table flowing with milk and honey and every good thing. This night, Yeshua honors Simon by sharing his table. His name no longer carries shame for him."

"Would that I could put my shame to rest as Simon did."

"You will no longer remember your shame on the day you forgive yourself as fully as Yeshua has forgiven you." Joanna took Zera's arm. "Come with me up to the house. Martha has offered those of us who are going to the banquet a special pleasure. She will provide towels and a private place where we can wash in the nearby spring and let the sun dry our hair and our garments."

They hastened to the spring where Zera secured the ampule in a safe spot under a tree. She joined Reah and Joanna, who were already splashing and squealing in the cool water—like they were young girls once again. When they had had their fill of play, they washed their hair and dressed. Then they helped one another comb and braid their long hair.

Reah finished Zera's final braid and pinned it back away from her face. "My lady, when a ray of sun strikes your amber eyes, they glitter like gems."

A thorn of fear jabbed at Zera's throat and lodged there. "Perhaps I should not go. Simon's guests may be sickened at the sight of my cat eye."

Joanna laughed. "If they are not sickened at the thought of eating with a former leper, your cat eye will not dampen even one man's taste for the rich food served at the banquet."

Zera retrieved her ampule of perfume and placed it back around her neck. Throughout the afternoon, splinters of her shattered dream poked at her memory.

In her mind, she heard Yeshua say, "My head has not been anointed before men." Why was that needed? And if it was needed, why had it not yet been done?

They walked to Simon's house, Joanna and Reah a couple of paces ahead. Zera lagged, sifting her thoughts.

"Simon's house is a mansion." The words spilled from Joanna's lips. "I am told, not only are his banquets memorable for the exotic food and exciting company, but that the opulent furnishings of his home are a sight to behold."

"I will always treasure our simple meals so close to Yeshua at the cookfires in the field. But what an honor to share a banquet with Him this evening." Zera thought back to the poor, starving widow at the Temple and how Joanna had generously given her the cloak. Zera had spent her last mite to redeem Reah. She had no more gold to give.

A new notion seemed to swim just under the surface of Zera's mind. But her flickers of insight vanished as fast as the tiny fish in the spring that flashed silver in the sunlight.

She walked unawares behind the others. *My head has not been anointed before men.*

HaShem, open my mind to Your meaning, Your will. She drew her brows down as if the force of her frown would draw the hidden meaning from her mind.

Come, let us reason together. Zera, what is an anointing? That still, small voice had come to her again.

An anointing was the setting apart of a prophet, priest, or king for the Lord's purposes.

Flashes of her dreams rushed back to her.

And what is needed for an anointing?

Fragrant, perfumed oil. And someone called to carry out the anointing. Zera cradled the ampule at her neck. *Perhaps this perfume was returned to me for such a time as this.*

Zera entered the house and was drawn quickly into the busyness of setting out the meal. The men were led to reclining couches. Yeshua was ushered to the place of honor.

Simon the Leper sat at Yeshua's right hand. "Lord, would You offer the blessing over the bread?"

The room went silent.

Without thought, Zera's hand moved to the ampule.

Yeshua kept still. His face carried no worry, no impatience. He waited in holy silence.

Who is there to anoint My Son?

Now, Zera was sure she had seen with the eyes of her heart. Messiah means Anointed One. She would not let Yeshua enter Passover without an anointing. An anointing as prophet, king, and high priest.

Yeshua looked at Zera and nodded ever so slightly. His face was filled with such love and acceptance that her feet were drawn of their own accord to the place where He reclined.

With one swift movement, she broke open the alabaster ampule and slowly poured the perfumed oil on his head. The glistening joy in Yeshua's eyes matched the tears in her own.

A stunned silence captured the room. A holy silence. A musky, but sweet aroma filled the air. And tinges of ginger and turmeric wafted to Zera.

No one spoke. No one moved. It was as if no one dared breathe. The awe-filled silence seemed to stop time.

Then evil reared its serpent head. The disciples nearest Judas Iscariot began to grumble. One stood and pointed an accusing finger at Zera. "Why was this fragrant oil wasted? It might have been sold for much money and given to the poor." His tone was indignant, but it did not ring with one note of true concern for the poor. Others raised their fists and added their protests to his.

The raised fists reminded Zera of all the fists holding rocks at the Temple. The fear. The sheer horror. Had she misunderstood? Had she once again done something wrong? She sank to her knees. This time, had she failed Yeshua?

Joanna and Reah came forward and helped Zera to her feet and drew her away from her accusers.

For the flutter of a honeybee's wing, Zera did not dare look at Yeshua. But she gathered her courage. One look at the quiet blaze in Yeshua's eyes reassured her of His approval.

Yeshua turned to the sowers of chaos and raised a hand. The room fell quiet once again. A quiet awaiting a just judgment.

"Why trouble this woman? For she has done a good work for Me. For you have the poor with you always and may do them good whenever you wish. But Me, you do not always have. This woman has done what she could. In pouring this fragrant oil on My head, she has anointed My body for burial. Assuredly, I say to you, wherever this gospel is preached in the whole world, what this woman has done will also be told as a memorial to her."

Zera's spirit took flight. Yeshua was pleased with her.

"Let us take our places with the women." Joanna led Zera to the table of women. Reah followed.

Simon's wife stood. "Come Zera, sit at my right hand. You have the wisdom of Esther, who understood the times and purpose for which she was born. You honor our table with your presence."

Zera glanced at each woman and saw approval and acceptance in their eyes. "I never intended to anoint Yeshua for His burial." Zera took her place on the reclining couch next to Simon's wife. "But at least He will not go to His death without the outward signs of consecration as priest, prophet, and king."

Joanna reclined next to Zera. "Even though you did not fully understand your call to anoint Him, HaShem still used your willing heart."

Rhea found a place to sit farther down the table. "Praise HaShem, for Yeshua has restored your good name."

Zera took a small portion of fried fish with olives and tomatoes. The women ate and talked. Zera slowly took bites of her food. When she had finished, she rose and spoke to Simon's wife. "A thousand thanks for your kind invitation. I find I am overcome and need a moment to myself."

Simon's wife rose. "Follow me. I will take you to my favorite place."

Zera went with her to a garden, and Simon's wife pointed down a path. "You will find a beautiful fountain just beyond the grape arbor." She embraced Zera, then took her leave.

Zera touched the empty ampule around her neck and sat on the wall by the fountain. She cried tears of living water. She would not be forever known as Zera the adulteress, but as the woman who anointed the Messiah.

Zera's heart seized, her mouth went dry, and her palms slicked. Yeshua said Zera had anointed His body for burial. His death must be at the doorstep.

Chapter Thirty-Eight

House of Lazarus
Day of Preparation, Thursday morning

Zera

*Z*era stood at the cookfire. "I will stir the embers and heat the flat stone."

Joanna looked up from the *matzah* dough she was mixing. "Zera, have you searched our camp and removed all food with leaven?"

"Yes, I woke early this morning, and not because of the babe I carry." Zera's mind was pulled back to the events of last night, and her hand went to the empty ampule hanging under her robe. "Let me speak aloud the worry that fills our minds. Does not my anointing imply Yeshua's sure and soon death?"

A look of anguish and sorrow spread across Joanna's face. "I wish my mind could read some other meaning. But Yeshua has said it will be so. He warned The Twelve that He will be crucified and die. But they do not seem to hear."

Reah came closer, her arms loaded with garments. She held up a robe. "The time until Passover sifts through the sandglass, and we must be ready. I have taken every garment into the fig grove and shaken each one free of crumbs. I will wash my hands and come help."

"Zera, is the flat-stone heated?" Joanna turned the dough over. "It is time to knead if I am to have the *matzah* finished in the allotted time."

Zera dipped her fingers in water and flicked them at the stone. "The water sizzled, the flat stone is ready." She wiped her damp hand on her tunic. "Please forgive my ignorance, but we were Herodians, and Joram hired more observant Jews to see to our preparations for Passover. What is this time allotment of which you speak?"

Joanna blew a stray lock from her brow. "If the dough is worked too long, it is considered fermented or leavened. I will need you or Reah to help form the flat rounds."

Reah sat next to Joanna.

Zera looked toward the house. "Martha is coming our way. And she looks distressed."

Martha's face was somber, and her stride determined. "We have much to do and too few hands. But the mother of our Lord would speak with the woman who anointed her son for burial." Martha's tone carried no hint of what Miriam may have to say to her.

Martha turned and Zera scurried around the fire, joining Martha as she walked up the hill to the house. Her demeanor did not welcome any questions.

Martha reached the door, opened it, and ushered Zera to an inner courtyard. "I will leave you now, I have *matzah* to make."

Miriam sat on a stool in the sun, mending a garment. "Martha, you are always busy. Busy doing good works for others. I will come in a few moments to help knead the dough."

"Miriam, stay here and pray. You are not needed to make bread." Martha's soft voice was stern, but it cracked in a way that spoke of her love for Miriam.

"If my hands are busy making *matzah*, my troubled mind will be freed to pray for my son."

Miriam looked from Zera to Martha. "And staring at the unleavened bread will keep my mind fixed on Him. For He has taught He is the Bread of Life. And was He not born in Bethlehem, or Beit Lechem, which means the House of Bread?"

Not until Zera spoke with Miriam at the Temple did she consider that even before Yeshua's birth, Miriam had borne trials. Trials because she was the mother of the Messiah.

Martha's face crumpled. "I will never look on Passover or *matzah* with the same eyes again." She went to Miriam and hugged her. Then, she offered a brave grin and pointed to the door. "I will leave you and Zera alone and help Joanna with the day of *matzah* making."

Zera's heart squeezed as if she were the dough kneaded beneath Joanna's hands.

Miriam patted a stool beside her. "Come, Zera, tell me what led you to anoint my son last night?" Her tone was curious, not angry.

"Sometimes I hear this voice inside my head, or ..." She waved her hand and the thought away. "Or maybe the voice is from my soul." Zera's cheeks flamed. Miriam would think she was a madwoman.

"Perhaps you hear the voice of the Lord. But take great care. Not every voice or stray thought comes from the Lord. Yet, I believe I have learned to know that voice. It first came to me when I was a young girl." Miriam picked up her sewing and began to mend.

The kneading of Zera's heart relented. She told Miriam how she came to the decision to anoint Yeshua, the vitriol of some disciples, and Yeshua's confirmation that He was pleased with her choice. "But I meant to anoint Him the Messiah, not anoint Him for burial."

"HaShem speaks to those who listen, even if they do not fully understand. You understood in part, but now you know you have fulfilled His will." Miriam threaded the needle again.

Zera rejoiced. She had listened to the still, small voice. "Yeshua says His sheep know His voice and hear Him. And He and the Father are One." Zera touched Miriam's hand. "What must we do now?"

"We must prepare for His death and burial." Miriam shivered as if the chill running through Zera ran through her as well. "And pray for the friend who will betray Him."

"Yeshua will be betrayed by a friend?"

Miriam handed Zera a threaded needle and a linen towel to mend. "It is foretold by the prophets that the Messiah will be betrayed by a friend."

"Yeshua teaches we must pray for our enemies. I will pray from obedience, but not from my own will." Zera set to mending.

"Is that not the way of it so often? Prayer is a sacrifice of our will to the will of the Lord. You must remember, whoever betrays Yeshua will be someone close, someone He loves as a brother."

Miriam was a woman of strong courage and faith. Zera hoped she would have the fortitude to bear the death of Yeshua with the same bravery as His mother.

Miriam rose and rang a small bell hanging from a pillar in the courtyard.

After a few moments, Emet came running up to Miriam. "How may I serve you?"

"I must send a message to Yosef of Arimathea. Do you know his house?"

"Yes. If you write, I will run."

"No. We must not commit anything to writing. Go to his house and ask that he comes here with all speed."

"I will return with him soon." Emet ran off.

Zera knew there was a question on her face, but she waited for Miriam to see it.

"Yosef bought an unused tomb in a garden on the Mount of Olives many years past. He must make sure it is opened and waits in readiness. If my son dies close to the Passover—" Miriam's voice broke with a sorrow that seemed too heavy for her to bear. She took several breaths. "—we will have need of a tomb that has been prepared."

Mary of Bethany came in with Lenah. Mary kissed Miriam's brow. "My heart breaks for you. Have you any need of us?"

"A blessing on you both." Miriam welcomed their embraces. "You have come in time to go to the markets and purchase burial spices."

"Oh, Miriam." Lenah's voice stuttered over her sorrow. "I well remembered how we rushed to find enough burial spices when Lazarus was taken so quickly. I have already sent servants to the markets, and Lenah and I have begun to prepare strips of linen and the shroud."

Miriam turned the stark white of a Lily of the Valley and dropped to her seat on the stool. "Every year at Passover Seder, I would look at my son and be glad we could together say *Next year in Jerusalem*, as the wish for Messiah to come. But I have known since before His birth that He was the promised Messiah. And there would be a time when we would say, *This year in Jerusalem*."

"And this Passover is nigh upon us." Zera's voice was the quietest of whispers.

"When I heard He had overturned the tables of the moneychangers in the Temple, and angered so many men of power, I feared that this Passover, we would be apart." She shook her head as if she could not believe her own words. "The time has passed so quickly. It seems like merely a year past, He was a babe in my arms. A month past, He was amazing the Torah scholars at Temple." Miriam placed both hands over her heart. "It could have been only a week past, He turned water into wine at a wedding in Cana."

"It seems to me only yesterday He raised my beloved brother Lazarus from the dead." Mary of Bethany bore the same look of awe and wonder on her face as when she had first seen her brother back from the dead.

Miriam took Zera's hand. "But I must face the hard truth. It was the will of HaShem that Zera anoint Yeshua for burial. And that truly happened. Merely last night." Miriam sank to her knees and cried as only a mother can mourn. A mother mourning her firstborn son.

Zera's babe kicked within, and she placed both hands over her belly. She prayed for the child's safe birth and for a long, full life.

Lenah knelt beside Miriam and held her. Mary of Bethany and Zera moved closer to Miriam, and they, too, sank to their knees to mourn with her. A mother whose son had foretold the horrific manner of His death.

Martha came running into the courtyard. She stopped and her face filled with compassion. "Blessed are those who mourn, for they shall be comforted." She knelt, raised her hands over them, and spoke soothing words. "The Lord is my Shepherd, I shall not want ..." The others continued, speaking the psalm as a soft prayer. Zera joined them. "Yea, though I walk through the valley of the shadow of death, I will fear no evil, for thou art with me ... thou anointest my head with oil ... Surely goodness and mercy shall follow me all the days of my life and I will dwell in the house of the Lord forever."

Miriam rose from her knees and sat on her stool. Zera sat beside her. Martha looked to the others. "Let us all leave Zera with Miriam." Martha's tone was kind and calm. She sounded as gentle as her sister.

Mary of Bethany smiled through her tears and took Martha's hand. "Come, sister, there is a Passover Feast to prepare."

Chapter Thirty-Nine

House of Lazarus

Nisan 13, Thursday evening near sunset

Zera

Zera spent the day with Miriam, fasting and praying. The other women joined them in turn, offering warm hugs and shared tears.

"This morning when Yeshua took His leave of me ..." Miriam's voice stumbled then crumbled as if it had been dashed against sharp rocks. "He said ... My son said ... 'This morn is the last time we share bread until My work is finished.'" Resting her head against Zera's shoulder, Miriam cried out. "My son, my son ... my beloved son ... would that I could take Your place."

Zera's heart shattered, sharing the agony of another mother. Miriam. A chosen mother. A mother chosen for this moment in time.

Miriam straightened and picked up the mending in her lap. "Zera, do you know where Yeshua will be this evening?"

"I do not. Knowledge of the place The Twelve share the meal tonight has been kept secret, even from them."

"I am glad." Miriam stood. "The wicked friend who betrays my son will not know of the place beforehand. Yeshua has safeguarded the last supper with His disciples."

Miriam's voice was steady, accepting. She did not weep. Her eyes did not brim. It was as if her well of tears had run dry. Spent. Empty. Like the broken ampule that hung around Zera's neck.

"I must rest before the ordeal set before me begins." Miriam rose, took a step, and faltered.

Zera stood and took her arm. "You are weak from fasting. I will walk with you to your chamber."

They walked at the pace of a snail creeping in the midday sun. Miriam offered Zera a weary smile.

When they reached Miram's chamber, Zera settled her on the raised sleeping pallet and smoothed back her hair. Over the course of one day, Miriam had aged. Aged so profoundly, she seemed an old woman. Zera kissed Miriam's brow.

Miriam placed her hand on Zera's babe within. "You will be such a good, loving mother."

"I will need to fill the shoes of both mother and father for this little one."

"The Lord will provide."

The baby kicked against Miriam's hand. She laughed and her eyes dimmed to a distant place. "New life ..." Her voice faded to a contented whisper. "I remember the birth of my son, Yeshua. Such a joy."

Zera could barely press back tears. "I will depart so you may rest."

"Please wake me if there is news." Miriam closed her eyes.

Zera slipped from the chamber, left the house, and walked toward the field. The sun sank into a blood-red sky slashed by blades of gold. Zera shuddered and gathered herself. She must be strong. Strong for Miriam, for her friends, for her babe within. Her friends had held her up when she was shamed and alone. She reached the cookfire where Joanna and Reah sat on a log speaking quietly. "Any news?"

Joanna shifted, making a place between them. "Yosef of Arimathea has come."

Zera looked back up toward the house. "Miriam will want to speak with him, but I loathe to wake her."

Reah patted the log. "There is no need. Yosef has sent word to his servants to ready the tomb. He will stay at the House of Lazarus until morning."

"Joanna, why would he not want to be in Jerusalem?" Zera sat between Reah and Joanna.

"Yosef believes word from the disciples about the fate of Yeshua will come here first." Joanna gestured toward the house. "And Theo has returned and Lazarus is safely hidden."

Zera rose. "I would greet Theo."

"You have been fasting with Miriam. You must break the fast for the sake of the babe." Reah motioned for Zera to sit back down and handed her a *matzah*.

"I will eat on the way to see Theo at the house."

"Stay. Be at peace. Yosef and Theo have need to speak in private. They make plans to shelter the disciples in diverse places, if needed. Though I do not believe Yeshua would sanction it, some of His disciples may offer resistance when He is betrayed."

Zera's heartbeat throbbed in her ears. "We must be as wary as serpents, but as harmless as doves. We must plan what we are able, then stand firm. Stand with faith in Yeshua. Stand with faith in HaShem who sent Him to dwell in the midst of us." *Lord, what more will befall us before the sun next sets and Passover begins?*

"Look, Theo comes." Reah pointed up the hill.

Theo hobbled toward them, leaning heavily on his crutch.

Zera hurried to embrace him. He put an arm around her and sighed. A sigh that seemed to carry the weight of worry of all those who waited at the cookfire. He stepped back and eyed Zera with a smile. "I have only been absent a short while, but I believe the babe has grown."

"Perhaps. And the babe kicks more strongly. Most often at night." Zera rubbed her back. "Come, Theo, sit with us. You are weary with well-doing."

They joined the others. Joanna prepared some warm wine. Zera shared with Theo the happenings of the last days. Her dreams before she felt compelled to anoint Yeshua. The harsh judgments from some of the disciples. Yeshua's defense and praise of her. And the shock of His revelation that she had anointed Him for burial.

A war of emotions played across Theo's face. "That He has declared His death yet again overwhelms my spirit with sadness. But your anointing of Him has swept away your shame, and makes my heart overrun with gladness."

Zera pulled the rock from her waistband. "Yet, I still carry this rock."

Joanna brought the warmed wine. "Have you carried that rock since the day you were accused at the Temple?"

"Yes, it is with me always."

Reah looked at Zera with a mixture of sympathy and surprise. "I never knew you carried that rock—such an unceasing accusation. I pray one day soon you will cast it far from you."

Clashing sentiments colored Theo's countenance. "It is no light matter to surrender feelings one has carried for so long.

Even when they no longer serve. Or perhaps never did. But HaShem will show you when and where to leave that remembrance rock."

"I hope for that day." Zera tucked the rock back at her waist.

Joanna offered warm wine to Theo.

He smiled but waved it way. "Though it is not law but tradition, I fast with the firstborn sons. We must all sleep now. Yosef and I are certain there will be news before daybreak. And we must be ready for whatever is to come." Theo lay down in his bedroll and spread his cloak over himself, pulling it up to his chin.

Reah and Joanna prepared their bedrolls. Zera spread the fire so it would burn down to embers.

"What if we hear nothing before morn?" Zera stretched and yawned. Sleep was coming fast upon her.

Theo rolled to face her. "If Yeshua is accused and arrested, any trial before the high Council of the Sanhedrin must be conducted after break of day. Trials at night are not legal."

"The growing child within is sapping my strength. I am so weary I can barely move to my bedroll."

Reah helped Zera lower herself to the ground. "My lady, Joanna and I will bed down farther away on the warm side of the fire. Where you sleep is too cold for those of us not with child."

Zera stared at the stars flung across the heavens. The moon high overhead was round and bright. Wonderstruck at the handiwork of the Creator, peace gently enveloped her. How could anything evil come to pass on such an awe-inspiring night? She drifted into dreamless slumber.

Something vexed Zera's rest. A sound. The snap of a twig. Zera tensed. Someone was near. She peered through slitted lids. Emet was quietly taking a tunic from Theo's bundle. He crouched and headed toward Zera. Just as he passed her, she grabbed his ankle. He covered his mouth with the tunic, muffling his gasp. He knelt by her. "My lady, it is not what you think."

"Why have you need of a tunic?" Zera sat up.

"There is a young man in the fig grove who has need of it."

"Why?" Zera could see Emet's cheeks flush even in the dim light.

"Because he seems terrified. He shivers with cold ..."

Emet looked down.

"And he is naked."

Chapter Forty

House of Lazarus

Nisan 14, Thursday, middle of the night

Zera

Zera kept her voice low. "There is a naked man in the fig grove?" She wanted to cover her ears and not hear what came next.

Theo stirred, eyes opening as Emet tucked the tunic under his arm and continued speaking.

"He is like me. A young man, beardless, but of an age to bear witness. He was so frightened he could not speak."

Theo stood and glanced toward the others still sleeping. "Emet, I will go back with you." Theo rummaged in his bundle and pulled out a cloak. "He will need this as well."

Zera rose. "Both of you, take great care. This young man may not be of sound mind. Or perhaps he is possessed and has come to seek Yeshua to cast out his demon."

Emet shook his head. "He is of sound mind, But I see fear in his eyes. Something has left him terrified."

"Come. We must go find this young man before he wanders away." Theo left with Emet.

Zera poured watered wine into an iron pot and placed it in the embers to warm. The wine began to simmer, and Zera ladled some into a clay cup.

Theo returned with a young man. He was now clothed in Theo's spare tunic and cloak. His teeth chattered, and his whole body trembled.

Theo helped the young man to the log, and they both sat.

Zera brought the warmed wine to him. "You are safe here. This will warm you."

He put the cup to his lips and drank the whole of it. She took his empty cup, filled it once more, and brought it to him.

Theo's worried eyes and mouth were drawn tight. "He still shivers."

Zera brought one of the blankets from her bedroll, taking care not to disturb Reah and Joanna, who had not wakened despite the noises surrounding them. She placed the blanket across the young man's shoulders.

For a moment, he noticed her and smiled, then lapsed back into himself.

Zera and Theo sat quietly with him on the log. The man of mystery seemed more boy than man. And he stared blankly into the embers.

Theo's worried face softened with compassion, and he eased his arm around the young man's shoulders.

A notion came to Zera of how they might draw him from his daze. "Young man. The man who sits beside you would understand your terror all too well."

Theo glanced toward Zera. A question on his face.

"I know this because Barid told me. In the days after your

brutal beating, you did not speak. And you stared with empty eyes."

Theo looked at the young man. "Zera speaks truth. I know what it is to be affrighted beyond reason. So fearful only a numbing daze seems safe. But I have learned, it is healing to speak of it with others."

A spark of attention came into his eyes.

Emet came running, Yosef trailing behind.

Zera put a finger to her lips. Emet came close to the log, reached into his cloak, and drew out a large *matzah*. "You must be hungry."

The young man took it and began to eat.

Yosef stepped into the light from the fire. "I can see you have had a great fright. But if we are to help you, we must know the cause of your trouble."

The young man still stared blankly.

Theo gestured to himself. "I am called Theo. How are you called?"

The young man scrubbed his face with his hand as if he could wash away his terror. "I am named John Mark. But call me Mark."

Yosef sat beside Mark and patted his knee. "You are from Jerusalem. Your mother is a friend of mine. As was your father." He looked to the others. "She is a follower of Yeshua."

Theo shifted to face Mark. "Can you tell us how you came to be naked?" His voice was soft, calm, without demand.

Zera noticed Reah had awakened and was listening from her blanket. Yosef gestured for Zera to take his place. She sat next to Mark. "Tell us what has happened so we may help."

"I ... was seized ... arrested ..." He buried his head in his hands.

Zera placed a hand on Mark's back. "You are safe here.

Perhaps you could begin with the first thing you remember of this night."

He looked up, the daze had vanished. "I swept our upper room, helping my mother prepare for guests. Later, Yeshua and his disciples partook their meal there." Mark stopped speaking, and stared blankly, seeming caught in a fishnet of tangled thought.

Zera took great care to keep her own panic from her tone. "And did your guests leave in peace?"

"Yes. Their manner was loving. The way of close family, even brothers."

Zera glanced at the others. Something dire must have happened after Yeshua left. "And then?"

"I helped my mother, and the servants set the room to rights. It was nearing the midnight watch when I went to my chamber and fell asleep." Mark's eyes changed, dark terror dawned again on his face. "A great pounding at the door made me look below from my chamber window. Torchlights. Temple guards. A mob wielding clubs, thirsty for blood."

Zera wanted to cry out, but she must keep silent. Any disturbance now may shackle his tongue.

"I rushed downstairs wearing only my loincloth. The door shook and the hinges weakened at the sound of each blow. I sent my frightened mother to the back room."

Mark's face hardened and he stopped speaking.

HaShem, please give him the strength to go on.

Yosef brought Mark a cup of water.

He took a sip. "When I opened the door, Judas Iscariot barged in with Temple guards and demanded to know the whereabouts of Yeshua. When I told him I did not know, he glared at me with the sharp eyes of a vulture." Mark's chin began to tremble. "I said Yeshua was not there, but Judas swooped in and shoved me to the ground. At his order they ransacked the whole house, breaking pottery, strewing linens, and overturning furnishings." He licked his lips and drank more water.

"When they found no one, Judas told the Temple guards that he knew where Yeshua would go. And they hastened out the door."

No one moved. No one spoke.

"I ran to my mother and told her to bolt the door behind me and open it only when she heard me call."

Now that Mark had again found his voice, words spilled from his lips.

"I had to warn Yeshua that He had been betrayed and made my way the Garden of Gethsemane. But a great multitude with swords and clubs already surrounded Him."

Mark swatted at a fly buzzing near his ear. "Yeshua turned to Judas, His face full of loving sorrow, and mourned that Judas had betrayed Him with a kiss.'"

Joanna sat beside Zera. "I knew Judas was a thief. But now he has betrayed Yeshua. May the name Judas Iscariot forever be joined with the title *traitor*."

Zera flashed a look at Joanna. A warning to keep still. She turned to Mark. "Please, we would hear more."

"The Temple guards moved to lay hands on Yeshua. Peter drew his sword and struck the servant of the high priest, cutting off his right ear." Mark shuddered and his hands shook. "There was a flood of blood, and his ear was hanging by a thread of flesh."

Zera's heart stuttered and would not keep a steady beat. The servant of the high priest had been attacked. Maimed. Had Yeshua and the disciples all been slain by the sword? Was the man in front of her the sole survivor?

Yosef leaned toward Mark and put a hand on his shoulder.

"You have suffered a great shock. Be still a moment and carry on when you are able."

Mark took several deep breaths. "Yeshua told Peter to put up his sword and warned that all who take up the sword will perish by the sword."

"What compassion. Even when seized by His enemies, our Good Shepherd cares for His sheep." Yosef's voice and face were filled with admiration.

"Yes. None were slain. Then a most wondrous miracle was wrought. Yeshua touched the servant's ear and it was made whole. The man's hand went to his ear, and he began to tremble. Many in the mob crowded around the Temple guard to confirm what they could not believe their eyes had just witnessed. The ear was whole and clean, though blood still stained his tunic."

Zera's heartbeat steadied. "The mob witnessed Yeshua's power and His mercy. Surely, He must be safe."

"Yeshua then turned to the chief priests, the Temple guards, and the elders, who had come for Him. He reminded them that every day He was in the Temple courts teaching peacefully. But they seized Him and led Him away."

Zera gasped and began to weep. "I have just awakened to a nightmare."

"The disciples scattered like sand in a windstorm." Mark's tone was one of brewing anger. "Not one of them had the fortitude and faith to stay and be seized with Him."

Theo hands trembled, and he clasped them together. "I know what it is to suffer a beating beyond bearing. At the threat of such pain, I fear I would have failed Yeshua and fled along with the disciples. Mark, what more do you know?"

"The disciples escaped, but I was so stunned I did not move. A guard caught me by the arm, but I wrenched free. As I ran, the guard caught hold of my loincloth, but I kept running, and it pulled away."

"How did you come to be here in the fig grove?"

"My only thought was to find a place of safety. My mother and I have oft been guests at the House of Lazarus. I knew here I would be sheltered. I was so afraid, I ran without thinking, without stopping, for the whole two miles from Jerusalem. "I ran ..." He flushed and looked away. "As bare as the day I was born."

"How terrifying. I am glad you escaped the guards." Zera's voice trembled, tears filling her eyes.

Mark's face darkened like a thundercloud. "The disciples left Him alone. Amidst a brood of vipers."

Zera hugged herself as if that would keep her heart from being cleft in two. "Yeshua went willingly with His enemies—a sacrificial lamb to slaughter."

Chapter Forty-One

House of Lazarus

Nisan 14, Friday before dawn

Theo

"Where would the Temple guards have taken Yeshua?" Theo rose from the log.

Mark stared into the fire, silent and still.

Yosef swung his cloak onto his shoulders. "To the Temple stockade. We must go at once to Jerusalem. The guard at the Jerusalem gate may know me. If so, for a token of thanks, he will let us in the guard's side door before daybreak."

Emet rubbed his eyes and stood. "I will fill the waterskins."

Reah rose from her blanket. "And I will gather provisions. You may have a long wait before you learn of Yeshua's fate."

Theo picked up his crutch. "Mark, where would the disciples go?"

Mark looked at those around the cookfire. "I do not know. They fled in every direction."

Yosef slung the strap of his leather travel sack across his shoulder. "Think back to anything you may have heard."

"When I was helping serve, I heard the one called Peter say he would never deny Yeshua. The others all agreed they would never forsake Him. But Yeshua said Peter would deny Him thrice before the end of the cockcrow watch."

"It seems Yeshua knew even Peter would flee." Zera helped Reah wrap the packet of provisions for the two men. "Would the disciples return to your home?"

"No. Judas Iscariot was last with them there. The disciples would assume that spies watch my house. And they would never place my mother in danger." His face took on new panic. "My mother. I pray nothing has happened to her. I must go home." He stood and turned to leave.

Zera grabbed his arm. "Mark, you have been seen and almost captured. If you return home, danger may follow you to your mother's door."

Theo gestured for Mark to sit back down on the log. "We will go to your mother's house and see that she is unharmed." Theo judged the path of the full moon. "It is well past the cockcrow watch. Yosef, what think you? It seems to me there is little more than an hour until first light breaks."

Yosef looked up. "Yes, it seems so. But be at peace. I doubt Caiaphas can summon a quorum of the Council to conduct a trial. The members of the Sanhedrin will refuse to come on Preparation Day."

Joanna offered each of them figs from a small basket.

Theo did not take any figs. "I am a firstborn. I shall fast until the Passover begins."

He glanced at Yosef. "You are the eldest here, how should we proceed?"

Yosef looked to the heavens, swaying in prayer, consulting

HaShem. "Theo and I will travel without delay and the women should come at daybreak."

"Miriam." Theo's mouth went dry. "Someone must wake Miriam and tell her the dreadful news."

"She will want to be near her son." Zera rose from the log. "Reah, please go awaken Lenah, who is like a daughter to Miriam. Lenah will gently tell Miriam the devastating tidings of Yeshua's arrest."

Zera offered a *matzah* to each one at the fire except Theo. "Take, eat. Bread for those who must hurry to their destiny." She turned to Theo. "If you and Yosef go ahead, how will we find you? Jerusalem brims with Passover pilgrims."

"We will bring Emet." Yosef took a second matzah. "When we know the meeting place, we will send him to wait at the Nicanor gate and bring you to us."

Theo, Yosef, and Emet bid farewell and hastened to Jerusalem. Theo hobbled along the Roman road, grateful for the full moon and his crutch. The guard knew Yosef and let them through the side gate before daybreak.

Yosef hurried them through the dim streets. They came to a large two-story house. Yosef stopped at the carved cedar door that bore fresh scars.

"See where the mob bashed their clubs against this door." Theo knocked and waited.

Silence. A long silence. The breathless silence of an empty house. Theo tugged at Yosef's sleeve. "Mark told his mother not to answer the door. Announce yourself."

"It is your friend from Arimathea come to sell you my finest goods and bring news of a young man you know."

Theo pointed to the side of the house. "Move there where you can be seen from an upper window."

Yosef looked toward the East. "We are near the House of High Priest Caiaphas. There are many torchlights in the courtyard and a warming fire. People must have been there for hours. Once our duty is completed here, we must hasten there and find out what has happened."

The door opened a crack. "Yosef, is that you?" A woman's whisper.

"Yes. Mark made his way safely to us in Bethany."

Mark's mother flung open the door pulled Theo and Yosef inside. Emet barely slipped in behind them before she closed the door.

"Praise the Lord for His mercy on me, a widow. Yosef, what has befallen my son?"

Theo stepped forward. "Mark was watching when Yeshua was arrested and was seized. But he wrenched free and escaped." Theo's cheeks burned. He had spoken out of turn, blurted his thoughts again. He was more like Peter than he would care to own.

Yosef smiled and gestured toward Theo. "This is a follower of Yeshua, my friend Theo. He has told you our news. Have you any of your own?"

"Come, let us sit." Mark's mother ushered them into the front room.

When Theo stepped aside, Mark's mother gasped. "And who are you?"

Emet flashed his most endearing smile. "I am Emet, and I am always hungry."

Mark's mother's eyes opened wide, and she laughed the laugh every indulgent mother shares. "My son has the same complaint. Go that way to the kitchen. I am sure we can find a cure. Tell Anna, the cook, to feed you." She turned back to Yosef and Theo. "Please forgive the disorder." She gestured to clusters of damaged chairs, many with broken legs. "These chairs on the right are still sound."

Theo arranged several chairs, and they sat. "Mark told us about the attack on your home."

Mark's mother waved a hand. "Praise HaShem, it was only broken things and not broken people."

Yosef rested his hands on his knees and leaned forward. "Please tell us what has happened to Yeshua, the disciples, and anything else that may help us to rescue them."

"Nicodemus came less than an hour ago and told me all he had learned. Caiaphas called a meeting of select members of the Council—only those who seek to condemn Yeshua to death. Many gave testimony, but no two agreed. Caiaphas then sought a confession."

Anger sparked in Theo's chest, and he pounded his crutch on the stone floor. "Under the Law of Moses, a man cannot be compelled to testify against himself."

Mark's mother nodded. "And Yeshua wisely remained silent."

Yosef shook a fist. "I would have relished overturning the tables at their sham of a hearing."

"Yeshua bested them at all their questions, but then He declared He was the Son of Man whom they would see coming with the clouds of Heaven."

The look of disbelief and dread dawning on Yosef's face made Theo's palms slick.

"What then?" Yosef pressed his hands to his temples.

"The high priest tore his clothes and declared Yeshua guilty of blasphemy. He has been sent to Pontius Pilate at the Antonia Fortress to await Roman judgment."

Yosef groaned. "What sin, what evil leaven has infested the Council?"

Theo wiped his palms on his sleeves, jumped to his feet, and gathered his courage. "The sun has risen. We must go to Pontius Pilate." He turned and called. "Emet, we go."

Emet returned with a young girl. "First, you must hear this servant of Caiaphas."

She stepped forward. "I am a new-born follower of Yeshua. Emet told me you seek news of the disciples."

Theo's breath caught. Could this girl be a spy for Caiaphas? "What news have you?"

"I am sure I saw one of the Twelve warming himself at the courtyard fire. I asked him if he knew Yeshua, but he denied knowing Him. If he would have owned that he was a follower like me, I would have helped him hide. I asked twice more, and he denied Him twice more—each time looking more frightened and suspicious of me."

Theo's spirit settled. The girl was no spy, her witness rang true. "Do you know this man's name?"

"He spoke with the accent of Galilee. Someone near me said his friends call him the Big Fisherman."

"That would be Peter." Theo tensed, bracing for bad news. "Do you know where he is now?"

"When I finished serving, he was gone." She looked over her shoulder. "I must go before I am missed and struck with the rod for my laziness."

"Blessings, sweet one." Emet waved a farewell.

"Keep your mind on the task before us." The vexation in Theo's voice made Emet look toward him.

They went out into the streets once more. People bustled around them on every side. They had not walked far when a procession of Temple guards, chief priests, and elders blocked their way. They prodded a man whose hands were bound behind him with their staffs.

Emet jostled for a view. "Yeshua has been beaten. Even His face is bruised and bloody."

Theo's stomach roiled. Emet's raw whisper unleashed a

slew of memories—the fiery darts of fear and pain and outrage Theo had nursed since his beating so long ago.

Yosef stepped in front of one of the priests. "Where are you taking Yeshua?"

"To Herod, by order of Pontius Pilate. Now let me pass." The priest's arrogant tone was only surpassed by the scathing look on his face.

"First, tell me, what was the verdict of Prefect Pontius Pilate." Theo could hear from the Yosef's tight tone he was trying to keep some semblance of respect.

"The Prefect found no fault in Yeshua. But what would a Roman know of the Law of Moses?"

The pride in the priest's tone made Theo want to trip him with his crutch. "Priest, why would Pontius Pilate order an innocent man to be taken to Herod?"

"Pontius Pilate learned Yeshua was from Galilee. Thus, he sent him to Herod for judgment from the tetrarch over that territory."

Yosef stepped away from the procession and let the priest pass.

Theo grabbed Emet's forearms. "Run to the Temple, wait at the Nicanor gate, and bring the women to Herod's Palace."

Emet darted through the growing crowd and disappeared.

"Many years past, I sent your friend Samuel of Shechem to Herod." There was a hopeful note in Yosef's tone. "That trial was conducted by Caiaphas, Pontius Pilate, and Herod. The same three men who today judge Yeshua. And a just verdict was rendered."

Theo waved to Yosef signalling him to follow the slow-moving procession. "Samuel told me the three rulers would have tripped over Justice and left her shattered at the judgment seat. But cunning Queen Herodias intervened and acted as Samuel's advocate."

"But there is no one to advocate for Yeshua." Yosef walked past Theo and through the wide, deep arch leading to Herod's Palace.

Theo hobbled slowly. The royal stable was built within the wall of the arch, and Yosef waited for Theo on the far side. Theo, his strength flagging, stopped to rest where horses were hitched just outside the stable.

Yosef cupped his hands at his mouth and kept moving away with the crowd trailing Yeshua. "I will go ahead and secure a place close enough for us to hear."

Theo called after him. "We must pray Herod's heart is moved to mercy."

"That Old Fox has no heart." Theo knew that voice. The charioteer, Auriga Maximus. "And not the smallest bone in Herod's body is moved to mercy. Unless it serves his greedy purposes."

Auriga stood in the shadows grooming a magnificent black stallion. There was something eerily familiar about the way he used a brush in each hand to groom the horse.

Theo drew closer. A wave of memories crested, then crashed over him. A memory of his childhood friend—a small boy running through the colonnades of the Winter palace in Jericho. A memory of that friend—a young charioteer grooming his first horse. Then, that friend running for his life.

Now, ten years later, Theo realized that same friend stood before him. But now he had a long blond beard and hair past his shoulders.

Theo's knees turned to wet wool, and he grabbed his crutch with both hands.

"Auriga, my friend, do you not know me?"

Chapter Forty-Two

Theo

Theo stared at Auriga. "Can you not look past the cripple and see your lost childhood friend?" Theo's chest tightened, his breath bound.

Auriga stopped brushing the stallion, turned, and studied Theo's face.

"We were great friends, once. Before I was a cripple. Before you came to be known as Auriga Maximus."

Then Auriga's face flooded with joy and wonder. "Etan, is that truly you who stands before me?" Auriga's voice cracked and trembled.

"Yes. But I have only now remembered that was my name. For more than ten years, I have been called Theo. I was beaten nigh unto death, and my memories were driven from my mind. Now, some memories come back to me without warning."

"My only friend has risen from the dead." Auriga threw his arms around him. "Etan, you were well named. You are *enduring.*"

Theo tensed and pulled away. "Years past, I saved your life and your first victor's purse. And for this I expect nothing. But I hold one trespass against you. And for that I expect an accounting."

"Speak. I would make amends."

"I cannot reconcile my memories of you and your well-known heroics in the hippodrome with your sins against Zera."

"We chose to follow our passions."

Theo saw no remorse on Auriga's face, heard no repentance in Auriga's voice. Theo's blood simmered, a warm flush of fury heated his cheeks and fueled his angry stare.

Auriga flinched. "From the moment Zara and I were caught together, I have regretted my betrayal of her trust and the threat to her life."

"She is no longer known as Zara, but Zera. You expect me to forgive the unforgiveable much too readily." Theo's fury loosed his tongue. "Zera overheard you quarrel with Joram after your victory in Caesarea. I cannot fathom how the friend I once knew could plot the seduction and murder of a woman."

"Ever since the day I sold my honor to Joram, the gods have turned against me." Auriga grabbed Theo's shoulders. "Please, Etan, you must believe me. Joram played me false. Zera had three times asked him for a divorce, and I desperately desired my freedom. Joram told me he wanted Zera to be caught in adultery, so he could demand a divorce and keep her bride-price. He vowed he would stay silent about her adultery and set me free. He did neither."

"But—"

"Please ..." Auriga held up a hand. "I never, never, knew Joram plotted Zera's death by stoning so he could steal her inheritance to cover his half-witted wagers."

Theo's blood still simmered. "What did you think would become of a disgraced, divorced woman with a cat eye?"

Auriga looked away and pressed his brow into the stallion's withers. After a long moment he turned back to Theo. "I was a wealthy slave and fond of Zera. Expecting to be freed, I harbored a foolish fantasy that she would still want me, and as recompense I could provide a comfortable life for her as my wife."

"Your wife?" Theo could not keep the disbelief from his tone.

"Slaves cannot marry, but freed men can."

Theo's blood cooled, and his spirit calmed. "If it is any comfort, Zera has forgiven you even though she believes you were plotting her murder."

"Etan—"

"The man called Etan is a murky memory. Call me Theo."

"Theo, how can this be?"

"Zera is a follower of Yeshua, the man whose life now stands in the balance before Herod. He teaches us to forgive not only our friends, but also our enemies. Especially our enemies."

"And you, Theo, the only man I ever called friend—will I ever earn your forgiveness?"

"You can never earn forgiveness."

Auriga looked as if he had been struck in the stomach.

"Forgiveness is a gift. I choose to forgive you." Theo clasped arms with Auriga. "It is the forgetting part of forgiveness that may take some time."

"My friend, we have time." Auriga stepped back and crossed his arms. "A few moments ago, you said you saved my life. But I know nothing of this."

"I remember hiding with three other men, high on the cliff at the last blind curve on Jericho Road. One spotted you, walking alone. He knew you won the final chariot race and would have the victor's purse. They decided to set upon you, steal the gold, and kill you. I remember their laughter brimming with bloodlust."

Auriga shot him a look of shock. "Stealing is one kind of evil, but murder is a seven-fold worse abomination. Why were you with them?"

"I do not know." Theo's mouth went dry. "But they were Zealots who sought to overthrow their Roman oppressors. You came around the bend into the tight curve. They were three, I was one. I did the only thing I could to save you. I harnessed the strength of my own terror and shouted."

"I heard someone shout *Run, Auriga, run*. And I fled. Even though the bandits chased me, I outran them. I have never forgotten that kiss with death. Your call rang out across the cliffs, but the way your voice echoed, it could have been anyone."

"Auriga, did you not wonder when I did not return to Jericho?"

"Your close kinsmen went to search for you. They returned with your bloody, shredded cloak found many miles away on the outskirts of Jerusalem. They showed the cloak to your uncle, the overseer. He always believed you had been attacked by a wild beast." The stallion whinnied and Auriga gentled him. "Do you remember anything more?"

"No. But I have a nagging sense that I knew the bandits."

Auriga raised a brow, and his face flashed the unspoken question.

"I know deep in my bones that I was never one of them."

"Theo," Yosef called out, coming back to the gate. "We cannot get close enough to hear, and Herod has already begun his audience with Yeshua."

Auriga stepped forward. "Follow me to a side enclave in the audience hall. A place where neither of you will draw attention, but you can see and hear what fate befalls Yeshua."

Just as Auriga finished speaking, Emet brought Joanna, Reah, and Zera to Theo's side at the stable.

Zera glanced toward Auriga, gasped, and stepped back pulling the other two women close so they shielded her rounded belly.

Auriga's face blanched when he spotted Zera, but then it became a marble mask.

The women clung to one another, their faces drawn and distraught.

Joanna turned to Yosef. "We rushed ahead. Lenah went to wake Miriam and will bring her soon."

"Come." Auriga led them up several steps to a secluded area between two pillars in the audience hall. "I will leave you now but be on your guard. Whenever Herod is involved, life often takes dangerous turns."

Auriga left and relief flooded Zera's face. Did Zera truly believe that Auriga had not seen that she carried his child? Did she not notice Auriga's eyes narrow when he first caught sight of her or see he had glanced her way several times?

"We can see above the crowd." Zera looked at the others. "Where is Yeshua?"

Yosef peered around a pillar. "When I left before, He was standing near Herod, but now He is not there." Yosef's face was grim.

Herod stood and arranged his fine blue mantle over his long red and yellow striped tunic, making sure that the long fringes fell neatly from the sleeves. He straightened his dark blue turban, lifted an arrogant chin, and looked down his long nose at the crowd. "I was exceedingly glad when Yeshua was brought before me. I have asked Yeshua many questions. But no answer has been given. I have asked for a sign, a miracle to prove he is the Messiah. And no miracle has been worked. He dares to mock me." Herod clapped his hands three times. "Behold what becomes of such a man."

A nervous laugh ran through the crowd and an evil foreboding crawled from Theo's gut up into his throat.

Yosef, his hand trembling, grabbed Theo's arm. Zera gasped and took his other arm.

Herod's soldiers brought Yeshua, dressed in a rich scarlet robe, back to the hall.

"Now you look like a king. Call down an angel and set yourself free."

"If you are a miracle worker, show us a sign and we will believe."

The mockery of the soldiers brought Joanna and Reah to tears. Theo felt Zera tighten her grip and heard her grind her teeth.

"Who do you think you are?" Herod's tone was full of scorn. "You cannot even save yourself." Herod stepped within three paces of Yeshua and glared. But it seemed he could not bear the weight of Yeshua's stare. Fear flickered across Herod's face. "Guards, take this false Messiah back to Pontius Pilate."

Theo whispered to Zera. "Herod would not know the true Messiah if he tripped over him in the road."

Zera put a finger to her lips. "Take care. The walls have ears."

Theo turned to Emet. "Run back to the Nicanor gate and bring Magdalena and Miriam to us at the palace of Pontius Pilate."

Theo and Yosef ushered Zera, Reah, and Joanna through the palace courtyard teeming with a loud crowd on the brink of a riot. They neared the open iron-barred gate that led into the palace courtyard of Pontius Pilate. The priests and elders stood in a perfectly spaced row, straight and stiff like the tall bars of the gate.

Zera put her hands over her ears, but that would never block the priests' hostile shouts against Yeshua.

"Yeshua is a blasphemer."

"He is a false Messiah."

"If Yeshua is not sentenced to death, his treasonous teaching will bring the wrath of Rome down upon all our heads."

The throng pressed in around Theo. "Yosef, I do not see Yeshua."

"The Romans would take Him inside the palace to Pilate. But the priests will not go in and become unclean for Passover."

A nearby man turned to them. "As he did this morning, Pontius Pilate will come out to the priests as a sign of respect for the Passover feast."

Several paces before they reached the gate, Emet brought Miriam and Magdalena to them.

Theo shouted. "We must stay together. Women link arms, and we men will protect you."

Just as they reached the gate, a trumpet blared, and the Roman guards began pushing the heavy gate closed.

Miriam lunged forward. "My son. I must not be parted from my son."

Zera pulled her back. "It is not safe for you to be parted from us."

The iron gate clanked shut and the Roman guards bolted it with a long iron rod. The crowd fell silent as if suddenly aware they were penned in the courtyard, at the mercy of the Romans.

Miriam reached through the bars toward the empty portico before them. "My son, my son, where have they taken you? I am here."

Miriam's grief-stricken moans seemed to blanket the crowd with a shroud.

Where had they taken Yeshua? A chill crept forward from the back of Theo's neck and clawed its way down into his heart. Yeshua spoke of His burial when Zera anointed His head. Theo shivered at the memory. By the setting of the sun, Yeshua might already be dead.

Chapter Forty-Three

Antonia Fortress, Palace of Pontius Pilate

Nisan 14, Friday near the 2nd Hour

Zera

Zera watched Lenah gently guide Miriam's outstretched arms back through the iron bars.

"Zera, you were wise to keep Miriam outside the gate." Yosef put his face between the bars and scanned the courtyard. "There are guards posted on the perimeter. If violence erupts, those inside have no way of escape."

"Look." Zera grabbed the gate. "There is a gap in the curtains at the back of the portico. Someone is coming."

Pontius Pilate strode onto the wide platform, dressed in a fine white toga with the broad purple stripe reserved for Roman rulers. He was known to be arrogant and ambitious and brutal.

Pilate raised his right hand. "As a sign of the magnanimous

mercy of Rome, it has become a tradition to release a prisoner at Passover each year."

Hope in her heart fluttered to life.

Miriam clutched Zera's arm. "Surely HaShem will spare my son just as He spared Isaac—the son Abraham was commanded to sacrifice."

Zera held Yeshua's desperate mother.

Yeshua, beaten and bruised, his hands bound, was brought out and shoved next to Pontius Pilate on his right.

Zera gasped and her babe punched upward, stealing her breath.

"Here is Yeshua of Nazareth. A man I have found to be without fault. And Herod has not charged him with any offense that warrants death."

The crowd jeered, and Pilate took a step back. A flicker of confusion crossed his face.

The Roman guards surrounding the rowdy crowd drew their swords. At the sight of the swords, the crowd went still.

Zera whispered in Theo's ear. "Even a pagan like Pontius Pilate can see our Yeshua is a good man."

Yeshua slowly looked over the crowd as if He could read the souls of each one. Some wept. Other faces were stony. A reflection of their hate-filled hearts.

Pontius Pilate lifted his left hand, and another bound man was dragged into place on his left. "Here is Barabbas, a murderer and a thief." The rough-looking man did not even look up. "I give you a choice."

Miriam clutched the gate. "Choose Yeshua. My son is a righteous man."

Her cry was swallowed by the screams of the frenzied crowd. "Barabbas. Barabbas. Give us Barabbas."

Lenah placed a hand on Miriam's hand. She turned and fell into Lenah's embrace.

Zera heart slammed like a battering ram into her breast-bone. "Where are the masses who will cry out for Yeshua? The multitude who wanted to crown Yeshua king only six days past?"

Theo's eyes flashed, his mouth drawn tight. "The priests and elders have packed the crowd with their faction and stirred up false fears."

The thunderous cries for Barabbas grew into a frightening frenzy. Pilate looked as shocked by the rampant hatred aimed at Yeshua as Barrabas looked hopeful that he would be freed. Pilate stared with a fierce frown at the loud crowd until their cries died. "Release Barrabas."

The guards unbound him, and he slunk away.

Pontius Pilate turned to his Praetorian Guard and pointed to Yeshua. "Two of you, punish him."

Yeshua held His head high.

Zera saw no surprise on His face. No anger. No fear. What she saw instead was a look of peace, a peace beyond all understanding.

Yeshua turned to Pontius Pilate with a look full of compassion.

For the blink of an eye, Zera was sure she saw a flicker of uncertainty on Pontius Pilate's face. But it was quickly replaced by the confidence of an arrogant patrician. He left the portico and retired inside the palace.

Two guards brought Yeshua down the steps and into the courtyard. One guard tied Yeshua to a post in the center and bared His back. The other guard uncoiled the whip and laid the first stripe.

Miriam cried out with every crack of the lash. She sank to the stones beneath her, crumpled on her side, and wrapped her arms about her legs.

Zera sat on the ground and eased Miriam's head onto her

lap. Joanna, Reah, and Lenah knelt by them, praying for mercy for their beloved Yeshua.

Finally, the cutting lash was silent. A sorrowful silence lingered.

"Mourning melts my heart." Miriam pushed up and looked at Zera. "But I must stay with my son in His pain, not lapse into my own."

Zera helped Miriam stand. She clung to the gate.

Yeshua was hauled to His feet, His face ashen, His body slumped. The guards dressed Him in a royal robe of scarlet. A soldier had plaited a crown of thorns and pressed it onto His head. Then they brought Him back to the portico and shouted, "Hail, King of the Jews."

Pontius Pilate returned, stared a long moment at Yeshua, then lifted his hands. "Behold the man. Know that I find no fault in him."

The chief priests and elders chanted, "Crucify him. Crucify him."

Pilate sneered at them. "You take him, you crucify him, for I find no fault in him."

Several priests shouted protests.

"You know that we cannot."

"By our law, he deserves death."

"He made himself the Son of God."

"But he has done nothing wrong under Roman law." Pontius Pilate looked upon Yeshua with what seemed fear born of suspicion. Pagans believed in sons of the gods.

One chief priest stepped forward. "If you let this man go free, you are no friend of Caesar. For whoever makes himself king, speaks against Caesar."

Pilate's face flooded with fear.

Yosef put a hand on Zera's shoulder. "All of you, be ready to run. The priest has just accused Pontius Pilate of treason."

"You say he made himself King of the Jews." Pilate gestured toward Yeshua. "Should I crucify your king?"

The priest gave Pontius Pilate a smug smile. "We have no king but Caesar." Others took up the chant.

Yosef's shoulders slumped. "Pilate will not have the courage to counter such a cunning political threat."

Miriam dropped to her knees. "Lord, be with my beloved Yeshua in the valley of His death."

"Bring me a basin and water." Pilate gestured and a servant scurried away. "I am innocent of the blood of this just man."

Yosef raised a hand as if to teach a fine point of law. "Pilate cannot absolve himself. He is the only one present with authority to issue a sentence of death. We Jews lost that right many years past."

The servant returned with a pitcher and basin.

Zera's anger sparked. "Pilate makes a great show of pouring the water and washing his hands." Her stomach soured. "He surrenders to the evil chaos surrounding him."

Pilate dried his hands. "I will write the charge to be nailed to the cross." His lips were drawn as taut as his tone. He turned, took the wooden sign and quill handed to him and wrote the charge.

Zera's sight darkened at the edges, and she reached for Yosef. "What charge can Pilate write for a man he has declared innocent?"

"This is to be nailed to his cross."

The chief priest took the sign from Pilate's hand.

Pilate crossed his arms. "Priest. Read it aloud to the crowd."

"The Prefect of Rome has written in Latin, Greek, and Hebrew. 'Yeshua of Nazareth ... The king of the Jews.'" The priest's face flushed blood-red. His tone plunged from victory to defeat, and he pushed the sign back toward Pontius Pilate. "You must write Yeshua *said*, 'I am king of the Jews.'"

"I have written what I have written."

Theo pulled Emet close. "Go to Herod's palace. Find Prima the dovekeeper. Tell her to send word to Shechem that those who follow Yeshua must pray. Yeshua is to be crucified this very day."

"I will run as fast as a hare chased by a hungry dog." Emet sprinted into the crowd.

The gates were pushed open and most of the crowd departed. But Miriam did not move. "I will wait and walk with my son to His cross."

Zera drew Theo close. "Look there, lingering near the gate is the man called Barabbas."

The man skulked by, and Theo grabbed his arm. "Why have you not run away? Are you going to the cross to gloat? To see Yeshua die in your place?"

Barabbas looked up and met Theo's eyes.

Theo let go of Barrabas as if he had touched a red-hot branding iron. "I know this man." Theo's face went gray. He dropped to his knees and fainted dead away.

Chapter Forty-Four

Palace of Pontius Pilate

Nisan 14, Friday, nearing the 3rd hour (9 am)

Theo

Paving stones dug into Theo's back. He opened his heavy eyes and waited for the spinning to ease.

"Theo, you fainted." Zera's hands cradled his head. "I will put a cup of water to your lips."

"Firstborn fast ..."

Yosef leaned over Theo, worry lines like cracked desert sand deepened around his eyes. "A tradition, not law. At least take some water."

Theo sat up and drank. He looked over and saw Miriam sitting with Reah and Lenah on a low wall, praying.

Theo got to his feet. "Where did they take Yeshua?"

"Pilate's soldiers have not brought Yeshua out from the palace." Yosef handed Theo his crutch. "He will be taken to Golgotha—the Place of the Skull."

At the thought of crucifixion, Theo's stomach felt sour and heavy. "I must sit."

Quaking from head to heel, Theo took the arms of Zera and Yosef. They led him to the low wall, away from the others, and sat on either side of him.

Yosef drew *matzah* from his pack. "You must eat if you would keep vigil with Yeshua in His hours of suffering."

Theo forced himself to eat some of the flat, dry bread. It did nothing to soften the heavy lump in his stomach.

A curious look dawned on Zera's face. "Before you fainted, you said you knew the man called Barabbas."

A leaden lump of sadness stuck in Theo's throat and stole his voice. He could only nod.

Zera moved into the nearby shade. "How came you, a good man, to know a thieving, murdering Zealot?"

Theo took a deep breath. "He was the leader of those who beat me and left me for dead."

Yosef stood and shook his fist. "How galling. The man who maimed you forever is pardoned in place of our loving Yeshua."

"There is more ..." Bitter bile surged upward, burning in Theo's chest. "Barabbas is my kinsman."

Zera's hand went to her throat. "Then am I—"

"No, you and I share my mother's bloodline. Barabbas and I are kinsmen through my father." The burning made his throat tighten. He could barely croak. "The other two who beat me were his brothers."

"Those bloodthirsty bandits." Yosef spat on the ground. "Do you remember why you were with them?"

"Because I was young and witless and did not heed the warning of Zera's father."

A patient quiet fell upon Yosef and Zera. A quiet that held no judgment. A quiet that encouraged an unburdening of the truth.

"Zera's father warned me that my kinsmen were drawn to a violent faction of Zealots. That night, they asked me to help keep watch over their flocks."

Zera stood and rubbed her back. "But why were you beaten?"

"To pass the time, we climbed onto the cliffs. When I realized my kinsmen were going to rob a man coming down from Jerusalem, I called out and he escaped." Theo took a sip of water and a deep breath, hoping to still his shaking hands. "They tore at me like wild boars."

Zera touched Theo's arm. "Do these memories help or hinder your quest to forgive your enemies?"

A sudden knowing prickled across Theo's neck. "It is HaShem who has appointed this time for me to remember."

Rough voices and hobnailed footsteps made Theo look up. The soldiers escorted Yeshua from the palace. He struggled under the weight of His cross, dragging it over the stones. He strained with every step.

Sorrow and horror ran through Theo's veins.

The crown of thorns left Yeshua's cheeks streaked with blood. But His face bore a calm perseverance, an acceptance of His impending death that was beyond the smallest splinter of Theo's understanding. He looked from Yeshua to Miriam. Her face mirrored the face of her son. "How is it that you both bear this crushing burden with such calm courage?"

"Like Yeshua, I have yielded my whole heart, my whole mind, and my whole soul to the unfathomable will of HaShem." She reached toward her battered and beaten son. "It is written that the Messiah will suffer and—*by His stripes we are healed.*" Miriam spoke through the strangled sob of a mourning mother. "I know not how His agony will bring healing. But I will suffer with Him and trust HaShem. Or I will go mad."

As soon as Yeshua reached the road, a great multitude followed Him, some wailing, some praying.

Zera moved into the crowd, gesturing for Theo and the others to follow. "Come here with me, beside Yeshua so He can see we have not abandoned Him in His hour of darkness."

After a few steps, Yeshua fell to his knees.

Miriam ran through a gap in the crowd, stumbled, and reached toward Him. "My son, my son. I will not leave You to face this trial alone. I am with You in Your suffering until the end. Only death will part us."

Theo knew Miriam's haunting vow would stay in his ear all the days of his life. Yeshua looked up and met His mother's eyes. Something unfathomable happened between them. It seemed to Theo as if each drew strength from the other.

Yeshua struggled to rise and trudge on, bent under the weight of the cross.

The soldiers pushed the crowd back and Theo brought Miriam to the women. Zera embraced her and Miriam gently laid her hand on Zera's rounded belly. "I remember the first time Yeshua ever fell." Miriam's voice sounded faraway as if she spoke to no one and everyone. "He wanted so badly to walk. His hopes were much greater than His little feet and His balance."

She took a deep breath and began to walk faster. "Every mother wishes, after that first fall, that her child would never fall again. But she knows that he will. And every mother wishes to be there to soothe every disappointment, every wound."

Yosef leaned close to Theo. "Yeshua has fallen twice more. He may not live through the walk to Golgotha."

Reah pointed. "Look, Miriam. The Romans have forced another Jew to carry Yeshua's cross for Him."

"May the man who carries my son's burden be blessed a thousand-fold." Miriam walked with more determination.

The crowd left the city and came to the place of execution outside the wall, at the base of the hill called Golgotha.

Zera gasped. "The way the morning sun strikes the rocks, the image of a skull is unmistakable."

A wave of revulsion ran through Theo's veins. "It is about the third hour."

"The time of the morning sacrifices." Zera shivered and hugged herself. "I have never been in this cursed place."

"Nor I." Theo gestured to lone olive tree on a rise nearby. "Let us take Miriam there, up on the rise. There are some boulders where we may rest. It is a ways off from the horror, but Miriam can sit in the shade of the tree and be assured that Yeshua will see that she is here." The group followed Theo and settled on the boulders.

The soldiers put Yeshua's cross on the ground. He dropped to His hands and knees. They went to lay hold of Him, but He waved them away. Then He crawled onto His cross and stretched out His arms and legs.

Theo's heart pounded, his breath seized, and his hope shattered. "HaShem, how can You allow this murder of Your Messiah? Your prophet?"

Yosef put His arm around Theo. "Just days ago, Yeshua wept, 'Oh Jerusalem, Jerusalem, the city that kills the prophets.' Yeshua told us He came up to Jerusalem to die, but my ears refused to hear."

"My son goes to His death like a lamb to slaughter—sure it is the will of His Father." Miriam flinched each time the hammer struck an iron nail. And with each flinch Theo's stomach wrenched into a tighter twist.

The centurion signaled, and the soldiers raised the cross, dropping the end into a deep hole with a heartrending jolt. "Father ..." Yeshua's voice carried over the crowd with the strength of a prophet of old. "Forgive them, for they know not what they do."

Theo felt as if one of the heavy, iron nails had been driven through his soul. He had fought granting forgiveness, hardened his heart—even as he prayed for his enemies each day as Yeshua taught. Even when he desperately desired his own miracle but did not dare ask. Even when he knew forgiveness of others was the way to eternal life.

Yeshua's eyes were soft and gentle, filled with compassion for His tormentors. In the midst of His agony, Yeshua had forgiven those who crucified Him. He had shown Theo the face of pure forgiveness.

Theo fell to his knees. He would echo Yeshua's prayer. "Father ..." Theo lifted trembling hands and voice to heaven. "Forgive those who crippled me even though they meant to leave me dead." A warm tingling ran through him, settling on his shoulders like a comforting mantle on a cold night. His heavy yoke of hate began to vanish like a vapor.

Quarrelling soldiers cast lots for Yeshua's garments. Theo rose, his prayer interrupted, cut off by gambling greed.

Zera came to him shaking her head. "Much untold woe has come from the casting of lots."

Theo hugged her. "Praise HaShem, you have been set free from a life as wife of a mean-spirited gambler." He looked over her shoulder and spotted Barabbas lingering in the shadows. Theo took leave of Zera, strode toward him, and spoke with a gentleness that would have pleased Yeshua. "Are you here to pray for the man who dies in your place?"

Barabbas, an accursed look on his face, met Theo's eyes. "Yes, for I am wholly guilty, and Yeshua is wholly innocent. But I also come to pray for those crucified with Him, for that center cross was meant for me." Barabbas gestured to the two men on crosses now hoisted into place on either side of Yeshua.

A Certain Mercy

A deluge of dread washed over Theo. "They cannot be ..."

"Yes. The others are my brothers."

Chapter Forty-Five

Golgotha, The Place of the Skull
Nisan 14, Friday at the 6th hour (noon)

Theo

Theo studied the faces of the crucified men who crippled him. "They have suffered such beatings." Tears blurred his vision. His heartbeat drummed a merciful dirge for the men he had just forgiven. "Had you not told me they were my kinsmen, I would never have known."

"I deserve to die with my brothers."

Theo brought his hands together. "Pray for them who suffer such pain."

"HaShem would never hear my prayer." Barabbas ripped the neck of his tunic.

At the sign of mourning, Theo took his hand. "Barabbas, look on them. Yeshua, in the center, I came to love, but those on either side, I came to hate. Yet, they all have endured humiliation and torture for hours." Theo raised his hands. "HaShem, have mercy. Bring a swift end to their anguish and agony."

"You pray in my stead? You pray for those you hate?" Barabbas looked as if he could not fathom such a baffling thought.

Theo's heart pounded against his breastbone. Pounded like a hammer driving the final nine-inch nail of hate from his chest. His soul lifted like a dove taking flight.

Theo drew in his first peace-filled breath since his beating. Even from the cross, Yeshua had taught him to pray for his enemies.

A crowd of mockers stopped on the road at the foot of the crucifixions. Their shouts carried across the hills.

"Save yourself."

"If you are the Messiah, come down from your cross."

From a hill, a few paces beyond Barabbas, the chief scribes and elders cried out.

"Let him come down from the cross, and we will believe in him."

Then Theo's kinsman on the cross at Yeshua's left hand turned toward Him. "Are you not the Messiah?" His tone cast stones of contempt. "Save yourself. Save us."

"Do you not fear HaShem?" The man crucified at Yeshua's right hand called out to his brother. "We receive the wages due for our deeds, but this man has done nothing wrong." His voice was reverent, repentant. "Yeshua, remember me when You come into Your kingdom."

The noise of the crowd died. "Truly, I say unto you, today you will be with Me in Paradise."

Barabbas sobbed and dropped to his knees. "Praise HaShem. One of my brothers has been redeemed."

Darkness descended, covering the land. Theo checked the high sun, shrouded in a smoky haze. It was near the sixth hour.

A Certain Mercy

A cutting wind blew across Golgotha, and Theo went back to his friends.

The darkness persisted, then deepened. For hours, time seemed to slow. No one spoke. Many stared at the blood-soaked ground at the foot of the crosses. By the ninth hour, the mockers had left, sure the blackened sun was a portent of evil. Others feared it was a sign of oncoming judgment.

Yosef came to Theo's side. "The winds whip wildly across the rise. Perhaps, we should take the women away."

Miriam stood and faced them. "I will not leave my son until He draws His last breath. As long as I am in His shadow, I am safe."

Zera came to Miriam's side. "And we will not forsake you."

Lenah, Reah, and Joanna added their 'amens.'

The disciple, John, walked toward them.

Yosef stepped in front of him. "Where are the other disciples?"

John glanced toward the elders partway up the other hill. "I do not know. I have seen no one, heard nothing. I have been at the foot of Yeshua's cross since morning."

"John, in this darkness, I can no longer see my son's face."

He held out a hand toward Miriam. "Yeshua asks for you."

She took it, and he led her down the hill.

Theo and the others followed at a respectful distance.

Barabbas moved closer to his unrepentant brother's cross, and the man spat upon him. Barabbas walked to the foot of his penitent brother's cross, lifted his hands, and began to pray.

As Theo came near, he heard his penitent kinsman say to Barabbas, "I pray you will find a new way. The way of Yeshua."

John brought Miriam close to Yeshua's cross and stepped back.

Yeshua's chin was slumped onto his chest. Miriam lifted her arms toward Him and murmured something. He raised his head and gazed at His mother with such tenderness, such love. The love of a faithful son. A love that did not wane even in the midst of His pain. "Woman ..."

The word was filled with respect, yet He had not called Miriam 'Mother.'

Yeshua drew a labored breath and turned His head toward his disciple, John. "Woman, behold your son."

Miriam nodded to John, and he came forward beside her. She placed a hand on his sleeve.

Yeshua looked at John with a steady, trusting gaze. "Behold, your mother."

John placed an arm around Miriam, pulled her close, and nodded.

Now Theo understood. Yeshua had relinquished Miriam, His mother, to the care of another. John would care for her, take her into his own home, love her as his own mother.

John brought Miriam, overwrought and shuddering, back to the boulders. He took his cloak and placed it over her, for the day had grown cold as night.

Theo and the others joined them.

At the ninth hour, Yeshua cried out, "*E'lo-i, E'lo-i , la'ma sabach-tha' ni.*"

Zera turned to Yosef. "I did not hear all the words. Does Yeshua call for Elijah?"

Yosef shook his head. "No. He said, '*My God, My God, why have You forsaken Me?*'"

Theo's stomach pitched like a ship on the Great Sea. "Does Yeshua believe HaShem has forsaken Him? Was all His suffering for naught?"

Miriam looked up at them, her eyes glistening. "Yeshua knows He is not forsaken. He draws strength and comfort from the first words of a psalm of King David. In my spirit, I have prayed the psalms with Yeshua for hours."

"I thirst." Yeshua's parched voice carried on the wind.

Someone nearby poured *posca*, the sour wine of commoners, on a sponge from the sea. They bound it to a branch of hyssop and lifted it to His lips.

Yeshua pushed up and cried out. "It is finished." He breathed His last breath.

The ground trembled beneath their feet. Rocks broke off and fell from Golgotha.

Many fled the quaking earth like scurrying rats. Nearby, the ground cracked open and fissures spread in all directions.

Yeshua's faithful followers fell to their knees and clung to one another, praying.

Confusion flared in Theo's mind and set the cauldron of panic in his stomach simmering. Were those who stayed with Yeshua destined to die with Him today? *Lord, please let me live in the blessed freedom of giving and receiving forgiveness. The path of mercy Yeshua has just shown me.*

The centurion, awe in his eyes, but fear on his face, raised his lance and pointed it like an accusing finger toward the chief priests and elders. "The earth moves. Truly, this was the Son of God."

A Roman messenger ran up from the road to the centurion. "You are to speed their deaths. Break their legs and take the bodies down before the Jewish Feast."

Theo stared up at Yeshua, grateful that His agony was finally relieved. Now His face was a picture of peace.

A soldier broke the legs of Theo's kinsmen. Their ghastly groans curdled his stomach. The soldier moved toward the centurion. He pointed his iron hammer at Yeshua. "Shall I also break these legs?"

"No. He is dead. And we dare not break the bones of the Son of God."

"Son of God?" A look of fear invaded the soldier's face.

"We must not awaken the anger of a powerful god. But we must certify to Pontius Pilate that this man is dead."

The centurion lifted his lance and thrust it into Yeshua's side. At once, blood and water flowed from the wound. "He is undoubtedly dead."

Theo's thoughts scuttled between his throbbing temples. He went to Zera and drew her aside. "Yeshua promised my repentant kinsman on His right that he would be with Him in paradise this very day. He was too weak to last past sunset, but my kinsman could have lingered for days. With broken legs, they will die today. Yeshua knew."

"Yeshua knew every jot of our lives." A new knowing seemed to dawn on Zera's face. "Could it be He also knows every jot of our lives after death?"

"We cannot begin to fathom all He knew."

Zera placed her hand over her child within. "We must cling to the hope that we will see Him again at the Resurrection of the Dead on the Last Day."

"But Yeshua said He would be raised on the third day. And He promised the thief that they would both be in Paradise today. It is yet another of His baffling riddles. A mystery that plucks at my mind and plagues my soul. How could Yeshua—already dead—raise Himself from the grave?"

Chapter Forty-Six

Golgotha

Nisan 14, after the 9th hour (3 pm)

Zera

Z era looked up at the three crucified men. She must cling to the precious memory of Yeshua in life and scrub away the painful picture of Him in death. "Theo. What will happen to the bodies?"

"By custom, they are left up as a warning. But because the Passover feast begins at sunset, the Romans conceded to take them down. They will throw them into the Valley of Gehenna."

Yosef joined Zera and Theo. "You must pray for me. I go to Pontius Pilate and plead for Yeshua's body."

Theo looked toward the crosses. "It is dangerous to openly align yourself with a man condemned by Rome."

Zera followed Theo's gaze. A glimmer of hope lightened her chest. "Look, off to the side, that centurion is Longimus from the Inn of Three Centurions. He must be known to Pilate."

Yosef walked toward him. "And Longimus declared Yeshua the Son of God. We will pray that HaShem moves him to help us."

Zera and Theo followed.

Longimus caught sight of Zera. She braced her child within and picked her way across the rocky ground. They must be quite a sight—a richly robed man with a silver-streaked beard, a cripple with a crutch, and a woman great with child. "Please, sir, a word."

"Speak, woman."

"We seek permission to bury Yeshua, but Pontius Pilate must give his leave."

"Woman, why come to me?"

"Because you are Pilate's trusted centurion. Because the Lord revealed to you that Yeshua is the Son of God. And because above all, it would be pleasing to Yeshua's Father in Heaven."

"How do you know this? Show me some sign."

Zera gazed at the dark sky and prayed. *HaShem, lay Your hand on my heart, give me the thoughts to pray. And lay Your hand on my lips, give me the words to say.*

While Zera was still looking up, the black sky suddenly cleared, the low sun blazed bright, blinding their eyes.

"There is your sign." Zera met the centurion's eyes just as her own eyes were struck by a ray of golden light.

Longimus studied her face. "Your cat eye. Are you a prophetess, then?"

What should she say? If he thought she was a prophetess, would that give her sway? Then she remembered the still small voice. "At times, I hear the voice of the Lord."

Longimus jerked his chin toward Zera. "Was this man you seek to bury the father of your child?"

Perhaps if Longimus thought her child was left fatherless, he would take pity. "This child has no one to call father."

Longimus pointed to Yosef. "Come with me to Pilate."

Yosef hastened away with him.

John brought Miriam to the foot of the cross.

She looked at one of the soldiers. "Please, sir, I would hold my son. I beg you, grant a mourning mother a peaceful parting."

Zera's breath caught at the sight of the soldier's stern face. But when Miriam reached up toward Yeshua with open arms, the soldier's face softened. "Every soldier here has a mother who may grieve for him one day."

He nodded to the other soldiers who pried the nails from Yeshua's hands and feet.

John helped Miriam sit on the ground, and the soldiers gently laid Yeshua across her lap. She touched the blood on His cheek and removed the crown of thorns. A thorn pricked her finger, and her blood mingled with His. "Since the moment the angel Gabriel told me You would be the Son of the Most High, You have also been blood of my blood and bone of my bone." Miriam stroked His hair and rocked Him. "My child, my child. Your suffering is finished."

Zera felt as if her spirit had been crushed by a great grinding stone. A mother was never meant to live longer than her children.

The soldiers took the thieves down.

Yosef returned with a linen garment and a shroud draped over his arm. He hurried to the cross, showed a parchment to the soldiers. "Pilate has granted me permission to bury this man's body."

The soldiers left, carrying the other two bodies to Gehenna.

"Magdalena and Miriam, come with me. I must show you where we lay Him."

John and Yosef covered Yeshua with the burial garment. They slowly lifted Him from Miriam's lap.

Zera could see Miriam was loath to let her son go. She leaned toward Yeshua, her fingers stretched out for Him.

Lenah helped Miriam to her feet, and they walked arm in arm behind the men who carried Him away.

"Reah, please go back to Bethany. Help Mary and Martha with any guests until they have no further need of you. Then, send word to Barid to come for you."

"Yes, my lady."

A servant came to Theo and Zera. "Master Yosef begs you stay with him in Jerusalem. The followers of Yeshua should stay in small groups outside the city, not camp in the field in Bethany. To gather together may bring the wrath of Rome to the door of the House of Lazarus. I will wait on the road."

Zera, suddenly aware of the silence, looked about. The soldiers had left. Their friends had taken their leave. Only she and Theo remained. The sun was fast sinking behind the black skull of Golgotha.

"Come, Zera, let us depart."

"I would have a moment alone."

"I will wait with Yosef's servant."

Zera walked to the cross where Yeshua had been crucified. She turned and looked to the west, where the sun was buried in a sea of dark red sky. Then, she looked to the east, where a fiery blood moon rose over the land.

She sank to her knees and the empty ampule brushed against her chest. A keening cry clotted in her throat, smothering her next breath, her next word, her next sob. Silencing her mourning but not her gut-wrenching agony. A simmering anger seeped into her sorrow. Joram had rejected her. Auri had betrayed her. And now, when she finally felt safe, even admired — Yeshua had abandoned her. She would forever be alone.

HaShem, I still have vivid dreams of Yeshua as priest, prophet, and King. Has this all been a mirage in a dry desert? How does one keep faith in the absence of understanding?

Hold fast to the Truth you know.

Zera lifted her hands. "Yeshua was the Messiah, to that Truth I will cling." She touched the cross. Yeshua's blood anointed her fingers. A fiery rush ran through her, and a revelation flashed across her mind and heart and spirit.

"Beloved Yeshua. You pardoned my sins. How can I, in my pride, cling to my own condemnation?" With trembling hands, Zera took the remembrance rock from her waist sash. "I no longer raise this rock above my own head. I forgive myself the sins You have already forgiven." She lovingly placed the rock at the foot of the cross and left—her soul finally set free.

Chapter Forty-Seven

Jerusalem Mansion of Yosef of Arimathea
Nisan 16, The beginning of the Third Day after sunset,
Saturday evening

Zera

Zera reclined at the banquet table between Theo and Yosef. Yeshua was three days dead. For three days, she, Theo, and Yosef gathered for meals, but spoke little and ate even less. For three days, doubts loomed large, and faith shriveled like the cursed fig tree. For three days, fear made the disciples scatter and hide.

Flashes of Him came back to her. Yeshua saving her from being stoned—writing *zera, new beginning* on the ground. The look of love and approval He gave her when she anointed His head. Watching Him perform countless miracles that could come only from the power of HaShem.

"When Night gives way to Day, we women, who never

deserted Him, will go to the tomb and complete all that is required so He will rest with all proper respect."

Theo took Zera's hand. "Must you go to such a gruesome place of death? Think of the child you carry."

"Yeshua prophesied that I anointed Him for burial. He praised me in life, now I would be worthy of His trust in death and help complete the anointing."

Tears ran into Yosef's beard. "The tomb has been sealed."

Zera pushed up to sit. "But why?"

"The people were sorely afraid and railed against the priests. They took the earthquake, the darkness, and the blood moon as signs that Yeshua was a true prophet sent by HaShem after four hundred years of silence. The priests pleaded with Pilate to secure the tomb."

"And Pilate agreed, knowing the burial was not completed?" Disgust dragged through Theo's tone.

"Yes. A centurion stopped me on the road and demanded I take him to the tomb. A rope was suspended across the burial cave and closing stone. It was affixed with seven clay seals of Rome. Three great seals were stamped on each side of the entrance and one on the face of the stone. A *castra* of sixteen men was set to guard the tomb."

Yosef's stoic countenance cracked. "Then the women can do nothing at the tomb until the guards have left." Yosef rang a bell. "Zera, you must try to eat, for the sake of the babe. And Theo and I must keep up our strength. For only HaShem knows what the followers of Yeshua will face in the days to come."

The servant woman brought a platter of matzah and chopped olives mixed with garlic and onions. The aroma sickened Zera. She pressed a sleeve to her lips.

The servant woman moved the platter away. "It was the

same for me when I was with child. I will add ginger to your watered wine."

Yosef uttered a blessing over the unleavened bread, lifted a piece to his lips, then set it back down. "Yeshua was nailed to the cross at the time of the morning sacrifice and died at the time of the evening sacrifice. He hung there dying as the Passover lambs were slaughtered."

A morbid quiet descended over the meal. No one ate. No one drank.

The woman servant twisted a towel. "Master, when Yeshua died, the Temple veil was torn from top to bottom, exposing the Most Holy Place."

"That veil is so thick and strong that not even horses tied to either end can tear it apart." Yosef put a fist to his chest. "Surely it was the hand of HaShem. A warning of coming judgment."

A loud pounding at the door seemed to confirm Yosef's warning. Fear gripped Zera's racing heart, her sour-sick stomach, and her uncertain soul.

Yosef glanced at his trembling servant and rose. "I will go."

The pounding grew louder, stronger. "Open."

Yosef opened the door. Torchlight flared in the dark.

"I am Malchus, servant of High Priest Caiaphas, sent to search for the disciples who plot to steal Yeshua's body and claim He is risen. The body that was entrusted to you."

Yosef stepped aside. "My servant will show you and your men the house and the grounds."

Malchus signaled the six guards who entered. "Go. I will stay here so no one can help a hidden disciple flee." He turned to Yosef. "If the body goes missing, you and your friends will face judgment."

Theo pushed up from his couch and stood. "Who would risk their life to steal a body? Who would die for a lie?"

Yosef gave Theo a wry smile. "Yeshua is dead, the tomb is

sealed. If the body is missing, Malchus would have to believe in miracles."

Malchus gasped. Zera watched his hand move to his right ear. The ear Mark told them was cut off and Yeshua healed in Gethsemane.

The guards returned empty-handed and Malchus waved them out. "I see my men have found no one. For your sakes, I pray Yeshua's body remains in the tomb."

Yosef closed the door after him. "The wicked priests know Yeshua was our Messiah. It seems they are the ones with the faith and fear that He will be raised."

⸻

Mansion of Yosef of Arimathea
Nisan 16, The Third Day, Sunday before dawn

Zera

A breeze blew across the portico of Yosef's mansion, where Zera stood gazing at the sky. No crack of light. A sky dark as her dreams through the sorrow-filled night. She could scarce believe it was the third day since Yeshua died, though she had witnessed His hours of suffering with her own eyes.

"Zera."

She turned toward the voice. Lenah stood on the road near the gate of Yosef's house. There were several other women with her. "We go to the tomb. Call Yosef and Theo to come roll the stone away so we may enter in, sit by Him, and complete those things that are proper."

Zera went to the gate. "Lenah, the tomb has been sealed and a Roman guard set before it."

"Even so, we will go to the tomb, sit, and mourn." Lenah started on the way.

Zera hastened to come alongside her. "Surely the Romans will not deny us our grief."

While they walked, a brilliant dawn broke—far too uplifting for this downcast moment.

"Look toward the garden, Lenah. There is a glowing light."

Lenah dashed ahead and peered through the gate.

Zera picked up her robe and ran. "The tomb is open. It has been desecrated. The soldiers are gone." Anger and sorrow twisted a knot in Zera's throat. She opened the gate.

Lenah rushed to the tomb and stepped to the threshold, vanishing into the glowing light.

Zera and the others hung back and clung to one another. Watching. Waiting in fearful silence. Lenah did not emerge.

"Has our Magdalena been struck dead?" The woman's wail made Zera's stomach tighten.

"I cannot bear to see what further disgrace has been heaped upon His body." This woman's whisper set Zera's stomach churning.

The others went to the gate to wait.

Zera clung to her empty ampule, her heart pounding, pounding, pounding, with each step she took closer to the tomb.

After what seemed a night and a day, Lenah stepped from the tomb. She walked toward Zera, her face aglow. Then, her starry eyes looked heavenward.

"What did you see?"

"Praise the Lord, the tomb is empty." Lenah's voice was soft, and she sounded dazed. "I thought I saw the gardener, but He called my name. I have seen Yeshua. I must find the disciples." She ran off before Zera could even utter another word. Had Lenah's sorrow driven her to the brink of madness?

My sheep hear My voice, and they know Me.

The voice of Yeshua.

Zera's heart quaked and her limbs trembled. How could she hear the voice of the dead prophet so clearly? Had she lost her own reason?

Hashem, show me the truth.

A true prophet's foretellings are always fulfilled.

Yeshua said He would suffer and die, but He also promised to come forth from the grave on the third day.

And now, the tomb was empty. Could it be Yeshua was risen?

Zera's mind could not fathom what her soul already knew. She took off her sandals, for surely this was holy ground.

Nisan 16, The Third Day, Sunday late morning

Theo

Theo sat on the portico bench with Yosef, waiting for Zera's return from the tomb. Passersby stopped to share rumors that grew like leavening bread.

"The disciples have stolen the body."

"Women claim Yeshua is risen."

"There are wild reports that others have risen with Yeshua and gone to the Temple to show themselves."

Yosef stood. "Theo, rumors fly on the wind like chariots of fire, igniting hope of a revolt."

Other travelers called to them from the road.

"The disciples mean to burn the Temple to the ground."

"Yeshua will go to the Temple to be crowned."

Yosef arranged the rich black robe he wore to meetings of

the Sanhedrin. "I must go to the Council and quell these rumors that place the disciples at more risk of arrest and crucifixion." Yosef rushed away. He left Theo simmering in a stew of hope, fear, doubt, and confusion.

Zera ran through the gate. "The tomb is empty. Yeshua must be risen."

Theo leapt to his feet. "Did you see Him?"

"No. But Magdalena did."

Zera's joy was a bubbling brook. She took Theo's hand, pulling him into her running dance step.

Theo dug his heels into the ground like a stubborn donkey. "Zera, stop. The last time I laid eyes on Lenah, she was mad with grief."

"As were we all. Go to the tomb and see. There was a great glow. Lenah saw Yeshua. Spoke with Him."

Theo grabbed his crutch and hurried to the garden gate. John, the disciple, bolted past him. Peter came forth from the tomb muttering to himself.

As Peter passed by, he glanced at Theo. "Yeshua is not there." Peter's voice trembled. "Yet ... the graveclothes, the bindings are still tied, lying in place."

"When Lazarus was raised, there were many witnesses. He shuffled from his tomb still bound. I released him from his graveclothes. No one saw Yeshua walk from His tomb. No one freed Him from His graveclothes."

"The undisturbed graveclothes are witness to Yeshua's resurrection." Peter lifted his hands. "The facecloth lies off to the side. Yeshua must have folded it with His nail-pierced hands." Peter's voice was an awe-filled whisper.

He took hold of either side of Theo's cloak. "Magdelena came to me and said that Yeshua was risen. At first, I thought her demons of deceit had returned. And a woman's testimony is not accepted in court, so I ran here to see. But two men must give witness for a thing to be considered true."

Theo clasped Peter's arms and smiled. "The disciple, John, was with you. He is the second witness."

"Yes." Joy crept onto Peter's face, then crumbled. "Why would Yeshua show Himself first to Magdelena?"

Peter's words tore at Theo's heart. "Miriam once told me shepherds were the first to hear of Yeshua's birth. They, too, cannot bear witness."

"Why would the Lord choose shepherds?"

"Perhaps because Yeshua is the Lamb of God. And shepherds are the first ones called to attend the birth of a lamb."

"The Baptizer said Yeshua was the Lamb who would take away the sin of the world." Peter held his temples. "Who can fathom the ways of the Lord?"

Theo moved close and peered inside the tomb. There, a perfectly undisturbed cocoon of graveclothes lay collapsed along the cave shelf, a neatly folded facecloth off to the side.

A holy fire burned through Theo's veins, opening his mind and eyes to the truth. "Hallelujah. Blessed be the name of the Lord." He turned to the gathering crowd. "Go. Do not look for the living amidst the dead. Tell mother, father, sister, brother the good news. He Is Risen."

Chapter Forty-Eight

The Inn on Jericho Road
Ten days after the Resurrection

Theo

Theo fed the beasts in Barid's stable and considered the ten days since the tomb was found empty. The day after Theo and Zera saw the empty tomb, they fled home to Barid. Yosef fled to Arimathea.

"See who is here." The joy in Zera's voice was catching.

Theo clasped arms with Thomas. "He is risen. I have seen the empty tomb."

"He is Risen, indeed. I have seen Him. Touched His scarred hands and side. Eaten with Him."

Theo trembled, shaken to the core. "Yeshua appeared in the flesh—Not spirit, but body."

Zera eased onto a bench. "To see Him, touch Him. Hear Him teach." Zera's voice quivered with longing.

Theo cleared his throat, found his voice. "Tell us all you know."

Thomas moved to sit beside Zera. "On the third day, Yeshua appeared to all the disciples save me. I was walking back to the upper room with a basket of food. Overwhelmed by all that had happened, I was glad to go to the market alone. While there, a woman grabbed my sleeve and called, 'Yeshua.' When I turned, sorrow filled her face, and she rushed away. When we were young, I had been called the Twin because Yeshua and I looked so much alike."

"Tell me, Thomas." Zera took his hand. "What did you think when you first heard Yeshua was risen?"

"To my dismay, a woman had just mistaken *me* for Yeshua. Yet every man insisted that they had seen Him. Peter declared nothing could hold Yeshua, not even the wrappings of Death. I demanded to see Him, touch Him. On the eighth day after He was raised, He appeared to us all. Yeshua and I stood side by side. Both drawing breath, both partaking of food, both true flesh. The disciples are all witnesses. They can counter any lie that claims that those who saw Him were mistaken and instead saw me."

"The Lord has protected the Truth." Theo picked up a rake and began to clean the stalls. "How I wish I could see Him, tell Him I have forgiven my enemies."

"Yeshua told us He will meet us in Galilee. Word has spread, and many more than The Eleven travel there."

Zera rose. "Theo, we must go. And Barid will also want to witness Yeshua's victory over Death."

Theo looked up at Thomas. "When will Yeshua come?"

"No one knows. I will send word."

Barid strode into the stable. "A royal runner brought a message. Herod will stop here with his traveling party today on the way to the Winter Palace in Jericho. Thomas is a well-known disciple. If he is seen, Herod will have him jailed."

"The apprentice from the forge just brought back our repaired bridles. He can take Thomas to Dex at the forge in Jericho, well ahead of Herod." Theo hitched the donkey to the cart and led it outside. "Thomas, ask Sophia to send a messenger dove to the believers in Shechem, so they may come and see Him too."

Zera had fetched the apprentice and he climbed onto the seat. Thomas scrambled up beside him.

They drove off, and Theo called, "May the next meal we share be in Yeshua's presence."

Zera

Zera lifted round loaves of bread from the oven near the cookfire in the courtyard. The aroma of leavened bread after so many days of *matzah* made her mouth water. She brought a basket of fresh bread into the front room of the inn.

Herodias rushed inside, shut the door, and grabbed Zera by the arm. "Hide. Do not let Herod catch sight of you." She shoved Zera back into the courtyard.

Zera's mind swayed. She must find a safe hiding place. She would worry about the why of it later. She looked about and headed to the stable. Slipping inside, she spotted the backroom Barid had added for Theo when she and Reah had come to live at the inn. She moved past the stalls, into Theo's room, and closed the door. Then, she heard Theo leading a horse into the stable. A gap between the door and the doorpost allowed her to see this end of the stable. Someone led another horse in at the far end.

Theo put a saddle on the rail. "Leave that stallion in the far stall. I will feed and water him."

"Only I tend Herod's stallion."

She knew that voice. *Auriga.* The babe within moved. She had forgiven Auriga, but she had not forgotten how he had deceived her.

He led Herod's mount to her end of the stable. Zera pressed back a shiver of shame. Only the door and a few footsteps separated her from her former lover.

Theo hurried to Auriga and touched his brace. "Does this brace Dex fashioned keep your shoulder in place?"

Theo had not told her Auriga had been injured. Zera shifted so she could see the leather and metal brace binding Auriga's right shoulder.

"The brace helps. Theo, stop working. I must share a secret."

Just then, Barid entered the stable and hurried to join them. "We must talk. Herodias drew me aside and warned me Herod must not see Zera. She said Auriga knows why."

Barid shot Auriga a fierce look.

Auriga raised a palm. "Yes. I came to tell you."

"Is Zera in danger?" Barid's tone of command made Zera feel safe.

"Not Zera. The child Herod suspects is mine. He is still livid I can no longer race and provide him with wealth from winnings. It is Zera's ill fortune Joram left one final debt—and Herod holds it. If the child is a well-formed male or a comely daughter, he will call in the debt and take the child as a slave."

Zera clamped her hands over her mouth. She wanted to scream. She wanted to run. Lord forgive her, she wanted to murder Herod. She slid down the door and hugged her trembling legs. Then she shifted to peer through the gap.

Theo stood tall. "Let us reason together. If the babe is born when Zera is a widow, Herod would have a claim. But if Zera is married when the child is born, the child belongs to her husband. No claim can be made." Theo looked up at both strong men towering above him. "I will marry Zera, if she will have me."

She cared deeply for Theo and would marry him to save her babe. But she could no longer lie to herself and deny she had given her heart to another.

Barid stepped toward Theo. "No. I will marry Zera. The child's future will be more secure with me."

"Why? Because you are able-bodied and own this inn?" The bitter edge in Theo's tone sounded more like the man Zera knew before he forgave his enemies.

"Theo, peace my friend. You must know that I care for Zera. And Herod would not dare challenge me, a Roman citizen. I will acknowledge the child as mine as soon as we marry and, for good measure, adopt the child at birth."

"Think, my long-lost friend." Auriga clasped Theo's shoulder. "Barid's claim would be upheld under both the laws of Judea and Rome."

Barid clasped Theo's other shoulder. "And if the child resembles the father and not the mother ..."

Auriga pointed between himself and Barid. "Are we not perfectly matched? Like a pair of stallions for a chariot."

Zera studied them through the gap. Both blond. Both with eyes the color of the sky. Both brawny and strong. But Auriga was a young lion, Barid was a mature bear.

"Theo, look at me." Barid's voice was calm, but his voice quivered.

Zera watched as Barid stooped to meet Theo's eyes. "You do not love Zera as a man loves a woman. I do."

Barid loved her. Zera held her breath, hoping to hear over the drumming of her runaway heart.

"Barid, I saw you had grown fond of one another. But you cannot expect Zera to live with you as man and wife if she is not willing." Theo's voice was a cautious whisper.

"I would not. But it is my greatest hope that one day she will come to love me as I already love her."

Zera stood and laid her hand on the door, wanting to caress Barid's cheek and share her heart.

"My mother grew to love the Roman who adopted me. The man I was honored to call father."

Relief flickered across Auriga's face. "If Barid marries Zera, this child of mine will never be a slave."

"The child will be entirely mine." Barid glared at Auriga.

Theo stepped between them. "Barid, you must be told. Auriga was misled when he bargained with Joram. Auriga believed Zera would be divorced, not stoned to death."

Zera's eyes brimmed. Joram had lied to Auriga. The father of her babe had not plotted to have her killed.

"I have heard enough." Herodias appeared at the side door. "Even with the best intentions, it is never wise to plan a woman's future without her say. Theo, go fetch my litter bearers. Auriga, take Herod's stallion to him. He is more skittish than his high-strung mount." Herodias came close and peered into the crack at the backroom door.

Zera peered back at her.

Barid crossed his arms and leaned against a stall. "And does my queen have orders for me?"

"Yes." She came close to Barid, rose onto her toes, and whispered something in his ear.

Barid blushed crimson and walked to the door of the backroom. "Zera, my love for you is like the sun. New each morning, rising bright." His whisper was strong and sure.

Barid's soul was the other half of hers. He was the man HaShem had fashioned for her. Zera put her lips to the gap and spoke. "Barid, I love you like the moon and stars, through the darkest dark of each and every night."

Herodias turned to Barid. "Go. Now. Before Herod decides we have been alone here too long."

"Have faith, my Beloved, soon we will be together." Barid hurried away.

Zera opened the door, and the queen slipped in.

"My queen, you have risked Herod's ire to protect me. Why have you shown me such grace?"

The queen's face softened, her lips trembled. "I once had a daughter. A daughter I sacrificed to preserve my power. A daughter Herod defiled." The queen shook a fist. "I will never let Herod steal the innocence of another child. Or break the heart of another mother." Her face betrayed no emotion, but anger teemed in her tone. "One day, I will have my revenge."

Praise HaShem. He had moved a cunning, self-serving queen to show Zera and her unborn child mercy.

Chapter Forty-Nine

The Forge at Jericho

Iyar (May), three weeks after the Resurrection

Zera

Zera folded blankets in the front room of Dex's house at the forge. She placed them in a basket for the trip. "We are packing now, but when word comes from Thomas, we must be ready to leave for Galilee. I do not want to miss our chance to see Yeshua."

Sophia picked up a cloak. "I am glad for your help."

"And I am glad for the distraction. Waiting since morning for Barid to return with my marriage contract has me perched on the point of a needle."

"Can you remain carefully perched a little longer without being pricked? Come help me set out a simple wedding supper. But I promise you, Dex and I will host a special wedding feast after we return from Galilee."

The babe within turned. Zera's hand went to her belly. "The moving grows stronger."

Zera took Sophia's hand and placed it over the spot the baby had moved.

Sophia tilted her head, waiting. The babe kicked and she smiled. "Even the babe is excited for your wedding feast."

Gaius darted round the room, almost toppling stacks of supplies. Sophia handed him the sling. "Go practice, my little warrior. I will call when the meal is ready."

He ran out, swinging the sling in circles at his side.

Zera set out a pitcher of wine and a basket of bread. "The men will be hungry after the journey from Jericho."

Sophia put out olives and figs, cucumbers and cheese. "We will eat as soon as you are married."

At the rumble of an approaching cart, Zera's heart quickened, racing her feet to the door.

She spotted the donkey cart with Theo and Barid sitting high on the seat and two scribes sitting low in the back. Theo drove the cart up to the house and Barid, his face lit with joy, jumped down before the cart stopped moving. He ran to her, waving parchments above his head. "Zera, we brought the scribes to confirm your consent."

"I began to worry they may not come today." She nodded to the scribes and nestled under Barid's arm.

He guided her inside and set the parchments on the table. "We are soon to be wed." He kissed her brow. "These carefully drawn documents record our marriage under the Law of Moses and the laws of Rome."

"Praise HaShem, we will be together, and the child will be safe."

Two scribes walked in with Dex and Theo. The first scribe brought a quill and a jar of ink to the table. He eyed Zera's rounded belly and a faint smirk formed on his lips.

Barid shot him a glare that shouted *beware* and the scribe's face became as blank as an unmarked tablet.

Zera stood close to Barid, and he put a protective arm around her. Barid would always guard her honor and her heart.

The other scribe turned to her. "Zera, you are kinswoman of Etan of Jericho, also known as Theo. Do you freely consent to marry Barid, owner of the inn on Jericho Road?"

"Yes, a thousand times yes." She met Barid's eyes, and her heart soared like a caged bird set free.

"With you as my wife, my life is whole." Barid's hand cupped Zera's cheek.

Zera leaned into his gentle touch, willing his hand to linger.

The men signed the documents, the scribes affixed seals, and left for Jericho.

Barid lifted her chin and gave her a tender kiss. "My beautiful beloved bride. From this moment forward, I will shield you and our babe under my strong arm."

Dex poured the wine and handed each a cup. "Blessings on you both. May you enjoy the same contentment Sophia and I share."

Barid laughed. "I remember when all the young women and their mothers would make elaborate meals trying to attract you."

Sophia kissed Dex's cheek. "And you chose the woman who could barely cook."

Zera's cheeks warmed. "You are a good cook now, so there is hope for me."

Barid lifted Zera's cup to her lips and put his cup to his mouth. "Our first fruit of the vine as man and wife." They drank the wine and Barid kissed her lips.

Zera's heart skipped the quick steps of a wedding dance. "HaShem has blessed me with the love of a good and trustworthy man."

Sophia raised her cup again. "You and the babe are safe from the evil hand of Herod."

Barid gently touched her belly. "No one can take our baby from us now." Barid's tone was so sincere it melted Zera's heart like warm sealing wax, embossing his name on her soul.

"From the moment the ink dried on the marriage parchments, a peace has settled round my heart. Husband, where should we keep these precious documents?"

"There was a small carved chest among the things your steward brought to the inn. I will bring it here."

"And we will pack the carts." Dex and Sophia carried bundles outside.

Barid returned with the chest and set it on the table.

"Barid." Dex called out. "Please come. Things have shifted and my cart lists to the right."

Barid kissed Zera on the cheek. "This will take only a moment." He left her alone with the chest.

Zera lifted the lid and placed the documents within. When she lived with Joram, this chest had been filled with jewels. Jewels that did not soothe her soul nor fill the hole in her heart. She was struck by a sudden memory. Turning the chest over, she found the latches concealed by carvings and opened a secret niche.

Her gold hair comb studded with amber gems shimmered in the sunlight.

Zera's chest tightened, and her heart sank. Reah must have hidden it. Zera did not want such a reminder of Auriga Maximus. Her first thought was to cast it into the nearest wadi and let the next heavy rain wash it away.

HaShem, what would You have me do with this comb?
Pray and wait.

She wrapped the comb in a small cloth.

Barid came through the door. "You look as if you have seen a spirit from the shadowlands."

Zera went to him and took his hand. "I have seen a glimpse from my sinful past. And I must speak of it."

"I am listening."

Zera unwrapped the comb. "This was a gift from Auriga when he sought my favor."

Barid remained quiet, but his face took on a look of deep sorrow.

"I will never wear the comb."

"And I would not want the gold from its sale."

"Nor I. Not even for the babe." Zera took a deep breath and embraced the freedom of Yeshua's forgiveness.

Barid took Zera's hand. "We must trust that you found the comb for a reason."

Zera returned the comb to the niche and handed the box to Barid.

When they came outside, Sophia was running from the dovecote toward the loaded carts. "Finally, Thomas has sent word. On the fortieth day from the resurrection of our Lord, we are to travel at daybreak to Bethany."

Sophia hugged Zera. "We will see Yeshua."

Zera peered through her happy tears at the carts. "It will be almost three weeks until we travel to Galilee, not Bethany. But it will serve. By my reckoning, the babe will not be born for at least two moons."

Barid, Zera, and Theo returned to the inn, where they hosted travelers and counted the days until they would travel to Bethany. Over the next weeks, they served travelers who had been in Galilee. There were reports of Yeshua appearing to the disciples in diverse places. With each tale of Him, Zera's longing swelled, and time seemed to slow. She wanted to walk out the door and start on the journey to Bethany. But she must obey Yeshua's command.

One evening, at supper, Thomas appeared at the door. "*Shalom.*"

Barid and Theo welcomed him to the table. Zera readied a room for Thomas, then joined them. "Tell us of your time with Yeshua in Galilee."

"We first caught sight of Him on the shore when we were fishing. Peter jumped from the boat and ran to Him." Thomas grinned. "Some temperaments never change. We brought the boat in and joined them. Yeshua looked at each of us with such tenderness we felt great shame and sorrow. Peter had denied Him. We had abandoned Him." Thomas looked as if he would weep.

Zera gentled her voice. "Yeshua has a way of blotting out the shame for those who love Him."

"Yeshua asked Peter three times if he loved Him. Each time, Peter proclaimed his love and promised to tend Yeshua's flock of followers. Peter's three-fold denial was reversed, redeemed. Then, Yeshua forgave us for abandoning Him in Gethsemane. Together, we shed streams of soul-cleansing tears."

Zera tapped Thomas on the hand. "How did you pass the time with Him?"

"Yeshua opened our eyes to the scriptures in the Law, the Prophets, and the Psalms. He made clear it was foretold the Messiah would die as a sacrifice for our sins, vanquish death, and be raised to eternal life on the third day."

Theo stood. "You must help us understand the great mystery of this teaching."

"The Eleven still seek to grasp the vast sweep of HaShem's plan for the redemption of Creation. But when I was traveling, contemplating all that has come to pass, it came to me. The raising of Lazarus is a foretelling of eternal life in Yeshua's kingdom. And the release of Barabbas is a foretelling of how Yeshua took our place, bearing our sins on His cross."

Theo stood and clasped Barid's shoulder. "I pray for my kinsman Barabbas every day."

"Has Yeshua appeared only to the Eleven?" Zera's voice faltered with loss and longing.

Thomas turned to her. "Yeshua was seen by more than five hundred in Galilee. Wherever He appears, He speaks of His coming kingdom."

Zera swiped at her happy tears. "Thomas, when will Yeshua's kingdom come?"

Something flickered across his face. "Only HaShem knows the day or the hour."

"Will Yeshua journey past my inn?" Barid's voice was a mix of worry and unfettered excitement.

"He has gone ahead to Bethany to see His mother before He leaves us."

"Leaves?" Theo's croak sounded as rough and dry as the Judean desert. "But Thomas, Yeshua has just returned to us. He means to abandon us again?"

Chapter Fifty

At daybreak on the appointed day, Barid helped Zera into the back and placed a cloak around her shoulders. "The chill of the night has not yet lifted."

Zera pulled the cloak closer. "Thank you, husband. I never tire of calling you *husband.*"

"And I thank HaShem every day I can call you *wife.*" Barid climbed onto the seat beside Theo.

Theo could not hide the twitch of a suppressed grin. He flicked the reins, and the cart jolted toward Jerusalem. Dex and his sleepy family followed in their cart.

Zera revelled in the beauty of the amber dawn and the sunrise song of the birds. They passed the morning hours in bouts of contemplative quiet, soft conversation, and light sleep.

As they neared Bethany, Theo began to sing a psalm of ascent. "I lift my eyes to the hills, from where does my help come?"

Zera's soul thrilled. The Lord had used Theo's rich baritone voice to reveal that he was her lost kinsman. She looked to the Mount of Olives rising into a bright sky.

Theo stopped the cart and Barid pointed across the gathering crowd. "Just near those trees are our friends Samuel and Shamara, with travelers from Shechem. They sent word they will stop at the inn on their way home."

Zera looked. "Theo, two of them have their heads and faces veiled."

Theo squinted, then leaned close. "It may be Lazarus, and a woman called Yonah. I will follow after I see to the donkey."

Barid helped Zera down and they walked up the hill. "Look. The Eleven stand near the peak. Miriam, Mary, and Martha are just below.

"Where is Yeshua?" Zera turned to Barid.

Yeshua was suddenly with her and Barid. All else seemed to fade away.

A warm wave of joy flowed through Zera. "My Lord and my God."

Yeshua met Zera's eyes. She could see in His shining face that He knew. Knew she surrendered her shame at the cross. Knew she entered into a loving marriage with Barid. Knew her past, her present, her future.

She drew out the packet she had tucked in her waist sash. "Lord, what must I do with this comb?"

"Zera, what do you already know?"

"The comb should be used for the glory of our Father in Heaven."

Yeshua smiled at her. An ageless, timeless smile. "Bless the giver."

Bless the giver. The giver, Auriga, who feigned affection in exchange for his freedom? Zera tucked the packet away. An ember of anger sparked in her heart. "Lord, it is one thing to forgive and yet quite another to bless."

"Have I not both forgiven and blessed you?"

"Yes, Lord. Beyond measure."

"Zera. I bless the fruit of your womb." Yeshua placed one hand over the babe within her and raised the other to heaven. "This child will be a pillar of faith, an anchor of truth, and a light to the Gentiles."

Yeshua lifted His hand and stepped back.

Barid drew her into an embrace. "Our child has been blessed with a certain future." She smiled up at him, then turned back. "Where is Yeshua?"

Barid pointed to the peak.

Zera could scarce believe her eyes. Now Yeshua stood before the disciples, His voice carrying on the gentle breeze. "You will be my witnesses in Jerusalem, and in all Judea and Samaria, and to the ends of the earth."

"Zera, did you hear? Yeshua commanded his disciples to witness to the whole world. Gentiles, like me, who follow Him will surely gain a place in His kingdom."

Zera looked up at her beloved husband. "Yes, my love." She laid her head on his shoulder.

Yeshua looked beyond The Eleven to His many other faithful followers. He gazed at each one—a shepherd counting His flock, making certain not one sheep had been lost.

Once again, Yeshua opened His arms wide as He had on the Cross. In a moment that stretched beyond time, He seemed to embrace each one there, capture each face in His heart.

Yeshua raised His arms higher and looked up like a child reaching for his father. Somehow, He seemed to grow taller. Zera realized His feet were no longer touching the ground.

A jolt of understanding made Zera swallow a sob. She clutched at Barid's robe. "Yeshua, our Messiah, is taking His leave of us." He had walked and talked with her when she was frail and fallen. She had so much more to learn, to ask. How could she bear His absence?

"Yeshua may stay in Bethany tonight."

"No, Barid. Look at His feet."

"He is rising?" Barid's whisper was part worship, part doubt.

Yeshua slowly rose higher.

People began to murmur and point.

"Do my eyes deceive me?" Theo joined them, his face filled with awe.

Rolling white clouds surrounded Yeshua's feet. Zera did not want to watch Him leave, but she could not bear to look away. "I never expected I would witness Yeshua's return to His Heavenly Father." Trembling, she clung to Barid and Theo. She strained to keep sight of Him as His form slowly shrank, then vanished into the heavens.

"He is gone." Theo tapped his crutch on the ground. "And finally, I had resolved to ask for my miracle."

"I hear the regret in your voice." Zera touched his sleeve. "I am sorry, Theo."

"I am content to be freed from the poisonous draught of hate I drank daily." Theo turned to Barid. "I should have listened to your counsel."

Barid touched Theo's sleeve. "You are a good man, a loving man, and a forgiving man. You will be blessed. For you have learned to walk the way of mercy."

Two angels in blinding white robes appeared where Yeshua's feet had last touched the ground. One angel spoke to the crowd. "Men of Galilee, why do you stand staring into heaven? Yeshua, who was taken up from you, He will come again in the same way." The angels slowly faded from view.

The crowd was still and silent.

Zera rubbed her eyes, not sure what she had seen.

People began to whisper to one another and leave.

Sophia ran to Zera and took her arm. "We must cling to the promise that Yeshua will come again."

Zera pulled her close, unable to speak past the lump snagging her throat.

Barid, Zera, and Theo waited until the crowd had cleared, then walked toward a grove of olive trees circling a well where Theo had tethered the donkey. Zera drew water and they drank. Then Theo drew water for the donkey. "I will hitch the donkey and meet you down the hill on the side of the road.

Zera and Barid walked to a peaceful spot to wait.

Zera withdrew the comb from her waist sash. "I would ask your help. I want you to sell this and ..."

Zera drew in a deep breath and squeezed Barid's hand. "Go secretly and buy Auriga Maximus. Herod will set an exorbitant price for him, but the sale of the comb will cover the cost."

Confusion, then worry, overtook Barid's face. "Wife, Yeshua would not want you to take revenge. I know so little of HaShem, but I do know vengeance belongs to the Lord."

"Oh, husband, this is not for revenge. Auriga's greatest fear is to be a slave sent to fight as a gladiator—and die like his father in the arena. I believe Yeshua prompted me to set Auriga free. But he must never know his freedom came from me." She kissed Barid's hand. "What think you?"

"I was once a slave, finally set free by a master who believed in me." Barid gathered her into his arms. "My precious beloved, I will gladly do as you ask, but there is no surety that Auriga will use his freedom wisely. Are you certain?"

"Yeshua set me free from my guilt and shame and has given me a new life with you. To set Auriga Maximus free will mirror the mercy Yeshua offered me. Mirror the mercy Theo offered his enemies. Mirror the mercy and love and protection you offered me. Buying freedom for Auriga Maximus will free him, and free me."

Barid took the comb, then looked over her shoulder. He turned Zera to face the road behind them. "Look."

In the distance, a man strode toward them, leading a donkey and cart. "That man seems in a hurry. I wonder what is wrong."

"Nothing is wrong." Barid's face was filled with joy. "All has been made right. Look more closely."

Zera watched the man reach into the cart, pull out a crutch she knew too well, and cast it into the nearby olive trees. "Praise HaShem, it is Theo."

He dropped the reins and ran toward them.

Zera rushed toward Theo with open arms and embraced him. "Theo, my forgiving kinsman, healed and whole. The Lord offers all who love Him—a certain mercy."

Gratitude Interlude

"Feeling gratitude and not expressing it is like wrapping a present and not giving it."

William Arthur Ward

The creation of this second book, *A Certain Mercy,* was in many ways like birthing a second child. You must still nurture the first, and each one has different needs. Without the generous help of others—and the mercy of God—I could not survive or thrive in this writer's life.

I am grateful the Lord has given me Vince, a steadfast husband and an anchor to Him, both in writing and in sailing through the storms of life. I am richly blessed by our family— Andra, Karen, Lauren, Maisie, and Karlis, Viktors, Greg, Mikey, and Henry. Much love and thanks to you all. You are my haven of peace and mercy.

The Lord has also gifted me with brothers and sisters in Christ who pray for me—especially when I've retreated into my writing cave. Heartfelt thanks to the Thursday Night Bible Study hosted by Ken and Lindy Zinkgraf, and the Women-in-the-Word Bible Study led by Mary Jo Bohn and Joan Wendelburg.

Laughter truly is good medicine, and my friends—Peggy Dixon, Karen Eyers, Cheryl Gorman, Valerie Hawkins, Monika Hoerig, Jackie Mortenson, Lee O'Daniel, Noemi

Prieto, Barb Tock, Cece Wells, and Joanne Woodard—keep me healthy with heaping spoonfuls of joy. To my two groups of pickleball friends: thank you for letting me bring the comic relief and for embracing my "come-as-you-are" game. Special thanks to Mary Anne Wawrzyn for keeping us organized year-round.

It is said that music is prayer without words. I'm blessed by Rebecca Winnie, conductor of the Bel Canto Chorus Senior Singers, who keeps music in my life—and in my marriage, as my husband and I continue to sing together.

Many friends lovingly stepped forward to promote my debut novel, A Certain Man. Special hugs to those who featured the book in book clubs, helped place it in Christian bookstores, invited me to speak at luncheons and conferences, and wrote articles:

Deena Adams, Lori Aeschbacher, Susan Bares, Charlotte Castleberry, Roz Diederich, Sandra Merville Hart, Nancy Martin, Hyndie Stecke, Inga Seraphim, Linda Siehr, Deborah Stone, Linda Stolz, Marcia Schwager, and Monika Veldre.

Heather Greer and Tonya Ashley, my Scrivenings Press accountability partners—you are treasures. And Charla Matthews, my talented virtual assistant, thank you for helping me tame the social media dragon.

Writers' retreats are where fellowship, friendship, and craft are nurtured. I'm grateful to Susan Lindstrom and Becky Melby for organizing the Green Lake retreat in Wisconsin—a gathering of amazing writers and mentors of faith. The Holden Beach spring retreat, with Starr Ayers, Sandra Merville Hart, Deborah Sprinkle, K. Denise Holmberg, the founding members of the Facebook group Writing with the ERASERS, has been a wellspring of fun and encouragement.

Writing groups—Page 3 Word Weavers, guided by our devoted president Bonnie Beardsley, and ACFW-WI-SE, lovingly shepherded by Elizabeth Daghfal—have been a safe place for critique, fellowship, and growth in craft.

Mountains of gratitude to my writing champions and Wisconsin beta readers: Marilyn Malcom, Nancy Martin, and Michele Merens, for your insightful edits. A special thank-you to Susan Taylor-Boyd, who wielded her "tough love" editor's pen with grace and wisdom, prompting rewrites that added real depth to this story. Sabrina Savra DeCarlo and Michael Shuster also provided thoughtful, helpful readings.

The feedback from discerning readers has been invaluable. Hannah Lea Hazard offered critical insight on technical details and fine points of scriptural intent. She, along with Martha Thelen and Jan Hall, introduced me to the world of reader events. I'm also deeply thankful to Baiba Abele, Renate Dindzans, and Sarma Dindzans Van Sant for their careful critiques, which encouraged clarity, consistency, and stronger chapter endings. My heart is full remembering the loving, open arms of the Dindzans clan.

I am especially grateful to the consultants who enhanced the authenticity and heart of this story.

Brian Dainsberg, Senior Pastor of Alliance Bible Church, offered wisdom on shame and spiritual struggles and helped ensure scriptural integrity throughout.

Dr. Richard Marks gave valuable insights into the emotional complexities of shame, forgiveness, mercy, and redemption.

Vincent B. Davis II, an award-winning, bestselling author of ancient Rome, generously shared his historical expertise.

Suzie Edstrom, your hand-drawn maps enrich the biblical setting beautifully. And once again, Linda Fulkerson—your stunning cover design captured my heart.

Margie Lawson, PhD—my longtime writing coach and

friend—thank you for never settling. Your encouragement, edits, and brainstorming left fingerprints on every page.

To Amy Anguish (content editor), Kaci Banks (line editor), and Heather Greer (managing editor)—you helped lift the words off the manuscript and into readers' hearts.

Linda Fulkerson and Liana George, co-owners of Scrivenings Press—thank you for your wisdom, patience, and grace in bringing *A Certain Mercy* to life.

Soli Deo Gloria

Author's Note

My prayer for this book is best captured in the words:

> *"Let this be written for a future generation,*
> *that a people not yet created may praise the Lord."*

> —*Psalm 102:18, NIV*

Though I am neither a historian nor a biblical theologian, I have long been captivated by the study of Scripture and the history of first-century Judea.

Yeshua of Nazareth is both a historical and spiritual figure. His life and teachings are at once simple and profound, mysterious and compelling—tangible truth. *A Certain Mercy* is a biblical novel that seeks to dwell within the space of this verse:

> *"Jesus did many other things as well. If every one of them were*
> *written down, I suppose that even the whole world would not*
> *have room for the books that would be written."*

Author's Note

—*John* 21:25, *NIV*

I praise the Lord for His mercy—that He appointed for me to live in these times. While some are gifted with unquestioning faith, I find myself in need of reason and a ready defense. Without the full revelation of Scripture, I'm not certain how I would have responded to the reports of Yeshua of Nazareth—especially had I never witnessed His miracles or heard Him teach.

One of the challenges in writing these characters was portraying their fear, doubts, and confusion—even after Jesus clearly foretold His death and resurrection. We must remember: the fullness of revelation had not yet unfolded. I aimed to stay close to what they *knew, feared,* and *felt*—before the resurrection, before the outpouring of the Holy Spirit at Pentecost, and before the Gospels were written.

Even after the resurrection, when the disciples saw Him in Galilee, Scripture tells us:

"When they saw Him, they worshiped Him; but some doubted."

—*Matthew* 28:17, *NIV*

This is a profound statement. It suggests that faith and doubt can coexist. It echoes the plea of the father who cried, *"Lord, I believe; help my unbelief!"* (Mark 9:24). Just as Jesus healed that man's child, He did not reject His disciples—nor their worship mingled with doubt. Rather, *He opened their minds to understand the Scriptures* (Luke 24:45). He explained how the Law, the Prophets, and the Psalms all pointed to God's redemptive plan through the Messiah.

In *A Certain Mercy*, scenes drawn directly from the Gospels closely paraphrase the NIV and NKJV translations for clarity and to preserve the tone and cadence of first-century language. Scenes that take place "offstage" from the biblical record are fictional. Jesus, while dwelling among us, was certainly not a two-dimensional figure. Yet the Gospel accounts are often sparse in description, dialogue, and backstory. With much prayer, I've sought to create fiction that feels faithful—ensuring that His imagined words, teachings, and actions are in harmony with Scripture.

Pronouns referring to Yeshua are capitalized when spoken by characters who regard Him with reverence as a prophet or more. I chose *Miriam* as the name for the mother of Jesus to distinguish her from the many Marys in the Gospels. This convention, introduced in book one (*A Certain Man*), helps the reader differentiate among Mary Magdalene (whom I refer to as *Magdalena* or *Lenah*), Mary of Bethany, and others. Mark's mother, referenced in *Acts 12:12*, is left unnamed here to avoid confusion with yet another Mary.

A special thanks to Rebecca Winnie, whose inclusion of Hebrew repertoire in our Senior Singers concerts inspired the scene of voices lifted in praise—and Zera's recognition of Theo.

Writing about this time period—particularly the culmination of Jesus' earthly ministry—comes with unique challenges. Many historical details are unknown. Scholars and historians sometimes disagree. The Gospels do not contradict one another but offer varied perspectives—like multiple eyewitnesses recalling the same event with different emphases. The choice of perspective, the mountain of details, and the weight of research can be daunting. Any unintended errors are mine alone.

My hope is that *A Certain Mercy* blesses the reader and offers a window into the life, teachings, and extraordinary impact of Jesus of Nazareth. May you journey with the characters—hear Yeshua teach, see Him heal, and watch Him offer forgiveness from the cross. May you consider the radical events and redemptive claims of His story. And above all, may you learn to walk in the way of a certain mercy.

Blessings,
Linda Dindzans

For book club discussion questions, references, and bonus content, please visit:
lindadindzans.com
Facebook: *Linda Dindzans, Author*

About the Author

Linda Dindzans, M.D., is an award-winning author, speaker, and retired ENT surgeon. Writing Biblical fiction allows her to indulge her longstanding fascination with God's Word and a commitment to in-depth Bible study. *A Certain Man,* her debut novel, a tale of ancient Samaria at the time of Jesus, has received multiple awards.

She is grateful for this time to lay down her scalpel and pick up her pen as she follows a call to write. Linda is a guest speaker at national and regional Christian writing and worship conferences, church events and a facilitator for church and home Bible studies.

Several times per week, Linda can be found on the pickle-ball courts but has no aspirations to win a trophy. She is content to supply the comic relief .

Linda and her husband, a fellow physician, have been blessed with three adult children, a son-in-law, a daughter-in-law, and three grandchildren. Wisconsin is home, but they enjoy travel, photography, birdwatching, and singing with choirs across the world.

Also by Linda Dindzans

A Certain Man
A Certain Future—Book One

Mara is a young Samaritan beginning to discover her love for Samuel—and his for her. Soon she will be deemed mature enough to marry. Her hopes are dashed when her greedy father brokers a match with the cruel son of the wealthy High Priest of Shechem. When her loathsome betrothed is killed, her beloved Samuel must run for his life. Mara and Samuel struggle to survive and reunite during the treacherous and scandalous times of the Bible under the merciless rule of Rome.

Along the way, they are entangled within the snares of such notable figures as King Herod, Herodias, Pontius Pilate, Caiaphas, and Salome.

The heartrending tales of Mara and Samuel are interwoven with their desperate love story. Before either meets Yeshua the Nazarene face to face. Before He sets the political, religious, and spiritual landscape on fire. And before either Mara or Samuel are immortalized in the gospels.

Get your copy here:

https://scrivenings.link/acertainman

Stay up-to-date on your favorite books and authors with our free e-newsletters.

ScriveningsPress.com